The Pulse of My Heart

THE TAKEN SERIES
BOOK THREE

E. C. RODERICK

For all inquiries about this book contact:
E. C. Roderick
P. O. Box 453035
Los Angeles, CA. 90045

Cover Design: Mary Ann Smith

Editor: Candy Leonard

Library of Congress Control Number: : 2023923239

ISBN (Ebook): 978-1-7374357-6-1

ISBN (paperback): 978-1-7374357-7-8

ISBN (hardback): 978-1-7374357-8-5

Publisher: Sandy Pier Press
Los Angeles, California

Piracy Notice

There is only one happiness in life, to love and be loved.

—George Sand

One

The coach sways as we travel through the forest. I'm so tired... exhausted and bereft of sleep. Nights have been consumed with worry, making it difficult to drift into a dream.

It's been six days since we left Boston. The air is warm and fragrant with mountain flora and birds chirp throughout the surrounding trees. But it's warmer inside the coach, though a breeze enters the window and moves loose ringlet tendrils over my face. My stomach anxiously quivers as I anticipate our destination. I don't know what to expect when we arrive.

Will we find an explanation, letting us understand what happened to me? What if it happens again? Can the phenomenon be controlled? If not? Then, this forever is my home. But what if...? Could I really be lost forever? If the anomaly breaches again when I'm there this time, what's going to happen to me? Is the strange occurrence random? Systematic? What could it be...? Supernatural even? And, if there are no answers...?

A chill rolls over my skin and my blood runs cold. I shudder at the frightening possibilities running through my mind...

My breath shakily escapes me, and I try managing my breathing while gazing out the window. But I decide to rest my head

1

against the backrest of the leather seat instead, and the life inside me stirs. Tiny feet press against my lungs, causing my breath to grow shallower. My gaze turns toward his hand stealing beneath my cape, and he gently caresses my swollen belly.

"I don't know if I can do this," I whisper, turning my gaze toward him, meeting his eyes.

"Hold fast," Leif reassures me, carefully brushing my ringlets off the side of my face and placing them behind my ear.

"You know when you think that you've got the whole world figured out?" I ask him.

"Ye mean understood?"

"Yes."

"Aye," he says, looking steadily at me.

"And then it turns out you don't know a thing about it?"

"That ye have been mistaken?"

"Because of naiveté."

"Aye."

"Well, I feel like that," I tell him. His arm comes around me now, and he pulls me close against his chest. "I don't know what's going to happen. If anything will happen. But, if it does... I don't know, Leif. Anything can go wrong. I'm scared."

"Try holding this sentiment tae heart—fear not, fur whit is unknown has not given rise tae harm till it has been revealed. Yet, if ill becomes of us, ken that we shall endure nae matter whit passes amongst us. Recall whit we have already experienced and see that we live. Find strength in this and we shall overcome any menace," he tells me. I want nothing more but to latch onto his bravery and believe him, as he gives me a reassuring smile and kisses my brow.

The horses' hooves clack over pebbles in the dirt over the path.

Clack... Clack... Clack...

Dust stirs up into the air and flecks enter the window, making the air smell like earth. I'm uncertain of how much time we have left to travel before arriving, so I lean my head on his shoulder; too tired to wonder anymore.

Risking ourselves and our unborn child by journeying this far into the frontier this late into my pregnancy, jars me considerably. But he vowed that he'd bring us to this destination after the thaw to discover the anomaly that brought me here. It's our only chance before the baby's born.

I sense him thinking also as we continue traveling when he contracts his arm securely around me and he pulls me closer against his chest. The sway of the carriage begins lulling me, finally, and now it seems as if weights are pulling my eyelids closed...

❦

"Sylvie... Sylvie..."

I groggily open my eyes, hearing Leif's muttering lips speaking against my temple. My sight adjusts to the dim light inside the carriage, and I peer out the window of our coach. A river rushes by a low embankment, and the forest envelopes us. I know now that we've arrived.

I hesitate stepping outside the coach. Foreboding comes over me, but Leif looks at me with expectation and some discernible caution. Months ago, I thought I wanted to do nothing but this, dreaming about it daily: to come here and to know how I came to exist in this place in time. I wondered for so long if I'd ever see my family and friends again. Now, the answer was finally close at hand.

Except, fear suddenly sways me to change my mind. It holds me still, and I don't care to know the answers anymore. My gut clinches. I need to tell Leif to turn back for our haven in Boston. We have to go back.

God, I can hardly breathe...

Tiny fists double punch me from inside my womb and I look at Leif, realizing he is staring observantly at me.

"We are arrived," he says calmly.

I nod in response instead, despite myself, as he taps the ceiling with the silver grip of his fashionable walking cane. My voice catches in my throat to tell him to turn the coach around. But it comes to a halt, and Samuel, our coachman, is heard scraping himself off the driver's seat outside. He promptly arrives at the door and opens it.

"Thank ye, Samuel," Leif acknowledges him while shifting from me, stepping outside now into the fresh late spring air.

"Aye, Your Grace," Samuel replies politely.

I slide from my seat toward the door when Leif leans inside, proffering a hand for me to take. All hopes of avoiding this and returning to Boston are now gone. Slipping my gloved fingers into his hand, he clasps my hand with strength, easily assisting me from our coach, and my feet plant onto the ground. Glancing around our new surroundings, the smell of moist earth permeates my nose as I recognize the Hoosic River rushing by us.

"Do ye recall whaur tae go in the wood?" Leif asks me, calling my attention to him from scanning the enveloping trees surrounding us, flanking the path. I nod at his question. "Guide me."

I start pacing the road up stream and he follows, assisting me along the way. Leading him off the trail, we walk between the towering trees and soon, not far from the path, I suddenly recognize the basalt outcrop: Crazy Eye. I immediately cease my tracks and stand before it, staring at the point where time unraveled. My heart wildly hammers in my chest.

"Here. This is where it happened—where I disappeared... I awakened right over there the day we met." I point to the location directly before the pupil of the rock's eye suspended over a patch of bloodroot blossoms to the side.

"Do ye recall whit precisely occurred tae ye?" he asks curiously, appearing cautious now.

"That night, I got into a vehicle accident—everything was so confusing... I hit something unseen in the road while I was driving. When I got out of the car to see what it was that I'd hit—there was nothing. But I saw the damage done to my brother's car... That's

when everything really strange began happening." I compulsively move toward the flowers and stand among them in front of the "eye," looking up at it, striving to attempt making sense of it all. "I was standing right about here when it all started happening."

I proceed telling him in detail what occurred to me that fateful Christmas Eve night in twenty seventeen.

"Ye discovered yerself amidst the flowers whaur yoo're standing presently once ye had awakened?" he asks with a serious look of consternation on his face now.

"Yes," I tell him. He pauses in bewilderment and is pensive while we simply stand here together gazing around our surroundings, nonplused.

"'Tis deeply puzzling as I am confounded by the nature of this possibility," he says finally, interrupting the lull. I notice how severely furrowed his brow is. But it lifts high and his eyes suddenly widen when an unexpected ringing sound emits, startling us. We instantly realize it's resonating from the folds of my skirts and our gazes lock with alarm. Leif has the unmistakable look of fear on his face as I stare at him, stunned. He watches me retrieve my hidden cellphone I'd been carrying undisclosed in my pocket. Flummoxed, I look at the illuminated screen and stagger as I recognize the caller. My fingers shake as I receive the call and put the phone to my ear.

"Hello?" I say tremulously.

"Sylvie?" A male voice answers on the other end.

"Kyle?" I gasp and can barely breathe.

"Thank God you answered. I've been trying to get a hold of you," he says, sounding expressly relieved. "Yeah, it's Kyle. Where are you? You're late. I told you that I was going to call the cops if you didn't get back here in time, so I did, and now everyone's worried. So, tell me where you are 'cause I'm coming to get you myself."

"Kyle?" Saltwater swiftly fills my eyes and a tear immediately slips down my cheek.

"Yeah?" My breath catches and I uncontrollably begin sobbing.

"It's going to be okay. I'm coming for you, Sylvie. I'm leaving the party right now."

"Is it really you?"

"Of course, it's me. Who else would I be besides everyone else who's worried sick about you?"

"I—I—mean—how—" I stammer.

"Tell me where you are. You should've been back from the grocery store by now," he says. I think to put the conversation on speakerphone so Leif can hear my brother's voice also.

"Kyle?" I continue sobbing.

"Yeah?" he responds and Leif's eyes immediately widen as he's looking at me. He's thunderstruck and fear pours out of his expression as his face blanches.

"I love you," I tell Kyle.

"I love you too, of course. But you need to tell me where you are," Kyle demands, sounding even more worried and confused now, too.

"Tell mom and dad that I love them also, will you?"

"You can tell them yourself after I come get you."

"I miss you guys so, so much."

"Tell me where you are, Sylvie."

"I'm sorry."

"Why?"

"For damaging your car," I snivel.

"I don't care about that. I just need you back here with us where I know you're safe and okay."

"I'm safe. And, I'm okay."

"You don't sound okay. You're crying. Are you hurt?"

"No. I'm not hurt."

"Are you sure?"

"I'm sure."

"But you're crying, and you haven't come back yet. Something's obviously wrong. You've gotten into an accident and I'm worried about you. I've been calling you repeatedly and spamming you with *texts with no answer from you. Why didn't you respond right away?"*

"My phone wasn't working. The reception was so bad."

"Yeah, service around here does suck. Luckily, it's working now, though, and I got through to you, finally."

"Yeah."

"Now that I got a hold of you, tell me where you are so that I can come get you. Can you share your location with me? Or better yet, send me your coordinates."

"I can't," I sniffle.

"Why not?"

"Because my GPS isn't working."

"Are you by any street signs, then? Give me the name of a street and I can be there to help you in no time—"

Suddenly there's static erupting over the phone. It's loud, interrupting us. Kyle's voice cuts in and out. Then, abruptly, there's dead air...

My heart instantly falls to the pit of my stomach. I turn my gaze from the phone and return looking at Leif. He's staring at me flummoxed, and flabbergasted. The pallor on his face is ghostly. He's frozen motionless standing in front of me, petrified.

"That was my brother," I inform him, paralyzed as he with fear and confounded, while wiping tears from my eyes with shaking fingers. Leif absently nods in response.

"Mercy God," he barely utters under his breath. The ashen color on his face is so noticeable, he looks the way I feel. But he pulls forth a handkerchief from his waistcoat pocket and places it in my palm. I dab my damp eyelashes dry. "Why does yer discussion with yer brother nae longer proceed?" he inquires peculiarly.

"The transmission was interrupted."

"Och..." he responds blankly, sheerly bewildered.

My gaze falls to my illuminating phone in my hand, and my thumb accidentally swipes the timer app as I fumble to return it securely into my pocket. The app opens, and I see the timer set for seventeen hours, fifty-six minutes and six seconds. I stare abstractedly at the numbers for a moment, utterly baffled that my phone is somehow working when it shouldn't be.

"I—I think we should leave," I say to Leif, feeling inexplicably unnerved as we stand isolated in this forest location. "Something very strange is happening around here... My phone shouldn't be working at all. Nothing's making any sense..."

"I am also entirely mystified," he says, appearing exceptionally edgy also.

"I'm looking at my timer right now—and it's striking me so oddly..." I show him the set time on my phone's timer as a wild thought crosses my mind and shockingly registers. "Seventeen hours and fifty-six minutes. Do you see it?"

"I reckon," he responds meaninglessly.

"Seventeen fifty-six is the year I came here. And, six seconds matches the exact month I arrived. Is that a coincidence? Or could it mean there's a correlation?" I ask, feeling the tiny hairs on the back of my neck electrify and stand.

"I dinnae have the merest notion if thaur is a correlation. It is all extraordinarily perplexing," Leif replies with a questioningly look. He suddenly glances around himself at the sky and the enormous trees stir from the breeze passing through their limbs. He quickly returns looking at me with sharp unease, additionally shaken. "We ought tae take our leave, immediately."

I agree. He starts away from the outcrop overhanging the bloodroots, intending to guide me as he expects me to follow. Except, something outside of myself causes my hesitation. So, I remain, instinctively compelled to set the timer to twenty hours, seventeen minutes, and twelve seconds, remotely considering if by chance there's a quantum connection.

I open my mouth to tell Leif to wait pacing ahead before he goes any farther from me when an unexpected, distant, low frequency pitch pulses the earth. He freezes in his steps, and turns, facing me realizing that I'm not following him. As I look at him, an eerie expression washes over his face and he thrusts a hand for my arm, urging me away with him.

"Do you hear that noise?" I ask him as he tightens his grip around my elbow. He pauses and listens to the air.

"I hear naught." His brow furrows. He's looking extremely confused and is impatient for us to leave.

"That noise. It's a low pitch. I hear it," I say. He stills himself again to listen and briefly gazes up at the clear cobalt sky now beginning to cloud over.

"I merely recognize the mere soond of birds singing amongst the trees," he says, returning his eyes to mine.

"No—it's a low pitch sound, instead," I differ. "It's getting stronger in frequency. Don't you hear it now?"

"Solely the birds," he repeats. "Let us make haste tae take our leave. This place bestows an uncanny sentiment. I believe it cursed." He abruptly tugs my arm, urging us away from the outcrop.

"There has to be some kind of scientific explanation to all of this. Understandably," I counter frightfully as he forces us away. The unusual noise grows in intensity, becoming more distinct and rumbles the earth. Suddenly, the earth begins roaring and within a nanosecond quakes, throwing us apart from each other. I struggle stepping toward Leif as he fights his way toward me. But we only jar farther apart, and the distance between us grows.

Now aware of the raging sound resonating throughout the forest, and the earthquake happening, he panics as he strives capturing me. But he abruptly jolts backward and hurls airborne, crash landing on to his back. He's too far away from me now. Struggling to his feet, the noise continues intensifying causing pain in my ears. As the earth shakes, Leif makes it to stand and endeavors off balance to approach me. The mounting pain in my ears is unbearable and my phone accidentally slips from my grip to the ground when I suddenly bring my hands to cover my ears, trying to muffle them.

I scream for him. Trepidation is all I know.

"Sylvie! Sylvie!" he hollers for me in terror and stretches a hand

forth to grab me as I reach for him also. The tips of our fingers touch. He suddenly begins fading. Swirling light emerges around me, distorting my vision, blinding all that is seen. Desperately, I exert myself, searching for his hand in the whiteout. Then, gravity abruptly takes control and paralyzes me, catching me in a spinning centrifuge. I can still hear him calling, "Sylvie! I shall find ye! I shall find ye! Hold fast!"

A massive sonic boom unexpectedly erupts in the vortex, shredding the atmosphere. Leif's voice instantaneously stifles, and all sound mutes. Light recedes by the existence of darkness. It's cold now. Freezing. I free fall into a black abyss as matter dissolves around me.

"God, help me!" I frantically scream. The sound incapable of escaping my lips, I beg for the hand of God to save me. But, I fall, and fall... Nothing to grapple... I wonder when I'm going to hit the bottom of the universe before I die.

***

MY EYES FLING OPEN. I GASP AND FRESH AIR FILLS MY lungs. My body painfully aches. It feels debilitated as I stir to sit from lying near a patch of bloodroot blossoms. I'm not dead... and I'm thankful to my Savior.

As I struggle to my feet, I recognize Crazy Eye outcropped beside me. It's still spring and the air is fragrant with mountain flora. But I notice the vegetation. The trees surrounding me are no longer as tall with massive trunks, but spindly as many saplings encompass the area. The air also smells different, but the blue sky looks almost the same; it cleared from previously covering clouds. I also now notice, to my horror, the faint sight of a jetliner cruising high above in the atmosphere. My eyes immediately dart from the sky and nervously glance around my new surroundings as I peer through the woods. A sudden horrific feeling intensifies and washes over me as a paved road not too far away between the trees can be seen. A car whizzes by over it, electrifying my terror.

"Leif! Leif!" I cry, shaking, panicking, desperately scanning the area looking for him. But he's nowhere in existence...

Suddenly, warm liquid streams down my legs and a violent cramp arrests my abdomen, forcing me to crouch. The pain briefly passes. Beside myself, I begin searching for my phone that I remember dropping to the ground among the vegetation. Except, as I search, I can't find it anywhere and realize it's lost, disconcerting me further.

Disoriented and scared, I anxiously rub my eyes from tears, desperately needing to find my way back to him. Except, I know I'm lost. Stranded again from the one I love.

Abruptly, another cramp painfully clinches my belly, causing me to bowl over. I clutch my stomach, forgetting to look any more for my phone. Instead, I need to find my way out of the woods. So, I instinctively start walking through the trees toward the road. I'm in pain, and I'm terrified. But I'm getting closer to the paved road. As I arrive at the edge of the forest on to the shoulder of the road, my orientation is confused. Still, I just start walking along the road's side, desperately hoping to find someone to help me.

A vehicle approaches. It's a pickup truck and it begins slowing. The driver notices me and pulls the vehicle onto the side of the road and stops. The sharp, seizing pain returns in my belly and arrests me, bringing me down to my knees on to the ground. The aching stabs me. It's nearly too much to bear as it radiates from my stomach toward my back.

The male driver of the truck quickly emerges with a woman passenger, and they carefully approach. They have inquisitive looks as they introduce themselves. They seem kind and offer to take me to the hospital.

THE NURSE PUSHES ME IN A WHEELCHAIR TOWARD THE maternity ward. I arrive in a private delivery room, and she gives me a couple of hospital gowns. As she gives them to me, she stares at the way I'm dressed. I know she thinks my appearance is strange and thinks I'm weird. After she gives me gowns, she leaves, and I remorsefully begin undressing as I remember my past. Water pools in my eyes. I feel helpless and bereft of hope. Leif possesses me, and I sob.

Dressed in gowns now, I tearfully place myself over the bed when a different nurse enters the room. She catches me suddenly clearing my appearance and gazes at me with an empathic look. But she doesn't say anything. Instead, she instructs me to lie against the pillow and relax as she begins connecting me to a fetal monitor.

"Is it too late for me to have an epidural?" I ask her, clearing my throat. I'm trying my best to remain composed in front of her.

"We'll find out. My name is Jessica and I'm going to be your nurse," she says politely while taking my blood pressure. She gives me a kind smile.

"It's nice to meet you, Jessica. I'm Sylvina."

"What a pretty name."

"Thank you."

"You're welcome. Okay, let's see how far apart your contractions are and check your dilation. Then, we'll know about the epidural," she says cordially. I nod in response, gripped by nervous insecurity. "Do you know what you're having?"

"I don't—actually."

"A surprise then, huh?" I nod again. "Surprises are always so sweet." She smiles at me again and observes the fetal monitor for a moment. She takes the Velcro blood pressure cuff off my arm when she's finished. "Well, it seems you're having twins. A double surprise!"

My heart skips a beat when my attention attaches to the monitor registering the unexpected double heartbeats.

My thoughts run wild... **Twins? My God... What am I going to do? I'm not prepared for any of this. How can I do this all by myself? Oh Leif... Not without you.**

"You know, your husband can be in the room with you, if you want," Jessica suggests thoughtfully, intuitive to my apprehension.

"He isn't here." My voice cracks, and my eyes well. I blink and a single tear slips down my cheek.

"Oh." She gives a regretful look. "Would you like to call him to let him know that you're here?"

"He's away."

"I'm so sorry. Well, is there someone else you'd like to call, instead?

"Yes, thank you."

"Okay, let me first check your dilation and then I'll give the phone to you." She goes to the counter and places sterile nitrile rubber gloves over her hands. Lying on the bed, she begins gently probing me as I fight back the urge to break down and sob. After a second, she removes her gloves, tosses them into the hazmat bin, washes her hands, then reads the monitor again. "Looks like you're still good for an epidural. Now, I'll get the phone for you." She reaches behind my headboard and gives the phone to me, then retreats from the room. Alone now, I dial Dakota's cellphone and she answers. I'm apprehensive and relieved to her voice again.

"Hi. It's me," I say, breaking down, sobbing all over again.

"Oh my God...! Sylvie?"

"Yeah."

"Is it really you?"

"It's me."

"I can't believe it...! Where have you been? Where are you now? Please tell me. We've all been so worried sick about you. I can't believe it's you."

"I'm in Adams," I snivel.

"What?" She gasps.

"Yeah."

"You're in Adams?"

"Yeah?"

"Right now?"

"Yeah."

"I can't believe it! Are you okay? You're not okay, you're crying."

"Don't be worried."

"How can I not be worried? Of course, I'm worried. What happened to you?" she asks, sobbing now too as we're both overwrought from hearing each other's voice. But I pause, unable to answer her question.

"I need to ask you something," I blurt instead.

"Sure. What?"

"What year is it?"

"What year is it?" she echoes, sounding strange as she's crying.

"Yeah."

"It's twenty eighteen, of course. Why are you asking?"

"The date? What's today?" I pursue shakily.

"Tuesday. May first," she answers.

"May first?"

"Yeah," she says. Leif's birthday... I pause again, sobbing more. My soul weeps. "Sylvie...? Are you there? Are you all right?"

"I'm here."

"What's going on?"

"I'm not okay," I whisper unevenly.

"I'm so sorry. I want so badly for you to okay. No one's heard from you in five months. We have the police, and FBI searching for you. Where in God's name have you been? What happened to you? Can you tell me?" she prods compassionately, speaking through tears. I stay silent. I don't know where to begin answering her questions. I don't know how I can tell her anything. It's impossible. So, I pause. "Tell me—please. What happened to you? Where are you, exactly? Let me help you."

"I'm in the hospital," I choose to say.

"You are?"

"Yeah."

"Oh no! What's happened to you?"

"I'm about to have babies." The phone trembles against my ear.

"Babies? You're pregnant?" Dakota gasps.

"I'm having twins, and I'm in labor." I have no choice but to tell her this.

"Oh, my goodness..." She pauses. "I don't understand. How? I mean the last time I saw you, you didn't... I mean, you never told me anything."

"Please don't ask me to."

"But, did something bad happen to you?" she inquires anyway.

"Nothing like that," I respond. She exhales. I know she's relieved and grateful.

"So, were you seeing someone, then—that no one knew about?"

"It turns out."

"Oh... You told me that you weren't dating when we last saw each other. Why didn't you just tell me what was really going on?"

"I—I couldn't."

"Why not? You know you can tell me anything, Sylvie."

"You wouldn't understand."

"Of course, I would. I wouldn't judge you," she assures gently. I become quiet; there's no way of telling her anything about what's happened to me. "All right. I won't push you. Except, where did you go for so long?"

"Nothing makes sense for anyone..." I say to myself.

"I'm sorry things are so difficult for you right now. But you should know that I'll help you in any way that I can. Okay?"

"I can't express how much that means to me, Dakota."

"Of course, there's no need to thank me, Sylvie. We're family. Remember?"

"I know."

"Good." She pauses again. "So—you're pregnant. What are you going to do?"

"I don't know... I feel so alone."

"You're not alone. You have me. We just reestablished that fact —and you have Kyle, as well as your parents. We've missed you more than we can say. I'm so happy and relieved to hear your voice again. It's going to be okay, Sylvie. You're going to be all right," she consoles.

"Do you think you could be here with me? I know it's a stretch— being so sudden and everything. But I'm just wondering. I'd be so grateful to have you with me."

"I'll catch a flight outta LaGuardia tonight. I'll be there," she promises quickly.

"Really?"

"For sure."

"Thank you. You mean so much to me," I sob.

"You mean a lot to me too. I love you, of course. You should already know that," she replies, sniveling also. "Have you contacted your parents yet?"

"No."

"Please contact them immediately, Sylvie. They've been beside themselves."

"I'll call them," I assure her, noticing the anesthesiologist now entering my room to give me the epidural.

"They're going to be so grateful and ecstatic to hear your voice again also," Dakota says.

"I've missed them so much. More than words can say."

"That's exactly how they feel about you. They're going to be so happy to know that you're back. You have no idea. And, I can't wait to see you."

"I can't wait to see you also."

"Then, let me get off the phone with you so that I can book the soonest flight to come see you."

"Okay."

"But before I hang up, I hope you're feeling a little better now that we've talked."

"I'll be much better when I see you here."

"I'm on my way."

"I love you."

"I love you too, and I'll see you soon."

"See you soon," I reply.

***

I GAZE AT THEM, AND I BEHOLD THEM WITH MARVEL. I think of him. He possesses me, and my soul is comforted when I remember us as I see their small faces.

"Mom," my little son calls my attention away from my thoughts revisiting the day he and his sister were born. He's running from the ocean wave advancing toward his sandy feet and approaches me.

"Yeah, sweetie?" I say to him, admiring him. His skin is tan and sandy from the shore. I look at him and see his father's deep, crystal blue eyes and gilded head as it glistens beneath the brilliant sun.

"I'm hungry," he tells me.

"Would you like some strawberries to snack on before we go home?" I suggest. He nods. "Okay. Sit here on the blanket beside me, and you may have some." He moves toward the blanket and plops himself down next to me, facing the aquamarine waves as they rush in over the sand. I reach into the beach bag and retrieve a container full of fresh ripened strawberries. I open the container and give it to him. His little hand reaches inside, pulls out a large, red berry and he happily takes a bite.

As he eats, my gaze returns to the shoreline and my daughter notices her brother sitting with me away from the incoming waves. She dashes from the sand pail she was filling with sand and runs toward us as her damp onyx ringlets gleam in the sunlight, bouncing *as she now skips along her way. Her fair skin has started turning slightly pink over her bare shoulders. So, I reapply sunblock on her when she comes close and sits beside me, opposite her brother.*

"I want some strawberries too," she says in her tiny voice.

"Okay, you can have some," her brother offers kindly. He reaches into the container he's still holding and draws forth a large strawberry, giving it to her.

"Thank you," she says to him. He smiles at her and continues to feed himself another berry.

I watch them as they peacefully eat, loving their innocence and beauty. But for his complexion and the relaxed curls mussed over his golden head, my son is the spitting image of Leif as I imagine him as a boy. He's darling, and I feel my deep warmth of affection for him embrace my soul. Turning my gaze now toward my daughter as she also eats contentedly, I adore her equally. Recognizing Leif's complexion on her and the rose tint in her cheeks, sharply contrasting her long onyx ringlets and bright emerald eyes, I'm reminded of him completely. I smile at her, celebrating her with all my being, and she smiles sweetly at me in return.

They eat enough berries and dart back toward the water. I let them play for a while longer as they build sandcastles. They pack and move sand in and out of their sand pails while the ocean waves crash on shore at their little feet.

I realize, while watch them play, that they are gifts from Leif: that they belong to us in a way which is fundamental to our existence and to the love we shared. They are the beginning and the end of us, and this is how Leif and I came to be.

I close my eyes, remembering him well, longing for him, wanting him, needing him to be with me. My heart and my body return to aching for him as I yearn. I can't bear it. Then, the experience of that horrifying day erodes my amorous thoughts. I remember falling through time. The feeling of losing him rushes to my mind, and buries me without mercy as cold fear takes me all over again. Dark-

ness surrounds, and my heart races. My breath quickens and I think I'm going to die.

My eyes fling open, and my sight returns to my children radiant under the sun. They're shrieking with delight as they play in the wet sand and shallow waves. Calm restores me, erasing fear and my life is safe. But, immense aching from loss remains.

❦

THEN, HE APPEARS FROM THE BLACKNESS. FROM nothing he solidifies. So, I feel him. He touches me, and I languidly open my eyes as consciousness replaces the cobwebs of slumber, and my blood warms. The silhouette of his face comes into view when he hovers over me in the shadows of darkness broken by moonbeams entering windows in the room. His mouth presses over mine and my yearning manifests as I ache to receive him. He knows. He then enters me, joining us together. My legs wrap tightly around his hips, sealing the connection of consummation between us as my heart fills with joy. The warmth of his flesh tenderly moves against mine when he thrusts generously inside me.

I burn as he takes me. The taste of his skin, salty as I kiss him. The heat from his body encasing mine, spellbinds me with bliss as he brings us to climax.

Then, I shudder. My depths electrify and rock. Euphoric spasms consume me. He trembles with me as we embrace. Simultaneously, he erupts, seizing into oblivion. After, he collapses over me, satisfied, and I exist with him in bliss.

Suddenly, a bell emits, ringing throughout, disintegrating the spell between us and all which exists vanishes...

Two

The alarm on my phone buzzed and my eyes flung open, throwing me from deep sleep. My vision adjusted to the shadows of predawn, my heart still pounding as my body settled from the dream I'd just had.

I instantly reached for my phone over the nightstand beside me and turned off the alarm in a haze, feeling an empty echo in the pit of my soul, remembering that I was alone. It took me a minute to adjust as I lay in bed staring in the dark up at the ceiling. Haunted by another dream. One of the worst ones. The kind that contradicts reality, tricking your mind, and tortures your soul. Cursing you as it merged the subconscious with reality, making you question if it really in fact did occur. Except, most of it was actually real and imbedded into my subconscious, possessing me.

Memories haunting me in many ways uniquely manifested into my consciousness this morning as I continued feeling the strange residual effect of my throbbing cervix subsiding now from feeling ecstasy while dreaming of him. I knew him and had felt him so pristinely. Leif was the ghost visiting me. He would haunt me until I die. Becoming an apparition dissolving into nothingness the second I opened my eyes, he was gone, leaving me agonized. He possessed me, and he was my obsession.

As the haze from my dream began clearing, I was left in solitary bereavement. The reality I now lived was nothing like I'd ever experienced before. I was captive to what I had lost. An inescapable hostage to the past. Leif and I were real once. My love for him remained unbroken, and all I did now was to hold on as I desperately longed.

Torment was all I knew at this hour. My mind wouldn't release the dream from which I had just awakened and grant peace. The fixation branded my awareness, further tethering me to him in the four years that have passed. During days while simply functioning, my mind perpetually gravitated toward his memory. Many times, I found myself barely coping with the pain of missing him. During these times, I'd escape others for privacy to weep, and to simply be left alone since no one was capable of understanding.

Desperation often gripped me to be with him once more. I perpetually thought if I could make a wish that would come true, that I'd wish for escaping alone to the Berkshires to travel back to him, leaving my obligations behind and forgetting this world as if I had never known it. But the ironic thing about guilt, is that it forces honesty and selflessness. So, I was bound to admit that I couldn't run away. I couldn't abandon our children. I couldn't do it. Ever. I knew it would be a betrayal to them, and to Leif, and to myself. It would be an unreconcilable sin to us all. Because I loved them at heart, I accepted my current circumstances.

So, I was committed to the happiness of our children and to the stability of their lives. I meant to raise them in this society surrounded by the love and support from my family that included their friends. The thought of suddenly ripping my children from the security of their current lives, and extricating them from what they'd ever known in order to move them to a place that was not only completely foreign to them but might likely risk their lives, was unthinkable. The idea was also extremely cruel to my parents.

To take their only grandchildren away from them and disappear forever, hurt my heart.

Instead, I remain here alone lying in bed in solitude, feeling gut wrenched with a profound sense of loss unlike the time I'd lost my first husband, Matt. As the misery reached the core of my being every single day, I wasn't certain how I might last without Leif.

Saltwater had pooled in my eyes and silent tears were slipping down my cheeks. I rolled onto my side away from the moonlight still entering the windows and turned my face into the pillow, feeling the magnitude of our separation and wept a stream of anguished tears.

I'm unsure how long I grieved, but I noticed dawn had broken as fresh daylight was now entering the room. I turned my gaze toward the windows and watched the sun climbing the sky from the brink of the horizon, trying to settle from suffering. Retrieving my phone from the nightstand beside me, I glanced at the time: 7:00 a.m. Regarding the hour, I cleared my tearful face, deciding to finally get out of bed and headed for the bathroom to refresh with a shower.

Once showered, my emotions to an extent had eased to somewhat being bearable. So, I quickly tied my hair into a ponytail, dressed in a pair of leggings and oversized sweatshirt as I intended to exercise before going to work today. But before I did that, I strove pushing my sorrows behind and turned my focus toward preparing my children this morning for preschool.

I PACED THROUGH THE HALLWAY AND ENTERED MY KIDS' bedroom that they shared at the end of the corridor. The *Thomas The Tank Engine* nightlight situated on the dresser to the right of the threshold softly illuminated their nicely decorated bedroom.

Reaching for the lamp, I switched it off as warm golden hues seeped inwardly through the windows from the early morning sun, casting the room in a warm, gentle orange glow. The children were peacefully sleeping when I arrived between their toddler beds and moved to carefully awaken them.

"Hey, sweethearts," I greeted softly when I leaned to give each a tender kiss on the cheek, mindfully rousing them from slumber. Leila stirred beneath her pink Hello Kitty comforter and sleepily opened her eyes, focusing on me as she yawned. I softly stroked her plump, ruddy cheek as I knelt between their beds.

"Good morning, Mama," she said in her sweet little voice. "Is it time for school?"

"Yes, it is. We have to get dressed and eat breakfast," I said affectionately.

"Okay," she replied and groggily stretched before playfully rolling out of her low raised bed and hitting the floor with a giggle.

"Silly," I said, smiling at her as she now lay beside me on her back, gazing up at me. Amused, she giggled again.

"Is today when we have our birthday yet?" my little son asked me, awakening also. I turned my attention toward him and he sat up from his Star Wars comforter, gazing at me with eager anticipation.

"Well, today is Monday," I replied, smiling at him also. I was happy to give them a birthday week to celebrate, since I had to work over the weekend and couldn't properly celebrate their birthday on their actual day, which was yesterday.

"Yay!" they both cheered in unison.

"It's our birthday at school today!" Leila cheered again, picking herself up off the floor and jumping around the room with excitement.

"I'm four years old now!" my little Leif realized with equal enthusiasm.

"So am I!" Leila informed us.

"Are you bringing cupcakes to school?" Leif happily asked me.

His bright ultramarine eyes were big and round as he also leaped out of bed, and hopped with joy before me.

"Yes, I am," I confirmed pleasantly.

"Yay! Yay! Yaaay!" he expressed and did a little happy dance, causing me to laugh.

"I want a chocolate one," Leila told me as she stopped bouncing around and looked at me.

"I want a vanilla one," Leif said, settling himself from jiggling around too.

"Sure. You both can have whatever one you want," I replied, smiling at them both.

"Goody!" Leila expressed elatedly.

"Don't be late, Mom. Okay?" Leif warned.

"When am I ever late?" I asked as I turned my gaze toward him. He gave me a certain look that struck deep into my heart, reminding me of a look that only his father could give when he was serious.

"Well, you might get stuck in traffic," he said.

"We live only five minutes away from school," I replied, smiling at him. He didn't respond except maintained the particular look on his face. "All right. I promise I won't be late. I'll even get there a little early so that you will see that I'm there ahead of time."

"Good!" he responded, nodding his head once, ultimately satisfied.

"All right, now we need to dress and eat before we go," I directed as I straightened from kneeling on the floor.

"Okay," they agreed. I moved toward their dresser, retrieved their school uniforms, and assisted them as they freshened and dressed.

When they completed dressing with their faces washed, teeth brushed and hair neatly combed over their heads, we scampered down the staircase to the kitchen where I prepared them portions of yogurt, banana, and apple slices with pieces of toast, along with a bit of fresh orange juice for breakfast. While they ate, I made myself a glass of iced coffee and viewed all of the sprinkled cupcakes I had baked last night for their preschool class to celebrate their birthday.

This was the first year I hadn't bought them gifts to celebrate their birthday, since Dad requested that I not. Instead, he and Mom had made plans to take the kids to Disneyland for the upcoming weekend for their birthday. My parents were very indulgent with their grandchildren; they adored them immensely and had no hesitation of showing it. I loved that they loved them, and I loved that the kids equally adored their grandparents.

The kids spent much of their spare time at my parents' house as my parents were always willing to spend their time with them, enjoying themselves with them. Still, I felt really guilty not getting my kids anything for their birthday to celebrate. But Mom agreed with Dad, and insisted that I not buy anything for the kids. She promised me that the kids would overlook missing any gifts from me, because Dad had something extra special to give them when they visited them tonight to have dinner and cake with us. So, I relented to my parents' wishes.

When the kids finished their breakfast, we went to the foyer where they proceeded placing shoes on their little feet. As they did so, I collected their petite backpacks from the bench seat by the front door and patiently waited for them to finish covering their toes with shoes. In a moment, they'd completed the task and I assisted them with their backpacks over their shoulders once their sweaters were placed on them first. Finally leaving our house together, we entered into the cool, crisp spring air.

It wasn't a long walk through our Westchester neighborhood to school, since it was about a five-minute walk from home. I enjoyed strolling to school with them; it was a time when we had many curious conversations. The kids were inquisitive about everything and prattled on about their innocent thoughts and ideas. I found their curiosity was profound and existential, and it impressed me.

They often asked me about dinosaurs, the creation of the planets and the universe, and why Nature was the way it was. And, they also talked abundantly about God—wondering why He created things and made them the way they were. I discovered that I could easily answer many of their questions when it came to science. But when they asked me about God, I found the answers to be slightly more difficult, because I couldn't truly fathom God's will even though the Bible might grant us some insight about Him and His will. Instead, I would simplify those answers for them using my own perspective. Except, that seemed to satisfy them only a little as they continued to ask me spiritual questions, I thought that I had already answered. Consequently, these discussions tended to pique my own curiosity as I also tried fathoming God.

When we arrived at Immaculate Heart School, we entered through the side gate leading into the playground. We continued walking toward the back of the school until we arrived in the junior high school courtyard, where all the school children assembled at this location every morning in lines corresponding to their grade. Each grade was then divided into a pair of lines which corresponded to the children's gender.

At this moment, Leif and Leila released my hands and ran to their group of friends congregated in their grade. I glanced around, noticing parents gathering around the perimeter where their children had gathered, beginning to mingle, and socialized with each other also.

"Hey," my friend Heather suddenly appeared, greeting me as she approached my side where I had found an empty spot to stand behind the perimeter beneath the green awning, watching my children talk happily with their friends.

"Hi, how are you?" I asked turning my attention toward her now.

"I'm good," she said pleasantly. "How are you?" She was holding Mason, her five-year-old son's hand, and leaned to give him a kiss before he was sent running toward the kids assembling in their proper lines sharing the same class as my kids.

"I'm okay," I responded while tucking loose tendrils behind my ears that had escaped my ponytail in the breeze.

"Good," she replied naturally. "Happy birthday to Leif and Leila."

"Thanks."

"So, the party is Friday after school, right?"

"Yeah."

"At three o' clock?"

"Right."

"Okay, just making sure. I wanted to confirm it with my husband so he wouldn't make other plans for us to do something at the same time," she said.

"Oh, of course," I agreed.

"Mason is so excited for it. He's been counting down the days as if it were his own birthday party happening. So, we'll definitely be there."

"Great! It'll be fun," I said gladly.

"Yeah," she agreed easily. The morning sunlight caught the blonde highlights in her voluminous hair and I noticed her new haircut. She frequently complained about the length of her hair and the way it appeared before she changed its style.

"Your hair looks really nice," I commented.

"Oh, thanks! I told my stylist not to cut it too much since I wanna grow it out passed my shoulders like the way Brigitte Bardot had it. Do you remember her in Hollywood a long time ago?"

"Yeah, I remember her from the old movies. That style would look really nice on you," I complimented.

"Thanks. Yeah, I was thinking so too. It's been so long since I've worn it long. I don't know if I could wear it as long as yours, though. Yours is so beautiful with your ringlets down your back. I'd have to cut mine all off if I had it as long as yours, because mine would just look flat and straggly like *Cousin It*," she said, and I laughed.

"You're so dramatic," I said, amused by her.

"Trust me—it would," she giggled. "So, are you working today?"

"Yeah. Are you?"

Heather was a dental hygienist and was employed by her husband, Rick, who was a dentist and had a practice in town close to school.

"Nope. Not today," she informed me.

"Oh, that's right, today's your day off," I remembered suddenly.

"Yeah. So, I can help you with the cupcakes today if you want," she offered.

"Oh, that would be so nice of you. I could definitely use the help."

"I figured."

"Thanks so much. You're a life saver."

"No problem."

Suddenly, the school bell rang and surrounding conversations from everyone ceased. Announcements promptly began over the intercom, and birthday wishes were mentioned. As the speaker wished Leif and Leila a happy birthday, all their classmates cheered for them, causing their faces to light with happy excitement.

Once all of the school announcements had been concluded, the Lord's Prayer was said with everyone's participation followed by the Pledge of Allegiance. Afterward, the children were dismissed from the assembly and proceeded leaving the yard for their respective classrooms in an orderly fashion, with the youngest grades departing the congregation first.

Heather and I stepped between the boys' and girls' preschool lines and walked with our children toward their classroom building with their teacher, Ms. Lambert, leading the way. I held my children's hands as we normally did while walking toward the main school building where their classroom was located, listening to their classmates' innocent conversations as they excitedly discussed the birthday celebration expected today. When we soon arrived at the door to their classroom building, I kissed my children goodbye, wishing them a good day. They each kissed me back. Then, releasing my hands, they continued walking in line through the open doorway, vanishing inside the school.

Three

After leaving the kids at school this morning, I decided to jog around my neighborhood for exercise as my thoughts pulled toward Leif again. Desperate to center my mind before I went to work at my pediatric practice in Santa Monica, I needed this time to use for myself. Every day I did this, because I had to. Without this spare moment, the need to compose myself wouldn't exist. Crumbling before everyone's eyes wasn't an option.

But, today seemed harder from the start, despite my intention to focus on my responsibilities for the day. I couldn't shake the feeling of the dream I had last night from my consciousness. The memory of him was so clear this time, as if we'd never been separated. I wanted the sensation of him to remain impressed upon my soul and not dispel. But the compounding sorrow accompanied, so I beat the pavement with my feet. The distraction in particular while running drew me away from the present as I plugged earbuds into my ears and turned up the music to the calming song, *Emotion* sung by Destiny's Child inspired by The Bee Gees, breathing again the minute it flooded my mind.

Inhaling the fresh, cool air filling my lungs while jogging, a light breeze stirred, breaking across my face. A different state of mind came over me at the moment, and a sense of peace was beginning to fall onto my consciousness. The sadness had dimmed. My mind was settling, and I found nothing held my attention any longer. My mind emptied. My emotions disappeared.

Remembering Crazy Eye and the Berkshires, feeling heartsick, all went numb—granting me solace—for now. My focus latched onto the present, and the only thing I was aware of was the rhythm of my heart beating, my panting breath escaping me, the pounding of my feet against the pavement, and the music in my ears faded into the background. I was now running no longer for the exercise, but just running simply to run. It was serene. I was existing. It didn't matter where I was going, because I wasn't going to stop.

So, I ran—losing track of time…

When I realized I had turned onto Emerson Street and rounded the corner of 83rd Street, I recognized my titanium-white colonial style house coming into view and I automatically slowed my stride. Lightly jogging along the shrubs lining the white picket fence, I found myself entering through the gate. Panting, I walked the stone pathway until I reached the porch, finally exhausted despite my urge to continue running anywhere else down the street. Instead, I unthinkingly came through the front door and entered the foyer the moment my cellphone rang.

"Hello?" I answered as I was heading for the kitchen.

"Hey, it's me." Dakota's voice solemnly came through on the other end.

"Oh, hey," I replied, glad to hear from her while going to the cupboard and retrieving a clean glass.

"How are you?" she asked, sounding concerned and a little stilted.

"I'm okay," I said, moving toward the refrigerator now to fill my glass with cold water.

"Good," she said.

"How are you?" I inquired.

"I'm—okay, too, I guess."

"What do you mean you guess?"

"No, I'm okay—really. I'm just calling…"

"What's wrong?" I asked a little nervously, as she wasn't sounding like her typical buoyant self.

"Where are you right now?" she replied instead.

"I'm at home. I just got back from a jog," I informed her.

"Oh. You went for a jog?"

"Yeah, I needed the exercise."

"Right… I forgot that you do that."

"What's going on? You're not sounding like you normally do."

"Are you alone?" she asked directly, instead of answering my question again.

"Yeah," I said strangely, wondering why she was calling me.

"Good. I was hoping to catch you before you went to work—and while you were alone."

"What's going on?" I asked, now worried.

"Well…" she started, but paused. She sighed and I knew that something was surely wrong.

"What is it, Dakota? You're starting to scare me," I prompted.

"I'm sorry. I don't want to scare you."

"But you are."

"I just don't know how to tell you what it is that I need to tell you."

"Just tell me."

"I'm trying to. I am—I mean."

"Are you okay? Because, you seem unsettled or something and I'm becoming very—"

"Right now, Kyle and I are in the Berkshires at my parents' house for the week—house sitting while they're in Seattle visiting friends," she interrupted, informing me.

"Yeah?" I responded curiously.

"Well—there's a guy here—at the house with us. He just randomly showed up today," she continued anxiously.

"Who?" I asked, alarmed. Suddenly, I believed that she was experiencing a crime right now and was secretly informing me of it—that this man had broken into their house and was going to harm her and Kyle. "Are you being threatened? Do you need me to call the police?"

"No! No—nothing like that. We're okay. Seriously. Just listen to me. Okay? I'm sorry that I'm freaking you out."

"Yes, you are."

"It's not my intention. I'm sorry."

"I'm so confused."

"I know. Just listen," she urged.

"All right. I'm listening."

"The guy who showed up here is someone who we've never met before. He seems to be a foreigner—from the U.K., I'm guessing—given his accent. No big deal, I suppose. But, the very strange thing about him, though, is that he's weirdly dressed in a bunch of eighteenth century Revolutionary garb as a redcoat. He says he knows you. He also says he's a duke or something very strange like that, and gave us an extensive name, identifying himself. If I'm remembering what he said, he said that his name is essentially Seamus Stewart, and that he—"

"Oh my God!" I gasped, abruptly interrupting her. My hand catapulted to my mouth and my heart instantly ceased within the span of a beat, fundamentally shocking me. The world immediately came to a grinding halt. Everything around me instantly became surreal. I suddenly stared into oblivion, dangling in suspension, not believing any of this. "Leif," I uttered beneath my breath, flabbergasted.

"Yeah—he says that's the name which you call him by," Dakota responded oddly.

The glass I was holding was shaking and some of the water sloshed out, spilling to the travertine floor at my feet. I carefully turned away from the refrigerator, slowly setting my full glass of water on the white marble countertop over the island, as best as I could, before uncontrollably sinking to the floor with my back supported against the island cabinet, unexpectedly sapped of all my strength.

"It's impossible..." I whispered unevenly, dilapidated on the floor, utterly discombobulated. "How is it possible? This can't be real..."

"Wait. What? So, you know him, then?" Dakota asked, astonished.

"He's there? With you? Now?" I responded instead, tremulous throughout my limbs.

"Yes—he's here. So, you actually know him?" she questioned curiously again, sounding clearly confused now too.

"Yeah—I know him," I heard myself saying. My fingertips trembled uncontrollably against my lips as I strove to measure my quick, shallow breathing. My vision rapidly blurred. Water began pooling in my eyes while I remained collapsed sitting on the stone floor, trying to make sense out of the senseless. Simultaneous joy expanding my being, immediately uplifting me as countless thoughts swarmed my mind, overwhelming my ability to speak.

Dakota paused also, becoming silent for a moment, letting dead air come between us. Then, I heard her saying in a muffled voice to someone, "She says she knows him."

"She does?" I recognized Kyle's response. He sounded incredibly flummoxed—like I knew he would be.

"Yeah," Dakota said to him.

"So, who the hell is this guy?" Kyle questioned her, expressing his cutting skepticism.

"I don't know yet. Let me find out," I heard Dakota saying to him.

"Well, stop hesitating. We've gotta find out who this guy is right now," he told her.

"Be patient. She's upset," Dakota replied to him.

"How? Is she afraid or something? Afraid of this guy? Let me talk to her."

"Wait. I don't think she's afraid. She doesn't sound like it."

"But you just said she's upset."

"Yes. She's crying. So, let me handle this delicately," she insisted. Then her voice became clear over the phone again when she pursued asking me, "Are you all right to talk to me, Sylvie?"

"Yeah..."

"Okay," she realized in a compassionate voice. "I know that you're upset. I feel really bad that you are. But I'm going to have to ask you who this guy is, Sylvie—since he's here with us at the house, and we don't know anything about him. He swears that he knows you, and that you know him. And now, you're telling me that you in fact do know him. So, please tell me. Who is he?"

I desperately wished to answer her question: to tell her everything about him, to tell her all about us. But there wasn't any way that I could actually do that without causing more problems with my family. It was hard enough that I protected myself, including them, by holding secrets regarding my disappearance and my relationship with Leif. I guarded my secrets like I guarded my emotions whenever I was around anyone. Most of all when I was with my family. Pretending everything was fine, was easier than revealing a snippet that I was less than all right.

How could they understand any of it? They couldn't. The circumstances were impossible to overcome. So, I hesitated—not knowing how to respond without revealing everything that had happened to me and inspiring questions from her that I was not prepared to answer. Or, could not answer instead. So, silence was my salvation. Figuring out what to say instead was also impossible, because I wept.

"Sylvie?" Dakota said gently, calling my attention back to her.

"Yeah?" I sniveled.

"So, who is he?"

"He's, um..."

"Yeah? Who is he? Please tell me," she prodded carefully.

"He's their father," I croaked, struggling with tears, forced to inform her of that particular truth.

"Their father?" she echoed questioningly. But then, she suddenly inhaled. "You mean the kids' father?"

I blinked and tears unforgivingly slipped down my cheeks, soaking my face.

"Yeah," I sniffled, hearing my voice crack as I processed her complete astonishment, while stroking tears away with my fingers.

"Oh my God…" Dakota gasped again. Silence suddenly returned between us, and I was deeply insecure over her reaction; I imagined what she was beginning to think, and didn't want her misunderstanding my relationship with Leif.

"Please tell Kyle not to be mad at him," I implored instantly.

"He's kinda already," she admitted.

"He shouldn't be angry at him at all, though."

"Why not?"

"Because, there's no reason for him to be resentful," I said truly. She didn't respond immediately. Instead, she remained silent, giving me the distinct impression that my brother was absolutely furious at Leif. My breath shook as I drew it in, and I started saying, "It would mean a lot to me if Kyle treated him nicely. Leif's sincerely a very, *very* good guy. He did nothing wrong. He didn't abandon me."

"He didn't?" Dakota questioned seriously.

"No. He didn't," I told her honestly.

"That's very reassuring to know, because we love you, Sylvie, and we could never stand it if you were ever hurt by anyone."

"I know."

"In that case, I'll make sure to tell Kyle to support your wish."

"It would mean a lot to me. Thank you."

"You're welcome. We're just trying to protect you in case there was ever a problem with him."

"He was never a problem."

"Okay."

"So, please don't blame him for anything."

"All right. We trust you."

"Thank you."

"You don't have to thank us. I know that you're being honest with us about him. So, don't worry about anyone being upset," she stressed. "We're just worried about you—you know? Whatever it was that happened between you and him that separated the both of you from each other can be helped now, if that's what you want —of course.

"You've been silent for so long, Sylvie. For many years, I know you've been scared to tell us about what happened to you. But, just know we're here for you—always. Okay?"

"I know you are," I understood, grateful.

"Good," she replied. "I know that you've mentioned some things to your parents about what had happened the day the kids were born, when you returned from missing. But it wasn't every-thing. Kyle and I respect your feelings and we promised not to push you to tell us anything until you were ready, thinking it was best. But now that the father of your kids is here... things are differ-ent. I'm sure you're aware of that. Just know that we love you and we'll support you—no matter what."

"Thank you," I sobbed.

"We don't want you feeling like you have to run away anymore."

"I never meant to. I'm sorry—that everyone has been put through so much heartache because I was gone. I never meant to leave anyone. I didn't mean for it to ever happen."

Dakota released a compassionate sigh. "I know you would never intend to hurt anyone, Sylvie. It's not like that. *You're* not like that. But cope with us instead from now on, because we're all here for you. You're not alone. You never were."

"You're right," I acknowledged.

A pause ensued between us, and the lull lasted for a moment. Both of us, I sensed, had understood each other as we rested from our conversation. Although, I couldn't seem to stem my flowing tears as I struggled to stifle my sniveling.

"So, now what are we going to do?" she started again.

"I can't answer that right now," I replied, extraordinarily distressed.

"No—I'm sorry. I meant what plans should we make for him? Now that we know that you both in fact know each other, and with him being the kids' father, I wouldn't mind offering him one of the guest bedrooms."

"That's extremely kind of you. Thank you so much. I really appreciate you doing that for him."

"Well, he's family—so of course," she said.

"I promise that he won't be an imposition on you for too long, since I'm intending to pick him up and will be bring him back with me to L.A. to stay," I responded.

"Don't concern yourself over the length of his stay with us. Take your time in getting here."

"I can't ask that of you. So, I'll be catching a redeye flight tonight."

"There really is no pressure. But you do whatever you feel is best."

"Thanks for your understanding, Dakota. It's best that I fly out as soon as I can tonight," I replied sincerely.

"Sure, of course," she accepted sympathetically. "I'm wondering, though, if you'd like to speak with him right now. He's constantly asking for you. For some reason, I don't think he quite understands that you're not here with us right now, and I'm thinking that if you were to speak with him, it might ease his curiosity about you. He's very anxious to see you again."

"Absolutely, I'll speak with him. Is he nearby?"

"He's actually in the dining room right now having a cup of tea and a sandwich that I made for him. He said that he was famished. I guess that he hasn't eaten in a while," she informed me.

"I see."

"But I'm sure he'd definitely won't mind the interruption in order to speak with you while he eats."

"Whenever he's ready, I'll be ready too."

"All right, I'll give him my phone. Hang on a second."

"Okay," I replied.

I waited in silence while she took a moment to bring him the phone. My heart began hammering madly in my chest as I nervously anticipated the sound of his voice after it had gone dark for so long. But as I soon heard the phone shuffling between hands, I grew dizzy. My breath suddenly caught in my throat, and my blood ran warm, heating me. A strong spell of lightheadedness came over me, making me feel that I just might faint before a word from him was spoken.

"Hullo?"

"Leif?" I inhaled abruptly, staggered, when absolutely recognizing his voice for the first time again now coming through the phone.

"Sylvie!" he gasped, instantly recognizing me too. Copious tears flooded my eyes, obscuring my vision. Short of breath, it was difficult to breathe. Wholly mystified that I was hearing him call my name once more, I broke down and completely sobbed.

"Oh my God—I can't believe this is happening. It's really you..." I blubbered helplessly, fundamentally overjoyed.

"Holy God! I hear yer sweetness!" he expressed in sheer elation clearly emanating from his cracking voice. "How I have missed ye. Ye will never ken." His voice was hoarse, and I knew he was fighting back his own emotions.

"I might have an idea of how much," I wept.

"Ye micht, indeed," he agreed croakily. "Have I truly discovered the pulse of my heart?"

"Yes—you have."

"Tell me 'tis nae dream."

"It has to be real."

"Aye. It must."

"Leif…"

"Permit me tae hear ye say it again. How I have longed tae listen tae the charm in yer voice floating from yer lips."

"Leif. How? I lost you… I thought I'd never see you again. I never thought that you'd—"

"I shall explain how 'tis so, once I lay eyes upon ye again," he interrupted anxiously. "Tell me, whaur are ye? I must have ye within my presence." His voice was cracking, and I knew he was on the cusp of collapsing under the weight of his emotions.

"I'll be there to see you really soon," I told him, incapable of clearing my watery vision.

"How soon will it be?" he asked urgently.

"Tomorrow."

"The morrow?"

"Yes."

"Yet, my heart was set upon the immediate present."

"If I could be there today, I'd be there quicker than lightning."

"Then, ye remain far from me?"

"Yes."

"How many leagues?"

"Enough for me to need several hours to travel to meet you."

"Hours?"

"Yes."

"Micht it be how many?"

"About a day's worth."

"In that case, I must journey tae ye, instead."

"That'll be impractical."

"How micht it be?"

"Remember that I had told you about airplanes once?"

"Aye."

"One must be taken in order for me to see you as soon as tomorrow, and I'm the only one between us who can travel that way."

"Truly?"

"Yes."

"I see…" he responded, sounding slightly confused and obviously disappointed. "Then, I must bide patiently."

"Yes. I must be patient too—even though I'm fighting it," I said.

"As am I…" He drifted into silence for a moment. "I'm jubilant tae hear ye speak. Pray, tell me—how have ye been faring?"

"Well—I'm inexplicably better now that I can hear your voice again too."

"I understand."

"I know you do. Tell me how you've been?"

"I have had many difficult years since our separation."

"Me too."

He paused for a moment and our conversation lulled again. I heard him breathing and it fluctuated. He sniffled. "Sylvie?" he resumed, clearing his hoarseness.

"Yes?" I wiped my damp eyelashes with my fingers.

"I must ken about the bairn. Did it perish? I had a cursed dream once which unsettled my soul, and has tormented me ever since… I dreamt 'twas still upon birth." The tone in his voice was full of trepidation, and I realized the haunting had chased him incessantly, too.

"Nothing like that happened," I reassured.

"Nae?"

"No. Our children are alive, Leif."

"Children?"

"Yes. We have two of them."

"Do we?"

"Yes."

"Two?" he uttered, astonished.

"A boy and a girl."

"Twins?"

"Yeah. They're doing very well—strong, healthy, bright—"

"God Almighty!" He chuckled briskly. "'Tis an extraordinary blessing! Whit are their names?"

"Leif and Leilani."

"A tribute tae us," he recognized.

"Yes. I remembered you said that if we had a girl, that you wanted her to be named after me. And, that if we had a boy, then he would be named after you."

"I certainly recall it... Ye have honored me," he croaked.

"And, I'm thanking you," I replied instead.

"Fur whit reason?" he asked strangely.

"For giving them to me," I said. Leif suddenly paused in silence. His breathing shook over the phone. Then, he said, "Yoo're the lecht of my soul, and the ballad of my heart, Sylvie." I hyperventilated with more tears, unable to reply. "*Tha gràdh agam ort*," he uttered softly.

"I love you too," I managed saying through weeping. "Today's your birthday—in case you weren't already aware of it."

"Is it?"

"Yes. Happy birthday."

"Och. Weel now, I have been bestowed the greatest gift upon this day as I behold yer bonnie voice in my ear, knowing that we shall reunite."

"I've missed you more than I can express."

"It has been most bitter fur me as weel... These many years now spent in yer absence has altered me."

"How?"

"I am an old man now, Sylvie."

"What? You don't sound like you're old at all."

"Yet, I am. Ye will see once we meet again at last."

"Well—if it's any consolation to you, I've aged as well."

"Ye will always remain wet behind the ears," he joked, and I suddenly giggled.

"You still have your sense of humor."

"I do that, indeed, merely due tae yer present affect upon my heart."

"I'll happily take credit for keeping you young, and throw time by the wayside," I teased. He chuckled and my heart leaped delightedly as I found myself giggling again.

"Ye have kept yer wit also, I see," he said, humored also.

"Only because you inspire me," I replied.

"A perfect match."

"Yes."

"It has been too long."

"It has."

"We shall reconcile the time that has come betwixt us."

"I'm looking forward to it."

"As am I," he replied, causing me to smile. We both became quiet with each other for a moment. I sensed him missing me as I had missed him throughout all of this time. But strangely, we didn't seem to mind it anymore now that we were communicating again. So, we simply remained peacefully silent with each other, comforted by the fact that we could finally exist together at the same time at this hour.

It was a while before he and I were willing to end our conversation. Aware of each other, we were hesitant to let one of us go. Except, the time regrettably came to say goodbye.

"I don't want to say goodbye to you," I uttered softly.

"Dinnae say it," he said gently.

"But I need to let you finish eating, knowing how hungry you are," I replied. "And, I should also prepare for my journey to come see you."

"Is it farewell after all?"

"Just for now."

"Just fur now," he echoed.

"Yeah."

"I shall long fur the moment."

"I'll long for it too."

"Farewell, then, *mo leannan*."

"Farewell for now," I responded.

Next, I shortly heard the phone shuffling between hands again. Feeling elated now that everything had unexpectedly changed by the incomprehensible, I was beginning to settle from my exuberant emotions. Calmness secured me again, and filled my heart with rejuvenated hope and gratitude.

"Hey..." I heard Dakota now saying over the phone, recognizing the shock in her voice; I supposed she had heard Leif's entire side of the conversation, to my discomfiture.

"Hi," I responded, clearing my throat, now that my tears had begun drying. "Thanks for letting us talk. It's obviously been a while."

"Yeah, no problem. I'm glad that you guys were able to speak," she said. "So, you're flying out soon?"

"Yeah. I'm catching a flight out of LAX tonight, after I celebrate the kids' birthday this evening with my parents," I replied.

"Okay. We'll be here waiting for you."

"All right."

"Give my sweet little niece and nephew hugs and kisses from me and Kyle. We ordered a couple of gifts for them from an online toy boutique. They should arrive in time for their birthday party."

"Thank you so much. That's very sweet of you," I said.

"I'm sorry that we can't make it out there to celebrate this time."

"It's all right."

"Well, we feel bad about it. But Kyle and I will call them tonight to wish them happy birthday."

"They'll love hearing from you."

"We'll FaceTime them. The next best thing to actually being there with them. I know they'll like that."

"They certainly will."

"Great. I'm glad we'll get a chance to celebrate with them, even if it's remote."

"As long as they can see your faces, they'll be thrilled for sure."

"Us too. I'll let you go now. I know you've got things to take care of first before you leave."

"Thanks for everything, Dakota."

"No worries."

"Love you," I said truly.

"Love you too," she reciprocated equally.

I hung up the phone and removed my earbuds from my ears, thoroughly astounded and baffled that I had just had a live conversation with Leif. Truly surreal... I was left sitting on the kitchen floor overwhelmed by joy. All I could do was simply thank God, realizing His mercy and grace.

IT TOOK ME A HEALTHY MOMENT TO SETTLE MY NERVES and collect my composure. My vision had finally cleared from tears. I coincidentally glanced at the clock on the refrigerator facing me when I realized that I hadn't called my office yet. So, I took my phone up from off the floor where I had set it down beside myself after hanging up with Dakota, and dialed my work number. Samantha, the head nurse, promptly answered the call and I briefly explained to her that I wouldn't be coming into the office today, using the excuse of having a family emergency.

"Oh gosh! I hope it's not the kids?" she asked concernedly when I notified her.

"No, they're fine," I assured her.

"Oh, I'm so glad to hear that."

"It's a family matter involving a close relative."

"I see. Well, I hope everything works out for the best for your relative," she said sincerely.

"Thank you."

"Will we see you tomorrow at the office, then?"

"Not until next Monday," I informed her.

"Okay. We'll have Doctor Bailey cover your patients for you, instead."

"Thanks so much, Sam. I truly appreciate it."

"Not a problem."

"Thank you, anyway."

"Sure. Take care, then, and we'll see you next week."

"You take care too."

"Thanks."

"See you Monday."

"See you then," she said, concluding our brief conversation and we hung up.

Finally picking myself up off the travertine floor, I moved around the island and went out of the kitchen, heading up the staircase for my bedroom. When I arrived inside my room, I spotted my laptop on the nightstand at my bedside and retrieved it. Plopping myself on the bed with it, I activated it from sleep and began searching the airlines on the internet for the least expensive red eye flight I could find from LAX to Logan.

After comparing prices and flight times, I finally found the right one and instantly booked it. Then, hurrying to the bathroom, I took a quick shower, understanding that I had a lot to accomplish before arriving at school for the kids' birthday celebration today, including going to the mall to purchase some modern clothing for Leif that I was certain he would need.

Four

I rushed home from the mall and hastily packed clothes and toiletries that I had purchased for Leif into my rolling suitcase, along with my own belongings. Then, rushing down the staircase to the kitchen, I collected all of the nicely decorated cupcakes, beverages, birthday party themed paper plates, napkins, including party hats and placed them inside my Odyssey. Except, I realized that I had nearly forgotten the matching tablecloths before leaving the house. So, I ran back inside and grabbed them off the foyer bench where I'd left them. Finally shutting and locking the front door afterward, I hopped into my minivan and drove to school hoping to make it in time to celebrate before arriving too late.

Just as I had pulled into Immaculate Heart School's parking lot, I noticed Heather emerging from her Flex already parked. She waved at me as I turned my vehicle into the empty parallel parking slot beside hers, and waited for me to exit my car.

"Hey," she greeted as I opened my driver's side door.

"Hi." I was relieved to see her already here to help me. "Thanks for coming."

"Yeah, no problem," she said easily.

"I thought I was going to be late," I replied anxiously.

"You did?"

"Yeah."

"Busy day at work?"

"Not actually."

"Oh. Was it traffic?"

"No. I wound up calling in sick. So, I didn't make it to work today," I disclosed.

"I get it. That always happens to me when I have to be here volunteering the same time I'm supposed to be working."

"That's the case for me today."

"Was it hard to find someone to suddenly cover for you, though?"

"Fortunately, not. It worked out."

"Glad it did." Her eyes turned toward the cupcakes in the large, rectangular Tupperware cake containers with the party supplies resting on the back seats inside my minivan, when I promptly opened the passenger door. "Did you actually bake all those?" She appeared duly impressed, returning to looking at me.

"Yeah," I said.

"Wow, that's a lot of work," she recognized. I smiled knowingly at her and she giggled a little. "They look delicious."

"Thanks."

"Okay, so what can I help you with first to get this party started?" she asked willingly.

"If you wouldn't mind grabbing one of the cake holders, and the bag with the paper goods, that would be great," I suggested.

"Sure." She easily leaned inside the van to grab the items, and I reached inside for the remaining cake container and drinks on the other seat. Once we had the goods, I closed and locked the doors and we started away from the car. We walked and chatted while approaching the main building where the school's office was located. When we arrived inside, we entered the office, following protocol, and signed ourselves in as parent guests as we were pleasantly greeted by staff. Then, returning outside, we headed toward the back of the school where the lunch area was located. Green picnic tables beneath the matching awnings were evenly spaced around the area. Randomly selecting a table, we finally placed the party items down on to the surface, relieving our arms.

It was close to a half hour before the dismissal bell would ring. Having the time slot open, Heather and I began preparing for the birthday celebration. We proceeded setting party supplies over the picnic tables now shaded from the warmly shining afternoon sun by the overhanging awnings, making it pleasant as a light breeze stirred around us from the ocean not too far away.

While we were laying festive tablecloths over the tables, a couple of other mothers arrived early to wait to pick up their children from the same class. Sarah and Tammy made eye contact with me and we smiled at each other as they began lingering nearby, waiting for their children. They were typically the early birds like Heather and I were to pick up our kids from school. Noticing us preparing the lunch tables with birthday goods, they kindly offered their assistance and gladly joined us in readying the tables for the celebration.

The usual chitchat started between the group while we were setting paper dining places over the covered picnic tables. But I found it difficult to center on their conversation at the moment as my mind remained glued to Leif. I was unusually anxious. The anticipation building inside me to see him again was brimming, and it seemed time couldn't pass quickly enough before we reunited.

All I wanted to do was to abandon everything I was doing right now, only to behold his face. But guilt intruded, shaming me for having these feelings, since I was supposed to be placing my undivided attention on making my children happy today. Striving to concentrate on the immediate task facing me, I forced myself to focus on situating the correct number of mini water bottles I had purchased onto the table in front of me for the school children to have.

Since my conversation with Leif this morning, I felt suspended on a cloud while walking around in surrealism. Caught in a daze, my excitement for him was getting the best of my attention. I couldn't concentrate on the usual occurrences presently taking place around me. My mind simply wouldn't let me as it drifted away into the realm of fondly remembering my past with him. Distracting thoughts swirled in my head over him. The eager expectation of soon seeing him again shook me to the core of my foundation with happiness. After believing all hope for us had been lost, I was overjoyed.

"Are you okay?" I heard Heather inquire confidentially as she was distributing paper napkins next to plates beside me over the same table.

"Yeah. Why?" I responded as my attention was suddenly called back to the occurring moment.

"You're awfully quiet," she noticed.

"Oh—well—I just—have a lot on my mind," I stammered.

"Yeah? Like what?" she asked curiously. I hesitated telling her anything at all. I never spoke to her, or to anyone else for that matter, in detail about the father of my children. I kept as much as I could regarding him a secret, and buried it only to keep it safe from everyone. But when forced to refer to him because of my children, I made a cautious effort to limit any information about him, keeping it vague and at a minimum to my friends and acquaintances.

I was certain that no one on Earth would ever understand me —not even my family—if I attempted slightly revealing more— despite my most recent conversation that I had with Dakota today. But now Heather's light blue eyes were gazing penetratingly at me with clear curiosity. My heart began pounding in my chest as my stomach quivered with wild butterflies fluttering when I nervously returned looking at her.

"I got an unusual phone call today," I blurted despite my caution, surprising myself.

"You did?" Her eyes widened with intrigue.

"Yeah."

"Tell me about it. I hope it was an okay one?"

"It was—actually."

"That's good. Who did you hear from?" she inquired curiously. I automatically bit my lip and broke eye contact with her as I tucked a loose ringlet behind my ear, feeling my lips involuntarily curling a little upward. She smiled a bit quizzically at me, and I could perceive her wondering about my reaction when I returned to looking at her.

"I—I heard from someone whom I haven't heard from in a really long time," I started as I looked at her. The anticipation to know more was obviously expressed on her face.

"Who was it?" she prompted, observing me. I hesitated proceeding. The look in her eyes turned into puzzlement indicating concern, and now I perceived her questioning if the person I'd heard from was someone I had actually regretted as the little grin on my face disappeared. "Are you sure it was a good contact, and that the conversation was good?" she inquired, insightfully.

"Yeah—it was," I answered positively.

"Okay?" she responded skeptically, urging me to continue. Suddenly, I was concerned for myself in this new conversation with her. I realized immediately there was no way around it but to simply tell her a fragment of the truth. Unless, I preferred for her to think that something was wrong between us instead, and have her believe that I didn't trust her, ultimately damaging our friendship. But I did value our friendship, and I didn't want her believing the opposite. Except, as I currently thought for a second, she might feel a modicum of betrayal when I tell her a portion of the truth that I've kept hidden from her pertaining to my kids' father, since I became a parishioner here at the school's church several years ago. "So, are you going to tell me what's going on? Or will you leave me hanging?" she encouraged, half joking.

"No—I—I'm sorry for being weird. I won't leave you hanging," I faltered.

"Then, tell me. Who did you hear from?"

"It was my... I mean, I spoke with my kids' father today," I divulged confidentially, finally, feeling very nervous that I told her.

"No way." Heather's eyes suddenly widened again. But this time her mouth dropped.

"Yeah." I nodded.

"You're serious?"

"Yeah," I said, perceiving the shock on her face.

"Wow."

"I know."

"What happened?" she continued inquisitively.

"We just caught up with each other—that's all," I responded, aware that my hands were trembling a bit while I continued distributing water bottles over the table.

"I'm imagining that was a long conversation. Wasn't it?" she presumed, keeping her eyes on me while she continued setting down napkins on the same table.

"It wasn't long enough, actually," I admitted.

"It wasn't?"

"No." I lightly shook my head.

"Why not?"

"We got interrupted."

"Oh," she realized. "When did you guys last speak with each other?"

"Too long ago."

"Was it weird? After it being so long?"

"I can't say that it was weird at all—which might seem strange," I answered, glancing from the water bottles I was still distributing and meeting her gaze again. She nodded a little.

"I didn't think that you had any contact with him."

"I know. It was unexpected. He surprised me."

"So, it wasn't awkward at all?"

"No."

"I have to say that I'm really surprised. I mean—you know—because so much time has gone by since you guys last talked. I would've thought that there might've been at least a little bit of weirdness, or resentment—maybe," she said frankly.

"It's nothing like that," I replied.

"Then, what was it like for you?"

"It was actually comforting," I divulged honestly, holding her gaze for a moment before returning to placing more bottles of water over the table.

"Really?" she responded, tilting her head to the side, appearing surprised and skeptical.

"Yeah."

"Oh..." She nodded again, now contemplative. "So, there's no animosity in the slightest?"

"There isn't anything like that between us."

"Seriously?" She leaned and positioned another napkin over the table on the opposite side from herself as I set a new water bottle down in front of me.

"Honestly," I told her for certain. Her eyes bounced up from the table and looked at me again.

"I'm impressed. Seriously. You're generous, because I know I would be feeling so much differently if it were me. I wouldn't be so forgiving of Rick if we had separated and he contacted me out of the blue after I had his son. I even get agitated not hearing from him when he's out playing golf with his friends over the weekend," she disclosed. I didn't respond; I didn't know how to. "So, are you guys planning on seeing each other now that he's contacted you?" she continued asking, giving me a suspecting look. I nodded. She nodded also, acknowledging my intent for it to happen, while gazing thinkingly at me again. "Will you see him with the kids?"

"Not yet."

"That's wise. I don't suppose you'd want to overwhelm them."

"I suppose not."

"Yeah, I would think they'd need some kind of preparation before meeting him."

"I agree," I responded, recognizing my children weren't actually going to be afforded that opportunity, and I worried about it.

"How soon will you tell them about their dad?"

"After he and I meet—when we would have had the chance to discuss them first."

"That's reasonable."

"I think so too."

"You're nervous about it. Aren't you?"

"Can you tell?"

"Yeah," she replied. "Don't be, though. I mean, if you guys are on good terms, then it seems you'll be able to work it out with the kids more easily after you guys meet."

"Yeah," I said, considering her encouragement.

"So, can I ask what happened that caused you guys to break up?"

"It's difficult to say—and it's a long story."

"Then, give me the short story."

"The simple version would be that time came between us," I said, slipping a partial truth.

"Oh, you both grew apart from each other," she assumed understandingly. "That happens to a lot of couples."

"Yes, it does," I agreed.

"So, was it that he was taking too long to make up his mind to commit? And that you felt like you were wasting time, or something like that? I mean—I'm just presuming because you don't wear a wedding ring."

"No—I don't," I replied self-consciously, glimpsing at my ring finger. I'd stopped wearing my rings Leif had given me on my left hand. Instead, I had switched them to my right hand, because I didn't want my family asking me questions about his existence when they believed I remained widowed by Matt, knowing full well I could never explain Leif to them without causing emotional strife to everyone based on presumptions I let prevail due to my silence. Instead, it was significantly easier to let them believe, and accept, that I was a lonely widow who had an undisclosed romantic affair out of wedlock. And even though I had never told this lie to my friends, it's what they automatically assumed of me too. I was certain.

My previous friends knew about my tragedy with Matt, but plenty of my current friends and acquaintances never knew I was once widowed, and immediately presumed that I was either divorced or had my children outside of marriage. This is what Heather believed along with all of the other parents and faculty here at my kids' school. It was an uncomfortable feeling, since members of this parochial school were Catholic like me and strove to live by the Doctrine. But no one ever made me feel any shame for my perceived unorthodox circumstance. Instead, members of this parish school were sympathetic and understanding of people in general—which put me at ease for the most part despite my own hidden qualms. Only, now that Heather and I were talking about myself, I realized I was close to having to confront the reality of my past by exposing a portion of my secret to her.

"He didn't have a fear of commitment," I said to her.

"What was it, then?" she pursued.

"It was distance. It got in the way."

"Oh, okay. That makes sense. You guys suffered from a long-distance relationship."

"Yeah—something very much like that," I replied uncomfortably.

"That's hard. How far away from each other were you while trying to make it work?"

"He's from Scotland," I revealed.

"Wow. Scotland?"

"Yeah."

"That's definitely far," she sympathized. "Long distance relationships are always so tough." I nodded. "Is he still living there?"

"He's closer now."

"That's better. It'll be easier for you guys when you reconnect." She smiled reassuringly and I nodded again, agreeing with her. "So where is he living now?"

"He'll actually be moving here to L.A."

"Really?"

"Yeah."

"Will your friends get a chance to meet him too, then?"

"To scrutinize him?"

"Of course. Gotta make sure of him. That's all," she said with a little grin, trying to make light of my situation without meaning any harm.

"There's no need for that. I already told you that he's not a commitment phobe," I said, understanding her tacit indication as I returned a little grin of my own. "Besides, you're married."

"No harm in looking," she giggled.

"You're such a teenage girl," I teased, giving her a little smile.

"I know," she admitted without any shame, and we giggled together.

At that moment, the school's dismissal bell rang and the preschoolers were noticed leaving their classroom building as they began walking in our direction. They followed their teacher in respective lines while chatting excitedly with each other, anticipating being served cupcakes. I spotted my children walking happily with their classmates as they came toward the prepared party tables. Leif noticed me and smiled brightly with a vigorous wave. He suddenly got out of line, running to stake his place at one of the two picnic tables designated for his class to eat, or celebrate with parties.

"Mama!" Leila squealed happily with bright green eyes, noticing me also, and jumped out of line like her brother but ran directly toward me instead. When she arrived, she gave me a big hug. I embraced her and leaned to kiss her plump, rosy cheek.

"Now sit with your friends, sweetie," I gently instructed her after our hug and kiss.

"Okay," she replied cheerfully and eagerly ran to sit with her friends at the opposite table facing her brother. Ms. Lambert, their teacher, easily noticed me and approached as the children were gleefully placing party hats over their heads while assembling themselves at the tables.

"Hi," she said, kindly greeting me. She was a sweet teacher in her mid-twenties with dark auburn hair and amber eyes, and who was always fair and understanding to her very young pupils.

"Hi," I replied nicely as we now stood before each other.

"Are the cupcakes ready?" she asked.

"Their waiting," I informed her.

"Great! It's all the kids have been talking about the entire day," she laughed.

"Have they?" I responded, amused.

"Well, just look at them now. They're bubbling over with excitement."

"Then, I guess we shouldn't keep them waiting any longer."

"I agree. Let's have some of the parents help pass out the cakes, and then we can all sing Happy Birthday," she suggested.

"Sounds good," I agreed. So, Heather, Sarah, Tammy, and I began distributing cakes to the children, making certain to keep my promise to give Leif his vanilla cake and Leila the chocolate one.

When the cupcakes had been given to all the children, following Ms. Lambert's cue, we collectively sang Happy Birthday to my kids. Afterward, everyone began enthusiastically eating sprinkled cupcakes among giggles, screeches, and cheerful chatter between ourselves. There were several cupcakes left over from the serving, so I offered them to Ms. Lambert and to the three mothers who had helped me prepare the tables.

"Thank you so much," Ms. Lambert said as glad as the kids when she received the cake.

"Of course," I replied, smiling when she immediately bit into it.

"Mmm, this is so good," she complimented after swallowing.

"I'm glad that you like it," I said.

"I think you should have a bakery," Heather suggested, complimenting me also as she was enjoying her cake.

"My hands are already full," I self-deprecated with a modest smile.

"I bet. I can only imagine having twins and working as a pediatrician full time," Tammy understood when she stepped out from beneath the awning into the bright afternoon sun beautifully illuminating her cappuccino complexion.

"I know," Sarah agreed, nodding her strawberry blonde head.

"Then, keep it as a hobby and don't give up on it, because everything you bake tastes so good," Heather responded, continuing to encouraged me.

"Thank you," I appreciated. She smiled at me, taking another bite from her cake.

More parents now gathered by us at the surrounding unoccupied tables to pick up their children from different grades, since school was ending. But our children continued indulging in their cakes, and as other parents were already leaving with their children, the church bells chimed loudly into the air twice—suddenly making me aware that I still had not yet had the opportunity to call my parents to tell them of my unexpected travel plans. I also remembered that I needed to quickly arrange for someone to look after my children while I was gone, and was hoping that my parents wouldn't mind doing it.

Five

Once I arrived at home from school with my twins, I had them settle from their exciting day by placing them in their playroom to play quietly with their toys while I grabbed my phone from my purse and went to the kitchen to call Mom. Sliding over the window seat at the bay window in the breakfast nook to sit, I nervously inhaled and dialed her cell number, hoping not to seem odd or suspicious as we spoke.

"Hello?" she answered promptly after it rang.

"Hi Mom," I exhaled, realizing I had been holding my breath.

"Oh, hi sweetie! How are you?" she responded pleasantly.

"I'm good."

"That's good. I'm glad to hear it," she said.

"How are you?" I asked.

"Just fine, sweetie. Your father and I will be seeing you and the children in a couple hours, I suppose. What time is it?" she inquired. I glanced at the digital clock on the stove.

"It's fifteen after two," I told her.

"Okay, so, we'll see you at four," she confirmed.

"Okay."

"How was school for the kids today?"

"They had a really good day," I said, biting my lip as I watched my fingertips mindlessly draw light little circles in front of me over the table.

"Oh, I'm so glad to hear that they had a nice day. Did they enjoy their little party there?"

"Yeah, they did. It was great."

"How darling," she replied as I was wondering how I was going to ask her for the favor I needed.

"Hey Mom?" I blurted.

"Yes, dear?"

"May I ask a favor of you, please?" I heard myself saying anyway.

"Sure, sweetie. What is it?"

"Well, um... You see—I'm going out of town for a couple of days. So, I—"

"You are?" she questioned, interrupting me.

"Yeah, so, I'm wondering if you wouldn't mind watching the kids for me until I get back?"

"Of course. When are you going out of town?"

"I'm leaving tonight and I'll be back on Thursday during the day."

"Tonight?" she replied unexpectedly.

"Yeah. But, don't worry—I'll pick up the kids from school the day I get back—so you won't have to," I explained hurriedly, so that she wouldn't interrupt me again. "I just thought I'd ask you, because I'm kinda in a bind, since it's sudden and everything, and since you and Dad—"

"You're leaving tonight?" she interrupted regardless.

"Yeah."

"It's rather unanticipated."

"Yes, it is. I know."

"We're celebrating the children's birthday today, though. Must you leave so soon?"

"I have to, yes."

"Well, where are going? And Why?"

"To Boston."

"Boston?" she responded abruptly.

"Yeah."

"What for?"

"It's for work." I lied, feeling guilty about it.

"For work?"

"Yeah, a pediatric symposium at Harvard is taking place—to do with the latest vaccines and medications that will be made available soon to doctors and their patients," I lied again as the idea abruptly entered my mind.

"Oh, I see. But, couldn't you have known about this earlier than now? This is rather last minute."

"I'm sorry. I just got the conference notification only recently," I said, lying some more. She sighed and became silent. "I know it's an imposition on you and Dad. But I'm stuck—since I don't know any babysitters."

"Babysitters? You know how skeptical of them I am. So, don't even consider it. Your dad and I will come to your rescue and do it. You know that. I'm just not prepared for the short notice, and you know how we get whenever you travel far from us."

"I know."

"All right. Seeing that you have to go, apparently there's no other choice. So, we'll just take the kids home with us tonight after we finish celebrating their birthday."

"Well, I want to make it easier for you so that you won't have to commute with them from your house in Santa Monica to their school here, by offering you guys the guest bedroom," I suggested.

"Oh! Why didn't I think of that option? That will actually make it a lot easier for us. Thank you, honey."

"It's okay—you're doing me a huge favor. So, I'm the one thanking you."

"Thank you, darling, anyway. But there's no need for thanks.

It's what I'm here for," she said. "In any case, I do want to know what time you have to be at the airport?"

"I have to be there by eight o'clock," I informed her.

"Okay. It won't hurt us also to drive you there, since you're so close to it."

"That's really nice of you, but you don't have to do that. I'll just take Uber," I preferred.

"Are you certain?"

"I'm sure."

"Well, all right then. Your dad and I will be prepared to watch the kids for you while you're out of town."

"Thanks so much, Mom. You're really saving me. More than you realize," I replied gratefully.

"Of course, honey. Is that all you wanted to talk about?"

"Yeah."

"Okay. Then, I'm going to inform your dad about what we're doing once we get off the phone."

"All right. I better go, then. I have to get dinner started and bake a cake."

"Sounds fine. We'll see you soon."

"Okay."

"Goodbye, honey."

"Bye, Mom." I hung up the phone, feeling exceptionally relieved when I unexpectedly noticed Leif standing near me by the breakfast table dressed in his little black cape with his Darth Vader mask on top of his head and lightsaber in hand. He was staring at me, and I wondered how much of my conversation he'd heard while standing there.

"Are you going bye-bye, Mom?" he suddenly asked me. The look of disappointment was obviously discerned on his ruddy face.

"Yes, sweetie, I am," I said.

"Are you going today?" he asked curiously.

"Yes, I'm leaving today."

"But, it's our birthday party with Granddad and Nanna, and they're coming over to have cake with us," he promptly reminded me, looking sadly with his shoulders slumped.

"I know, sweetie. Don't worry though. I won't be leaving until you and Leila are tucked into bed, so I'm definitely not missing your birthday dinner with Granddad and Nanna tonight," I assured him.

"But, why do you have to go anyway?" he asked me, pouting.

"I have to go for business reasons," I said, trying to make him understand as best as I could. His brow furrowed and he appeared dissatisfied.

"Do you *have* to go do business?" he whined unhappily.

"I'm afraid that I must, sweetie."

"I don't like business. I never get to see you because of it."

"That's not true. I always see you."

"No, you don't."

"What do you mean? I always visit you at school when I volunteer for yard duty almost every day."

"That's different."

"How?"

"I'm at school, and you can't play with me there."

"Well, what about when it's the weekend, and I take you and your sister to rent bikes to ride at the marina sometimes? Or, when we go to the park? Weren't we at the beach recently, too?"

He thoughtfully pursed his lips, looking at me for a moment as he paused. He then folded his arms over his little chest and asked, "Will you be gone a long time on your trip?"

"No. I won't. You'll barely miss me," I promised him.

"Hmmm," he considered. I gently smiled at him and lightly stroked his soft, plump cheek.

"I'll be back on Thursday and I'll pick you up from school just like always," I assured him again. "Okay?"

"Okaay," he accepted, whining a tad this time.

"Come on," I said cheerfully, trying to enliven his mood. "Would you like to help me make your birthday cake?" He nodded. "Good. Go find Leila to see if she wants to help us."

"Okie-dokie," he agreed and ran out of the kitchen in search of his sister, seeming contented now.

Six

My parents arrived punctually at four o'clock in the afternoon at my house, and the kids were overjoyed as usual to see them. When they came through the front door, the kids rushed toward them, noticing their grandfather bearing a sizable gift box for them. Leif and Leila bounced around like ping-pong balls in delight, skipping after him as he moved through the foyer and hallway into the living room holding the beautifully wrapped gift box. Excited to know what was inside, the kids crowded him as he mindfully made his way between them. When Dad reached the center of the living room, he leaned and conscientiously placed the box on the cherry hardwood floor. Then, he proceeded carefully opening the lid of the box, revealing an adorable, little, white West Highland Terrier puppy.

"A puppy!" the kids exclaimed in unison, awed by the sight of the precious animal.

"Happy birthday, buddy," Dad said to his grandson, mussing his silky, golden crown. "You too, Sweet Pea. Happy birthday to my favorite little girl." He turned to his granddaughter and hugged her as he gave her a kiss on the top of her head.

"You've gotta be kidding me, Dad! A dog? Really? Who's going to take care of a dog?" I responded utterly surprised, and skeptical of having a pet. Dad gave me a guilty look and shrugged. "Dad?" I pressed for an answer, returning an unbelievable look at him.

"Don't worry, Mom. I'll take care of the puppy!" Leif assured me, appearing quite confident about it as he turned his innocent ultramarine eyes up toward me.

"Me too! I'll take care of the puppy too!" Leila promised happily with the same look while hopping on one foot.

"Mom?" I questioned, turning my gaze toward my mother.

"Yes, sweetie?" she replied, feigning ignorance.

"You knew about this all along and didn't tell me," I accused her.

"Let's just call it even for the sudden babysitting notice," she said with a smile. I closed my eyes and took a deep breath. Opening my eyes again after a second, I saw the kids adoring the puppy, and quickly understood that because it was a gift from my parents, I felt that I had no choice but to resign myself to the idea of having an animal in the house.

"Is it a boy?" Leif inquired of his grandfather as my dad stood in the room admiring his happy grandchildren.

"Yeah, bud, he's a boy," Dad answered.

"Yaaay! He's a boy!" Leif screeched excitedly. He knelt to pick up the puppy and awkwardly gathered the animal into his arms.

"Hey! You know what?" Leila squealed enthusiastically.

"What's that, Sweet Pea?" Dad asked, turning his attention toward her.

"We can name him Yoda!" she suggested happily as she moved to gently pet the puppy being held by her brother.

"Hey! That's a great idea!" Dad agreed in a chipper voice.

"Yeah! I like that name!" Leif declared.

"Well, I guess Yoda it is, then," Mom proclaimed. I couldn't help the smile on my face while shaking my head, hopelessly accepting my parents' gift to their grandchildren.

Watching everyone adoring the puppy, I abruptly remembered to retrieve my phone from the green marble console table in the hallway near the foyer and returned to the living room to take pictures of the kids enjoying their new puppy with my parents. After I had acquired a number of good images of the kids in particular, I retreated to the dining room with Mom and began setting the table for dinner with her help.

By the time six o'clock came, I had the children bathed and dressed for bed. Paying close attention to the time, when it became a quarter till, I had them tucked into their beds with their new puppy resting peacefully on Leif's comforter. Lastly, I turned on their night light positioned over their dresser, and reached for Leila's American Girl doll stored over her Hello Kitty toy-box in the corner on her side of the room. As I stepped toward her bed, I carefully placed her doll in her arms for the night.

"Do you have to go bye-bye, Mama?" she sadly asked me while cuddled with her doll.

"I'm afraid so, sweetie," I replied as I knelt between their beds.

"Aww, I don't want you to go," she whined when I leaned to kiss her forehead.

"Yeah, Mom. You can do business later when I'm a gown-up," Leif determined in a strict little voice and I turned my gaze toward him now.

"But it can't wait, sweetie. I have to go," I explained to him. He glowered at me, conveying his significant displeasure. "I'll be back very soon like I told you. Plus, you'll have Granddad and Nanna here with you while I'm gone, and you're bound to have a nice time with them. Also, you have your puppy now too, to keep you company." His brow relaxed a bit and he released a small sigh. I leaned and kissed his soft cheek, and he suddenly smiled at me.

"I will miss you, Mama," Leila said unhappily. I turned my gaze toward her and gently stroked the side of her silky head before leaning to kiss her delicate cheek.

"I'll miss you both too," I said as I straightened from kissing her. "The both of you promise me that you'll be good for your grandparents. Don't wear them out."

"Okay," they both replied, promising me.

"Good. Now, nighty-night. Sleep tight—"

"And don't let the bedbugs bite!" Leila interrupted with a giggle and Leif laughed also, making me giggle with them too.

"That's right!" I replied, smiling at them. "I love you."

"I love you too, Mama," Leila said.

"I love you too, Mom," Leif told me also.

"Good night," I said to them both.

"Good night," they responded together and I stood from kneeling between their beds.

Leaving their room, I left their door ajar behind myself and headed for my bedroom now. Shortly inside, I proceeded gathering my belongings, making certain that I had packed everything that I needed for this trip. When everything had been accounted for and packed, Dad brought my luggage downstairs and placed it by the front door as I waited for my Uber driver to arrive.

"Okay now, I want you to call us when you land in Boston," he instructed me with a serious tone while we stood in the foyer. Ever since I had returned from my disappearance, my parents had become particular over me and were sensitive over my wellbeing, understandably.

"I'll definitely call you," I promised.

"And, again once you get to your hotel room," he said.

"I will."

"Your mother said that you'll be back here on Thursday."

"Yes, that's right."

"What time on Thursday?"

"My flight is supposed to get in at one fifteen in the afternoon," I informed him.

"All right," he said, nodding. "Your mother also says that you don't need us to pick up the kids from school the day you return."

"Yeah, that's right."

"Okay." He nodded again. "Now give me a hug, and your mom a kiss before you go." So, I did and he gave me a peck on the side of my head afterward.

"I think your Uber ride is her now, sweetie," Mom informed us as she was peering out the front window.

"Okay, thanks," I realized and gave her another kiss on the cheek. She suddenly embraced me, holding me firm and kissed my cheek.

"Be careful," she said gently, then released me from her embrace.

"I will," I told her. Subsequently, I turned for my purse hanging on the coatrack hooks by the front door and tucked my phone inside of it. Dad grabbed my suitcase and opened the front door for me. He strode with me to my Uber car, now waiting at the curb in front of the house. As we approached the car, the driver popped the trunk open and got out of his driver side to assist Dad putting my suitcase inside the vehicle. When it was suitably place inside, the driver closed the trunk to his car, and Dad gave me one last hug and kiss before I opened the back passenger door and sat inside the car.

After Dad closed the door for me, my driver pulled away from the curb and began down the street through the neighborhood. But before we had driven too far, I turned my gaze behind my shoulder and caught a glimpse of Dad out of the rear window, watching me from the curbside as I was being driven away, until I disappeared around the corner into the night, gone from each other's sight.

It didn't take long for my driver to arrive at the airport and deliver me to the correct airline terminal. When I got out of the car, he popped open his trunk again and got out of the car to politely assist giving my luggage to me. After thanking him, I retrieved the handle to my rolling suitcase and walked through the large sliding glass terminal doors, eager to catch my plane.

Easily checking into my flight and checking my bag, I then breezed through the security checkpoint. Arriving at my departure gate, I noticed a large body of people already waiting to catch their flights also, and it seemed that I couldn't board my plane soon enough since I was extremely anxious for this trip.

Scanning the area for a place to sit among the crowd, I finally located a lone seat between a couple of exhausted looking women. I sat facing the dark windows that overlooked the tarmac with butterflies bouncing wildly in my stomach, waiting to catch my red eye flight non-stop to Boston. But, the wait was long. So, I tried preoccupying myself with my phone as I scanned the lates news headlines and read a few articles.

By half past eleven in the evening, passengers were finally boarding the plane, and I recognized from the number of people on board that this flight was a full one. I further knew that because of the amount of people entering this plane, I wasn't going to be afforded the comfort of an empty seat beside me to provide any space while I tried to relax. And, because of my amplifying nervousness, I was certain that I wasn't going to get an ounce of sleep tonight, despite being fully worn from the day. So, being crowded in my airline seat didn't matter anyway.

Now that I was alone and away from being distracted by family and friends, my mind became completely absorbed with thoughts centering around Leif. Anticipation jittered my stomach and abstracted my mind. My heart raced and the quivering in my gut, brought nausea close to me. The realization of seeing him again acutely stimulated my nerves down to my fingertips, and it became difficult for me to type while replying to texts from my brother when letting him know that I had now boarded the plane.

After we'd finished texting each other, I finally leaned my head against the headrest and attempted taking deep calming breaths, hoping to gain control over my reaction to my excitement. But it was proving to be a real struggle as I discreetly attempted to not acquire my neighbor's curious attention.

Then, the plane suddenly jarred into motion and we were backing away from the terminal gate, at last. Turning from the gate, the plane began taxing down the tarmac, headed for the runway, and I still tried forcing myself to relax. Thinking to retrieve my neck pillow from my large purse, I tucked it around my neck, believing it would help settle me as I wished to close my eyes and rest them. Naturally placing my head against the wall near the window as I leaned with my pillow to get comfortably situated, I hoped to gain a bit of sleep.

But my eyes opened again when I recognized we were now on the runway. The throttle opened, causing the jet engines to roar like thunderous wind as it howled, forcefully propelling us as we quickly began picking up speed and gaining momentum over the take-off strip. In a second, we were airborne, climbing into darkness as the city lights fell away from view, appearing like interconnected electrical lattices lacing the earth.

I watched out the window until the lights became indistinguishable from the eye, and nothing but moonlight lit the surrounding black night sky. The cabin inside the plane had settled as it was bereft of conversation now, and replaced by stillness with collective silence from slumbering passengers blanketing the atmosphere.

Once more, I decided to close my eyes to see if peace would finally come for me like it had for the rest of the passengers and take me to sleep. As I forced myself to relax, in a while, I did indeed begin feeling drowsy and was thankful that maybe I'd actually get to nap, as I needed to be alert enough to make the nearly three-hour commute from Boston to Williamstown.

Seven

When I awakened, I now felt relatively rested and fathomed that the plane was on its descent as I heard the captain's announcement over the speaker informing us of our approach to Logan. It seemed I had slept nearly the whole flight. I raised the window shade to peer out, and the day was newly born. Dawn had broken and the sky was already changing from dark Prussian blue to lighter tones of cerulean, and lavender, with ribbons of orange and gold streaking the horizon until the sun shone brightly overhead.

In approximately a half hour, the plane landed, taxing to the terminal and my heart catapulted to my throat, palpitating my pulse as it thundered within me. My stomach clinched and wildly fluttered. I thought I was going to be sick and in need of a restroom. Except after several minutes of convincing myself to remain steady, we passengers were finally let off the plane and I disembarked, forgetting my nausea as I swiftly headed for the baggage claim area.

Moments seem to distend as I arrived at the claim and impatiently waited for luggage to begin making an appearance on the carousel. Finally, when suitcases appeared and began dropping off the conveyor belt onto the carousel, I soon spotted the one belonging to me and yanked it off the turning platform. Raising its handle to pull it along the way, I promptly proceeded pacing through the terminal, looking for the rental car agencies.

I WAS GIVEN THE KEYS TO A WHITE FORD EXPLORER, AND placed my luggage in the back seat before hopping into the driver's seat and starting the engine. As I sat idling for a moment before driving out of the rental car parking lot, I called Dad as promised, informing him that I had safely landed. Subsequently, I set the GPS and carefully drove out of the lot, soon navigating my way out of the city.

I glanced at the clock on the dashboard and noticed the time: 9:15 a.m. Given the hour, I should be arriving in Williamstown at about twelve o'clock, I estimated. It had been four years sense I had seen this part of the country again and as I drove out of the city on route 90, all my memories of my disappearance returned, flooding back in a tidal wave of emotions I was fighting to keep at bay from overtaking me. It was almost too bewildering to realize, and overwhelming to bear. It being all so vivid.

I wondered how Leif was coping with being here now as I thought of him. He must be feeling significantly the same way I initially felt when I was first transported to his era. I was certain that he was deluged, and I wondered about the feelings along with the thoughts running through his mind.

Is he okay? I know he's gotta be dumbfounded and mystified by everything. I hope he's not too panicked or frightened by whatever's going on. I hope he's all right. I wonder how he is... Will he recognize me? Will he think I've changed too much? Will there be any difference between us now? What's he like now? What will be his impres-

sion of me? He said he's an old man. How can that be? I hope we haven't grown too much apart after all this time. I'm being such a nervous wreck! Get a grip, Sylvie!

The morning sun beamed brightly behind me and reflected in my rearview mirror, blinding my vision on the road as I headed west. I adjusted the mirror away from the direct sunlight and focused again on the highway, pushing my insecurities aside when I distinctly remembered what had happened between us. I remembered what he had told me the day I discovered him all alone in the woods in Concord mourning his brother, Finley. The time was after Leif had delivered the news of Finley's death to his wife, Elizabeth. Leif had reinforced us, binding me to him that day we were together alone in the woods in a way I never knew could be possible. The bond was earth shattering, and carried us through the eons. I never forgot that precise experience with him; I relived it every day now since he'd disappeared. Whenever I gaze at our children, pieces of him returned.

IN ABOUT AN HOUR AND A HALF, THE LANDSCAPE BEGAN changing, becoming more mountainous while driving through Springfield. I had just arrived into the western part of the state at nearly the halfway point, and my eagerness to see him escalated and intensified. But it wasn't until I entered the Berkshires and passed Pittsfield, did I begin uncontrollably trembling from sheer enthusiasm to finally see him.

By the time I arrived into Williamstown, I could hear the blood rushing in my ears. And my heart... my heart felt as though it would hammer straight through my chest. Recognizing the turn-off from the highway, and beginning through the winding mountain passage, I finally came onto the serpentine stone-laid driveway leading to the Rockport's residence belonging to Dakota's parents. As the driveway made its last curve, the titanium white colonial house with lampblack shutters came into perfect view between the trees.

I slowed the SUV to a stop directly in front of the house, feeling closely beside myself, nerve-racked. As my heart rapidly pounded in my chest, my limbs shook, my breath was short, my vision almost blurred with pooling tears, and a knot had formed in my throat as I emerged from my vehicle. Trying to remain composed, I conscientiously moved toward the front door and stepped onto the granite steps leading to the front door. As I stood there beneath the portico, I was suddenly arrested with hesitation, fearing to face my brother and sister-in-law. But as if someone else was guiding my hand up toward the brass door knocker, I watched my fingers grasp its handle and knock on the red door a couple times, forcing me to weather the pending storm.

Within seconds, it moved ajar and I recognized Kyle standing before me at the threshold with the door wide open.

"Hey," he greeted me soberly, just as I had expected.

"Hi," I replied self-consciously. He stepped aside and motioned for me to enter inside the house. As I stepped through the doorway, Dakota promptly appeared in the foyer beside him. I silently watched Kyle as he closed the door, very much aware of the awkwardness between us all as we stood there together.

"Hi," Dakota cautiously greeted me, suddenly giving me a hug with Kyle observing.

"Hi," I replied, hugging her in return.

"Oh, my goodness, you're shaking," she noticed as she held me. "Are you okay?"

"Yeah," I lied. She released me and scrutinized my face for a second. I sensed Kyle doing the same as he stood next to us silently watching.

"Are you sure?" she asked searchingly. I knew she perceived the lie.

"I've just been driving for three hours straight, and I haven't eaten anything since yesterday," I said, making an excuse. She glanced at Kyle and they exchanged tacit looks of slight skepticism.

"Well, I can fix you something to eat right now, if you'd like?" she offered, being thoughtful.

"Thanks. That would be great," I responded gratefully. I nervously turned my glance toward Kyle and began to asked, "So—"

"He's in the den," he interrupted shortly, informing me, though I was intending to make small talk with him first. Kyle tilted his head in the direction of the room down the hallway. I knew he would be upset with me, but I wasn't prepared for him to be this angry at me. I looked at him and he broke eye contact with me, clinching his jaw. He was livid.

"He's reading one of my dad's news journals right now," Dakota delicately informed me, being more considerate.

"Thank you," I said to her.

"Sure," she responded with a faint nod. "Would you like for me to take you to him?"

"If you wouldn't mind."

"Of course not."

"Thank you," I replied sincerely, and as I stepped aside to follow her through the hallway, I glanced toward the direction where we were intending to head and happened to recognized Leif emerging past the threshold from the den located halfway down the hallway. Sharply arresting my steps as our eyes immediately locked, my breath completely stole from me. I couldn't breathe as I stood there fundamentally stunned. Instantly seeing him, brought the dream into reality, and solidified. I couldn't believe it. It was unfathomable.

Without any kind of forethought, I immediately rushed toward him, leaping straight into his arms and tightly wrapped my arms around his neck, securing my legs around his hips also. Holding him so fervently, our bodies soundly pressed together and

I could feel all of his might holding me too. I couldn't breathe at all as he embraced me this soundly. His strength was immense. My emotions abruptly erupted from the dam restraining them, causing me to hyperventilate as I helplessly sobbed with elation into the curve of his neck.

The average world surrounding us now suddenly evaporated, and it seemed we were the only two existing in a realm where space and time suspended. No longer were we severed from each other.

Surrealism enveloped me, and I was utterly overcome. My heart, galloping too hard, I feared it would explode through my breast when I realized his hammering heart was felt beating as fiercely as mine. I clung onto the solidity of his body, comprehending that he was real. And, too frightened for the moment when I would release him, he would dissolve, returning to intangibility only to exist inside a haunting dream once more.

"Leif..." I blubbered, as profuse tears streaming from me, dampening the flesh of his warm bewhiskered cheek when I kissed him there. Over and again, I wept his name, reassuring myself that he was here—with me, concrete: that we were together, again—having survived the curse of time.

"*Sylvie*," he uttered hoarsely as I sensed him shaking also while holding me fervidly in his hard arms. The familiar aroma of his musky scent mixed with salt and sweat, filled my senses as I breathed him in, clearly reminding me of him from before and confirming more palpably the fact that he was inarguably real. Further adhering my body to his, I wanting to feel his flesh and sink into his bones. His heart, pounding synchronously with mine was robust and powerful as I felt the heat emitting from his body.

"Don't let go of me," I wept into his scraping cheek while abundantly kissing him over his face. "I haven't the strength to stand."

"I shan't ever let ye go," he replied in a cracking voice against my tearful cheek. His eyelashes were damp also, and salty as my lips passed over them. His cheeks, wet from the quiet flood of tears streaming from the corners of his eyes, brushed against mine and his breathing unevenly escaped him.

"You found me," I gasped over his lips.

"That I did, *mo ghaol*. That I did," he uttered against my mouth as he also trembled.

"How?"

"Yoo're a clever, lass... 'Twas the instrument which ye had left behind," he croaked between stifling tears.

"But I lost it," I wept.

"I discovered it whaur ye had dropped it in the wood," he wheezed. I only eased a little from his face enough to gaze into his eyes. He was older, I perceived. The crow's feet around his eyes had deepened, and there were lines around his face that I hadn't noticed before. We stared into each other's eyes, sobbing, viscerally overjoyed. Senselessly smiling at each other also, we began laughing and crying simultaneously. I leaned my forehead against his, and he seized my mouth with his tongue, kissing me with fervor, love, and devotion.

Kyle coughed and the normal world suddenly reappeared around us again, interrupting our reunion. I released my legs from around Leif's hips and he eased me back down to my feet onto the floor, remembering that we weren't alone. I turned my gaze over my shoulder and noticed Kyle and Dakota still standing by the front door appearing considerably stunned as they stared at us.

Sniffling as I looked at them now while clearing the tears from my face with my fingers, I noticed Kyle looking down at the floor now, trying to hide his embarrassment. Dakota unevenly glanced at her husband before returning eye contact to me. Her eyebrows drew together and I perceived the empathy on her face. But neither one of them spoke a word as they stood with us in the foyer, and the atmosphere immediately grew thick with awkwardness permeating around us.

Dakota cleared her throat and said, "Well, I should probably get you something to eat now, shouldn't I?"

"Thank you. I'd really like that," I responded appreciatively, still clearing my appearance.

"Okay—I'll be quick about it. I know you said that you're hungry and I don't want to keep you waiting. Seamus? Would you care for some tea?" she asked considerately.

"Aye. 'Tis most kind of ye, mistress. I thank ye fur a spot," Leif said courteously as he retrieved a handkerchief from his waistcoat pocket and politely gave it to me. I dabbed my eyes with it, noticing him wiping his damp eyes also with his cuff.

"Sure, I'll have some prepared for you—and please just call me Dakota from now on. There's no need to be so formal."

"As ye wish," he replied reticently.

"Great. Now, why don't you two go to the dining room and wait. I'll bring your food in there. That way you guys can have some privacy while you talk," she offered thoughtfully.

"Thanks," I said gratefully.

"No worries," she insisted, turning her eyes toward Kyle now. "Kyle, I need your help in the kitchen."

"Uh, yeah, sure," he stammered, suddenly looking at Dakota.

"Great," Dakota said and took Kyle by the arm, leading him out of the foyer for the kitchen.

When they shortly vanished from where Leif and I remained standing, I naturally glanced at him and gave him a soft little smile, meaning to return his handkerchief.

"Keep it," he preferred. "The day isnae yet done."

"You're right." I nodded, holding onto it instead. "Let's go to the dining room, then" I suggested politely.

"Aye," he agreed.

He followed me into the dining room and I closed the door behind us. We paced toward the dining table and he pulled out a chair for me to sit. He then moved a chair out for himself and sat close beside me. We sat in silence for a moment simply smiling and staring at each other, marveling over the fact we were currently sharing in each other's company again. I placed a hand over the table and he enveloped it in his. My eyes turned down toward our enfolded hands, and I noticed again how large it was compared to mine. I grinned, feeling a flood of happy tears welling in my eyes again as we tightly held hands. Taking the handkerchief he had given me, I dabbed away the tears in my eyes, incapable of forming any words to speak. But when I returned my gaze to his, he had already been staring at me, and I remembered how penetrating his eyes were whenever he looked into mine.

"You told me that you're an old man," I began, finding my voice and noticing how scratchy it sounded.

"Can ye not see that I am?" he asked.

"No," I said, shaking my head.

"Yet, I am," he replied.

"I strongly disagree."

"Do ye?"

"Yes, of course. You don't appear it at all."

"'Tis generous of ye tae say. However, I am an aged man."

"I would never know it, because I don't see that you're old in the scarcest bit," I told him as I studied his face, admiring it. He was still strikingly handsome, though he did seem older, but not old. Instead, he appeared to be a very attractive man in his mid-forties, perhaps? I wasn't sure how old he was anymore, given his appearance. Still, his ultramarine eyes were brilliant and alive, and the nearly undetectable gray hair hidden in his strawberry blonde whiskers only hinted at his real age. Even his hair remained deeply golden blonde, making him appear as youthful as he would ever be.

"I shall tell ye that till this moment of laying eyes upon ye, I was an aged man in more ways than one. I had grown weary in yer absence as I have longed half a score fur ye," he said earnestly. "Yet, presently, I am rejuvenated after those cursed, forlorn years weighing upon my spirit."

"Ten years?" I asked, shocked.

"Brutal years."

"That can't be right." I looked at him in confusion.

"How mightn't be?"

"It's been four years for me since I last saw you," I said, confounded.

"Ah, the reason fur it being that ye dinnae appear a day older than a single score," he complimented seriously. "Yet, how is it possible?"

"I don't know," I replied, shaking my head in confusion. "How did you find me, Leif?"

"I used yer instrument. Recall that I had indicated it?"

"Yes, I remember."

"Aye, weel, ye happened tae be correct when ye observed a correlation betwixt the timer and the year's date. However, at the beginning of my research, I couldnae understand how tae properly operate yer instrument. Yet, once I eventually understood the function of the timer, I returned every spring tae Fort Hoosic—tae the area whaur ye had vanished from me. I searched meticulously fur ye about the wood thaur."

"Every spring you returned there?"

"Aye."

"Alone?"

"Alone," he said. "Carefully listen tae me as I reveal tae ye that I had set the timer tae twenty hours and seventeen minutes—the precise time at which ye had left it—at which moment I had also operated the instrument. And whilst I stood before the rock with the strange eye in it, the world abruptly disappeared about me and landed me in an entirely new land as in this place." I gazed at him, flummoxed as he was explaining this to me. "During this occurrence I had remained in the wood, searching fur ye, and tae my dismay I couldnae find ye anywhere about."

"So, then, what did you do?"

"I had returned tae my own realm, entirely forlorn. Many years I had returned tae the cursed location near the Hoosic before the same wicked rock with yer instrument in search of ye, which took me through the bowels of existence.

"Till one winter's nicht, I landed and had wandered out onto a hard black road from the wood. As I did so, I came upon a brilliant pair of lanterns rushing toward me. Thus, I ran out of the way from the heading lechts—fearing that I would be killed by them. However, the lechts abruptly ceased in the midst of the road whaur I hid in the wood, and whilst I remained unseen, I observed a most bonnie lass emerging from a strange contraption that held those bricht lanterns. She was the most bonnie lass that I had ever seen. And as my eyes laid upon her, I told myself, 'I believe that I recognize this lass,' tae my heart's sudden delight. She was yer spitting image.

"So, I hastened out of the wood whaur I was concealed and commenced approaching her upon the road. The poor lass, however, was extraordinarily distraught and frightened—perplexed too, whilst standing alone before the strange contraption. When I arrived close upon her, compelled that I was, I reach tae touched her, merely tae see whether she waur not an apparition. My fingers gently felt her silken hair and I whispered tae her, intending tae settle her spirit. 'Sylvie...' I spoke tenderly tae her. Yet, at once, she vanished from secht—fading into air, returning into the darkness of that nicht," Leif explained and I stared at him completely stunned, feeling sudden eeriness creeping into my bones, and chilling my blood.

"Oh my God..." I gasped at the realization as my palm passed over my lips. Ice water immediately felt as if it were surging through my veins, and I shuddered. I sensed his hand firmly gripping mine in response. "I remember that exactly happening to me the night of my accident... I thought my imagination was running wild when I felt a hand slipping over my shoulder the moment I heard a man's voice calling my name. I swore it was a ghost, if I wasn't losing my mind—which I thought I actually was."

"I clearly recall yer revealing this tale tae me later. Once ye had told it tae me, I believed that ye waur being haunted."

"I remember the look on your face clearly expressing your belief of that."

"Whit was I tae believe? Spirits are weel knoon above the mere notion of slipping through time."

"Yes, I suppose so."

"Weel, due tae my present experiencing of having falling through time, I have since come tae understand that 'twas I who appeared tae ye that fateful nicht upon the road before we would have ever met," he said.

"You were looking for me before we'd ever known each other and I'd ever become lost," I realized, looking thunderstruck at him.

"A radical experience has occurred tae us, Sylvie" he said.

"Yes, it has" I agreed, nodding a little as I gazed at him, abstracted by the complete amazement of it all.

"It had been years before I had experienced that affair which brought me tae the road whaur I had believed that I had discovered ye at last. Yet, in the tenth year of my search of ye, I finally arrived in this year of our Lord twenty twenty-two, May—by using the method involving the timer within yer instrument."

"You're brilliant," I recognized under my breath while gazing at him profoundly stupefied.

"I am blessed," he said instead.

"I'm immensely grateful."

"As am I."

"But once you arrived in this time period, though, how did you know to come here, specifically? To this house to find me?"

"Upon learning how tae operate yer instrument, I inevitably discovered the particulars hidden within it, since I recalled the passcode fur it which ye had shown me earlier. Much about ye had been revealed tae me, and I understood the correlation betwixt your sister-in-law and her parents, once I had discovered the addresses within the ledger containing this sort of information within the instrument. Therefore, when I had arrived in this period, I had an inkling of whaur I must go tae discover ye at last. I met my fortune when I came from the wood and began pacing along the road, fur a pair of curious lads encountered me thaur and they kindly offered tae bring me haur in their horseless carriage yesterday."

"Oh..." I continued gazing at him, completely awed. "But, how did you keep the phone working? Wouldn't it turn on any longer?"

"Aye. Thaur waur bouts waur it wouldnae respond whilst in Boston. Yet, curiously, every instance I had returned tae the area near the eye in the rock, the instrument suddenly operated well," he said.

"Incredible..."

"Most certainly, indeed."

"I wonder..." I paused, trying to fathom how the anomaly of this phenomenon which happened to us could have occurred.

"Whit enters yer mind?" he asked, keenly observing me.

"Well, I don't know how to explain it, really... I can only think of it in simple terms."

"Pray, explain whit ye mean."

"I'm simply thinking that there must be some kind of really powerful electromagnetic interference in that area—something like the Bermuda Triangle maybe?"

"The Bermuda Triangle?"

"Yes, where explorers have lost navigation in the Bahamas and people have disappeared."

"Och." His eyes widened at the thought.

"Maybe Crazy Eye has something like that going on, where there's also some kind of invisible temporal anomaly that exists—somehow making my phone act like a time travel machine also when it's positioned in that vortex, creating a wormhole. It sounds so implausible, if not outright crazy. I'm not sure how my phone could ever be powerful enough to work like that, though. And, what are the controls? There're so many factors to understand that aren't known," I said. Leif only looked at me incomprehensibly, having no clue of what I was meaning. "But, what's also so very confusing, is that when I had set the timer to twenty seventeen, I was transported to twenty eighteen instead—five months later than from when I originally vanished—which makes me believe that I could never return to the exact moment in time of my disappearance no matter what, because I was already existing in that same moment in time. Except, here you are precisely at this moment in time to locate me without interference. Is that a precise situation occurrence determined by the function of time and the manipulation of the timer?"

"I cannae say," he said blankly.

"Neither can I. I mean, couldn't I have been returned to the year two thousand seventeen moments after I had disappeared since I wouldn't have existed then, filling that space in time along this timeline instead?"

"Such inquiries are highly complex," he replied, looking closely at me with a creased brow as he pondered it also.

"Yes, it is extremely complicated... But since I'm thinking about it, maybe it has to do with the fact I had lost my ability to return to that specific time just after I'd disappeared, because I had lost my grip on my phone when the time vortex had begun and the wormhole opened, effectively changing the date, propelling me forward a little bit in time several months into the future year twenty eighteen as it was existing. I don't know...

"I'm not an astrophysicist who studies relativity, or a mathematician whose focus is quantum mechanics. I'm generally hypothesizing without any parameters. Who really knows what's going on in the woods there that nobody else is aware of? But, something extraordinarily strange is definitely happening at that location," I concluded abstractedly, trying to figure it all out. The expression on Leif's face told me that he unequivocally didn't understand any of this, while he simply listened to me rambling.

"Whit ever the question, 'tis certainly one that cannae be

answered by ye or me—and mayhap by nae man, in truth, when it is an occurrence of the mystical sort," he said, thinkingly. I nodded in concert.

"Hmm. Maybe so—because today's science theorizes that it's physically impossible to survive quantum leaping. And the idea that my phone can determine quantum destinations is absolutely irrational."

"Yet, it very weel has the capacity tae make such a determination and we have thus survived the journey—a multitude of times."

"It doesn't make an iota of sense."

"Be that as it will. Ye and I face one anither this day, nonetheless."

"Maybe it doesn't have to make sense."

"Micht Nature make any sense in the merest?"

"Not at all."

"Then, except this truth as it relates tae the Natural world which cannae be explained—fur it simply exists as does God."

"I suppose I'll have to understand it that way."

"Aye. Thaur is reason, and thaur is faith."

"Yes, there is," I agreed thoughtfully.

"I have long held faith in our reunion. I merely questioned when it would come tae pass," he said softly. He paused and intensely stared at me, and I gently smiled at him, feeling the knot in my throat returning. "Upon hearing yer voice yesterday, I closely perished from joy when I realized my victory in discovering ye at long last."

Words couldn't express my utter happiness that he had triumphed in finding me as I gazed into his overjoyed ultramarine eyes. My vision began blurring again and tears slipped down my cheeks. I brought my arms around his neck, embracing him with all of my might once more and sensed his arms enfolding me. He drew me tightly into his chest and simply held me without speaking for an undetermined time. I locked myself onto him and felt him trembling as we embraced, as gasps escaped him while he breathed.

"I have knoon the ends of the earth, the bowels of time, and the frozen space betwixt celestial bodies as I have walked through the flame of the sun in my search of ye, Sylvie," he croaked breathlessly, as I also shook in his arms, weeping. "I would journey it again fur eternity merely tae have ye in my arms as ye are presently."

Not another word passed between us but the sound of sobbing gasps as we wept together. Tears continued flooding from our joyous souls. When I finally eased away a little from embracing him only to catch a glimpse of his face, I smiled at him and he chuckled, inspiring laughter from me as his arms remained tightly holding me. Suddenly, we found ourselves delightedly laughing, recognizing the absurdity of it all. But the dining room door moved ajar, and we released each other from our embrace when Dakota was noticed entering past the threshold.

"I've made you some bacon and scrambled eggs," she informed me as she placed the teak serving tray before me over the dining table.

"Thank you so much" I said appreciatively, clearing my appearance.

"No worries," she replied, giving me a compassionate smile. She removed my plate from the tray, positioning it directly in front of me. "And, I also brought you both some tea."

"Much obliged tae ye, Dakota," Leif said courteously in a reserved manner as he cleared his eyes with his cuff.

"Sure. Is there anything else I can get you guys?" she inquired hospitably.

"No, thank you. This is great," I said politely.

"In that case, I'll continue leaving you alone while you guys talk."

"Thank you," I said to her.

"Of course," she replied. "Kyle and I are going to go on our hike now for a little while. So, we'll see you in a bit."

"All right," I acknowledged. She smiled in response, then turned from us, retreating from the room. When she returned to the threshold, she quietly closed the door after herself, leaving Leif and me alone in privacy once more. As the both of us had composed ourselves again, I silently began eating my food while he proceeded pouring us some tea from the hot teakettle. A companionable silence existed between us as I ate and he drank his tea.

"So, it's been ten years for you since we last saw each other?" I began curiously after swallowing some the eggs I was enjoying.

"It has," he answered as he was about to sip more of his tea.

"That means you're forty-six now?"

"Aye, I am," he confirmed and took a sip from his teacup again. I nodded in response, regretting that it had been so long for him since we'd last seen each other, as I fathomed the discrepancy time had created between us as we lived within our separate timelines. I observed him drinking his tea and draw the teacup from his lips, returning it precisely over the saucer in front of himself. "And, ye? Are ye not thirty-eight years presently?"

"Yes," I said, realizing the larger age gap between us now.

"Ye dinnae appear a day older than twenty," he complimented again. "'Tis remarkable." I held his piercing, brilliant blue eyes as he perceived me and smiled softly at him. "Many may believe that I have robbed the cradle," he joked.

"Nobody would think that. I'm an old woman now, you know?" I laughed.

"Scarcely," he chuckled a little.

"Don't you see the gray hair on my head?"

"Thaur isnae any."

"You're not looking hard enough."

"Am I not?" His brow lifted high and his lips curved into a little smile, appearing suddenly surprised along with amusement.

"No," I giggled.

"Yer bonnie hair remains raven, however," he said.

"Well, if I'm as young as you perceive me to be, then you're not an old man like you say."

"Yet, my bones creek."

"So do mine."

"Dinnae say that we are both headed fur the grave, now," he replied with an unfavorable smirk.

"Should I tell the Grim Reaper to wait, then?" I joked a bit more.

"Aye. I am hardly finished with ye, yet."

"Yet? So, I'm disposable to you in that case?"

"Never."

"Neither are you. Don't be so bleak. You're too young for that mindset."

"Are ye reprimanding me?"

"Yup."

"Ye huvnae the reit tae do so tae yer husband."

"I differ."

"I am reminded of yer wit as ye mock me."

"I'd never do that."

"Would ye not?" he teased.

"Do you actually think so poorly of me?" I bantered in return.

"Need I remind ye of yer lesson?" he responded, clearly amused.

"Which lesson?" I asked curiously, looking innocently at him.

"Have ye forgotten?"

"I'm sorry. There were so many lessons to learn that you'd taught me."

"Then, I shall remind ye of the one tae mind yer husband, most importantly," he said attentively with a little wink.

"Oh. Of course. Well, I'm a little rusty, so please forgive me," I said, realizing his flirtation with me.

"Then, 'twill be my pleasure tae assist yer ability tae finesse yer manners," he determined.

"Will it, Your Grace?" I replied in an innocent tone and the smile on his face widened.

"I perceive not at all has altered betwixt us. Ye charm me, still," he chuckled and I giggled a little too. But suddenly he quieted and was now gazing genuinely at me while his lips relaxed into a soft grin. I held his penetrating gaze, which was abruptly making me feel strangely shy. He stared ardently at me for a moment without speaking further, and I wondered what thoughts were entering his mind. Then, I noticed the corner of his mouth distinctly curling upward, and a gentle look came over his face as the warmth in his eyes exuded. "Yet on a graver premise, tell me how have ye managed these past years?" he inquired in a soft voice.

"Working. I just worked," I gently answered him.

"Did ye?"

"Yes. It kept me from constantly thinking about how devastated I was because we'd been separated."

"Aye," he understood, nodding, seeming to be thinking also.

"Do ye continue tae do it?"

"Work? You mean?"

"Aye."

"Yes."

"'Tis presently unnecessary fur ye."

"But I also work to support myself and the kids," I said.

"As a physic aiding bairns, am I correct?"

"Yes."

"'Tis noble of ye," he said, nodding contemplatively. He brought his teacup to his lips again and I gave him a meek smile. I glanced down at the eggs on my plate, and decided to scoop a bit of them onto my fork, placing it into my mouth. A paused ensued between us, and I sensed him observing me quietly eat as he was thinking.

"How is Amity?" I inquired after I had finished the last bit of eggs on my plate, remembering her with fondness.

"She remains quite weel," he informed me as I met his steady gaze.

"I'm so glad to hear that she's been doing well," I said.

"She is a grown lass presently at the age of nineteen."

"Nineteen?" I echoed in complete surprise.

"Aye, she is."

"I can't believe it."

"'Tis stunning, I ken."

"Absolutely stunning."

"She's a bricht lass. She knows how tae read and scribe thanks tae yer tutelage."

"I'm so proud of her. I always knew she was capable."

"Yer faith in her ability has proven tae be her fortune," he said appreciatively.

"I'm really glad that I was able to encourage her development," I replied sincerely.

"Yoo're encouragement will never be forgotten." He kindly grinned at me, and I discerned the deep gratitude in his eyes.

"Well, I love her—so of course—I'd do anything for her."

"I ken," he said genuinely. "She carries the same love fur ye as weel. She misses ye greatly."

"I've missed her just as much too," I said truly.

"I reckoned so," he replied. Then, he suddenly sighed and the look on his face turned to concern.

"What is it?" I asked curiously.

"It pains me tremendously tae bare this news that I must, however, return tae her as she cannae be left alone."

"What?" I faltered. Suddenly, I thought I had been hit by lightning as my heart skipped a beat and my body tensed as it chilled with sheer alarm. "What do you mean?"

"I cannae remain. I must soon take my leave, fur I mean tae—"

"Don't leave me," I interrupted suddenly.

"I shan't ever abandon ye, *mo ghaol*," he said solemnly.

"You just said that you will," I replied, panicked.

"Understand me," he began, "I shall never abandon ye. Ever."

"I don't understand what you mean, then, when you say that you'll leave." My voice was suddenly shaky as I nervously looked at him.

"I may part from ye fur a time, yet I shall never abandon ye."

"How?"

"As ye and I have presently come to understand that we arenae prevented from moving about time, it is of nae consequence if I waur tae return from waur I come." he explained. "Pray, fear not."

"What if the phone breaks and you can't return here to me?" I asked anxiously, extremely worried by the likelihood.

"I have since seen that thaur are many instruments which are similar tae yers," he said. "Can we not obtain anither similar tae it in case it must be substituted before my departure?"

"Well—I—I suppose so."

"Aye."

"Except, what if the phenomenon is specific to the phone we already have?"

"A consideration, indeed, fur 'tis one I hudnae reckoned," he took into account, suddenly appearing puzzled. "Mayhap the experience is not precise tae our instrument, but that it can be manifested by other instruments as the one we already obtain. Do others not contain timers and operate in the same manner."

"Yes, they do. Just the interface varies."

"The interface?"

"Yes, the way it can be used by the one who uses it."

"Och, I see. Yet, the mechanics are the same, are they not?"

"Well, sure, the mechanisms to make it work are generally the same."

"Very weel."

"But what if using a different phone won't work because of their nuances?"

"Then, we shall discover if that is not the case in determining my being marooned haur. Do ye presently carry anither of the same sort of instrument upon yer person?"

"Yes."

"I shall use it instead tae try the concept upon my next departure."

"Are you going to leave really soon?" I inquired, abruptly panicked.

"I have only yet arrived."

"Yes, you have."

"I shan't take my leave before I seize this opportunity tae experience our happiness again." His hand mindfully moved a ringlet tendril off the side of my face and tucked it behind my ear. I could no longer hold his gaze and wavered from looking at him anymore when I dropped my eyes to the little food remaining on my plate. Worried, I thought I might cry. "Fear not fur us, Sylvie," he said softly. "Our separation wulnae ever occur tae us again."

"You don't know that," I replied quietly.

"I do ken so," he affirmed.

"How?"

"Faith."

"Faith?"

"Aye. It binds us. Do ye not see? 'Tis whit led me tae ye. It guides like a compass. Yoo're my north, Sylvie. We are tethered. Nae matter how far ye may lie, I shall find ye. I shall return, lass."

I returned my gaze to his. The look in his eyes was real, ardent, and full of promise, and the echo of the oath we'd taken long ago resonated in my bones. *We are tethered. Bound by blood. Amalgamated through the spirit in love. Unbreakable. Inseparable. United. Solid.* I faintly nodded my head, adhering to his faith, trusting him, knowing it was true.

"Ye believe me, then?" he inquired, making sure.

"I believe you."

"Guid."

"So..."

"Aye?"

"Where is Amity while you're here?" I wondered quietly, as I also wondered about the length of time he was going to stay and the new predicament we now faced.

"It was spring when I departed seventeen sixty-eight in this occurrence. As I had always sought ye during the spring season, I placed her within Beth's care till upon my return. Amity is sent tae Beth every spring throughout the summer season in order that her relationship with her aunt remains kindred. Thus, Amity remains with Beth at present," he explained.

"I see," I replied, nodding in acknowledgement. "How are Elizabeth and the girls doing?"

"They fare well. Beth wed again tae a fine merchant named Master Patrick O'Donoghue, and remains in Concord."

"I'm really glad that everyone's doing well."

"Aye. 'Tis a blessing—particularly after Fin's demise," Leif said solemnly, and I nodded in response.

"When I think of him, I think about how much I still miss him," I mentioned regretfully.

"I too," he agreed.

A pause ensued between us and I knew he was remembering the events that had occurred at Fort William Henry leading up to the last time he had ever seen his brother again. The pain was there. I could still see it in his eyes. But I also perceived that the trauma of what had happened to Finley while we were there at the fort had mellowed, and the memory of those tragic events we had experienced together had become distant; eroded by time.

"I desire tae ken..." he resumed while thoughtfully gazing at me.

"Yes?"

"Waur micht our bairns be?" he asked. The look in his eyes and the tone of his voice was soft and affectionate as he anticipated seeing them.

"They're at home—with my parents. They're taking care of

them while I'm here," I informed him. He nodded in response, looking disappointed that they remained away from him.

"I greatly desire tae lay eyes upon them," he said.

"I know—and, you will," I promised.

"When shall I?"

"Tomorrow," I said.

"Quite soon," he realized, nodding a little, seeming satisfied. "They are presently four years of age, are they not?"

"Yeah."

"We are blessed with two," he acknowledged, appearing mesmerized and thankful.

"Yes. We are," I responded, equally impressed, noticing the gentle expression on his face.

"'Tis a miracle that they waur born, fur I believed the only bairn we waur expecting had perished when I lost ye."

"I'm so grateful it didn't happen that way."

"I am most grateful fur it, as weel." He paused again for a moment, simply gazing into my eyes and I wondered what he was now thinking. "I am certain they are as bonnie as my wife." I smiled and he reciprocated a warm, gentle grin.

"I can show you what they look like," I offered as the thought suddenly came to mind.

"How?"

"I have pictures of them."

"I shall be greatly pleased tae view their likenesses."

"I took recent pictures of them during their birthday yesterday."

"We share the same birthday?"

"Yes, you do."

"I'm much surprised."

"So was I when they were born."

"It appears we are bound in more ways than one."

"You made sure of that," I said, smiling gently at him.

"An oath in blood can never be broken unless God wills it."

"I believe that because of you."

"I believe it as I see ye."

My throat became tight with a knot quickly forming in it, and I felt my emotions might carry me away again. I sensed his palm tenderly coming over my cheek and carefully stroking the pad of his thumb over my lips as he closely gazed at me.

"I shall very much like tae see their likenesses," he said in a low voice.

"Absolutely," I uttered softly, feeling my stomach beginning to quiver. "I have their pictures on my phone in my purse. But I left my purse in the car. I'll have to go get it."

"I shall bide fur ye haur in this chamber whilst ye retrieve yer purse." He was gazing at me with such intensity, I knew his attraction and affection for me, and thought he might yield with a kiss. But he only held himself closely staring into my eyes as he locked my gaze to his. I felt myself growing warm and my nerves tingle as I continued staring at him during this lull in our conversation, aware of my acute attraction to him, too.

"I'll only be gone a second," I whispered.

"Aye," he said mutedly.

His palm slipped from my cheek and I carefully withdrew from the dining table.

Eight

Leaving Leif at the table, I proceeded through the dining room and opened the door, stepping past the doorway into the hallway. I hurried through the hallway for the front door when Kyle unexpectedly appeared into the foyer from the living room the moment I had reached for the front door knob. The TV was on in the living room and I realized that he had been watching basketball before he and Dakota actually left for their hike.

"You dropped your keys on the floor when you came into the house," he notified me, pointing to them on top of the maple console table by the door.

"Thanks. I didn't realize that," I said apprehensively. I reached for my keys and opened the front door.

"Do you need help with your luggage?" he asked standoffishly before I had stepped outside.

"That would be great. Thanks," I replied as he unexpectedly caught my attention with the offer. He didn't respond except proceeded with me out of the house, and followed me to my rental car without expressing another word. Arriving together at the vehicle, I used the remote entry key to unlock the doors and reached for the back passenger door handle, opening the door. My suitcase was instantly visible on the back seat and Kyle lunged for it, yanking it out of the car.

"It'll be in the room you've used before," he said insensitively.

"Okay," I replied meekly. He turned away from me as I still stood with the car door open and observed him beginning to walk back toward the house, carrying my luggage. "Kyle?" I suddenly called after him. He stopped short from moving further and turned his attention, looking directly at me.

"What?" he replied, obviously impatient and irritated.

"You don't have to be such a jerk to me," I said, feeling hurt.

"I'm helping you with your suitcase right now, aren't I? So, I don't think you can call me an asshole."

"I didn't call you an asshole."

"Close enough," he replied, chaffed.

"Because you're treating me like shit. Why?" I responded strangely.

"Are you really asking me that question?" The look on his face was hard as he glowered at me.

"Yeah, because I can't read your mind," I said in a snarky tone, annoyed by his rude demeanor.

"You're not dumb, Sylvie. But if you took some social cues from us, you'd already know why," he snapped.

"But I don't know why. So, tell me."

"Fine. I'll help you figure it out, since I'm such a nice asshole. You lied."

"I haven't lied," I denied, looking at him, baffled, and surprised that he'd accused me.

"You did. To everyone," he blamed sharply.

"No, I didn't," I contested quickly.

"I'm not an *idiot*. So, stop the bullshit!"

"I'm not bullshitting you."

"You're so insulting."

"What did I lie about?"

"The fact that you told us that you weren't *dating* anyone, but then suddenly you turned up *pregnant* after skipping town. You told Mom and Dad when the kids were born that you never told your boyfriend that you were even going to have *his kids* when you were pregnant with them, and instead *skipped* out on him before he ever found out! You told us that you were never *kidnapped* and *raped* the time you *fucking disappeared* on us without a trace! I guess that part of it might shake out to be true, since your long-lost *boyfriend* has suddenly shown up on our front doorstep claiming he still loves you. Except, he has no idea where you are or how to find you. So, what gives, Sylvie? What the *fuck* is going on with you?" he angrily spewed.

"Nothing gives. Nothing's going on with me," I replied, diminished.

"The fuck there *isn't* something going on with you!" he countered, glaring at me.

"I'm sorry. I'm not trying to cause anything."

"Is that all you can say? That's rich," he scoffed sarcastically. "When are you finally going to figure it out?"

"Figure what out?"

"Your so fucking dense."

"I'm not dense."

"Apparently you are."

"You just said a minute ago that I wasn't dumb."

"My mistake."

"So, spell it out for me again, then."

"My question is, when are you going to figure out that the people who love you, *love* you? That it's your family who you should trust and lean on—no matter what—whenever there's a problem? Ever since Matt died, you shut down, pushing the people away who love you the most. And, ever since you've been back from having disappeared, you've been all that much worse. If it weren't for your kids, you probably would've given up a long time ago. You've been underestimating us for so long, Sylvie. You need to finally dismantle that wall you've built around yourself and get it through your *head* that your family cares for you and that we're on your side. You need to trust us, your family—because the only people who matter the most in this world, are the people who give a real shit about you, and would never *judge* you because they love you, and those people are *us*. So, give it up, why don't you?"

I stood there speechlessly staring at him, flabbergasted, and filled with indescribable guilt after listening to him berating me. I stood there unresponsive, because I didn't know what to say. What could I say, if anything? Nothing. His eyes stayed fixed on me for a moment anticipated my response. Except, there wasn't going to be one from me, he quickly realized as the frustration on his face piqued his complexion red.

"Like I said, your suitcase will be in the room you've used before," he concluded, then sharply turned away from me and continued walking back toward the house. He walked up the steps beneath the portico and vanished past the open entrance. I swallowed hard and averted my eyes from the empty front doorway, regretting the apparent deep strife I was causing my family to experience. I didn't know that I had been so transparent and they perceived me hiding the truth—and, that I was hurting them because of it.

A sigh escaped me as I despondently ran my fingers through my ringlets and tucked them behind my ears. Unnerved, I didn't know what to do with myself as I lingered beside the vehicle in the driveway for moments longer.

Until, I remembered that Leif was waiting for me to return to him to show him the pictures I had just promised. So, struggling to gather myself together, I inhaled deeply, trying to settle my troubled thoughts before showing myself to Leif again. Otherwise, I knew he'd also see right through me, and I dreaded him thinking anything was wrong. Only, plenty was wrong, I admitted to myself.

Still, I couldn't stall any longer than I had to compose myself and keep him waiting a minute more for me. That in itself would draw curiosity from him, if it hadn't already. So, I opened the front passenger side door, grabbed my purse out of the car and hastily shut the door.

WHEN I RETURNED INSIDE THE DINING ROOM, I FOUND Leif standing by one of the windows facing the side yard, simply gazing out of it, looking at the surrounding birch and maple trees. He turned his gaze from the window when he noticed me approaching, and our eyes met. A subtle, but warm grin eased over his face and my stomach fluttered. My heart pounding hard as it now began racing, caused me to suddenly forget my disturbance with Kyle as I gazed at Leif anticipating me.

"Hi," I said.

"Hullo." He was staring at me and I recognized the affection concentrated in his eyes.

"What?" I asked insecurely.

"Yoo're terribly bonnie," he said in a mild voice. His eyes skimmed the dark denim jeans and fitted, capped sleeve, black floral blouse I was wearing. "I can see yer shape."

"Can you?" I replied nervously.

"Ye ken that I can."

"Oh." I replied shyly, glancing down at my bootleg jeans.

"And, the bodice ye wear? Is it also common?"

"There're different styles. But, generally, yes."

He nodded in response and the discernible, quiet attraction in his eyes naturally drawing me to him was unavoidable.

"Would you like to see your children?" I asked, attempting to curb the yearning compulsion between us as we gazed at each other.

"Aye," he replied, nodding a tad.

"I'll pull up their pictures." I set my purse on the dining table and retrieved my phone from it. Then, pacing toward him while typing in my passcode, I tapped on the photo app and my recent stored images instantly came into view. I lightly pressed on the photo that I had taken of them at their birthday celebration yesterday, aware of him watching my fingers move over the phone's screen. When the closeup picture of our children popped onto the screen, I handed the phone to him for him to see.

He suddenly inhaled with a deep breath as his eyes immediately fell onto the image of his children for the very first time. It was a picture of them looking directly at the camera with large happy smiles while hugging each other.

"God Almighty!" He exhaled. "They are glorious." His eyes glued to their images in enthralling astonishment as silence ensued and lagged between us while he stared at them. I stood close beside him, gazing past his hand as he held my phone, admiring the image of them also.

"Leif looks just like you," I commented. "Except, his complexion is tan like mine. And he has some curls, but his hair is exactly the same golden color as yours. His eyes, nose and lips are yours, too."

"Aye," Leif agreed breathlessly.

"And Leilani—I call her Leila for short—I think looks more like me, except she has your really fair complexion," I mentioned also.

"She is the very spit of her mother, however. Her eyes as green as yers," he said, glancing at me. A gentle smile lightly curled his lips and the amazement in his eyes filled with affection, and welled with impending tears that didn't yet slip. But he cleared his throat as he choked, fighting his composure. I automatically reciprocated his smile as I felt my lips softly turning upward when I met his meaningful eyes again. Then, his eyes returned gazing at their likenesses, and he remained silent, simply staring at their little faces as if to imprint their images into his mind.

When he appeared satisfied after studying their images, his large thumb swiped to the next photograph and he discovered a second picture of them. He admired it also for a distended moment before he began slowly swiping through the rest of the photographs that I'd taken yesterday of them.

"Who micht these other bairns be?" he inquired curiously when he saw the images of our children's preschool classmates surrounding them while eating cupcakes.

"Those are their friends from school," I informed him.

"Our bairns attend school?" He turned his gaze up from the photo and looked at me with unexpected surprised.

"Yes, they do," I answered.

"Yet, they are not of age. Are they not?" he inquired, looking puzzled.

"It's only preschool."

"Whit sort of school?"

"It's school, but without the intensity of actual academics. It's for babies," I explained.

"Och..." He nodded contemplatively. "And Leila receives this sort of schooling as weel?"

"Yes. She does."

"Yet, she is a lass."

"Girls go to school also now. Remember when I told you everything about my own schooling?"

"I do recall."

"Well, that's the way it's now for all girls."

"However, I had believed that the lasses didnae share in the company of lads whilst being schooled."

"Some colleges and secondary schools remain that way, still. But for the former years it's generally coeducational," I informed him.

"I see..." His brow furrowed as he slowly nodded in acknowledgment, pensive. I didn't think he knew what sort of opinion to have of the novel idea of coeducation. But I sensed that he didn't agree with it, since he was silent.

"It's not a bad thing that they receive coeducation. It teaches the children how to socialize so they'll know how to ultimately engage in society at a later age," I said.

"Micht that be learnt strictly according tae their proper genders, however? I dinnea recall lads and lasses ever having difficulty learning their studies, or whit is expected of them later within society. Would thaur not be confusion amongst bairns should they join in the same schooling?" he responded genuinely.

"But I was never confused when experiencing being educated with boys. Besides, I think it's better to teach children to associate with each other while they're younger. It allows for them to understand social norms before they reach adulthood, so by the time they're of age they'll know how to appropriately respect each other as equals," I explained.

"Equals."

"Yes."

"I see. However, they micht learn such expectations separately, mightn't they? Lads and lasses differ from anither. Do they not?"

"Not when it comes to learning subjects, really."

"Yet, they are indeed dissimilar."

"Physically, yes."

"Aye. Lads are also executive and lasses are docile by nature, are they not?"

"What are you saying?"

"I am meaning that I'm maintaining concern that our lass micht experience an imbalanced challenge from the lads whilst attempting tae learn subjects within the school chamber."

"Oh. Well, I don't remember experiencing any sort of intimidation, or inferiority while learning with boys when I was small. So, I safely imagine that it will be the same for her. Besides, she has such a lovely teacher who is fair and understanding to all of her students—regardless of sex. Leila is really a confident little girl. She's bright and fearless like her brother. So, I don't think you should really worry for her," I assuaged.

He slowly nodded again, contemplating. The knit in his brow remained apparent, though, as he thought for a moment. I knew that he found the principle of coeducation unusual and difficult to accept. But, he didn't say anything further about it as he returned gazing at the remaining photos of our children while at school. When he had finished, he gently placed the phone into my hand. "I long tae hold our bairns," he said in a tender voice.

"I know you do," I said softly to him. "I promise you'll see them tomorrow."

"It seems an eternity," he responded. I carefully placed my palm on his billowy white linen sleeve and lightly caressed his hard bicep. He reached his opposite hand and gathered my palm into his. I sensed his large fingers tenderly caressing my hand and he raised my knuckles to his supple lips, planting a kiss on them. When he withdrew the back of my hand from his mouth, he returned his gaze to mine. I paused, feeling my blood surging, heating me, and I was suddenly stumped for words.

"I brought some things for you," I muttered when I found my tongue, very aware that he was still holding my hand.

"Did ye?" he replied, appearing surprised.

"Yes."

"Whit have ye brought me?"

"Some things I thought you could use."

"Och."

"Would you like to see them?"

"I expect so."

"All right. Follow me, then, and I'll show you."

With my hand still in his, I led him out of the dining room through the hallway and up the staircase toward the back of the house where my guest bedroom was located. As we entered the room, he released my hand and closed the door behind us, sealing us alone together inside. I spotted my suitcase on the floor by the dresser next to the window where Kyle had placed it, and I stepped toward it, hearing the little bolt to the door *click* as Leif remained standing by it. He lingered by the door, and I was aware of him watching me as I knelt at my suitcase to unzip it, revealing all that I had packed inside.

I pulled forth several pairs of jeans and slacks that I had purchased for him from Nordstrom. Uncertain of which material he would prefer to wear, I ended up bringing the two different styles for him to choose from. I also purchased several different style shirts for him to decide between, along with some toiletries for him to have. He also needed shoes, so I purchased a pair of leather loafers with his estimated shoe size that I'd brought with me in addition.

When I stood from my suitcase with the bundle of brand new clothing, I moved to lay it over the bed, spreading it out for him to see. I turned my gaze toward him while he still stood by the closed door and perceived a particular look in his eyes that I'd remembered seeing once before.

"I brought some clothes for you to have," I said as our eyes met.

"Thank ye most kindly," he replied.

"I wasn't sure exactly what to get you. So, I just decided to get you several things for you to choose from."

"Ye have brought me plenty, indeed, I see."

"Well, there're so many choices to choose from these days. I just wanted you to be happy with what you wear," I said as I unfolded a pair of straight-legged jeans in his tall size and held them up for him to see.

"Do breeches nae longer exist fur men?" he inquired.

"I'm afraid not" I said.

"Then, breeks it will be."

"There're also some shorts that I considered for you that I have brought with me. It's been getting warm lately, and I thought you might consider wearing a pair."

"Whit micht shorts be?"

"Those are cropped pants that aren't fitted like the breeches you're wearing now," I said. He glanced down at his breeches covering half his legs to his stockinged calves.

"Micht shorts accompany stockings?" he asked curiously as his gaze returned me.

"Not typically."

"Och," he realized as his eyes widened, appearing appalled.

"I understand your hesitation," I mollified.

"I reckon that sort of garment will scandalize me."

"No, it wouldn't," I giggled a little, despite the look on his face.

"Would it not?" he questioned sincerely.

"Trust me. No one here is scandalized by wearing a pair of shorts. They're very common."

"I shan't consider it, regardless."

"Whatever makes you comfortable. But, just know that I have a pair for you in case you might end up changing your mind."

"I shan't change my mind."

"As you wish, Your Grace," I replied innocently, smiling at him, and his eyes suddenly twinkled with a little smirk tilting his lips.

"I reckon yoo're being coy with me," he said.

"You think so?"

"I ken so." His grin widened, exposing the pearly gleam of his teeth, causing me to smile at him in return. He locked my gaze to his for a moment longer and suddenly I felt truly shy.

"So—do you have anything in mind as to what you'd prefer to wear?" I asked.

"Mayhap, ye will choose fur me." He started from the door, proceeding to remove the stock from around his neck, and stepped deeper into the room toward the chartreuse twill uphol-stered chair at the end of the dresser. As he arrived at the chair, I incidentally noticed his great coat and black tricorn hat had been placed there.

"Is this where you slept last night?" I asked.

"Aye," he said quietly, leaning slightly while positioning his stock over his coat already draped on the back of the chair. "Although, I didnae sleep a wink as I was immersed in thoughts regarding my anticipation of laying eyes upon ye again."

"Oh," I realized. He took his hat from off the seat cushion and placed it on top of the dresser. I glanced down at the clothes I'd brought sprawled on the bed and naturally began hanging them in the bedroom closet, aware of him observing me. I glimpsed at him while placing his new clothes on the hangers and our eyes met. He seated himself in the chair and began removing his boots off his feet. The hue in his face rose, I discerned, and I felt the heat in my own cheeks growing in intensity. I swallowed and my throat was dry, and wished for a sudden glass of water.

"I have missed ye, *àille dhubh*," he said in a low voice. My heart abruptly leaped in my chest and my body tingled as if I had suddenly suffered an electric shock.

"I missed you too," I replied softly. A wide grin curled his lips, further gracing his face and the glint in his eyes seemed lit by fire. He stood from the chair now with his boots removed and towered before it.

"Come," he said, urging me to approach him. I hung the last hanger with one of the new shirts I had brought for him upon the rod and strode toward him. As I arrived standing before him, he reached for my hand and drew me closer so that I stood directly in front of his broad chest. "Remain with me," he requested.

"I will," I agreed softly, holding his deep gaze as I understood him. Intensely aware of him, I knew I was going to buckle sooner than later.

He removed his scarlet coat, then proceeded unbuttoning the brass buttons down the front of his waistcoat, tugged it off his square shoulders and carelessly tossing it over the rest of his coats on the back of the chair without releasing me from his gaze. Conscious of what was occurring between us, I felt his palm carefully slip over my cheek when he caught my chin between his thumb and forefinger. He leaned, drawing my lips up toward his, and I sensed them tenderly coming over mine. He began gently kissing me with warmth and feeling, and I returned kissing him in kind.

I could hardly breath as we were kissing each other. It all felt completely surreal. Sublime, and true. I parted my lips, wanting to receive more of him, and his tongue thrust inside my mouth, causing me to sharply inhale from the power of his fervor.

Overwhelming me with his kiss, I understood how much he'd missed me. His tongue powerfully pushed and danced around mine, clearly reminding me of how we once were as the memory of him came flooding back to my senses. I anchored my arms around his neck, securing my body to his as he continued kissing me, wanting nothing more but to give myself to him as he took me, and feeling him again as we celebrated our reunion. His arms stole around my back as he drew me taut against his firm body, embracing me, and we lost ourselves in each other with our surroundings falling away.

He abruptly broke from kissing me and pressed his forehead against mine, panting. The intensity between us had begun mounting like never experienced before. It was palpable, and undeniable. His breathing was quick and heavy, and so was mine.

I heard him swallow hard, and felt his large hand carefully roving over my shoulder down the front of my neck toward my heart and rested, while still holding me firm with the other. The uneven stream of his breathing caressed my lips while his mouth hovered ever so closely to mine. He eased himself away from me a little and gazed into my eyes.

"Whit is it betwixt us which has bound us since before we ever wed?" he wondered.

"I don't know," I whispered, wondering too.

His gaze dropped from mine and he watched his hand move over my breasts. His fingers discover the petite buttons closing my blouse between my breasts and worked to unfasten them. I observed him as each button came undone. When my black, satin-lace bra became exposed, I noticed his lips curl into a little grin. He glanced up from it, meeting my eyes, and I discerned the questioning look in his gaze.

"Whit have ye?" he asked curiously. Still reeling from our kiss, my head was swimming, his face remained deeply flushed, and my chest quickly rose and fell as I took uneven breaths.

"It's called a bra," I said, lightly gasping, feeling a bit lightheaded.

"A bra?" he echoed. His brow lifted with interest.

"Yeah."

"'Tis different from stays," he observed, returning his glance down toward my breasts.

"Yes—they are," I responded breathlessly. His eyes met mine again, and the faint grin curving his lips, boldly widened. I sensed a finger find the edge of the lace covering my right breast and gently slip inside. It traced along the edge of lace against my heated skin. He glanced down, watching his hand moving along the ridge when I felt his gentle palm cover my entire breast, and tenderly caress. My bra cup slipped away a little by his hand, and his fingers easily discovered my protruding nipple and began stroking it with the pad of his thumb.

"It appears that yer bra isnae difficult tae remove," he said huskily.

"It would seem so," I whispered, agreeing.

"I reckon that I am fond of it." He grinned at me, and I felt my lips shyly curling upward.

His hand wandered past my breast as it slid up beneath my blouse over my shoulder, easing off my sleeve. He proceeded doing the same on my other shoulder until he had completely removed my blouse off of me, exposing my bra, entirely, and bearing my flat stomach to him. Sensing a finger slide beneath my left strap, my knees weakened as he drew it down my shoulder. He explored my undergarment with interest. My stomach fluttered and my blood heated me further as my mind began swimming. My body yearned with anticipation while he attempted removing it off me.

"How is it withdrawn?" he asked curiously in a semi-whisper, as I realized he was having difficulty.

"I'll show you," I said unevenly, reaching around myself with my fingers and snagging the closure. "It's released from the hooks in the back," I informed him, easily unhooking it, letting my bra slip from me. It fell to the floor, exposing my breasts.

"'Tis a wonder," he gasped, immediately taken as his eyes rolled over me half bare before him. I smiled nervously at him, and he grinned as the inspiration exuded in his eyes.

His hands slid around my waist and guided me toward the chair where he sat. He maneuvered me between his spread knees, and cupped my round breasts with his large palms, proceeding to caress them, fondly. I observed him as he touched me and sensed the warmth from his hands emitting on my skin. His thumbs rolled over my stiffened nipples, admiring the way they must have felt as his fingers lightly tugged them, electrifying my nerves. My mind was floating when he gazed up at me from where he sat while his hands massaged me with mesmerization.

A light moan escaped me and he moved his hands lower, discovering the front button to my jeans. He easily unbuttoned them but paused for a second, noticing the zipper. He curiously seized the zipper's slider and ran it up and down the teeth a couple of times.

"That's called a zipper," I said faintly, informing him. He suddenly glanced up at me in marvel.

"A zipper," he echoed, understanding.

"Yeah."

"Clever," he replied, returning his attention to the opening of my jeans, and proceeded mindfully pulling them down my hips, uncovering the top ridge of my panties. "Whit sort of uncommon garment micht this be? A chastity cloth?"

"No! They're called panties," I said, lightly giggling. He glanced up at me again, grinning quizzically.

"Why do ye wear it?" he inquired curiously.

"It helps to keep my clothes stay clean."

"Does it?" Leif gazed interestedly at me, coupled with enamor.

"Yes," I said, nodding a little.

"I see."

His eyes returned to his hands encircling my lower waist at my panty line, and I sensed them traveling around my lower back when they slipped beneath my panties and grasped onto each buttock cheek, splaying over them. He began massaging and kneading my buttocks, and as I felt him rubbing and squeezing me, I could feel the intense heat releasing from his hands burning my skin. A subtle groan eluded his lips as he leaned and sealed his mouth over my navel, branding his kissing mouth over it.

"*Mmm*," I lightly moaned when his scorching tongue thrust into my navel, fervently kissing it. My knees unexpectedly buckled, but I found his shoulders with my palms and steadied myself. His caressing mouth trailed from my navel and slowly passed over my stomach, raptly pressing his tender lips against my skin. The air cooled over my warm flesh in the wake of his steaming trailing lips, sending little chills over it. As he kissed my stomach, his palms began pushing my panties down below my hips along with my jeans, revealing my private tuft of hair. His mouth mindfully meandered lower until he was kissing me between my thighs. Struggling to remain balancing before him, I supported myself with my hands on his shoulders, hoping not to collapse.

"*Mmm*," he groaned as he deeply inhaled me, and I smiled.

Suddenly, I gasped when his fingers began spreading me apart, opening me for him as his tongue slip between my cleft and found my clitoris. He moaned as he licked and sucked while kissing me, carefully. I suddenly went limp before him and he buttressed me with his arm as I anxiously raked my fingers through his long, shoulder-length hair, feeling the burn from his mouth scorching the soft, sensitive flesh of my pubic area.

Then, his lips abruptly broke from me. Suddenly standing, he scooped me up into his robust arms, catching me by surprise, and strode toward the bed where he carefully placed me over the mattress. He seized my shoe and removed it from my foot, carelessly dropping it to the floor. When he tugged off my second shoe, he yanked the rest of my jeans and panties completely off me. Now standing at the edge of the bed, I anxiously watched him swiftly pull his shirt over his head, revealing his solid, well sculpted naked chest. He easily unbuttoned his breeches and they fell from his lean hips to his ankles. Immediately stepping out of them, he now stared at me with piercing, impassioned eyes, beautifully naked before me fully erect, and ready to proceed.

Crawling over the mattress and ceasing before me, he hovered and adhered his lips to mine with such fervor, I lost my breath. My lips naturally parted for him and he thrust his tongue deep into my mouth. My blood ran hot and my body ached as he sealed his lips to mine, kissing me with ardor. His tongue moved zealously within my mouth, and I thought I might faint as I returned kissing him. He groaned when I lightly scoured his back with my raking nails, wanting desperately to be with him.

My need for him was incomprehensible. It was frantic, maddening, potent, and determined. I had to be consumed by him as we merged. If not for the pure pleasure alone, then to satiate my need for the sustenance he brought me in order to exist.

As he feverishly kissed me, I knew he was confirming our solidity; he needed me, all of me, too—bearing out that I was not a mere figment of his imagination or an unconscious dream, but true to the existence of my form. And, ultimately validating our being one.

He pushed a solid knee between my legs and spread my thighs apart, and I sensed his formidable shaft brushing between my cleft, seeking my entrance. Then, in one vigorous thrust he surged into me, filling me to the end, and he moaned as he joined us together. I gasped at the sudden, powerful sensation of him plunging into me and was reminded by the overwhelming capacity of his organ. Taking him in, I adjusted my hips more comfortably, wrapping my legs snuggly around his hips, completely receiving him to the hilt. My body quickly remembered his touch and the sensation of him inside me, and gladly welcomed him.

"*Och*, Sylvie, *mo ghaol*... How I have missed ye so," he heaved huskily as his lips swept over mine.

"I love you," I gasped, taken by the complete sensation of him.

"I loove ye more," he rasped.

He drove himself with escalating force. My entrance opening and closing as he boldly surfed between my thighs, began swallowing me whole in an ocean of advancing euphoria. My body, inviting him on each thrust, begging him to return as my walls grew slicker, pulled me closer toward the apex where soon I would fall.

My body began tightening around him, my flesh gripping him, beckoning him to remain—to savor him for as long as we existed before our dissolve. The sensation of our union compelled me toward an ascending height I had never experienced before. It was imminently going to hurl me from this distance and crash me into a swirling abyss not yet known. So, I held onto him as he vigorously drew us closer toward this summit.

"Leif..." I panted sublimely.

"Aye," he rasped.

"Please... don't stop."

"We are too close," he half-whispered, breathless as he panted.

Excruciatingly close to our disintegration as the moment was quickly progressing, dictated how soon we would arrive. Helplessly, he thrust deeper and with more vigor, penetrating me to a new end when I believed all had already been discovered. But before he had reached the barrier of this unfamiliar depth, I was brought to the crest right before the fall when he surged in one last uncontrollable, insatiable thrust and I tumbled off the ledge.

I began shuddering in his arms. My chasm thundered as it violently pulsated around him. The sensation of my depths gripping and squeezing him, begging to keep him, sent shockwaves throughout my nerves as they were electrified, and launched me into pure ecstasy.

"Leif!" I cried out, soaring on a plane of joyous delirium. He released a guttural roar into the curve of my neck and his breath burned my skin. I was scarcely aware of him expelling himself, throbbing between my thighs, as his essence poured into me. My soul had been taken, and he was the reason.

But as I drifted downward, back to the consciousness of reality, I sensed his essence overflowing, filling me past my cusp, and knew that we had climaxed together.

He suddenly collapsed, nearly suffocating me while fully embracing me in his arms, satisfied. My legs slid from around his hips as I held him also. His seed escaped me while we embraced in silence for an undetermined moment, listening to each other's breathing finally settle. And, I could hear our hearts pounding in synchronicity until their rates slowed, returning to normal pulses.

Lessening my grip over his shoulders, I gently stroked his back while remaining affixed, still resting, unspoken. He grew flaccid in my arms, and my flesh began closing, forcing him out. Leif shifted and rolled onto his back, and I felt empty inside once more. Wrapping an arm around me, he drew me against his chest, holding me securely.

No words exchanged between us now. We simply rested together in silence consumed in bliss, knowing that the bond shared between us had awakened was avowed and complete.

Nine

I turned over in Leif's arms and placed my head comfortably on his shoulder while his palm gently stroked my bare back. He slightly shifted and crooked an arm behind his head against the pillows. I glanced up at him and smiled softly when his gaze tuned down toward me and our eyes met. His eyes smiled affectionately in return, and I sensed his lips tenderly coming over my brow.

"I can't believe you're really here and we're together. It feels like a dream," I said softly, loving the way his gentle fingers felt stroking my back after his kiss.

"It does feel as a dream," he agreed in a low voice. "I am mystified by the nature of our lives as it pertains tae time, and I thank the Lord Almighty with all my soul that 'tis nae dream as we experience one anither again."

"I thank God too," I said truly.

"We shall never separate again, Sylvie. Not ever. So long that I draw breath," he swore. I wrapped an arm around his chest, hugging him with strength, and he pulled me tight against himself. It became quiet between us as we continued resting peacefully with each other in the afterglow of our fervent lovemaking.

"You'll meet my parents soon," I mentioned quietly, lightly disrupting the silence between us, as I realized this fact was closely impending.

"Aye, I reckon that I shall," Leif replied. "'Twill be a great pleasure." I glanced up at him from where I was resting my head on his shoulder, and he warmly grinned at me. A little insecure smile slightly curled my lips.

"They're going to want to know everything about you," I remarked.

"I reckon they will," he replied mildly, appearing unfazed by the prospect. I nervously smiled a bit at him again. His eyes began searching mine as I gazed at him. I knew he could perceive my hesitation. "Whit troobles yer heart?" he inquired intuitively.

"I don't know what to tell them—about you... and me, now that we're together again," I disclosed diffidently.

"Why not the truth?" he suggested apparently.

"It's not that easy. They won't believe the truth. Nobody would—if I told them."

"Yet, did I not believe ye once ye had revealed the truth tae me? Therefore, why not them?"

"They won't believe anything about it, because they're practical people. They don't believe in the concept of paranormal activity at all. They're grounded in fact. Reality as we know it provides their logic without any consideration for anything that can't be proven. They don't stray from that thinking—even though they're Catholic and believe in God and the Mysteries of Faith. If I ever told them what happened to me, and how we met, they'd send me to a shrink," I explained.

"A shrink?" Leif gave me a puzzled look.

"Yeah. Someone who's known as what we call a psychologist. A doctor who analyses people's psyches for their mental health," I stated.

"Och. I see," he fathomed.

"Yeah... So, I'm kind of in a predicament, since they would

undoubtedly consider my story not even close to being farfetched, but completely ungrounded in reality."

"Would ye not contemplate exposing the truth tae them by demonstrating proof, as ye had shown me?" He asked reasonably.

"How? By bringing them to Crazy Eye?"

"'Tis certainly a notion, however."

"Then what? We all disappear together?" I replied, posing the possibility. "What would happen if we did that?"

"They would stand nae choice but tae believe ye, in that case."

"Sure. But I'd have to tell them everything about the truth prior to that ever even happening, and they'd never believe me in the first place without thinking something was wrong with me. They're already worried about me as it is, since I've refused to tell them anything at all about my disappearance."

"I see..." he replied, pensively. "Yet, I am able tae substantiate yer tale now that I am haur with ye."

"That's true... Except, I'm absolutely positive that they'll be insulted."

"Slighted?"

"Yes."

"In whit manner?"

"They'll feel that their intelligence is being mocked. Especially, because they've never met you," I said. "Trust me—they won't ever believe it."

Leif pensively stared at me. He paused speaking further. I clearly perceived him meditating.

"Ye say that yer parents show concern fur ye as ye have refused tae speak of yer disappearance?" he inquired after a moment.

"Yes."

"I reckon that ye must have mentioned a wee bit concerning it. Whit did yer family say once ye had returned tae them without me, alone and bairned?" I awkwardly looked at him, nervous, and broke my gaze with him. "Tell me," he pressed. I returned looking at him, wondering how I was going to tell him what I had done to explain it away to my family as he waited determinedly for my answer. "Ye fibbed tae yer family," he keenly conjectured, answering for me as he read the look in my eyes.

"Yes," I admitted guiltily.

"Sylvina." The look on his face coupled with his tone obviously conveyed not only disapproval, but disappointment too.

"I'm sorry," I said.

"Those words are fur yer family. Not me." he said. "Whit have ye informed them of me?" I hesitated responding. "Ye have mentioned me, I am certain, fur the fact that our bairns are born. Now tell me. Whit have ye said of me?"

"Well, I—I—told them that I was seeing someone—a man... But I never told them who it was—just that I had been seeing this man without them actually knowing about it," I began explaining, "and, for whatever undisclosed reason, we didn't work out."

"Work out?" he questioned strangely.

"I mean, that we couldn't come to a mutual understanding benefiting us," I explained.

"Ye told them that ye had a tryst?"

"Yes."

"Whit else did ye tell them of us?"

I heard the earnestness in his voice, but the appearance on his face was unintelligible. I knew he was dissatisfied with me, though I couldn't see it.

"I told them that it was my fault that we didn't work out—that I needed time to clear my head because..." I paused, knowing he further wasn't going to like what I was about to say.

"Aye?" he prompted, regardless.

"Because I wasn't expecting to become pregnant by him, and I was terrified of what I was going to do—since I didn't want to commit to him because of Matt."

Leif stared at me, deeply pensive and unresponsive. I became silent also, wondering what thoughts were going through his mind along with his feelings.

"I dinnae blame ye fur missing yer departed husband," he said genuinely. "I also perceive the depth of your loove fur me by the lie ye have told. However, I am dismayed."

"Don't be," I replied sensitively.

"Yet, I am."

"I can't tell them the truth, Leif."

"'Tis not necessarily the reason fur my dismay, fur I understand why ye have told them the falsehood."

"Then, why?"

"I fear that I have been deemed a wicked, dishonorable man tae yer family's belief as a result."

"Why would you ever believe that? That's not at all true."

"It is, because they must believe that I never claimed yer virtue. Thereby condemning ye tae shame as ye bore my bairns out of wedlock," he explained.

"Please don't think that. I promise you that I'm the one who's poorly perceived by them. I'm the bad guy in the whole scenario. Trust me. They sympathize with you over me."

"I cannae imagine it. Yoo're their daughter who has been shamed."

"It's not true."

"How is it not?'

"Because I ran away from you, that's why. My family believes that you never knew about our kids, because I told my family that I never told you that I was ever pregnant. So, according to them, you never knew—and they're furious at me because of that," I said. He stared at me without saying anything again, appearing shocked and gravely contemplative. "What are you thinking?" I asked delicately.

"I dinnae care fur yer being scandalized," he said, perturbed. "I am gravely concerned, presently, regarding yer family and fur the difficulty that lies before us." I nodded a little, acknowledging him. "We must come tae a resolution by some means. Yoo're bearing unwarranted disgrace. 'Tis unacceptable. I must protect yer honor in any manner that I can, Sylvie."

"I'm grateful to you for that," I replied truly. But I was just as concerned as he was—even more so—because there was no escaping and denying my family this time. Kyle instantly came to mind and I suddenly very much feared having to face him again after experiencing the recent outburst of his angry tirade.

"Yoo're troobled that I can clearly perceive."

"I am."

"I regret seeing the weight ye bear."

"I know."

"Permit us tae have faith in yer family. Will ye not? If their fondness fur ye is true, as ye have claimed it tae be, thus I have reason tae believe this grave matter may be met with a fairness betwixt them," he said encouragingly, despite the dour feeling he knew that I was feeling.

"I can only hope so," I replied.

"Then, hope." He pressed his lips over my brow, bestowing a tender kiss, comforting me.

"Are you angry with me for lying about you?" I asked, despite his affection.

"Nae. I am not. I understand yer trial tae guard whit we ken," he said, drawing me snugger into his arms. "We shall come upon a resolution tae settle this complex matter regarding yer family. Ease yerself as ye will, fur we shall see it pass."

I held onto him with an arm secured around his chest while he continued embracing me, wanting to believe him. We became silent with each other, and I sensed our thoughts run parallel as I remained thinking about having to encounter my family. Fearing the outcome of their reaction once they learned that the father of my children had unexpectedly returned to me after four years of his absence, made me skeptical. I didn't know what to do... How I was going to begin to explain it to them—without causing more strife I knew was inevitable, because I had lied?

So, I lay there with my head resting on Leif's shoulder chained to my troubling thoughts in silence until I felt the urge to shower. I started withdrawing from his restful embrace and his arm tensed around me, preventing me from easily slipping away from him.

"Whaur micht ye go?" he asked curiously.

"I'm just going to take a shower," I said.

"A shower?"

"Yes. I want to wash."

"Och, in the privy closet?"

"Yeah."

"Very weel," he understood. "I have the urge tae use the chamber pot. Waur micht I discover it?"

"In the bathroom where I'm headed. Follow me and I'll show you. Except it's called a toilet instead of a chamber pot."

"Och..." he responded simply, and released his arms around me.

We started from the bed together and he followed me into the bathroom where I pointed him to the toilet. I lifted the toilet seat for him and indicated for him to relieve himself into the bowl. As he was using the toilet, I turned for the shower and rotated the nozzle, letting the water flow and warm. He had quickly finished using the toilet, so I flushed it for him. He stood at the bowl, observing the contents swirl down as it disappeared out of the bowl while fresh water filled it again.

"Whaur micht it have all gone?" he asked inquisitively, mesmerized.

"To the sewer," I answered, incapable of holding back my amused little smile.

"Truly?"

"Yes."

"Quite novel," he said, impressed. I continued smiling at him, then turned for the bathtub and began running the water, filling it for him.

"The bathtub is filling, if you would like to bathe," I offered. His brow raised as he noticed water coming from the spout and pouring into the tub. He appeared duly captivated as he stared at the filling bath.

"Aye, of coorse. I shall care indeed tae bathe," he agreed. I nodded and proceeded obtaining a couple of washcloths and bath towels from the towel closet in the corner, making them available to us. I placed the fresh towels onto the sink counter as he stepped into the tub and sat, while water continued pouring into it. Easing himself comfortably leaning back, he stretched out in the warm water, and released a pleasurable sigh. After giving him a fresh bar of soap and washcloth, I turned the water off for him when the tub had sufficiently filled and hopped myself into the shower to begin washing.

As I completed showering, Leif noticed me emerging from the stall, and also decided to remove himself from the bathwater in which he was comfortably relaxing. Dripping wet, he reached for one of the towels on the counter and gave it to me. Thanking him for it, I received my towel from him and quickly proceeded drying off, staving the chill coming over my skin. While drying myself, I sensed him watching me and I glanced at him, meeting the warmth in his smiling, sparkling crystal-blue eyes. His gaze never wavered from me as he retrieved his own towel to dry off, locking my eyes to his while he also began drying himself. Affection was clearly visible in his gaze, and so was the enamor. Suddenly shyness slipped over me, and my cheeks grew hot. A large grin swept his lips, and I knew he could see through me. Unable to withstand the intensity of his stare, I broke his gaze, feeling weak for him again as the temperature of my blood began to rise.

"I have to get the toiletry bag. Excuse me. I'll only be second," I said diffidently, not knowing why he could make me feel uncertain like an insecure schoolgirl. He nodded in response and finished drying himself when I began withdrawing from him.

I hurried out of the bathroom, wrapped in my towel, for my suitcase to grab the toiletry bag and returned as he had just concluded drying off also. He folded his towel, neatly positioning it back over the counter. Placing the bag on the opposite side of the counter, I proceeded unzipping it, revealing the contents inside.

"Would you like to shave?" I asked, withdrawing a razor and shaving cream. He raised a hand to his bewhiskered cheek and rubbed his jaw with his fingers.

"Micht ye care tae do so fur me?" he asked, noticing the type of razor I was holding that was uncommon to him from the straightedge he was used to using.

"Of course, if that's what you prefer," I replied simply.

"Aye, it is."

"Okay," I agreed, and retrieved his folded towel from the counter. I moved the toilet seat lid down, and placed his towel over it. "Have a seat here," I suggested, indicating the place over the covered toilet.

He moved to sit and I reached for the shaving cream. Snagging the washcloth also from the nearby towel rack, I wet it with warm water from the sink and brought it to his face to dampen his cheeks, rugged jaw, and neck. Then, I took the shaving cream canister and it sprayed like whipped cream into my hand. Aware of him as he interestedly watched in silence, I moved toward him and stood between his parted knees, carefully beginning to spread shaving cream over his lower face. When his square chin and jaw were covered, I automatically wiped my hands clean on my towel covering me, took up the razor among my fingers and began shaving his face.

He sat motionless and silent while I drew the razor carefully down on the side of his whiskered cheek. When the hair was being scraped away from it, the concentrated silence between us was tangibly noticeable. As I mindfully drew the razor repeatedly over his face, his youthful appearance emerged with definition and strength the second the hair on his jaw was completely removed. I leaned in close, shaving his upper lip now, unexpectedly sensing his hands stealing over my bare thighs beneath my concealing towel. They began wandering upward, until possessively resting on the side of my hips. My towel was hitched up my waist by his hands, exposing my pubic area, and distracting me from concentrating on shaving his upper lip clean.

Conscious of him, I tried ignoring the sensation of his touch while focusing on cleaning the rest of the hair off beneath his chin and neck. In a few minutes, though, all of it had been removed, and his face appeared the way I had remembered it. He was striking. Breathtaking, as I couldn't help admiring him while examining the work I'd done.

I leaned to collect the dampened washcloth and ran it under warm water in the nearby sink. Ringing it out while remaining before him, I gently wiped his face clean from leftover shaving cream. As I wiped the bit of it off the side of his cheek, his palms lightly roved farther up my waist and caressed my sides. He continued gazing up at me while seated, and I was aware of the intensity of his searing eyes on me.

"There," I said weakly, returning my gaze to his when I had concluded. "I think we're all done."

"Are we?" he replied huskily.

"Yeah."

"Splendid." He moved his hands higher up my abdomen, loosening my towel until it unraveled and slipped to my ankles. He found by breasts and cupped them. Beginning to tenderly fondle them, he caught my stiffened nipples between his fingers and lightly pulled and twisted them, causing my breath to seize. Suddenly grasping my waist again, he wedged his knees between my thighs while I stood before him. "Come haur," he semi-whispered, maneuvering me astride his lap.

"Why?" I replied, perceiving the flare in his eyes.

"I shall like tae offer ye a seat," he coaxed. I giggled in response, reading the clear intention on his face. "Ye have kept me patient fur a wee too long. Dinnea tarry, Your Grace," he ordered.

"As you wish, Your Grace," I complied in an innocent tone with the same formality, smiling at him.

"Ye wish tae taunt me, I see," he said, grinning back at me.

"I would never taunt you," I denied, recognizing the inspired look in his eyes.

"Yoo're shameless." His grinning gaze was jovial and glimmered with enchantment.

"Maybe," I giggled.

"Ye ken that ye are so," he chuckled a little, urging me lower onto his lap.

"So, what if I am?"

"I would admire ye fur it."

"That's encouraging."

"Indeed, it is. Now, serve yer master as he pleases."

"Certainly, Your Grace." I gently wrapped my fingers around the shiny head of his shaft and slowly lowered myself further with caution, guiding him between my cleft and into the wetness of my depths, straddling him, completely.

"*Och*," he groaned as I instantaneously moaned, feeling him entering me. "Yoo're tremendous." I smiled unevenly at him, and the grin on his lips slightly slackened as his gaze suddenly glazed over with a dreamy glare.

The penetration was unusually deep in this position, and closely too much to bear, causing my breath to flutter. He immediately filled me to capacity as my body took a moment adjusting around him, when I abruptly felt the pressure of him distinctly pushing against my cervix. I sat on his lap, motionless, feeling the strength of his power lending no yield that I recognized. My body hadn't been worked to receive him like this in a long time, and I knew that I could end up being sore if we began too soon.

Sensing me, he gripped my hips and began deliberately rocking me. Slowly, he swayed me back and forth, working my flesh to loosen around him, grinding his head into my cervix. In a moment, I felt my depths relaxing, taking him in without discomfort and receiving him with pleasure. He was churning inside of me, rocking my uterus with delight, and I moaned as I began escalating.

The dreamlike expression in his eyes and the languid grin on his lips attracted me as the visible emotion on his face turned confident with rapture. I began taking over from him as he rocked me, and my hips naturally found their rhythm. The sensation of his shaft stirring my depths, enamored my core and the blood coursing throughout my body heated me thoroughly, melting me from within. He cupped a breast and drew my nipple between his lips, enhancing my pleasure and inciting a moan to elude me. Lightly catching it between his teeth, he drew it back into his mouth and massaged it with his dancing tongue, suckling it with delight.

I accidentally shifted off kilter from his lap and he steadied me, fastening my hips down on him as I took hold of his shoulders. Slowly and deliberately moving my hips, I could feel him at the ceiling of my cervix, stirring my uterus while I milled myself over him down to the root, wanting more. He moved a hand to my second breast and gently began groping it as his mouth remained latched onto my first one. Fervently teasing it while he suckled, sent amplifying shockwaves of pleasure throughout my depths, right to my fingertips and down to my toes, as I climbed toward the summit. He released his mouth from my nipple and cool air stimulated my dampened skin left behind from his moist kiss. He moved his lips to the other nipple, achieving the same delirious effect.

I thought I would die while feeling him adoringly kissing me there. He caused my nipple to swell and ache from sensitivity as he ravenously bestowed attention to it. Suddenly withdrawing his lips, he gripped the back of my head, driving my lips down onto his and thrust his tongue into my mouth, kissing me with ardor.

My lips automatically parted, inviting his amorous tongue to explore my mouth as it stole my breath. All the while he kissed me, his hand continued tenderly fondling my breast, making it more tender to his touch, as I continued grinding myself over his groin.

"That is it, *mo ghaol*... Come tae me," he said hoarsely when he let me go from his powerful, impassioned lips. Our eyes locked and he steadfastly fixed my gaze to his.

"I'm coming Leif," I panted. Observing my face with pleasure, he was precisely aware of me as I perceived in his dream-struck eyes the potent, yearning desire he had for me billowing within him. His breath shortened and a gravely groan eluded his lips.

"Ye fit so weel about me. 'Tis maddening," he growled. "Tell me 'tis nae dream."

"It's not a dream," I uttered shakily.

"Och, ye grace me so," he groaned as I felt his hands beginning to knead my buttocks, anxiously. "Ye grant me such joy. Ye will never ken the magnitude." I smiled unevenly at him and a lazy grin curled his lips, making him appear spellbound and stupefied with lustfulness.

Gazing into his eyes, I could also see him aware of my body tightening around him and he hardened like stone, articulately penetrating me with fervor, while climbing toward the crescendo.

"How I have longed fur ye," he rasped in hushed tones. I leaned my lips over his and kissed him, intently, with longing and desire. "Tell me a secret," he half-whispered against my lips as I was kissing him.

"You know all of my secrets," I muttered over his mouth.

"Do I?"

"All of them."

"I fear not."

"How do you know?"

"I ken ye weel, *ceisdein*."

"How well?"

"Weel enough tae ken that ye shy away from my request. Now, tell me one that ye have not yet disclosed tae me."

"Like what?"

"As in how shameless ye truly are," he groaned again. I giggled bashfully, perceiving that he did know me well by the instinctive look in his spellbound eyes.

"If I'm shameless, it isn't my fault," I moaned as I continued unabashedly kissing him.

"Would it not?"

"No."

"Explain."

"You've corrupted me."

"Have I, now?" he replied, amused, as I felt his lips widen into a large smile against mine.

"You know it," I accused.

"Have ye not permitted it?"

"No, Your Grace," I panted against his mouth.

"Hmm... Do ye protest?"

"I can't say that I actually do."

"Then, ye permit me."

"But it isn't fair."

"How micht it be unfair?"

"Because, you tempt me."

"Yet, ye seduce me entirely. A man husnae the choice but tae fall prey tae the charms of a siren."

"So, it's my fault?" I giggled.

"Aye," he replied, smiling in return.

"How, precisely?"

"I am enslaved by ye. Thus, I have nae will but tae express my whole devotion and loove fur ye, which will cause my further debauchment of ye."

"Is that so?"

"Quite so."

"I see."

"Aye."

"So, I must be very powerful to make you so weak."

"Truly."

"Then, satisfy me well, Your Grace."

"As ye ride me with pleasure," he moaned between our kisses. I withdrew my lips from his and continued rocking my hips as I ground myself over his groin. He hardened further, feeling like an iron rod penetrating my uterus while it churned against him. He moaned more when he sensed the final reach of my depths, and I knew that he was close to his dissolve. Eliciting groans while riding him, I sensed him feeling every detail of my depths offered to him. The sensation of him as I swayed, weakened me while drawing him to the very end.

Then, the plummet from the summit came, and the two of us fell.

Suddenly, my motion over him ceased and I seized. My body shuddered in the wake of electrifying convulsions pulsing between my legs, quaking my depths. My flesh radically clamped down on his shaft, and vehemently contracted with pristine pleasure. The sensation of electrical shocks pulsed throughout my nerves, trembling my body, and cramping my toes.

I helplessly collapsed against him, wrapping my arms around his neck, securing myself to him, wanting to retain the sensation of what was happening around his penetrating shaft. His arms immediately came around my back, soundly embracing me, and I felt the heat of his breath emitting from his parted lips as he stifled a feral roar into my neck. I sensed his testicles fiercely throbbing between my thighs as he exploded, expelled himself into my cavity.

We shook in each other's arms, both of us gasping. His heart hammered against my breasts as his slackened lips pressed against the rapid pulse in my neck. The moment yanked us from the real world surrounding our souls and hurtled us onto a plane of pure rapture, and we soared together as if in a fantastic dream.

Gliding downward, back to the real realm, serenity ensued and we sat there together returning to our senses, listening to our heavy breathing settle, conjoined, tightly embracing. As the moment silently passed between us while affixed, and satisfied, each of us knew that we belonged to the other, and we simply stayed adhered as time drifted.

Moments later, his heart rate began slowing and I finally sensed him growing flaccid. He naturally slipped out of me, leaving his aftermath warmly streaming from me as my heart was calming. We continued holding each other in silence, feeling the placidness between us and not wanting to disturb it. Burying my head into the curve of his neck, he securely held me in place within his arms. We were comforted and reassured by letting the tranquility around us remain.

Ten

I awakened in Leif's arms as he still slumbered. Daylight entering through the windows had dimmed, and I wondered about the time. I carefully stole from his sleeping embrace so not to disturb him, and quietly walked toward the dresser where I had left my phone. Gathering it up off the dresser, I read the time: 5:00 p.m. Several hours had passed, I recognized, as Leif and I had remained secluded in the guest bedroom.

Engaging Kyle again was intimidating as I anticipated it. I felt a mixture of chagrin and relief that I hadn't encountered him since Leif and I had entered the bedroom. Knowing Kyle was incredibly upset with me, my desire to avoid him was strong. I was apprehensive to encountering him again, and wished I could steer clear of him until it was time to take Leif with me to the airport when we leave. But, avoiding Dakota made me feel guilty and embarrassed. She hadn't voiced any disagreeable opinions or feelings to me about my circumstance, and I wanted to keep the peace with her, even though I was certain she may have shared Kyle's concerns. Still, she always exhibited understanding and acknowledging that, made me understand the awkward position she was in.

She was my friend, and I loved her. So, my admiration for her ran deep. Being a guest in her parents' house as she tried helping me with Leif, made me very disinclined to ignite any sort of ensuing argument between the three of us—particularly with Leif observing and being new to my family's dynamic. I only wanted to show Dakota my utmost love and gratitude for her.

Appearing in front of her again before leaving for the airport was unquestionable as I was expected to share dinner with her. Therefore, I knew that I was going to have to face my brother again before the evening ended. I was so uneasy about the thought it made me nauseous.

Compounded by more guilt when I suddenly remembered that I hadn't yet called my parents a second time to inform them of my fake hotel arrival as promised, I immediately went to the bathroom, quietly closed the door for privacy and gave Mom a call. After apologizing to her for my communication delay and explaining to her that I simply had become preoccupied with business, I hated that I was telling her another lie.

Hanging up the phone when our conversation concluded, I collapsed sitting on the edge of the tub, simply thinking about the mess I was in and wondering if there was really ever going to be a solution.

Leif seems to think so. He has more faith in my family than I do, apparently. I should hope like he does... For all our sakes, I hope he's right.

After a moment of just quietly sitting there and thinking about it all, my stomach growled and I realized my hunger as my stomach was further unsettled. I was certain Leif was going to be as hungry too when he awakened. So, I stood from my place on the tub's edge, and swiftly refreshed myself.

Opening the bathroom door when I'd finished, I emerged into the bedroom again and noticed Leif still sleeping. Deciding not to awaken him, I had the idea to sneak us both a few snacks from the kitchen before having to face my brother at dinner. So, I dressed and left the room for the kitchen.

As I was approaching the kitchen entrance to obtain snacks and drinks from the refrigerator, I heard voices resonating from within the room. Dakota and Kyle had returned from their hike and were in the middle of a conversation when I nearly entered past the threshold. I stopped short, realizing that Leif and I were the topic of their discussion, and listened.

"They've been MIA for a while since she's arrived. What do you think they're up to?" Kyle asked.

"They're likely catching up," Dakota answered.

"I bet," he derided.

"Cut them some slack. It's obviously been a while," she replied.

"Why should I cut her any slack? This whole ordeal is her fault," he said.

"I know. But, ever since Matt died, she's had a hard time coping with life in general, and I know that she hasn't been emotionally accessible to us since then. So, maybe with her ex here now, things could change," she responded understandingly. Kyle didn't respond. "You just need to be patient with her, Kyle."

"For how much longer, though? We've been patient with her for years now already. Enough's enough. She needs to finally snap out of it and stop feeling sorry for herself. Life's too short for wallowing in self-pity. All she does is push us away when we're right here in front of her for whatever support she needs. She runs away from anyone who challenges her. She can't keep running from her problems for the rest of her life. They'll always be there for her to confront no matter where she goes. So, when is she going to just stop avoiding her problems and stop running?"

"Only she can answer that—and all we can do is let her know that we're here for her whenever she's ready to talk to us."

Kyle sighed, sounding frustrated and said, "She might wake up one day all alone before she figures that out. I'm not saying that we'll ever abandon her. But I am saying that Mom and Dad aren't spring chickens anymore, and you and I aren't getting any younger either."

"Show a little faith in her."

"I'm trying." A pause ensued and the conversation drifted.

"So, what do you think about him?" she resumed asking.

"I don't know anything about him," he said flatly.

"Well, you at least have to have a first impression about him, don't you?" Dakota asked curiously.

"He's different, I guess," he said skeptically.

"What do you mean?"

"He's wearing American Revolutionary garb, and he hasn't bathed, if that should tell you anything—obviously."

"Well, maybe he's eccentric and participates in one of those historical societies where they reenact important events. As for his hygiene? I'm assuming it's because he's European."

"I'm pretty sure Europeans don't live in the Stone Age, Dakota," he said sarcastically.

"Of course not. I just meant that I don't believe that they bathe as much as we do—either because it's cultural or because they're such environmental conservationists," she replied. "Either way, Sylvie did say that he was a nice guy. So, I believe her."

"I guess," Kyle responded, sounding skeptical regardless.

"Well, obviously he still has strong feelings for her. Didn't you see the way he was hugging and kissing her when she greeted him?" she questioned.

"Yeah," he admitted.

"So, evidently, he's missed her—quite a bit, I'd say. And, did you see the way she reciprocated?"

"Kinda hard to ignore," he confessed ironically.

"Sure is," she agreed genuinely. "So, unless you're blind, there still seems to be feelings that exist between them."

"Another thing I don't get," he remarked.

"Why?" she asked.

"Because if it were me in his situation—not knowing that I had fathered a kid with a woman that I had been supposedly dating and loved? And that she had broken up with me for some unsubstantial reason to hide the fact she was even pregnant by me? I'd be fucking pissed off when I found out about it. So, yeah, I kinda do sympathize with the guy in that case," Kyle said irately.

"Okay. I'm not going to say that I don't understand your perspective, because I really do. I just wish—"

"And, I mean, what the hell is she going to tell our parents now that she's going to fly home with this guy back to L.A. and she's forced to introduce him to them? What do you think they'll say? What about the kids? What will she say to them?" he interrupted.

"I don't know," Dakota responded.

"Of course, you don't. Not even she knows," he said.

"Well, I know that you're really upset about it. We all are. But you should probably calm down, because she's going to find out how mad you are at her now that she's here," Dakota warned.

"She already knows how angry I am," Kyle disclosed.

"How?"

"I confronted her in the driveway when I helped bring her luggage into the house."

"Please tell me you're joking?" she replied regretfully.

"It was important that she hear it from me," he said instead.

"Oh, Kyle—why? It's the wrong time to be having this discussion with her."

"There's never a right time to have this conversation with her. I had to get it off my chest. She had to know it from me."

"Still, you could have picked a different time to talk to her, though, when it would be slightly less stressful, or wouldn't have been inopportune because she's just reunited with her ex. I mean, her ex scarcely knows anything about what's been going on with her—he just found out about the kids today. He seems like a really nice guy, and we shouldn't make him feel uncomfortable, because you decided to argue with your sister now."

"I wasn't going to tell her over the phone."

"Well," Dakota sighed. "This is definitely going to cause drama."

"We could use some drama in order to get her to be finally honest with herself, and with everyone else around her. The lying has got to stop."

"I agree with you about the lying, but you need to be civil about it with her. We don't need any bombs going off. That won't serve anyone's purpose, since it could backfire."

"The bomb went off when her ex-boyfriend suddenly showed up here. So, if it backfires, whose fault is that?"

"Give Sylvie some credit. I mean, she did immediately fly out here to see him when she could have easily denied him and told us to send him away instead. And, she does also intend to take him home to L.A. with her. So, she is actually taking a step forward in the right direction."

"Yeah, well, we'll see how this pans out knowing how skittish she is. So, excuse me if I seem doubtful. And now that there're kids in the mix, I'll find it extremely difficult to forgive her if they wind up getting hurt because of her selfishness in not facing the difficulty of the decisions she's made. She ran away from him once, who's to say that she won't do it again?"

"Sure. But I get the feeling that things have significantly changed for the better for her now that he's entered her life again."

"Well, if he's as good of guy as she claims him to be, then he won't let her go this time without a fight now that he's learned the truth about her having his kids."

"So, you should be encouraged by that, because he might very well make it difficult for her to abandon him again, and force her to no longer be afraid of trusting someone again, since she won't be able to actually ignore him because of the kids," Dakota said. "Let's also recognize the fact that he did seek her out again—even though it's been a long while—to finally see her. That's definitely gotta mean something about his determination."

"I guess that's encouraging," Kyle considered.

"Good. Now, we're about to have dinner together. Can you at least try to be civil with her while we eat?"

"You don't have to worry. Like I said, I got it off my chest. She knows where I stand," he said firmly.

At that point in the conversation, I turned away from the threshold and made my way back up the staircase for the bedroom, feeling extraordinarily glum.

RETURNING INTO THE BEDROOM, I DISCOVERED LEIF lying in bed awake among the pillows gazing up at the ceiling. His eyes shifted down toward me as I was closing the door behind me to our room. Our eyes met and a grin eased over his lips.

"Ye stole from me," he said.

"Yeah." I paced toward the bed and sat on the edge beside him.

"And, yoo're attired." He took my hand into his and gently stroked my knuckles with the pad of his thumb.

"Yeah," I responded simply.

"I wonder whit time is it?"

"It's a little after five o'clock."

"Is it?"

"Yeah." I smiled at him and the grin on his face broadened. "Are you hungry?"

"Aye, quite famished."

"Well, dinner is being made right now. I'm assuming it'll be done really soon. Probably by the time you finish dressing, it'll be ready for us to eat. We can go to the kitchen, then," I replied.

"Och, very weel. I shall promptly attire myself," he said,

encouraged. I automatically gave him a little grin and he naturally smiled with heart in return as he proceeded removing himself from the sheets.

I observed him crossing the room for the closet where I had hung his new clothes as I continued sitting on the bed, thinking about the conversation I'd just overheard between Kyle and Dakota. I was distracted by it, disturbed by the fact that I was forced to betray them and that they had felt my betrayal to them. I was also very apprehensive to face Kyle again so soon for dinner, understanding now the depth of his anger toward me.

My gaze stilled on Leif as he was mindfully selecting his clothes while my abstracted mind remained consuming by my troubled thoughts. He ultimately decided on a pair of brushed twill khaki trousers and a powder blue, long sleeve cotton button-down shirt.

"Shall I not have a waistcoat?" he inquired curiously as he faced me.

"Hm?" I responded blankly, when I realized, he was talking to me.

"It seems that I wulnae have a waistcoat," he recognized.

"Oh! Yeah—I'm sorry—they aren't made to wear anymore," I answered.

"Och," he realized.

"Don't worry, though—I promise you'll look very nice and presentable in the shirt and pants you've chosen for yourself to wear," I assured.

"Very weel," he accepted. I naturally moved from the bed and assisted him in dressing as I held his clothes for him to take. He stood before the mirror attached to the closet door as he was dressing, taking note of his appearance as he tucked his shirttail into his kakis once I had buttoned his shirt down his chest for him. "I presume a neckcloth disnae accompany this style of shirt that I am newly wearing?"

"It would be called a necktie instead. But I didn't think to bring one for you, because I thought you might like to appear more leisurely. You know, more typical like everyone else," I explained.

"I see," he responded simply. When he was soon dressed, he gathered the new hairbrush that I had brought for him off the top of the dresser and began running it through his long golden hair. "I huvnea a ribbon tae gather my hair into a queue," he realized suddenly.

"It's okay. You shouldn't worry that you don't have one. Your hair looks really attractive the way it is," I guaranteed. His eyes shifted from viewing himself in the mirror toward me as he brushed his hair. Our eyes met and the mild grin curving his lips dissipated as his gaze turned searchingly when he looked at me.

"Yoo're burdened. I apologize," he said seriously as I noticed abrupt disappointed clouding his face.

"No! I'm sorry. There's no reason for you to apologize at all. You haven't done anything. I'm so sorry that you suddenly feel that way," I stammered regretfully.

"Then, whit troobles ye?" he asked earnestly.

"It's Kyle," I started, feeling deflated.

"Kyle?" he responded with surprise as his brow lifted.

"Yeah."

"Whit of him?"

"He's really angry at me right now."

"Fur whit reason?"

"Because he senses that I'm lying to everyone about everything, and he made no hesitation to tell me about it earlier today when I went to get my purse from the car," I explained.

"I see," Leif replied, appearing sedate. "Whit was yer response tae him?"

"I didn't say anything to him."

"Not a word?"

"Nothing. I mean what could I say? He's right—and everyone feels hurt because of me."

Leif paused and merely gazed at me, looking impassive. But I knew that he was contemplating and felt sympathetic regarding the entire situation in which we all found ourselves.

"Nae doubt we are in a quandary," he said after a second. I nodded in response. "Weel…"

"Well, what?" I asked worriedly.

"Given the nature of the truth will remain unrevealed tae yer family, we shall bear the brunt of their wrath and accept it," he said. "In doing so, we shall hope fur their forgiveness." I looked at him in dismay. "'Tis the only course we may take tae amend this situation."

"I don't think their anger with me will ever pass."

"Have faith in the loove that they hold fur ye, *ceisdein*. Ye are their loving bluid. Take care tae act accordingly and their anger will pass."

"How are you so sure? I've known friends who've had simple disagreements with their families that have caused major rifts between them."

"I refer tae my own experience. Bluid is thicker than water. Forget not the strife we shared betwixt us upon my brother's demise. Did we not surmount it?"

"We did."

"Aye. So will ye surmount this discord with yer family," he encouraged. I nodded at the realization and accepting his words, if only to hope. He turned his gaze from me and returned the hairbrush over the dresser, now freshly attired and groomed.

"I guess dinner might be prepared by now," I mentioned apprehensively.

"Then, we shall dine with yer family and enjoy it. Hold fast, alrecht?" he replied.

"I'll try," I said honestly. I sensed his thumb and forefinger carefully gripping my chin, and he tilted my gaze up toward his.

"Be brave, Sylvie, fur I ken that ye are." He gently kissed my forehead, then released my chin, letting my gaze fall away from his.

Eleven

Kyle and Dakota were seen in the kitchen, chatting, as Leif and I entered. Noticing us, they immediately ceased their conversation and silently observed us approaching them where they sat at the island counter. Awkwardness was palpable in the air, heightening the anxiety I was already feeling. Kyle was already sitting comfortably at the dining counter with a beer while Dakota continued setting dining places over it. The inquisitiveness in their gazes was discernible, and I was insecure about how this dining experience was going to unfold.

"Hey!" Dakota greeted abruptly with an inviting tone as she appeared happy and interested to see us, attempting to ameliorate the discomfiture in the atmosphere also.

"Hey," I replied, smiling a little.

"Hey," Kyle welcomed, appearing aloof. I felt his anger still, and knew he was trying to repress it as he gave me a tacit look before his eyes acknowledged Leif.

"Sir," Lief responded politely to Kyle, recognizing him also.

"Here, come have a seat," Dakota quickly offered us, motioning toward the empty seats at the island.

"Thanks," I said, striding with Leif toward a pair of empty

chairs. Aware of them staring at us as they silently watched us taking our places to join them, amplified my anxiety about eating with them.

"I'm just now finishing up setting dinner places for everyone. I hope you don't mind takeout," Dakota informed us.

"Takeout is fine," I replied, trying to push my nerves aside.

"Great. I hope you like Thai, Seamus, because that's what we're having," she said easily with a smile. I glanced at Leif and noticed his brow faintly drawing together.

"He doesn't eat Thai food—I think," I said nervously, speaking for him instead.

"Oh no!" Dakota regretted instantly, looking worried. "I should have asked what kind of food I should pick up for everyone to enjoy. I just wasn't thinking. I assumed everyone enjoyed Thai. I'm sorry."

"Pray, dinnae be concerned. It will please me tae experience it," Leif said politely. Dakota glanced at Kyle and he shrugged.

"Well, I don't want you to feel obligated if it's not what you prefer. I can easily order you something else to eat instead—if that's what you'd actually like," she suggested. Leif looked a little blank and hesitated.

"He said he'd be pleased to try Thai food. So, give it to him," Kyle told Dakota.

"But I just want to make sure. That's all," she insisted, uncertain.

"He's okay with it. Right?" Kyle shifted his gaze from Dakota to Leif, confirming the fact.

"Aye," Leif responded, cluing in.

"See?" Kyle returned his attention to Dakota. "Everyone's happy. No need to worry."

"All right," she accepted with a small shrug. "Thai for everyone it is."

I noticed the uneven smile on her face as she glimpsed at Kyle, and knew she was also uncertain about what to expect between us all. Cumbersome silence ensued and we simply sat gazing at each other with empty glances while being together at the island. Kyle suddenly turned his attention toward Leif and cleared his throat when he finally asked, "Do you want a beer?" breaking the awkwardness.

"Aye. I thank ye," Leif replied politely. Kyle easily removed himself from his comfortable location at the dining counter and moved to the refrigerator, retrieving a fresh beer bottle. He popped the cap, tossed it in the trash hidden in the cabinet beneath the sink and gave the cold bottle to Leif.

"There ya go," Kyle said, trying to be friendly, insinuating the beer he'd just given him when returning to sit in his chair. He saluted his own bottle to Leif before taking a swig from it again.

"Appreciated kindly," Leif responded, drawing the bottle rim to his mouth after glancing at its opening.

"No problem," Kyle replied after swallowing.

Leif wasn't used to drinking chilled alcohol and his brow lightly furrowed as he withdrew the bottle from his mouth, swallowing it after a sip. I observed Kyle watching Leif as he drank his beer, wondering what he was going to say to him next. Whatever was going to fall out of Kyle's mouth, I was hoping it wasn't going to be confrontational, because I knew he was suspicious of him due to the way they had just met.

The room had returned to clumsy silence as Leif sat silently drinking his beer with all eyes on him. But he seemed unfazed by it, or at least on the surface he did. He was a skilled poker player, I remembered, and knew how to keep his cards close as he guarded his opinions and emotions. So, whatever discomfort that I assumed he might actually be feeling now, it was well hidden and no one would ever know. Instead, he simply sat in the company of their scrutinizing gazes imperceptibly assessing his beer as he continued to mindfully drink.

I noticed Kyle slowly rotating his own beer bottle in front himself on the dining counter as he was scrutinizing us, while we continued sitting in silence. His eyes shifted from Leif onto me and I saw the fury on his face as his lips tightened into a line. He held my gaze for a moment, impressing the heat of his anger into my eyes and all I wanted to do was shrink away. Except, I was compelled to keep his stare since I couldn't hide, and he knew that I was trapped as I perceived it in his eyes. At that moment, he decided to look away and returned his examining gaze toward Leif.

"So," Kyle started, interrupting the uneasiness in the air again. Leif's gaze had remained on Kyle, studying him while he was boring his irate eyes into me.

"Aye?" Leif replied impassively as he set his beer down in front of himself on the counter from taking his last sip.

"Where are you from?" Kyle asked directly.

"I was born in Scotland," Leif replied evenly.

"So, you're British," Kyle said.

"Aye."

"Is that where you're living now?"

"Formerly, it is waur I had resided," Leif disclosed.

"Where do you live now?" Kyle questioned.

"I have property lying in Boston."

"Boston?"

"Aye."

"You moved all the way from the U.K. to Boston?"

"U.K.?"

"United Kingdom?"

"Aye. Of coorse."

"That's a big move. What made you do that?"

"I have interests," Leif said bluntly.

"Interests..." Kyle reiterated in absorption.

"Aye."

"As in investments?"

"Correct."

"Would my sister be one of your investments?" Kyle inquired candidly.

"She is," Leif declared directly. Kyle paused, nodding silently, in response. He appeared ruminative, and I wondered how many more interrogating questions he was going to ask him.

Dakota began serving everyone their food and I politely asked her for a couple of forks—each for Leif and me—knowing Leif was unfamiliar with the use of chopsticks with his meal, and wanting him to be comfortable eating his food in everyone's company. She kindly gave the forks to me and smiled. Returning her smile, I remained silent as I watched her finally serve herself a plate of food after everyone else had been served, and move to seat herself at the counter with us. I gave Leif his fork and we all began eating. Leif hesitated for a second as he noticed Kyle and Dakota eating with chopsticks before he attempted using his fork to eat his noodles like everyone else. Mimicking the way I was using my fork, he quickly mastered the noodles onto his fork and began mindfully eating.

The conversation dropped as we ate, except for small comments between Kyle and Dakota regarding the pleasant taste of the food. I was glad for the lull to occur since it distracted us and allowed for us to focus on eating, and sparing me the disastrous propensity for a mistake happening as Kyle probed Leif.

"So, what do you do for a living?" Kyle pursued questioning Leif after a moment while we ate. I felt myself stiffen with nervousness again as my eyes landed on Kyle the minute he asked this question.

"I am a retired major of the British armed forces," Leif answered reservedly.

"You were in the army?" Kyle asked.

"Aye," Leif said.

"I guess we have a little in common, then. Our dad served in the marines," Kyle replied.

"Admirable of yer father," Leif acknowledged respectfully.

"Where did you serve?" Kyle continued.

"He was in Afghanistan," I blurted, nervously inserting myself into the conversation. Everyone's gazes turned toward me, and I swallowed hard, feeling dry in my throat. I immediately reached for my glass of cherry Coke and took a sip.

"You were in Afghanistan?" Kyle redirected his attention toward Leif, looking at him intently.

"Yes, he was," I abruptly answered for Leif again. Leif turned his gaze toward me and I couldn't read through his unexpressive expression. But as my eyes bounced back toward Kyle's, his blue eyes hardened and narrowed on me.

"Our dad served in Vietnam and in Iraq," Kyle said as he returned looking at Leif.

"Aye, Sylvie has informed me," Leif said, shifting his gaze back toward Kyle.

"How long were you in Afghanistan?" Kyle asked.

"Far too long for anyone, really," I blurted again, nervously answering for Leif. But, Kyle furrowed his brow and gave him an unusual look.

"Dude, you're sweating. Are you okay?" Kyle curiously asked him, suddenly seeming a little concerned. My glance shot toward Leif and the crimson hue on his face along with tiny beads of perspiration on his brow were clearly noticed.

"Is it the food?" I swiftly conjectured as I looked concernedly at Leif, realizing he'd just taken a large bite of drunken noodles. He quickly swallowed the food in his mouth and coughed, clearing his throat. "A little too spicy?"

"Oh no, I'm so sorry. I should have made sure to order the food with mild spice. I wasn't thinking. I just assumed medium spice would be fine for everyone. I'm so sorry," Dakota interrupted abruptly, looking truly worried for him.

"Nae, pray dinnae be distraught. The spice adds delight tae the palate," Leif graciously replied, sounding hoarse and scratchy, as he glanced at her. The worried look on her face quickly eased and she appeared reassured as she returned a sympathetic smile at him.

"Here, let me get you some water. It'll help ease the spice," she suddenly suggested. Promptly leaving her plate of food, she retrieved a glass and filled it with water from the refrigerator. Presenting the water to him, he graciously thanked her, taking the full glass from her and chugged it to its last drop. Observing him settling from the spicy food, Leif resumed taking a swig from his beer bottle and placed it back on the counter in front himself before returning his attention to Kyle, who'd been closely scrutinizing him.

"And ye? Micht ye be an apprentice of a sort?" Leif inquired of him, resuming the subject of interest.

"Interesting way of asking about a person's living. I'm a stock analyst," Kyle said, appearing a little more easy-going now.

"Whit micht that be?" Leif inquired curiously. Kyle gave him a strange look with a little smirk.

"You know, I try to determine the future activity of the market in order to help people invest their money," Kyle said obviously.

"As in trade?" Leif asked.

"That's right," Kyle responded.

"Intriguing," Leif replied genuinely.

"I find it to be. It's exciting to see it when the market goes up. Not so bad when it dips. But when it crashes, investors get nervous and want to pull out. So, you have to use a bit of psychology by reminding them it's the long game they're playing to calm their anxiety—unless you short stocks—because it's the nature of the market to rise over time—as you probably already know since you have interests," Kyle explained. "Big investors usually ride out the market volatility. It's really small investors who typically get skittish when the market tanks."

"Aye," Leif responded simply, appearing interested in what Kyle was saying.

"So, how long have you been here in the States?" Kyle asked curiously.

"I huvnae been haur fur long," Leif answered. He was being vague, and my nerves were beginning to calm as Kyle seemed to be accepting his answers without suspicion or dislike. He appeared to be warming up from his cold mood while engaging Leif in conversation. It was relieving, in spite of his angry feelings toward me.

"How do you like it here in the Sates, Seamus?" Dakota asked pleasantly, now inserting herself into the conversation as we continued eating our meal.

"From whit I have already experienced, I find it fascinates me," Leif said honestly. Dakota smiled at him, and I suddenly knew she approved of him.

"I'm sure that you must find it different than from where you're originally from. How have you adjusted?" she asked interestedly.

"I find that I have grown weel accustomed tae America, as I dinnae foresee my return tae Great Britain," Leif said.

"Well, I'm glad that you have adjusted well. But, if you still find yourself at a loss, don't hesitate in letting us know if we can do anything to help accommodate you," she offered nicely.

"'Tis most kind of ye tae present such a provision fur me. I am much obliged tae ye, indeed," Leif replied with sincere gratitude.

"Of course! Don't even think about it." She smiled at him again, then shifted her gaze and smiled at me. I smiled at her in return, feeling slightly more reassured and at ease.

"So, tell us how you and Sylvie first met?" she inquired inquisitively.

"'Twas upon a lonesome road whaur we first encountered one anither. She claimed her car had broken," Leif responded truthfully.

"So, you helped her," Dakota surmised.

"Aye," Leif said.

"That was extremely nice of you. Not many people would stop to help if you were stranded on the highway—except a police officer. You were like her knight in shining armor to the rescue," she said sweetly. I felt Leif glancing at me and I shifted my gaze, meeting his heartened eyes. He furtively grinned at me, appearing suddenly boyish, and my lips automatically curved into a little diffident smile in response.

"So, you're headed out to California," Kyle said to Leif, witnessing our reaction to each other.

"Aye," Leif said, nodding his head a tad, returning his attention toward Kyle.

"What time's your flight?" Kyle asked, unexpectedly turning his attention toward me.

"We have to be on the road by six in the morning in order to be sure to catch our flight at eleven," I answered, discerning his frustration with me had diminished somewhat as he now looked at me.

"Too bad it's such a short visit," Dakota said regretfully.

"I know," I responded, feeling similar.

"I'm going to miss you," she said.

"I'll miss you too."

"I wish we had longer to catch up in person. I'm hoping that our plans stick to come out and visit you around Thanksgiving. It'll be so nice to see the kids and your parents again."

"It'll be nice to have that time to celebrate with you too. I'll mark it on the calendar."

"Perfect. Kyle and I will be sure to see that our plan to visit you works out." Dakota glanced at Kyle.

"Yeah, sure. She makes all the plans around here. I just tag along for the ride," he half joked. A little smirk tilted Leif's lips, as I sensed he had become amused. Kyle shrugged as he caught the expression on Leif's face. "Cheers," he said and tapped Leif's beer bottle with his.

"Cheers," Leif replied, grinning more apparently.

"What are ya going to do?" Kyle asked rhetorically. "I know. I'll have another beer."

"I too, if yoo'll please," Leif requested politely.

"You bet. Can't leave us guys hanging out to dry," Kyle half joked again.

"When have I ever left you hanging out to dry?" Dakota asked Kyle with surprise.

"We'll talk about it later. Now's not the time," he hinted.

"See what I have to put up with? He's ridiculous," she said with a smirk as she glanced at me, causing me to giggle a bit.

At this point, the ice had somewhat melted with Kyle and the conversation carried on more affably between him and Leif, and obviously with his wife, Dakota. And even though he was no longer conveying his anger toward me while we continued conversing, I still sensed his resentment. Despite it, though, dinner progressed smoother than I had anticipated and for that, I was tremendously relieved and glad.

Twelve

After dinner Leif and I returned to the guest bedroom more than ready to retire for the night. It had been a long eventful, deeply emotional day and the tole of it had taxed us both. Although the evening was relatively early, I felt as though I hadn't slept in days. As I restfully lay my head on Leif's shoulder in the dark, I considered that it was just as well that we'd fall asleep early tonight, so that I'd have enough energy in the morning to drive us to Boston in order to catch our flight to L.A.

I sensed Leif gently stroking my bare arm as I rested on him, surprised that he hadn't already fallen asleep. I was certain that he was more exhausted than I was, considering he'd just arrived from traveling through time. Instead, I knew he was thinking and it made me wonder.

"I'm surprised you're not sleeping yet," I said softly to him.

"I'm also surprised that yoo're not either," he replied in a low voice as he continued stroking my arm. "Why do ye not yet close yer eyes and rest? Fur I am certain ye are considerably weary."

"I'm only awake because you are. Are you all right?"

"Aye, I am, of coorse."

"Then, why aren't you sleeping?"

"I cannae help myself from pondering."

"About what?"

"How I am immensely grateful that we are reunited, and 'tis not a dream this occurrence. I have dreamt of ye every wakeful and restful moment of my existence since we separated that cursed day," he said.

"I've dreamed about you and that day all of the time, too. And now, my wish has come true," I responded.

"My prayers have been answered as weel," he replied. "The Lord giveth whit the Lord hath taketh."

"Yes, He did."

"I am pleased tae have met yer brother and his wife."

"You are?"

"Aye. They are most kind and generous," he said. "'Tis evident tae my perception that they hold great affection fur ye. Yer brother may be angered by ye, yet I dinnae believe that he would ever shun ye."

"How do you know?"

"I suspect that if he husnae already shunned ye, then he likely never will."

"You believe that?"

"I do."

"Hmm... He's livid with me, though. It frightens me, because I think he might never forgive me."

"We shall endure, Sylvie. His wrath will settle sooner or later. 'Tis his pride that may hinder him, instead. A man's pride is paramount tae his esteem, and may fault him in knowing whit is just. Yet, if he adores ye as much as I reckon that he does, then 'tis my belief he will come about one day," Leif comforted.

"I really do hope you're right," I replied.

"'Tis always better tae hope raither than not. Hope permits fur chances tae be granted that otherwise wouldnae exist," he said. "Now, rest yer weary head fur the nicht. Dinnae be troobled any longer."

I felt his lips tenderly pressing against my brow in a kiss, soothing me. I decided to do exactly as he said and closed my eyes, intending to finally quiet my worried mind. I drew in a long breath and exhaled, relaxing at last, as he secured an arm around me and fitted me snugly against his body. Feeling sound with him embracing me again like he used to when we lay together centuries ago, I was contented for the moment, believing that nothing could ever truly eclipse my joy now that he was here with me.

Leif and I awakened before six o'clock the next morning to prepare for our flight. Once we were showered and dressed, I made sure that all of our belongings were packed. He gathered my suitcase from me as we proceeded making our way in silence through the dark house while Dakota and Kyle remained sleeping.

I placed my purse with my suitcase by the front door where I had requested for Leif to leave it, then we turned for the kitchen to share a light breakfast of cereal, toast, and coffee. Once we had finished our meal, we left the Rockport's house as we stepped outside into the predawn darkness.

After loading ourselves into the Explorer and starting the engine, I noticed Leif's eyes suddenly widen with wonderment as he stared at all of the lights on the dashboard.

"Do ye ken how tae operate this mighty contraption?" he asked with uncertainty.

"Yes, I do," I replied confidently. I put the vehicle into gear and began slowly driving around the bend in the driveway.

"It appears raither difficult tae ken how tae manipulate such a transport," he mentioned, sounding skeptical, as we began on our way toward the highway.

"It's easier than it looks. Don't worry. You're in safe hands." I said.

"I pray that I am," he responded under his breath.

"You are without a doubt." I smiled at him and he did the Sigh of the Cross over himself.

"The lanterns are brilliant—as bricht it seems as those I had first encountered upon the road the fateful nicht I had witnessed ye in the snow before yer horseless contraption," he remarked. I glanced at him from the steering wheel, and his gaze remained fixed ahead as he was viewing the dawning scenery out the windshield.

"The headlights are illuminated by an electrical current created and sustained by the battery charging the car," I explained.

"As in the one within yer instrument?" He turned his awed gaze toward me, observing me as I drove.

"Similar to that. Only more powerful," I replied.

"Intriguing." His eyes shifted from me again, returning to look out of the windshield at the road and surrounding woodland passing us by. "Thaur are many novelties within this new world which fascinate me." I smiled at him. "Fur instance, how is it that we travel swiftly without the use of horses?"

"It's done through either a battery or by gasoline," I answered simply.

"Gasoline?"

"Yeah. Gasoline comes from oil deep within the earth and is pumped out by drills, then later refined for usage. It's used to combust engines in order to power them."

"'Tis all a marvel," he commented, sounding extraordinarily impressed. I had connected to the vehicle's navigational system and the chat bot spoke over the speakers, telling me which turn I needed to take in order to direct me back onto Route 2, heading out of Williamstown.

"Who speaks?" Leif asked suddenly, caught off guard, glancing around himself.

"It's the vehicle's GPS system, navigating me as I drive," I informed him, aware of his unease and the question on his face. "Don't worry. It's just a computer speaking. It's not a person."

"Och…" he responded. "A computer similar tae that within yer instrument?"

"Yes, similar to the one in my phone."

"I see. How many leagues must we journey before we arrive at our new destination?" he inquired curiously, abruptly changing the subject. I quickly sensed his eagerness to meet our kids.

"Well, everything's measured in miles now—so, if I'm calculating correctly, I'd presume about eight hundred, give or take a little—maybe?"

"Eight hundred?" he echoed, astounded.

"Yes."

"Ye journeyed from such a great distance in merely less than a day tae meet me?"

"Yes."

"Remarkable," he replied, mystified. "Thus, we shall visit our bairns within merely hours."

"That's right. It won't be long from now."

"In spite of it, I am most eager tae lay eyes upon them at last."

"I know," I replied, understanding. I was anxious for him to meet them too.

Although our kids had never known their father, they had missed him, tremendously, as they compared themselves to their friends who were fortunate to have their fathers in their families. So, I was expecting our kids to be elated when they finally met Leif as I looked forward to his inclusion into their lives. Words couldn't express how happy I was that the final completion of my family was realized. A dream that I could only yearn for many years, until now.

Leif became silent and returned to gazing out the windshield and passenger window as I returned my full attention to driving along the road ahead of us. But I sensed him thinking, and because I wondered about him, I asked him about it, starting a new conversation between us. I was relieved to learn that it wasn't anything troubling that pertained to Kyle's disagreement with me, or my relationship with my parents after the lies that I'd told them. Instead, Leif was simply inquisitive about the modern age in which he currently found himself. He asked me many questions about the government and social structure of my society. He also had many questions about technological advances that were being used today.

But after seeming satisfied with all these particular questions he'd asked, his inquiries inevitably turned toward our children. He asked me countless questions about them; what it was like when they were born, who delivered them, what had occurred afterward, about their schooling, adventures, and pastimes. The conversation between us was limitless and lasted the entire nearly three hours it took us to arrive into Boston.

It was a little after nine o'clock in the morning now, and the fresh morning light radiated brightly, illuminating the tall buildings surrounding us as their glass facades facing the sun reflected sunlight. Leif stared out the car windows, captivated in awe, as he observed countless cars crowding the streets and passing us by now in the busy roads. While I continued driving us through the city, he stared at pedestrians quickly pacing up and down the sidewalks headed for work.

"The lads wear cropped hair and nae hats," he remarked, noticing.

"Yes, it's common," I replied while maneuvering the SUV through the crowded streets, on our way to the airport.

"And, the lasses wear short skirts and breeks with nae caps or pinners upon their heads," he commented further.

"I think it's been the style for women since the nineteen twenties," I said naturally.

"Has it?"

"I believe so."

"I see," he fathomed. "Micht we have a glimpse of *Taigh Gràs*?" he inquired curiously.

"I'm so sorry, but I don't think we have the time to visit it if we're to arrive home in time to see the kids," I replied regretfully. I didn't have the heart to reveal to him that I doubted our eighteenth century home still existed—not even in remnants.

I discerned disappointment in his composure and I felt awful about not being able to accommodate him. He drifted into silence and the conversation between us finally faded as I continued driving us. As we made our way toward the airport, I knew he was contemplating his surroundings again, and hoped that he wasn't too overwhelmed by the new environment in which he found himself.

Within moments, we arrived at Logan and my biggest concern now was how I was going to get him through security without a proper ID card. I hadn't really dwelled on the problem long enough to devise a better solution, and suddenly realized just how significant the dilemma was. It wasn't going to be easy to explain to Leif about the problem, because he was going to ask me many sorts of questions regarding it that I couldn't simply answer for him. It was going to be difficult for us to simply board the plane as it wasn't like in earlier days due to present day government restrictions placed on airlines and passengers in order for us to fly. So, I was a little more than apprehensive to attempt my plan to fly with him as I anticipated our encounter with flight authorities. Instead of revealing all of this to him, I kept quiet along with hiding my anxiety from him in order not to raise his concern, praying that somehow we'd be able to board our flight.

After returning my rental car to the proper agency, we arrived at our airline terminal. I slipped my hand into his and led us inside the crowded terminal for the check-in line to purchase a ticket for him. As we waited in line with other travelers to obtain his ticket and our boarding passes, I was aware of his silence as he discreetly glanced around himself, taking in his new surroundings here at the airport. With my hand remaining in his, I gently contracted my fingers, drawing his attention. His eyes turned toward mine and I softly smiled with reassurance, though I was anxious to successfully get us through this stage of miraculously gaining a ticket and pass for him. His lips curled into a small grin and his eyes sparked with uncertainty, though he also seemed to be reassured by the confident lead I was appearing to take to steer us through this world unfamiliar to him.

When it was our turn to arrive at the ticketing counter, the male ticketing agent promptly greeted us and requested for us to pass our IDs to him for his information and verification. Silently nerve racked, I proceeded retrieving my ID from the wallet in my purse. As I gave him my ID, I quickly did a mental assessment of his friendliness and determined his likely willingness to assist me with my impending problem the second my eyes landed on his mocha face. His brown eyes kindly smiled at me. I smiled in return and I took the calm initiative to succinctly explain to him, as innocently as I could as I lied, that Leif had unexpectedly lost his ID while traveling and we had just noticed it missing from his wallet.

"That's unfortunate," the agent said with a hint of sympathy as he gazed professionally at me when looking up from my ID, that I'd just given to him upon his request.

"So, I don't know what to do since my husband and I are traveling together, and we have to make it back home in time to pick up our kids from school this afternoon," I expressed nicely, appearing genuinely worried as he returned his eyes to me after looking at my ID. Then, he looked at his computer again and began typing.

"Hmm," the agent mumbled, appearing considerate of our serious dilemma as he'd just finished typing into his computer. His eyes returned to mine and he handed my ID back to me, appearing doubtful.

"Is there anything that the airline can do to help us in this situation?" I asked with a pleading look.

"I'm afraid not, unfortunately. Regulations," he said, regrettably.

"So, there's no extra paperwork I could fill out that's pertinent to help for verification purposes for the airline? I mean, it's really an emergency. We're kinda stuck, and anything you could do to help us out would be extremely appreciated," I expressed worriedly, feeling the heightened pressure to get us back to L.A. Also, I was aware of Leif not focusing on the conversation with the agent while he was constantly glancing around himself at our surroundings, making him appear like an unusual candidate for flying.

"What's your name, sir?" the agent asked, directing his attention toward Leif now. Leif didn't respond while in the midst of being distracted by everyone and everything around him, until I gently placed a hand on his bicep. He suddenly turned his attention toward me and his eyes locked onto mine with startle. The unexpected look on his face told me he was beginning to freak out. "Your name, sir?" the agent asked him again. Leif abruptly turned his eyes toward the agent and stared at him in bewilderment as he didn't immediately respond.

"He's asking for your name," I said to Leif, referring to the agent.

"Och—aye—'tis His Grace, the Duke of Monteith," Leif stammered. The agent's brow furrowed as he gave Leif a weird look.

"He means your given name," I clarified uncomfortably while observing Leif's uncertainty for the first time since ever knowing him.

"Och—certainly—'tis Leif Charles Seamus MacLeod Fitz-James Stewart," he told the agent with pride.

"Stewart?" The agent questioned curiously.

"Aye," Leif replied definitively.

"Where are you from?"

"I originate from Scotland, if it pleases."

"Europe."

"Aye."

"You don't share the same name as your husband?" the agent asked, now turning his eyes toward me.

"I'm a bit of a feminist," I joked unevenly.

"Right. Nothing wrong with that, I suppose," the agent replied unemotionally, nodding a little. "Well, I see that you've already purchased a ticket for yourself."

"Yes, that's right," I responded politely, hoping this might lead to our benefit by some miracle over the fact the agent now realized that not only was Leif a foreigner, but also that he and I had different last names.

"Seeing that your information checks out, what I can do is go ahead and issue you your boarding pass. But unfortunately, I won't be able to sell a ticket and do the same for Mister Stewart."

Leif, clueless to the circumstance and to what was occurring around him, resumed fidgeting at my side. Observing the new environment in which he found himself, his distraction was obvious and heightened my insecure anxiety of the perception of appearing suspicious to the agent, and to anyone else watching us. When I nervously glanced at Leif, he looked rattled and I knew he was struggling to remain unassuming and controlled. It was obvious to me that he was certainly alarmed.

Forget it.

Suddenly, I decided not to pursue this avenue with the airline any longer. I realized right then that it was futile attempting to fly commercially with him, sensing his extreme unease being here at the airport surrounded by abundant and uncontrollable stimuli— and that it was apparent there wasn't going to be any way to obtaining a ticket and boarding pass for him. Flying restrictions were tight and severe.

"Thank you. But I'll forgo my flight. We need to be together when we arrive in L.A. since our kids will be expecting him with me when we do," I explained as composed as I could in a polite tone to the agent.

"I see. Sorry I can't be of any more assistance to you," he said. I gave him a weak smile in response. "Is there anything else that I can help you with this morning?" he asked.

"No, thank you. That will be all," I replied hastily, absolutely anxious about the whole situation.

"All right. Then, have a nice day."

"You too," I replied to the agent, feeling defeated and thwarted while tucking my ID back into my wallet again, and shoving it into my purse. After zipping my purse closed, I grabbed Leif's hand and promptly led him away from the agent's counter.

Thirteen

"Damn it," I cursed in a low voice. But not low enough, apparently, as Leif heard me and I sensed his eyes immediately turn toward me as I was forging a trail for us through crowds of travelers in the airline terminal, while leading him by hand.

"Is there a matter?" he asked, sounding obviously concerned.

"Just a hiccup," I replied, trying to minimize the panic in my voice as I kept my eyes ahead of him on the crowd I was splitting us through while hurriedly pacing us.

"How do ye mean?"

"My plan for us didn't work."

"Nae?"

"No."

"Why not?"

"You don't have an ID."

"A whit?"

"Verification of who you are. It's necessary to do anything important here."

"Och. Yet, mayn't I acquire this order in some manner?" he asked unknowingly, sounding extremely puzzled.

"Not easily."

"Wouldnae the master at the stand assist in acquiring it fur me, however?"

"He's not the proper authority to issue that sort of thing. We have to go somewhere else."

"Mayhap a visit tae the governor is in order tae acquire this sort of document which is of import."

"It's not that simple anymore."

"Is it not?"

"Unfortunately, not."

"I see. Waur instead micht we go tae acquire it?"

"Don't worry. I just came up with another idea to get us where we need to be."

"Whit notion have ye?"

"Simply follow me," I advised as I continued moving us through hordes of people.

Meandering through the terminal while towing him, I scanned the area for a vacant place to sit. As we came through a stream of people, my eyes landed on an empty bench by a wall several feet ahead. Making a dash for it before someone else would occupy it, I hastily led Leif with me toward the bench. Gladly arriving at it within seconds, I dropped myself down on the bench and sat as Leif placed himself sitting close beside me. Immediately removing my phone from my purse, I promptly began scouring my contacts list, suddenly remembering one of my old friends from Harvard Medical School currently living in Bedford.

Quickly retrieving his phone number, I called him without any hesitation and asked him for the dire favor that I needed from him. Not one to ever fly commercially, the one person I swiftly knew had a Gulfstream jet and had a pilot friend who flew him around the country on a whim was my possible solution to our facing obstacle.

Once I placed the call to Dr. Micheal Richards, he immediately recognized my voice and a cordial conversation began between us as we briefly caught up on each other's lives after a couple years of missing contact. When he learned of the bind that I was in as I'd explained to him that I was stuck in Boston on the pretense of having missed my original airline flight, and the urgent need to return home this afternoon, he was pleasantly willing to help me without accepting any compensation from me. Utterly grateful to him for his kindness, he proceeded acquiring some necessary details from me in order to make prompt arrangements.

Once he'd gathered a little information from me containing the number of passengers intending to fly, amount of luggage, catering preferences, that's when he learned that I'd gotten married again and was traveling with Leif. Having remained a bachelor, the tone in Micheal's voice sounded regretful while he lamentably joked about his loss for not romantically pursuing me sooner when he had the chance. But he politely offered his congratulations to me for my new marriage with Leif, after a playful scolding that he'd given me for not having visited him while currently being in the Boston area. Still, after accepting his kind words, he quickly resumed to the matter at hand, giving me instructions, and assured that he'd get me back to L.A. without a further hitch.

When I hung up from speaking with him, and now having concrete travel plans successfully made for Leif and me, I took note of the time and shoved my phone back into my purse, completely relieved that I had such a contact in my friend, Micheal, and that the situation was swiftly and finally resolved. Glad about this new flying arrangement for Leif and me, my anxiety had diminished considerably.

Now, I had to focus on getting us to our next destination in a timely manner in order for us to catch our flight out of the Boston area. Arriving in time to pick up the kids from school was possible again. Because of our current circumstances, I was also alleviated that I was going to be able to keep my promise to my parents regarding my return, thwarting any chance for worry, concerns, or questions from them.

As the dilemma appeared settled, I glanced at Leif and found him entranced while blatantly staring at crowds of people passing us by, sizing them from head to toe as if they had antenna sprouting from their crowns. He appeared more than nonplussed, and I perceived his reaction to being culture shocked as it was clearly setting into his awareness. Conscious of the time again, and pressed to arrive at a different airport to catch our private jet in time, I was constrained to begin a thoughtful conversation with him about the thoughts running through his mind, as I wished to ease his discombobulation and uncharacteristically tense disposition. Instead, I seized his hand with mine and stood from my seat on the bench ready to lead him away with me once more. His gaze suddenly turned upward toward me as his attention from the crowd was interrupted.

"Let's go," I gently urged him.

"Waur to?" he inquired as he began standing from his place on the bench while holding my hand.

"We have to go to a different airport now to catch our plane ride to Los Angeles," I informed him.

"Och," he replied simply, appearing clueless.

I proceeded leading him through the terminal again in a different direction in search of the baggage claim where we left for outdoors. When we arrived where all the taxis and shuttles were waiting, I stopped us from walking any further and grabbed my phone from my purse again to launch my Uber app. Promptly requesting a ride from the app, within five minutes an Uber vehicle appeared for us and we approached a large black Suburban. Without hesitation, our driver emerged from the car and opened the door for us to enter.

As we were seating ourselves, he kindly assisted placing my luggage into the trunk. After I'd promptly buckled Leif and myself into our seats, our driver had closed the trunk and returned to his driver seat. Pulling the vehicle away from the curb, he began driving us away from Logan Airport and out of the city of Boston toward Hanscom Field where our private flight was waiting.

THE ENTIRE FORTY-MINUTE DRIVE TOWARD BEDFORD where Hanscom Field Airport was located was ridden in Leif's silence. While our driver was fairly inattentive to Leif's unspoken demeanor as his eyes remained glued to his passenger side window, peering at the scenery whizzing past us, our driver was proving to be genial and charismatic as he lightly conversed with me on related topics involving various encounters experienced while he traveled in certain locations about the country when on vacation. Thankfully, the conversation easily passed the time as we traveled, and made Leif appear presumably aloof and at ease to our driver upon our journey to Bedford, at least.

When we finally arrived an hour ahead of our twenty-minute expected arrival time to board the plane, our driver kindly unloaded us from his vehicle before the airport's doors. After thanking him, I slipped my fingers into Leif's hand and led him into the airport. Scanning our new location, by all accounts this place was a significantly smaller vicinity containing noticeably lesser crowds of people.

Unfamiliar with this airport as we proceeded indoors, I was glad to be promptly met by a fixed base operator who graciously escorted us to our chartered jet's departure gate facility to wait to board the plane. Once we were inside our terminal, I was introduced to the handling agent and gave my name including the information that Micheal had given me for her, along with my ID, as she requested. While she verified my identity, I instantly became immensely fearful again that Leif would be prohibited on this plane also due to his lack of ability to produce a proper ID card upon request.

But when she returned my ID to me, she didn't ask for Leif's though she was aware that there were going to be both of us flying. Instead, she simply smiled at us and had us both go through a rapid pre-flight session. After the session, Leif and I were cleared to fly, completely relieving my anxiety.

Entirely alleviated now that we were free to board when the plane was ready for us, I suddenly released my breath as I guided Leif toward a pair of plush chairs positioned by the windows facing the tarmac for us to sit. Several planes were visible through the windows parked at different gates. Just as I was about to take the opportunity to text Mom to inform her of my traveling status when I retrieved my phone from my purse, Leif straightened from his seat. I watched him stepping toward the large windows where he came to stand, and wondered about him as my attention settled onto his standing figure.

Still silent, he gazed out at the planes as a couple took off into flight, and another landed safely onto the ground. He stood with his back toward me, dressed in a fresh, crisp white cotton dress shirt, and beige slacks. His loose hair hung long, slightly past his shoulders. He kept his hands clasped behind his back while quietly gazing out the window, observing, and discernibly contemplating. I stood from my seat, stepping toward him to gaze out the window with him, and gently placed a hand on his firm bicep.

"Hey," I said, calling his attention away from the windows. Our eyes met, and I certainly perceived him thinking, and his insecurity.

"Aye?" he responded at last.

"Are you okay?" I asked, wanting to know his thoughts.

"Aye."

"Are you sure?"

"Aye. Why do ye inquire?"

"Well, you haven't spoken a word since we were at the other airport and came here."

"I merely ponder. It is all."

"About what?" I asked, looking inquisitively at him, searching his unwavering eyes as he stared back at me.

"'Tis quite a complex society in which ye reside," he noted. I shifted my gaze out toward the parked airplanes in front of us, considering his observation.

"Yes, I suppose it is," I said objectively, returning my gaze to his.

"Significantly."

"In comparison, absolutely," I understood, clearly remembering the society from which he came.

"How micht one not become muddled?"

"Being here, I suppose, any individual would become used to seeing so many people after a time—as things become understood by the way this society is ordered," I said thoughtfully.

"Yet, 'tis highly designed," he replied.

"What do you mean? Like socially?"

"I huvnea an understanding of the current politics."

"Well, objectively and rather specifically, nothing's changed all that much. People are still placed into danger because of politics, and the elite who move within governing circles still manipulate and kill for self-preservation as they hang on to power to rule countries and societies," I stated, drawing a comparison to the past.

"The presence of science is striking," he commented in addition.

"But, you're familiar with Benjamin Franklin and his writings. Remember?"

"Aye."

"Well, his experiments and discoveries ushered in a new age of science. The era in which he lived is known to us as the Age of Enlightenment."

"Do ye speak of the Age of Reason?"

"It's synonymous, yes," I responded. Leif slowly nodded in thought.

"How micht it have all occurred?" He spoke under his breath in amazement as the question sounded rhetorical. He looked meditatively at me, and I faintly heard a hint of doubt in his voice.

"I know the overwhelming feeling you must be feeling."

"'Tis stunning."

"I know."

"I ken yer compassion fur me as I felt it fur ye," he replied and I nodded.

"Only we know like no one else does," I acknowledged.

"Aye." He turned his gaze from me and glanced over his shoulder at some of the people around us for a minute. Then, he returned looking at me. "It appears many manage with purpose."

"You mean the crowd seems hurried?"

"Aye."

"It's not like that everywhere, though. The pace slows outside of cities. Most of the country is still rural and the lifestyle there would probably be more recognizable to you."

"Micht it?"

"Most likely."

He glimpsed over his shoulder again and briefly studied a woman sitting slightly near us with her eyes glued to her phone, then returned looking at me.

"Therefore, such fine instruments which I have witnessed in use haur wouldnae exist in those places of which ye speak that remain rural about the country?"

"They do exist, actually. Nearly everyone has the latest technology at their disposal no matter where they live in the country."

"Certainly?" he responded, lifting his brow, appearing impressed.

"Yes. The government takes initiatives to expand latest technologies across the country."

"It appears the enlightenment of all transcends my knowledge as I stand haur. Whit I ken is obsolete, and I fear my ignorance may be a hindrance."

"I understand the shock. It's one thing to be told about this place, and very much another to experience it," I sympathized as we spoke quietly between us.

"Quite."

"But you'll learn how to navigate here, just like I had to when I first came to your place. Believe me, it's just on the surface that things seem complicated here."

"Micht it be?"

"Yeah, I believe so."

"In whit manner?"

"Well, in the first place, people here are far from noticing other peoples' differences, because they're generally too unaware."

"Are they?"

"Yes, in general."

"Why?"

"Because, they tend to be self-absorbed with their own inter-ests," I fathomed honestly. Leif's brow furrowed and he appeared either puzzled or disturbed by this assertion.

"Does one not care fur anither any longer?" he questioned regrettably with a surprised look on his face.

"They do—for the most part. But they have a tendency to either look the other way when it comes to regarding others, or they simply accept them—depending on the community as it varies across the country—generally speaking. Many people simply tolerate other's differences likely because individualism is admired so much."

"Och," he responded faintly with his brows still drawn together.

"So, what I'm trying to say is please don't worry about being judged—if that's your concern. No one would really care about your originality. And, as far as you not being technologically savvy? That's something that's not too difficult to overcome. Just think of how you've already learned to use my phone—plus more."

"In whit respect?"

"Well, you found me, didn't you?"

"Aye, I have."

"Well? That was a highly complicated mission, and you succeeded. So, give yourself credit, because it's undoubtedly due."

He didn't respond, except maintained looking at me. As we stared at each other, I perceived his reception to what I was saying when his brow relaxed somewhat. A lull ensued between us and he shifted his gaze from me when he glanced around himself some more. He was observing the people sitting in the surrounding chairs waiting to board their plane, and at one man who'd just come from the restroom. After a minute, he returned his eyes to mine.

"Thaur are plenty middlings," he remarked.

"Yes, there are," I replied. "Most of the country is."

"The rest hold nae titles?" he wondered curiously, forgetting what I'd told him about the social strata here.

"No. They don't." I shook my head a tad. "There isn't a monarchy."

"I seem tae have forgotten since ye last informed me," he remembered now, and I nodded in acknowledgment.

"Other countries still have monarchies and aristocracies, though."

"The gentry?"

"Not since the Civil War experienced here."

"I see..."

"The classes here are separated between the wealthy, middle, and poor," I continued, informing him.

Leif nodded in response, realizing the differences compared to his own society, and appeared meditative. It seemed he couldn't take his eyes off the public, since he curiously glanced around again at our surroundings, pausing momentarily before returning his gaze to me. "The masses... Thaur are a mixture," he commented, noticing various people's ethnicities.

"They've all originated from different countries around the world and have immigrated here," I responded.

"Why have they come?"

"To seek a better life than their original countries offered them."

"Fur liberty?"

"Yes—to escape political persecution, for religious and economic freedom, to have a chance for a better life. Everyone who wanted freedom that they otherwise wouldn't have had due to oppressive governments has come here seeking this chance for themselves. Once the country was established and autonomous, it just continued to grow with more people. People simply multiply, you know?"

"Their forefathers sought this?"

"Everyone but the slaves." Leif didn't respond, but the look in his eyes appeared receptive to this damp realization.

"With exception tae those within bondage, waur not the forefathers of these descendants banished haur, nonetheless?"

"Many ancestors were, yes," I acknowledged, remembering his case with the Crown.

"Aye," he acknowledged also and paused momentarily. "Fur those who have come of their own volition, this land affords such possibilities fur happiness without reprisal?"

"Yes, in comparison to many other countries, it does. Even those who were forced to come here in the past through slavery, although it's been a frightening challenge for them and for society as a whole to experience, have achieved freedom and success."

"'Tis difficult tae believe." His eyes shifted again toward the window in front of us and adhered to a plane taxying away from its gate for takeoff, when suddenly my phone chimed inside my pocket, drawing my attention away from our conversation to the new text message I had just received. I reached a hand toward my back jeans' pocket where I now tucked my phone and pulled it forth, noticing the new text displayed on my home screen which had come from Mom.

Unlocking my phone to see the full text, I read that she was letting me know that the kids were doing well and wondered whether I had arrived at the airport already. I quickly replied, texting her that I had in fact safely arrived, and that I was certain to pick the kids up from school once I had landed back in L.A. We texted briefly back and forth for a moment, and after she sent me her love and wished me a safe flight, I tucked my phone back into my pocked, suddenly remembering my argument with Kyle.

Mom didn't seem to know anything regarding Leif as we communicated just now. Neither did she seem aware of the argument I had with Kyle. So, I assumed Kyle hadn't already informed her of Leif's sudden appearance and that he would be accompanying me home. Instead, Kyle respectfully left this information up to me to disclose to our parents. Still, I was incredibly nervous and worried about the whole situation all over again, as I thought about how I was going to introduce Leif to our parents while freshly remembering the feeling of Kyle's outrage toward me.

Strangely, though, I wasn't too worried about introducing Leif to our children, because they had always wanted their father involved in their lives, and I thought they'd be happy to finally meet him. Being so young, I didn't think their adjustment to him would be significant at all, so I didn't feel intensely concerned in this regard and believed their introduction to him would proceed fairly well.

It was really the reaction of my parents on which I was focusing, and for many reasons I feared their responses. Concerns about it raised and lingered at the forefront of my mind. I was primarily scared that they were going to accuse me of lying to them about my relationship with Leif just like Kyle had done—although it was true that I had lied. I was frightened to tell them anything about us, because it was complicated. I feared their reactions also because

I was likely to expose the level of falsehoods I'd been compelled to tell them as I struggled guarding the truth from them.

And, if they found out a sliver of the truth about what I'd hidden from them, I knew they were sure to be angry at me for it—along with being disappointed and hurt for not trusting them with knowledge pertaining to my relationship with Leif in the first place. In which case, I was convinced my parents would not be so yielding with forgiveness toward me if they were under the impression that I had chosen to lie to them at all. So, I worried about the impending friction this whole circumstance was going to cause. If my confrontation with Kyle was any indication, it was simply a matter of time closing in on me before it all exploded directly into my lap. The apprehension gripped me, and it was distinct. I was afraid of it all going wrong.

Suddenly our fixed base operator approached me, disrupting my thoughts, and informed me that it was time for us to board the plane. I glanced around myself, noticing few other passengers were assembling themselves to depart also on a different flight and I garnered Leif's attention. His eyes turned toward me when I placed my hand on his bicep as he became suddenly aware of me.

"It's time for us to go," I informed him. "Are you ready?"

"Aye," he said simply. I slipped my hand into his, leading him away from the windows and we proceeded following the operator outdoors as he led us to a vehicle which was going to drive us toward the plane waiting for us over the tarmac.

When we arrived at the jet, we climbed the stairs and enter the aircraft. As we embarked inside the craft, I offered for Leif to occupy one of the plush seats by the window as I proceeded taking the one beside him. When we sat ourselves in the seats, I leaned to gather his safety belt and buckled it over his lap, catching a glimpse of the wonderment on his face. He appeared much like a child as he glanced around at his different surroundings inside the jet, minus the talkativeness and the inquiries I was certain were running through his mind.

When it was assessed by the sole flight attendant that we had properly settled into our seats, the hatch was sealed. As the flight attendant took her seat also, the aircraft immediately began driving over the tarmac headed for the runway.

"We're on our way now," I said quietly to Leif and smiled reassuringly at him, as I was desperately relieved to be successfully leaving the Boston area for L.A. with him. He gave me a small, uncertain grin, then returned silently looking out the window as the plane continued moving us along.

When we soon arrived at the runway and had been positioned over it, the jet's engines revved. Leif abruptly swung his gaze toward me and I placidly met his eyes as the engines were howling. The apprehension was perceivable in his eyes. I reached my hand over his and wove my fingers between his, giving him reassurance as I gently squeezed my hand.

"It's all right," I uttered softly to him to put him at ease. He didn't respond. But the concerned and fearful look on his face diminished slightly. Then, the howling engines abruptly began to loudly roar and we were instantly pushed ahead at great velocity over the runway. Leif's eyes suddenly widened, and as we still held hands, his tightly contracted around mine.

"I have experienced this sensation before," he said under his breath.

"It doesn't last long," I reassured, knowing his alarm, and reading the question in his eyes. "You'll see sky and clouds the whole time."

"Will I?"

"Yes. There's no darkness," I promised. "You can see us soaring right now, if you look out the window." I directed his attention toward the window to see us lifting off. Immediately the earth fell away from us as the sight of trees, roads and building structures diminished, becoming indistinguishable to the eye. He gazed closely out of the window as we continued ascending. He was unspoken, merely watching us gliding upward into the bright cobalt sky.

When we reached cruising altitude, Leif continued gazing out the window, observing us entering misty clouds and returning into glaring sunshine surrounded by brilliant, pristine sky. He was enthralled. Awed far beyond the innocence of a child, I perceived him. Well aware of him simply soaking in this experience, I knew not only was he thoroughly impressed, but frightened too. Then, when the plane had hit an unexpected bout of turbulence, the silent alarm blatantly returned to his face as he immediately stiffened in his seat and his eyes shot toward me.

"It's only air turbulence," I calmly informed him, attempting to quell his apprehension. He also gave me a strange look conveying he didn't know quite what I'd meant when a sudden thought registered on his face.

"Ye mean as it is upon the angry sea?" he asked discreetly.

"Something similar to that, yes. But it'll pass sooner than an ocean storm," I assured him.

"I pray so."

"It will." I gave him a gentle grin, assuaging his concern and slid my palm over his knee with a little squeeze, encouraging him. He covered his hand over mine, entwining our fingers and secured them.

When the turbulence ended, his hand remained linked with mine. As our flight proceeded smoothly, he never released our joined hands—even when he finally lulled into sleep.

Fourteen

When we finally landed at the LAX, it was mid-afternoon—fortunately still early enough for us to get settled in at home before I had to pick up the kids from school. Once I had my luggage and we were driven toward the airport building, we were delivered to the area where road transportation via taxis and shuttles were easily available. As we stood at this location, I promptly called an Uber driver to pick us up from here at the airport.

Within a few minutes, our driver arrived and Leif and I entered a white Tesla. Filled with anticipation for us to arrive home at last, I continued sensing Leif's discombobulation; he remained silent for hours since we left Boston, and while riding in the vehicle from LAX to this point. He sat motionlessly while he merely kept gazing out of the window beside himself as our newest scenery was rushing past us while riding along congested streets.

I kept curiously wondering what particular thoughts were running through his mind. There wasn't any doubt that the impression of this new environment encompassing him now was making a significant impact on him. I also anxiously wondered about his anticipation on finally meeting his children for the first time.

After snaking our way through creeping street traffic for a while, at last the speed increased and we were now cruising on the road. It wouldn't be long now that we'd finally exit this current street for the one leading directly into Westchester. As we rode along Sepulveda Boulevard and soon turned a corner off the road, we were now driving through my neighborhood.

It seemed the time journeying until this point had suddenly fast forwarded when I suddenly noticed my house coming into view. My heart leaped from nervous excitement as my stomach quivered also the moment our Uber driver slowed his car and parked at the curb, stopping us in front of my house. When he immediately popped the vehicle's trunk, I emerged from the car with Leif stepping out after me and moved behind the car to withdraw my suitcase from the trunk without the driver's assistance. The minute I lugged it out of the car, Leif promptly snagged it from me and assisted bringing it to the ground.

As Leif held my luggage now in his hand, I thanked our driver as he got out of his car to closed the trunk before he proceeded returning into his vehicle. I watched for a second as the car began driving away from the curb, heading down the street, realizing Leif and I were finally left alone to ourselves.

We stood there together on the sidewalk for a minute, simply looking at each other a little nonplussed and anticipatory. I smiled at him, breaking the awkward spell between us and he reciprocated a little grin. Turning my attention toward the house now, I started through the white picket gate with him following me up the stone pathway to the front door. Taking my keys from my purse, he observed me unlocking and opening the facing door. As I pushed it ajar, we quietly entered the house together, stepping into the foyer. Inside now, I closed the door behind us, anticipating what was next to come. When I turned from the entrance, I met his gaze as he had already been staring at me.

"Welcome home, Leif," I said benignly.

"Thank ye, *mo ghaol*," he said in a gentle tone. "Hence, we have arrived."

"Yes, we have," I replied, smiling at him.

"We are in the city of Los Angels, the state of California, whaur ye and our bairns waur born, and waur ye and the remainder of yer family reside," he understood.

"Yes, that's right."

"Weel..." he paused and glanced around at where we now stood in the foyer.

"Yeah?" I prompted. His eyes suddenly returned to mine.

"I am most taken," he said, appearing duly amazed.

"Well, please don't faint. I don't think I could catch you from falling and hurting yourself if you do," I joked a little. He lightly chuckled and his dark blue eyes lit and sparkled.

"I shall very much mind myself," he promised, reciprocating my smile.

"I'll hold you to it."

"I am certain ye will."

"All right," I acknowledged, aware that he was still holding my suitcase. "Why don't we go upstairs for a minute to put away the suitcase? And then, I can show you around the house."

"Very weel," he agreed simply.

I started through the foyer toward the staircase, and climbed the steps with him following close behind me, carrying my luggage. As we arrived at the top landing, we rounded the banister and strode together through the hallway until we shortly arrived at the open doorway to my master bedroom. He shifted aside at the doorway, intimating for me to precede him into the room. So, I proceeded inside with him directly pacing behind me.

When we entered deeper into the room, I paused, noticing he did too and observed him interestedly gazing around the bedroom, taking in its décor: the light sea-grey painted walls, white trim and baseboards, fine crème colored linen drapes over the many windows, the long deep-set window bench seat with a yellow ochre cushion and matching pillows over it, the large barn door to the walk-in closet with a full length mirror on it, the cherry hardwood floors, the crème colored wool area rug, and the California king sized bed with a pastel grey down comforter with many sea-green and white accent pillows against the teak headboard.

"Do you like it?" I asked, because he hadn't said anything.

"Och, aye. 'Tis a grand chamber," he said, turning his gaze toward mine. He smiled openly at me, inspiring my own grin in return.

"I'm so happy that you do," I replied gladly. The strong daylight entering the room made the large space appear crisp and ordered in its modern interior design.

"This is yer own hoose?" he inquired, as I admired the way his gilded head was illuminating like a halo in the sun rays enveloping him where he stood by the windows.

"Yes, it is," I replied.

"'Tis charming. Whit have ye named it?"

"Nothing."

"Indeed?"

"Yeah."

"Whyever not?" He gazed at me obviously surprised with a mixture of confusion.

"Well, I haven't thought about calling it anything," I replied honestly.

"Have ye not?"

"No. I haven't."

"Curious." His brow drew together a little as he gave me an odd look.

"Well, people don't really name things anymore like they used to," I said, answering the silent question in his head.

"Why so?"

"I don't know." I shrugged a little. "Maybe they don't feel attached to things nowadays, I guess—in general."

"Micht ye not feel a sort of an attachment tae yer home, however?"

"Sure, I do."

"Then, mayhap name it."

"What would I ever name it?" I asked indiscriminately.

"Anything which fancies ye," he recommended.

"Like what? Serendipity? Something like that?" I giggled at myself, unexpectedly thinking of the whimsical name.

"'Twould be a splendid name," he responded encouragingly, with a mild grin.

"Serendipity?" I gave him a quizzical look.

"Whyever not? 'Tis raither a fitting name from whit I have already observed of this hoose. A delightful name fur a fanciful abode."

"Well..." I said, perceiving the inspiration in his eyes. "If it pleases you, then *Serendipity* it is."

"Does it not please ye as weel?"

"Sure, it does."

"Thus, 'tis approved and settled." I smiled at him and noticed the little wink he gave me, causing my smile to widen. "Now, whaur micht I place this parcel?" he asked, abruptly remembering that he was still holding it.

"Oh, on the window bench is fine, thank you." I pointed him to the area and he noticed it. He strode across the room to situated my suitcase suitably over the bench, then returned his attention to me once he had.

"Would you like to see your children's bedroom?" I suggested next.

"Aye, it will be favorable," he said as he benignly gazed at me.

"Great. Come this way with me," I urged softly, struck unexpectedly shy by the way he was staring at me.

I turned for the open doorway and he strode with me out of my bedroom. Leading him in the opposite direction through the hallway toward the end, we arrived at the children's bedroom and entered it together. As we stood inside their room, his eyes slowly swept around the area as he remained motionless with his hands clasped behind his back. I noticed a gentle grin easing over his lips while he studied the arrangement of their room.

The room especially catered to their interests: the character bedding on their two different wooden toddler beds facing us at the opposite side of the room, the wool tufted animal kingdom area rug, matching drapes, the built in bookcases filled with books and toys, the décor creatively divided between Hello Kitty and Star Wars, two toy boxes in the corners of the room were also noticed until his gaze finally landed on the *Thomas The Tank Engine* night-light on their dresser by the door where we were standing.

"I have never observed a nursery as cheerful as this," Leif commented when he returned his warmhearted gaze toward me. "'Tis gleeful."

"Do you like it?" I asked, noticing how true his eyes were.

"Verily indeed," he said and I smiled at him.

"Would you like to see their playroom also?" I offered, encouraged by his pleasant reaction.

"Thaur is anither chamber as weel fur them?"

"Yes, where they like to play inside if they aren't outside in the yard playing instead."

"I shall fancy tae see it."

"Okay, it's this way."

I started out of the kids' bedroom and began pacing through the hallway again when Leif ceased following me. He suddenly noticed all of the framed pictures hanging on the walls of the children which I had taken of them from the time they were born until recently. He was enthralled by their images and began intently studying them.

"Our bairns are extraordinarily bonnie," he remarked warmheartedly as I stood close to him, gazing at the pictures also.

"Yes, I think they're really adorable too," I agreed softly.

I walked him through each photograph experience of them

hanging on the wall, explaining it all. He interestedly listened while thoughtfully examining the photographs. When we finished gazing at the last photograph decorating the hallway wall, I proceeded touring him through the rest of the house by first showing him the two remaining guest bedrooms upstairs, before bringing him downstairs to see the living room, den, dining room, kitchen and finally the children's play room. He scoped all of the toys and art supplies lining the room in shelves and cubbyhole boxes when his observant eyes landed on the *Thomas The Tank Engine* train table with scattered LEGOs on it, before noticing the large wooden doll house, art table and child's pink tea table with matching chairs.

"'Tis a most fanciful chamber," he commented, appearing obviously pleased.

"They love it in here," I said, suddenly recognizing the puppy my parents had given the kids trotting up to me. I scooped him up into my arms, acknowledging him with gentle rubs behind his ear.

"Thaur exists a pup also?" Leif asked as his brow raised in surprise.

"Yeah, my parents just recently gave him to the kids for their birthday," I said.

"Had they?" His large hand moved to carefully pet the animal and gave the puppy an affectionate rub over his tiny head.

"He obviously likes you," I remarked, noticing how much the puppy was enjoying the affection Leif was giving him.

"Does he?"

"No question."

"He is a handsome laddie," Leif complimented. "Micht he have a name?"

"The kids named him Yoda?"

"Yoda. Whit sort of name have the bairns chosen?" he inquired strangely.

"They named the puppy after a fictional character from a story named Star Wars," I said.

"Och. I read those words upon our laddie's quilt."

"Yes. Your son will tell you all about the tale, I'm sure, once you two meet. He's very fond of it."

"I am certain tae enjoy him informing me of it."

"I know you'll find it fascinating. He's a very enthusiastic storyteller," I assured and Leif smiled.

Subsequently, we withdrew from the playroom and I brought him through the living room again. We exited between the sliding glass doors, entering outside into the grassy backyard where the kids played on their swing set, and in our swimming pool which laid just beyond the fire pit among the bordering tall wooden fence lined with towering Italian cypresses.

"'Tis grand! 'Tis reminiscent of Bath!" he commented, extremely impressed as I showed him the pool, after setting the puppy down behind the surrounding pool fence in the grassy yard.

"This is where the kids and I like to swim," I said.

"Micht the bairns be as proficient as ye?"

"They're fairly skilled. They've been swimming since they were three years old. I have them still taking lessons from the same instructor who's taught them since then. But every time they get into the pool here at home, they'd rather play than practice. I guess it's nearly all the same, though, as I think about it. I mean, as long as they're in the water, they're bound to exercise at least a portion of what they've learned from their instructor whenever they play."

Leif nodded slightly in response, appearing to consider my explanation. He glanced around a bit more at the backyard, noticing the tall trees lining the entire perimeter of the tall fencing, creating privacy from my neighbors.

"Do ye keep a garden?" he asked, returning he gaze toward me.

"Unfortunately, not. I just don't have the time to keep one. Although, it would be really nice to have something," I answered wistfully, remembering the luscious gardens Elizabeth used to keep and the ones we had at *Taigh Gràs*.

"Micht a servant maintain one fur ye?"

"I don't have any servants."

"Indeed?" He looked at me abruptly surprised.

"Yeah."

"Then who assists ye keep hoose?"

"Just I alone."

"Truly?"

"Yeah. I mean sometimes I hire a cleaning lady to clean the house for me, but that's about it."

"As charming as it is, 'tis a bit of a grand hoose fur ye tae maintain alone, is it not? Ye must have servants tae mind it, as weel as tae govern the bairns," he said.

"But I can't afford to pay for servants. And, I'm okay. The children and I are doing well without that kind of help."

"How is it possible?" he questioned seriously.

"For instance, there's daycare after school for them to attend until I can get them after I work. And, there are also my parents who live not that far away from here who are available to help me when I need them," I explained really. Leif looked at me without a word, seeming to ponder as he stared unwaveringly at me. I got the inkling he didn't agree with my situation.

"Whilst it appears yoo're maintaining order, I dinnae care fur yer burden," he said.

"But I'm not burdened," I replied.

"How is it possible that ye are not encumbered without having any assistance since I have been absent? Fur, I believe that ye have been hampered indeed. Dinnae spare me the truth, fur I am awaur of yer position being similar tae that of a lone widow with bairns. Whilst certainly our bairns are inarguably a blessing, 'tis nonetheless a hardship that ye have been enduring whilst not receiving the adequate assistance ye deserve, and indeed of which ye are in need from at least a single maid," he countered.

"I hate thinking of it like that," I regretted, but knowing he was right, to an extent.

"Yet, it is the truth. Yoo're not a widow any longer. I'm haur fur ye," he reminded, as he glanced at my bare wedding ring finger.

"Thaur is nae need fur any pretense betwixt us, Sylvie. Might'n ye agree?"

I became silent, suddenly feeling immensely guilty that I'd removed the rings he'd given me from my wedding hand in order to suitably portray my situation in public, which was false. I realized just then, through my lies to my family and friends regarding my relationship with Leif that I had essentially denied him, rejecting that he had ever existed, nullifying him in my world.

"I'm sorry... very sorry. I've just been afraid for so long—of what my family might think or say to me, because you weren't here with me when I returned while being pregnant. Or, how to explain it to my friends without them prying and judging me, or gossiping about me.

"I know that I shouldn't worry about those things and I shouldn't let it affect me... but I do worry about them, because it does negatively affect me—actually. I guess—I'm not as strong a person as I thought I was, since I care so much about what other's think. I'm so sorry for hurting you too, Leif," I responded in an inadequate voice, feeling horrible, on the verge of tears.

"I dinnae fault ye, Sylvie, fur the falsehoods ye have told tae yer family regarding whit has taken place in our regard. We have been harmed in many ways, such as by the war. Yet, time has caused us the most determent. We huvnea been spared by it. Yer family included.

"However, ye must nae longer fear our bond—as it soundly stands through it all. I shan't ever abandon ye, and time wulnea ever steal us away from one anither again. Understand that I am present, and yoo're nae longer burdened by being alone without me," he said.

I kept my eyes averted on my naked wedding finger as I nervously picked beneath my nails, unable to look at him, fearing I might cry if I did as a knot had lodged inside my throat. I caught the sight of the wedding rings he had given me on my right ring finger and stared at them.

"I swore that I'd never take off your rings," I muttered.

"I dinnae perceive that ye have. The rings remain upon yer finger as we stand," he said. I realized he was staring at the rings on my finger too, as I kept gazing at them, and understood that he was forgiving me. I carefully proceeded withdrawing the rings on my right hand to place them rightfully on my left ring finger where he had originally placed them. "Permit me," he offered gently, noticing my shaky hands. He carefully took my hand into his and mindfully began removing the rings. I quietly watched him slipping them over my finger, returning them to my left hand. "Thaur. The same as the day we had wed."

I gave him a tearful little smile, and he gently touched my cheek with the palm of his hand, cupping it. I felt the pad of his thumb tenderly brushing my bottom lip as he stared intently into my moist eyes.

"Thank you," I uttered softly in deep appreciation of his forgiveness.

"Thaur isnae any need fur thanks, *mo ghaol*. I ken that ye huvnea forgotten me," he said.

"I never forgot you," I replied. A subtle grin curled his lips, and the immense affection was apparent in his eyes as he carefully wiped a slipping tear from my cheek with the pad of his thumb.

"Nor I have ever forgotten ye," he said. I smiled a little at him also. "Nae more rumpled spirits betwixt us as we place pretense aside henceforth."

"No more," I agreed. The mild grin on his face was reassuring, inspiring me to smile in return the same way. The church bells abruptly began ringing, resonating throughout the neighborhood, seizing my sudden attention. Interrupted, I suddenly realized that school had just ended. "Oh no!"

"Whit is it?" he inquired strangely, unexpectedly concerned.

"I'm sorry to be sudden, but school's just ended and it's time for me to get the kids now," I explained.

"Och," he understood.

"I can't be late," I replied anxiously.

"We shan't," he supported. "Whaur micht the schoolhouse lie?"

"Only a few blocks away from here."

"Then, let us depart."

I turned from him, starting away from the pool with him following me and we exited through the surrounding gate together. As the gate automatically locked after us, we started toward the house. Rounding past the fire pit, I found Yoda lying on the stone and scooped him up into my arms, before we entered out onto the lawn again and approached the back of the house. As we returned inside, I returned the puppy to his feet and he trotted away, then swept through the hallway for the foyer and grabbed my phone along with my keys off the console table.

Leaving through the front door now, I quickly shut it closed, locking it. Leif hurried with me down the steps and strode along the stone pathway, through the picket gate. The gate instantly latched itself behind us as we stepped onto the sidewalk, and he and I immediately began walking away from the house, heading toward school.

Fifteen

As we walked together, I caught Leif examining more of his surroundings, scrutinizing the neighbors' houses, lampposts and trees lining the streets. His eyes also studied the cement sidewalk on which we were walking.

"There are plenty hooses about that lie closely together," he remarked observantly.

"Yes, there are," I acknowledged simply.

"Is there nae privacy amongst them?"

"A lot of them have tall fences or trees to create privacy—especially in their backyards."

"As do ye," he understood.

"Yeah."

"Do all also have horseless carriages?" He noticed all the neighbors' vehicles parked in their driveways or along the curbs, while some drove by us, heading down the street as we strode.

"Not everyone has a car. But I believe that most people own some kind of a vehicle," I speculated, enjoying him as we strolled together.

"In which case, whaur have all the horses gone?"

"A lot of them are on ranches or run wild in the middle of the country."

"Och." He meditatively nodded his head, realizing. A woman jogger unexpectedly appeared around the corner we were now rounding and passed by us, dressed in petite black running shorts and a sports bra. Leif craned his neck and blatantly stared at her as she ran past us, continuing on her way. His eyes instantly bugged and shot back toward me once she was out of view, glaring at me in utter shock. "The lass is unclothed!" he expressed outlandishly, clearly looking at me with wide eyes and gaping mouth, utterly appalled.

"No, she's dressed appropriately for running," I giggled, unable to help my reaction to him.

"Indeed not!" he sputtered, aghast, appearing deeply embarrassed as his face flushed hot pink.

"But that's what women wear here when they run," I calmly informed him.

"Scandalous! Micht from whom is she running?"

"From no one."

"I'm puzzled. 'Twould seem a man is giving her chase."

"You don't have to worry. No one is chasing her. She's exercising, instead."

"Exercising?"

"Yes, to stay fit."

"Abominable!" he said stoutly, reiterating his appall.

"Considering, I can understand your point of view very clearly. But the way she's dressed is acceptable here these days. The clothes she's wearing are designed for exercising—which she's doing. I assure you, she wouldn't appear like that in a professional setting," I explained.

"I say!" He unbelievably shook his head, obviously dumfounded and disapproving.

"I hope you'll not have a heart attack now that you're here in this time period with me, after all we've been through," I half joked, trying to make light. He scowled at me, and I giggled.

"My heart nearly arrested presently," he bantered back.

"Don't scare me."

"Then, permit my traipsing efter that lass in order tae toss my coat about her tae conceal her nudity!"

"She's not naked," I giggled.

"On the contrary!"

"Her privates were covered, and she hasn't broken the law."

"Is the whole of this society libertine?"

"What if it were?" I replied, teasing him a little. He suddenly became speechless, stumped for words as he continued gazing at me in astonishment.

"Are ye telling me that it is true, then?" he asked sincerely after finding his tongue.

"I don't know if that woman is libertine or not. But I can tell you that this society has cast off many aspersions regarding both genders and sex. Now whether that's a good thing or not is still debatable," I said.

"My word," he replied thinkingly, still appearing shocked.

"What?" I asked curiously. He shrugged a little.

"Merely, 'tis my opinion that whether anyone who chooses tae be libertine is truly of nae consequence tae me, so long as it remains unseen in order that the whole of society disnae become degenerate."

"I agree about protecting the innocent," I said as I thought about his philosophy. He nodded in accordance. "So, you really don't care if someone is personally libertine?" I asked, a little surprised.

"As I said, so long 'tis not flaunted within the public forum."

"Then, to each his own? As long as it's kept private?"

"Aye."

"So, what does that say about you?"

"That I am not innocent of whit may take place within society, but that I call fur the circumspection of such conduct."

"But you don't care how people conduct themselves in private as long as they're respectable in public?" I inquired, somewhat surprised by the suggestion of his libertarian position.

"Aye."

"But do you agree with libertine behavior?"

"I shall say, as I make ye awaur of me, that I am an imperfect man. Therefore, far be it fur me tae rule or pass absolute judgment upon anither man who disnae sacrifice his life fur God."

"Well, certainly no person is perfect."

"'Tis generous of ye tae say. Yet, some micht be more so than others."

"Hmm, I suppose... Is your imperfection that you're libertine?" I asked curiously, directly looking at him. He gave me a sidelong glance and smirked.

"Are ye not already familiar with me?" he implied.

"Well—I—I mean, I guess that I am," I stammered.

"In which case, ye micht ken the answer tae yer inquiry."

"Well, I suppose I never really considered that idea about you before."

"Had ye not?" He gave me a surprised look.

"Not really."

"Yet, we have kent one anither in an irregular manner."

"How?"

"I have laid hands and lips upon ye whaur the Pope forbids."

"Oh—well. Yes, but—I don't know—I just thought it was natural," I said, feeling a little embarrassed.

"'Tis natural. As natural as sin."

"But we haven't sinned. We're married."

"Before then?"

"We loved each other. Nothing's wrong with that."

"Within the confines of wedlock, aye."

"Do you really believe we were sinning by fooling around before then?"

"Ye waur innocent. I was wicked."

"What do you mean? I could have contradicted you—and I was a widow."

"I swayed ye as I am an imperfect man."

"You're not a monk. Besides, even priests aren't perfect because they're human. Remember? So, cut yourself a little slack, because I for one, am glad you're not a stiff."

"A stiff?"

"Yes. A prude."

"A pietist?"

"Exactly."

"Och," he chuckled a little. "Be warned that ye have liberated me."

"Have I?" I asked, smiling at him, intrigued.

"Without any doubt. Ye may regret it," he insinuated. I giggled, enjoying his flirtation with me.

"How much should I be worried?"

"Quite," he said.

"I have to say, then I'm a little scared," I admitted, wondering about him.

"Fear not. I am as gentle as a cub."

"A cub?" I giggled, looking skeptically at him.

"Aye."

"You're definitely not that."

"Then, whit micht I otherwise be?"

"I'm not sure. But maybe you're a full fledge beast," I said. Leif chuckled again, clearly entertained. "You're laughing because it's true." I couldn't help giggling also.

"Declare me such as ye fancy," he said, grinning boldly at me.

"As I fancy?"

"Aye. Ye do fancy me? Do ye not?"

"Good heavens, you're unbelievable." I shook my head at him, smiling also.

"Ye think me incredulous?"

"Absolutely."

"Ye charm me."

I smiled at him again, suddenly feeling shy, as the distinct grin on his face settled into a playful smirk. The look of enamor glinting in his eyes relaxed his face. He seized my hand into his and I glanced away from him, smiling, feeling my heart skip in my chest, and my blood running warm. A helicopter unexpectedly roared over our heads and his glance abruptly bounced up to the sky while it sped away as soon as it had appeared. "Whit is that?" he asked abruptly, quickly startled.

"It's a helicopter," I calmly informed him.

"Och... The skies are alive."

"Yes, they are. Particularly in the city. But if we were to go to the country, it would be a lot quieter than here."

"Indeed?" he asked, becoming at ease again.

"Yes."

"Hmm..." he contemplated, dropping his gaze from the sky, and looking at the various arid vegetation surrounding us as we continued walking. "'Tis not entirely green haur, is it?"

"We're actually located in a desert."

"Truly?"

"Yes."

"Curious. From whaur is water derived?"

"Water is irrigated from the Colorado River far away from here. But we also get a bit of it from groundwater supply."

"Intriguing..." I glanced up at him and smiled, noticing the fascination on his face. He caught my glance and grinned in return. I released my palm from his and slipped it securely around his solid bicep as we proceeded on our way. Soon the school could be seen from the next block, and I was glad that we weren't going to be late picking up the kids after all as the final dismissal bell had just rung.

When we arrived at the front of Immaculate Heart School, Leif noticed the church connected to the right of the school's building. "'Tis a Papist institution?" he asked with apparent surprise, noticing the sign fastened to the entry gate beside the parking lot with the school's name on it, along with the Virgin Mary statue beneath it.

"Yes, it's Catholic," I replied.

"One may attend without any reprisal?"

"Yes, of course. There're a lot of different types of religious schools that people may attend without being attacked for it." He didn't respond except his brow raised, conveying a remarkable expression on his face. "Things have changed."

"Greatly, it seems," he commented as I led him through the school's pedestrian gate into the parking lot.

After entering the parking lot, we strode toward the preschool and kindergarten lunch area to wait for the children to emerge from their building when I noticed they hadn't come outside yet. As we proceeded toward the area to wait for them, I had grown quite nervous about introducing him not only to our children, but to the parents belonging to their classmates as they were also assembling and waiting for their children to arrive from the classroom building.

Parents congregated by the picnic tables where I had served cupcakes a couple of days ago when I recognized some friends in the midst of conversations: Heather, Maria, and Dave, stood out among the group of eight parent friends and acquaintances with whom I was most close. Heather instantly noticed me approaching the area with Leif while she was in the middle of lightly discussing with them, and waved at me. I reciprocated waving at her and she smiled with another urging wave for me to quickly join their chatting group.

When Leif and I arrived beneath the awning at one of the picnic tables where my friends were standing and conversing, Heather ceased speaking among them, turning her attention toward us. My heart raced, jackhammering in my chest as I antici-pated introducing Leif to everyone—especially to her.

"Hey!" she happily greeted me.

"Hi," I replied nicely, equally glad to see her.

"How are you?" she asked.

"I'm good. How are you?"

"Not bad. We missed you the past couple of days. Where have you been?"

"I went out of town," I answered, feeling jittery inside.

"Oh? Where'd you go?"

"To Boston."

"Oh, nice. What took you to Boston?"

"I had a conference," I lied.

"Was it any good?"

"Yeah, it was informative," I lied again.

"Well, it's nice that you're back. I didn't know you were going out of town."

"I didn't want to bore you with the details of it, since it was work related."

"I understand," she replied with a smile. Then, her eyes imme-diately bounced from me to Leif with acute interest before shifting questioningly back toward me. I hesitated for a second as she looked anticipatory at me. I wondered how I was going to intro-duce her to Leif without raising her shocking surprise and curios-ity, knowing that I was going to suffer being the subject of gossip now. Except, there was no way around the gossip, or denying my marriage to Leif without causing detriment between us after the last promise we had just made to each other before our walk here.

"I'd like for you to meet, Seamus, my husband—the twins' father," I said nervously, introducing her to him, finally. Heather's eyes instantly bugged as round as silver dollars. Uneasily ignoring her sudden reaction, I swiftly glanced at Leif, saying to him, "This is my friend, Heather. Her son, Mason, is in the same class as our twins and is friends with Leif."

"'Tis a pleasure tae make yer acquaintance, Mistress Heather," Leif said politely and slightly dipped his head to her in a reserved manner.

"Yeah—it's a pleasure, also," she stammered, suddenly looking at him and smiling. I could tell by the pleasant but interested look on her face, and the sparkle in her eyes, that she found him attractive. She abruptly returned looking at me and the expression on her face now was full of curiosity and puzzlement. "Congratulations—I should say? If I'd known that you'd planned on eloping in Boston, I would have gotten you a gift. But then again, it wouldn't have been a secret, wouldn't it have?"

"It's okay. You don't need to give us a gift," I replied insecurely.

"But I should," she said willingly. I could easily perceive that by not accepting her desire to please me with a gift, I'd be obviously hurting her feelings.

"Well, if you'd like, then I'll be grateful to receive it," I accepted nicely.

"Great! You've given me another excuse to shop," she giggled guiltily, and I smiled. Then, her curious eyes returned to looking at Leif. "So, Sylvie told me a little bit about you—that you're from Scotland?"

"Aye. I am from the isle of Skye," he informed her politely.

"Oh, nice. How long have you been in the States?" she inquired.

"Not till recently," Leif said modestly.

"How do you like it?"

"I fancy it."

"Nice. Is this your first time visiting L.A.?"

"L.A.?"

"Yeah, Los Angeles."

"'Twould be so my first visit haur, aye."

"Have you seen much of anything of the city yet?"

"I fear not."

"Well, maybe you guys could take a trip over the weekend—

you know? Drive down to Laguna or up the coast to Ventura to sightsee or something like that. My son loves Laguna Beach whenever we go. Cute shops and everything. Take the kids with you. I'm sure they'll enjoy it. Remember when we went to Mission San Juan Capistrano?" she asked, turning her attention toward me again.

"Yeah, I remember," I replied.

"The kids enjoyed that trip so much," she said.

"They did," I agreed, then she glanced back at Leif, thoughtfully including him in the conversation.

"Yeah, it was a great trip. But we went there for a school field trip, though. All the kids love Sylvie whenever she volunteers to chaperon for a class field trip. She's so great with them—patient, easygoing, attentive, funny, you name it. She's such a great mom, and a dear friend. We all love her around here. We want nothing but the best for her. She deserves it," Heather said smilingly. Leif merely gazed at her without responding and I knew he was thinking, forming an opinion about her. I wondered if he found her to be an acceptable friend and whether he'd like her. He must have understood her meaning and took offense to it because he simply stood there, impassive. An awkwardness ensued and Heather smiled unevenly at him. I sensed his opinion of her was unimpressive and would remain unspoken, unless he cared to inform me of it—or unless I asked.

"Again, 'tis a pleasure tae make yer acquaintance," he said politely after a second, regardless.

"I'm sorry for rambling. It's a bad habit of mine," she apologized.

"No, it's okay. You don't have to worry about it," I assuaged, ameliorating the discomfiture I knew she felt. Believing it was not her intention to insult him, I was aware, though, of her inclination to be protective of her friends. But I immediately sensed from the look on her face that she suddenly recognized her ignorance over the details regarding my past with Leif, and that she might have drawn a mistaken conclusion about him.

"Well, we're looking forward to the birthday party tomorrow," she said a little awkwardly as she changed the subject.

"I'm glad," I replied, giving her a reassuring smile.

"Is the whole class coming?" she inquired.

"Everyone responded 'yes' to the invitation, so I'm expecting a full house."

"Well, let me know if you need any help with it. I can arrive early if you want."

"Thanks so much. But I think I'll be okay. Everything's pretty much already prepared."

"All right, then we'll see you on time."

"Sounds good."

She smiled at me and seemed better at ease now. I coincidentally shifted my gaze from her when I realized several friends in our parent friend group had ceased chatting with each other, and had been listening to our conversation. We gave each other acknowledging smiles, as the discomfort inside me remained; I knew that I'd given them significant fodder for gossip now, and regretted it.

But when the children finally began appearing from their building, I was glad to be spared my friends' scrutinizing and inquisitive gazes any longer as I turned my anxious attention from them to our children pacing in their respective lines with Ms. Lambert leading them toward us. When they reached the benches, the children were instructed to sit at the picnic tables until their parents arrived to collect them. Leif followed me as I excused myself from my friends and moved toward Ms. Lambert. She noticed me and gave my children permission to leave their seats at the table to come to me.

"How was their day?" I asked her.

"They had a good one," Ms. Lambert nicely informed me.

"Great," I replied gladly.

"Yeah, no worries," she said.

"Mama!" Leila expressed happily as she rushed toward me with open arms and gave me a big hug.

"Hi, sweetie!" I responded, giving her an affectionate hug and kiss as I knelt to receive her in my arms. "How are you?"

"Good," she said definitely.

"That's good," I responded, happy to see her bright, smiling face.

"Hi Mom!" Little Leif said cheerfully as he ran up to me also. I reached for him and took him into my arms also with a sweet hug and kiss.

"How are you, sweetheart?" I asked him.

"Good," he replied easily.

"That's nice," I replied.

"Did you bring Yoda?" he asked eagerly.

"I'm afraid not, sweetie," I replied as I straightened from them.

"Aww, I wanted to show him to my friends. They said they wanted to see him," he expressed disappointedly.

"Okay, well, then I'll bring him tomorrow for you, so that you can show him to your friends. Is that okay?" I responded, observing his sad blue eyes.

"Yeah, that's okay," he considered. "You won't forget, will you?"

"How can I forget with you around to remind me?" I lightly tapped the end of his little nose and he smile at me. He slipped his hand into mine and I lightly grasped Leila's hand with my other hand, ready to depart the school grounds. Leila and Little Leif then waved goodbye to their friends as we started walking away from them toward the parking lot, with their father following slightly behind us.

"Where's the car, Mama?" Leila inquired as she noticed that we were pacing out of the parking lot onto the sidewalk instead.

"We're walking home today, because I didn't drive from work to pick you guys up. So, I walked from the house instead," I answered.

"Oh," she realized.

"Are you done with business from far away, Mom?" Little Leif asked me.

"Yes, I am," I said.

"Good," he responded, satisfied.

"Yeah, good!" Leila agreed emphatically as she nodded her head once.

"I missed you both," I said to them.

"I missed you too," Little Leif said.

"Me too," Leila said.

"Did you have fun with Granddad and Nanna?" I asked.

"Yeah," they both said in unison.

"We had lots of fun!" Leila said happily, as she was skipping while we walked.

"What did you do together?" I asked.

"Granddad and Nanna took us to play at the park, and we had pizza for dinner," Little Leif said.

"Oh, that sounds really nice," I replied.

"We wanna go back to the park and play some more. Can you take us there today, Mama?" Leila asked.

"Yeah, Mom. Can you take us?" Little Leif asked also, eagerly anticipating.

"I'm sorry, sweethearts. It's going to have to be another day. Unfortunately, I just got back home from flying and I'm a little tired," I said.

"Okay," Leila accepted easily, still skipping along while holding my hand. Little Leif glanced over his shoulder, hearing footsteps pacing closely behind us, then turned his eyes upward at me.

"Mom?" he started curiously. My heart was frantically pounding in my chest now, because I knew what was coming.

"Yeah?" I responded.

"There's a man following us," he noticed. Leila also curiously glanced over her shoulder and stopped skipping.

"I know, sweetheart," I said, and Leila turned her questioning glance upward at me also.

"Who is he?" Little Leif strangely asked me, seeming worried. I took a deep breath, closed my eyes, and exhaled as I brought the children to a standstill in their steps.

Occasionally they had asked me questions about their father —about what he looked like and who he was. They sometimes wondered why he wasn't present with us, and I never knew quite the right answer to tell them. Except, I would tell them that their father was a very good and kind man who loved them with all of his heart and soul. And, if he could be here with us, he undoubtedly would be. Only, he couldn't because he was prevented as a result of him living so far away, which usually quelled their curiosity for the time being—until now. Now, everything was on a collision course. I wasn't certain how I was going to handle this...

What am I going to say to them? What can I say to soften their shock? How are they going to take this?

When I opened my eyes, I saw them strangely looking up at me. I had no idea how I was going to introduce them to their father. All the previous scenarios that I had fabricated in my head had gone out the window, because they didn't apply to the reality facing me right now.

Aware that Leif had ceased his walking also and stood close beside us, observing, I released the children's hands and turned them around to face him. Leif benignly smiled at them and the expression in his eyes was warm and friendly.

"Remember what I've told you about your father?" I started carefully speaking with our children as they strangely gazed up at me.

"Yeah," Leila responded curiously.

"Yeah," Little Leif answered, also in the same odd manner.

"Well... this man here—standing with us—is your father," I cautiously told them. The words automatically spilled forth from my mouth, while I was hearing the careful tone, I was taken with them.

"What?" Leila asked as if she hadn't heard me. Both of their eyes suddenly grew round with stark surprise as their mouths gaped.

"He's your father," I repeated gently, making sure they'd heard me and understood.

"He's our *dad*?" Little Leif expressed under his breath, sounding really confused. I glanced up at Leif and I could easily see the enthrall, and affection on his face as he stood there before his children simply staring at them in awe.

"Meet your children, Leif," I said gently to him. "This is Leilani. And, this is Leif." I gestured to the children for him to greet.

"Hullo, bairns," he said kindly to his children. They didn't respond except wondrously and strangely stared up at him, speechless.

"Aren't you going to say hello?" I prompted them.

"Hi," Leila said oddly in a shy tone.

"Hi," Little Leif responded the same way.

"Your father has come a long way to see you," I said conscientiously.

"Where did he come from?" Leila asked me. I struggled to answer her.

"Scotland. I have come from Scotland," Leif said abruptly. I weakly smiled at him, feeling relieved that he answered her for me.

"Oh. How far away is that?" Leila asked him in her little voice.

"'Tis thousands of leagues away, I reckon," Leif said. Leila gasped as her eyes simultaneously widened again.

"Leagues?" she asked in confusion.

"They're like miles, sweetheart," I said to her.

"Oh," she replied innocently.

"How can you be our father?" Little Leif asked suspiciously.

"I wed yer mother. That is how," Leif answered.

"Then how come I haven't seen you before?" Little Leif asked.

"He was kept from seeing you, sweetheart," I tried to explain. "But, he's here now. Aren't you glad?"

Little Leif didn't respond, except studied the very tall man standing before him.

"Are you going to be with us for good?" Leila inquired.

"Aye. I am," Leif promised unequivocally.

"So, we have a dad now?" she asked me.

"You've always had a dad, sweetheart. You just hadn't met him until now," I said.

"Oh," she realized. The children became noticeably quiet for a moment. They seemed awkward as Leif and I stood together observing them. I wondered what they were truly thinking as we stood in their uncomfortable presence.

"Mom?" Little Leif started after a minute.

"Yeah?" I responded attentively.

"I wanna go home now," he suggested innocently.

"Okay," I agreed, reading his uneasy demeanor. I glanced at Leif with some hesitation. He gave me a subtle nod, and I turned with the children in hand when the four of us quietly resumed our walk toward home.

Sixteen

When we entered the house, Little Leif hurried up the staircase without a word with Leila following behind him. I knew something was wrong with him in particular, and I had to fix it. I uncomfortably glanced up at Leif as we both remained standing by the front door in the foyer, and could perceive in his eyes that he was aware of something being amiss with his children also.

"I'm sorry," I said regretfully to him. He slightly nodded in acknowledgement.

"I fathom that I micht have displeased them," he presumed with noticeable disappointment in his eyes.

"You haven't done anything wrong to them at all," I assured. "I'll talk with them. I'm sure everything will be all right when I do. Will you excuse me for a minute?"

"Aye, of coorse," he said.

"Thank you. Please make yourself at home. Hopefully, I won't be long," I suggested. He nodded again and I turned from him, heading toward the staircase.

When I arrived at the top landing, I paced through the hallway knowing I'd find them in their bedroom. As I entered their room, I noticed them relaxing over their stomachs on their tufted area rug playing with their new puppy. Mindfully approaching them, I made myself comfortable, sitting on the floor beside them.

"Hey," I gently started, garnering their attention. "What's going on? What's bothering you two?"

"Nothing," Leila said, sounding honest. I looked at Little Leif and he shrugged his shoulders, though, confirming my speculation of his mood.

"Are you sure that nothing is bothering you?" I asked them both. I looked at Little Leif, especially, and he sighed a little as he tried placing his full attention on petting Yoda, instead. He remained quiet for a moment as I watched him enjoying their puppy.

"At school, Timmy said that I wasn't lucky, because I didn't have a dad," he divulged, finally, after a minute.

"He did?" I was somewhat surprised and regretful by this news.

"Yeah," Little Leif said.

"When did he say this to you?" I asked.

"I don't know." He shrugged a bit.

"Well, was it today?" I asked curiously.

"No," he said.

"So, was it a long time ago, then?"

"Yeah, it was a long time ago."

"I'm sorry he said that to you. That wasn't a very nice thing for him to say," I acknowledged. He didn't respond while still preoccupying himself with their puppy. "Of course, everyone has a dad —just like everyone has a mother. Otherwise, we wouldn't be here on Earth," I continued, hoping that he was listening to me.

"But, mine wasn't here when Timmy said it to me," he said.

"Well—I'm very sorry Timmy said something inconsiderate to you, and hurt your feelings," I mollified as I tenderly stroked his silky hair. "Of course, you have a dad. You know that, don't you? Just like I've always told you. Remember?"

He nodded a little, pausing to speak further as he paid more attention to their playful puppy.

"Why did he say that to me, though, if everyone has a dad?" he resumed innocently after his small lull.

"Maybe he didn't realize that everyone does," I answered honestly.

"Oh."

"Sometimes it's hard for others to imagine themselves in other people's places, so they think that others are supposed to be just like they are. Except, everyone is different—and our family was a little different from his when your dad was away from us," I explained. "I also want you to understand that because your dad was away, doesn't mean that he didn't love you. In fact, he loves you very much—so much that he couldn't wait to finally meet you the second he could have the opportunity."

"But what took him so long to come here to us, then?" he asked, finally turning his little face toward me with understandably hurt eyes. I inhaled wondering how I was going to answer his innocent question and comfort him. I exhaled at length, dreading what to say. If I wasn't treading carefully, I could possibly damage both of their relationships with their father before it ever got started.

"Well, he was in the military... and he was so far away—that he couldn't come see us sooner than now," I explained mindfully.

"Oh," he considered thoughtfully. "So, he was in the military fighting bad guys?"

"Something like that," I said.

"Oh..." He became quiet for a moment, staring at me with unwavering eyes, and I perceived him pondering before he returned his attention to fondly pet Yoda again.

"You know, this is a really new place for your dad to be where we live," I started.

"It is?" Leila asked strangely.

"Yes, it is," I replied.

"How come?" Little Leif inquired.

"Well, your dad doesn't know much about things here, because he's from somewhere very different than from where we live. And since he has been away from us for so long, everything to him is a little strange. So, I'm sure your dad is feeling a bit uncertain about everything at the moment. Just like you're probably feeling about him right now. Curious and strange, right?"

"Yeah," Little Leif considered.

"So, because of that, it will be easier for you to understand each other. But you know what would really help you and him feel better?"

"What?" he inquired curiously, returning interested eyes toward me.

"Well, it would be really nice if you and your sister helped make your dad feel comfortable by being nice and talking with him. I'm certain he would love that, and he'd be interested in anything you have to tell him," I suggested lovingly.

"He's big like Chewbacca," Leila chimed into the conversation, making a random observation, and inciting a smile from me.

"Yes, he's very tall," I agreed. "So, what do you think? Do you think that you can get to know your dad and help him feel comfortable here?"

"I guess so," Little Leif responded openly, encouraged.

"I can too," Leila said willingly.

"Good. That's very nice of you both." I paused for a moment, simply watching their demeanors. "So, how are you feeling about that idea?"

"Good," Little Leif answered genuinely, appearing thoughtful as he looked at me.

"Me too," Leila agreed.

"That makes me very happy," I said.

"I'm happy too, Mama," Leila said while smiling at me.

"Me too, Mom," Little Leif responded also with a contented expression.

"That makes me even happier that we're all happy," I replied, smiling at them.

"Goody," Leila concluded cheerfully, and I turned my smiling eyes toward her.

"So, will the both of you be all right, now?" I asked.

"Yup!" she said confidently and Little Leif nodded in accordance.

"All right. I'll leave you both be, if that's the case," I said, feeling better about them. They sincerely seemed comforted now, so I leaned and kissed each of them on the tops of their little heads, then left their bedroom, leaving them alone for now.

When I promptly returned downstairs, I discovered Leif in the kitchen sitting at the bay window in the breakfast nook gazing out of it at the front yard.

"Hi," I said as I came close toward him, attracting his attention as his eyes shifted and met mine.

"Hullo, *ceisdein*," he said mildly.

"Are you okay in here?"

"Aye." Although he said he was all right, I sensed his insecurity. "How micht the bairns fare?"

"They seem better now," I said.

"'Tis guid tae ken."

"They're just surprised to see you, really."

"Weel, I am unfamiliar tae them, therefore I assume they micht be a wee bashful of me."

"You shouldn't worry, though. They just need a moment. I'm sure the three of you will be best friends in no time," I assured, smiling gently at him. He grinned a little in response. "Are you hungry?"

"A wee bit, aye," he admitted.

"Okay, I'll make some snacks before I start cooking dinner. The kids are usually hungry too once they're out of school."

"I see," he replied simply as I moved to the cupboard and retrieved several plates. I went to the refrigerator and pulled out some cheese and apples. Placing everything on the island, I drew forth the cutting board from the counter top and started cutting apples. Leif quietly watched me slicing them as I lightly informed him about the kids' usual activities away from school. Within a minute or two, however, the children were noticed entering the kitchen as they detected their father listening to me talking to him.

"Hi," I greeted them. "Are you hungry?"

"Yes, I wanna snack," Leila said.

"Okay, sweetie. How about you, Leif?" I asked our son.

"Yeah, I'm hungry," he said.

"All right, I'm making you something right now," I said. He nodded and stepped toward his father who was standing facing them at the opposite side of the island.

"Do you want to see something?" he shyly asked his father.

"Indeed. Whit will ye show me?" Leif responded interestedly. We exchanged positive looks as he subtly grinned at me in response to his son.

"Okay, follow me," our son said and proceeded out of the kitchen.

"Pardon me, *mo chridhe*," Leif said to me with a lingering gentle grin.

"Of course," I replied, reciprocating his faint smile, and he followed his son out of the kitchen with Leila at his side.

After I had finished slicing apples and cheese and arranged them on a platter, I gathered some crackers also, placing them next to the cheese. I took the wooden walnut serving tray from the counter, and placed the snacks along with fresh cups of iced water on it. Now gathering the tray, I paced out of the kitchen and headed for the children's playroom where I heard their voices emanating. When I entered the room, Leif and the kids were surrounding the craft table, talking with each other.

"And, whit does one do with these LEGOs?" Leif inquired captivatingly.

"You build and make things with them," Leila said.

"Och," Leif replied with captivation.

"Yeah, like I made Luke Skywalker's starfighter," Little Leif said excitedly, showing their father the craft, he had constructed.

"I see. 'Tis most intriguing," Leif said sincerely. "Now, whit does it do? This starfighter?"

"It's a starfighter jet. It fights in outer space," Little Leif explained.

"Och, does it truly? Amongst the stars?" his father responded, astounded.

"Yeah," Little Leif said.

"Yet, who micht this Luke Skywalker be?" his father asked, as I set the snack tray over Leila's tea table.

"He's a Jedi Master," our son informed him.

"Whit is a Jedi Master?" his father asked curiously.

"A Jedi Master is a good guy. They know how to use the power of the Force to fight the Sith Lords. And, the Sith Lords are the bad guys, because they want to take over the Empire for evil," his son explained.

"Och, is that reit?" Leif responded significantly amazed and enthralled as his brow shot up.

"Yeah," our son replied.

"Look! I made Princess Leia!" Leila expressed proudly, showing off her LEGO construction.

"Did ye now?" Leif turned his mesmerized gaze toward our daughter.

"Yeah! Do you want to see her?" she asked eagerly.

"Indeed, I do," he replied nicely. She passed him the little figurine she had made. Leif carefully examined her little toy between his large fingers. "Och, yer princess is quite bonnie. Now tell me of her?"

"She's a Jedi too," Leila said cheerfully.

"Is she indeed?" Leif looked at his daughter with surprise.

"Yeah, and she's a princess. She comes from the planet Alderaan," she informed him.

"Och, I huvnae ever heard of such a planet," Leif said as he gazed intriguingly at his daughter.

"You haven't?" she asked with surprise.

"Nae," Leif responded, slightly shaking his head.

"Oh," she realized innocently.

"We could watch the movie about Star Wars, you know? It shows Luke Skywalker and Princess Leia in it," Little Leif offered kindly to his father.

"And it shows scary Darth Vader!" Leila warned forebodingly as she pantomimed.

"Och, who micht Darth Vader be?" Leif inquired as he smiled at our daughter's theatrics.

"He's a Sith Lord," Little Leif promptly informed him.

"Och, weel I say!" Leif expressed remarkably.

"Do you want to see it with us?" Leila asked.

"We'll watch the movie about the story after dinner," I nicely chimed into their conversation, attracting their attention toward me.

"Yay!" the children cheered. Normally after dinner, on school nights, I had them immediately prepare for bed and promptly tucked in for the night. But tonight was a very special occasion, so I was more than happy to be flexible with their schedule this time. The children quickly resumed talking happily with their father, and he attentively listened to them while they shared more about their toys with him. Observing how pleasantly they were all getting along, I decided to leave them for the kitchen to start preparing dinner.

I PREPARED MEATLOAF, MASHED POTATOES, AND GRAVY along with mixed vegetables for dinner tonight, and while we sat around the table enjoying our meal, Leif remained silent and observant, listening to my conversation with our children discussing their day at school. They were expressive and also liked telling innocent jokes at the table which generally had me giggling with them. When I occasionally glanced away from them as they were talking, I caught Leif gazing at me from across the dinner table at the opposite end. His lips were subtly upturned, conveying warmth and gratification. I returned gently smiling at him, and the affection in his eyes deepened. For the first time we were all together, a family, one that was our own, and appearing full of mirth.

After dinner was completed, I excused the kids from the dining table, leaving Leif and me alone, at which time I began clearing the emptied plates left behind by them. When I came toward Leif to gather his empty plate with the others, he reached for my hand and lightly held it in his.

"They are most charming," he said benignly, referring to our children, approving of them. I felt his thumb tenderly stroking the back of my hand when I gazed down into his stellar, deep blue eyes while he was still seated.

"Thank you," I said demurely. "They're really enjoying your company."

"As I am verily enjoying theirs. They are merry," he determined.

"Generally, they are. They've missed you, though."

"As I have missed the lot of ye," he said earnestly. I smiled at him again. "Thank ye fur serving tae me a most palatable meal, *ceisdein*."

"You're welcome. I'm glad that you liked it," I replied. "While I'm taking care of the dishes, would you care to read?"

"Yet, micht ye care fur a bit of assistance?"

"It's all right. I can manage."

"Yoo're certain?"

"Yes, of course."

"Then, I shall bide fur ye, if 'twill please ye."

"Okay. I'll bring you something to read while you wait instead."

"'Twould be nice, thank ye."

"Sure." Setting the dishes back over the table, I withdrew from him and paced out of the dining room for the living room and collected the *National Geographic* magazine from off the end table by the sofa. When I promptly returned to him as he remained seated at the dining table, I gave him the magazine to read and he thanked me. Then, I proceeded clearing all of the dishes off the table again, and went to the kitchen. After rinsing the plates and utensils, and loading them into the dishwasher, I gathered the clothes from my suitcase left in the laundry room before serving dinner and loaded them into the washing machine, along with his soiled attire from the 18th century to clean.

Once I had finished those tasks, I bathed the kids and dressed them for bed before we settled together in front of the TV to watch the movie they had wished to see with their father. Now ready, they immediately rushed down the staircase eagerly seeking him to join them in the den to watch the big screen TV. As they flew through the hallway, the kids easily found him still seated in the dining room reading the magazine I'd given him.

"Are you ready to watch the movie with us?" our son asked expectantly, suddenly calling Leif's attention from reading.

"I reckon so," Leif responded fondly as he looked at his kids standing before him with innocent faces, happy with anticipation. He straightened from his chair and the kids turned from him, excitedly running ahead of him out the room. He glanced at me and I gave him a little encouraging smile to follow them as we stepped out of the dining room together for the den.

When we arrived into the next room, the kids were discovered already seated in the large sectional sofa ready to view the movie. Leif approached and found himself a place to sit on the sofa also. The kids eagerly shifted themselves closer toward him in order to sit beside him, and the happy smiles on their faces I was admiring deeply kindled my heart.

Glancing at Leif, I smiled; the sight of him surrounded by our children heartened me with pure joy. He reciprocated grinning at me, and the heartfelt expression in his eyes exuded wonder, blithe and enthrall, and I knew he was as happy as I.

I moved to sit on the sofa next to Leila while Little Leif remained seated on the opposite side next to his father. Leila shifted slightly more comfortably as she snuggled against me with her doll in her arms when I turned on the TV. Pressing the correct app on the screen, the video library was located, and I found the Stars Wars movie for which we were seeking—*Episode IV, A New Hope*.

The kids had fallen to sleep during the movie, and I wondered if Leif was nearly as spent as the kids and I were. But when I glanced beside myself to see him still watching the movie, I realized he was captivated and remained wide awake still viewing it. Then, when it finally ended, the tole of the day was surely weighing on me and I was unquestionably ready for bed.

"How did you enjoy the movie?" I asked him as I turned off the TV.

"I believe that I raither fancied it," he replied actually.

"So, you understand the story, then?"

"'Tis a tale betwixt guid and evil, is it not?"

"Yes, it is," I replied when I gathered Leila from off the sofa into my arms as she was now sleeping.

"Then, I understood it regardless of the mesmerizing particulars," he said easily, observing me holding Leila. "Permit me tae carry the bairn in yer stead."

"No, it's okay, I can manage. But if you would carry Leif, that would be great," I suggested.

"Aye, of coorse." He leaned and scooped Little Leif up into his robust arms as he also slept, then followed me out of the den through the hallway, up the staircase until we arrived at the children's bedroom. He helped me tuck them both into bed. Subsequently, when the children were nicely blanketed, we left their room for our own.

Now entering the master bedroom, finally, Leif closed the door behind us and I went to the bathroom ready to undress for a quick shower. He followed me into the bathroom deciding that he wished to wash himself also, preferring the use of the tub. So, while I showered, he bathed, and I couldn't wait to sink into the pillows for the night.

When I had finished showering, he also had just emerged from the bath water and toweled himself dry. While drying myself also, I moved into the bedroom and retrieved a night garment from my dresser. Slipping it on, I watched him emerging from the bathroom into the bedroom once he completed toweling himself dry. He strode naked across the room toward the bed and comfortably slid beneath the covers. As he was settling his head against the pillows, his gaze seized mine when I moved to turn the bathroom light off. With it now switched off, I shortly climbed into bed and joined him beneath the covers.

"What?" I modestly asked him as his eyes were adherent on me.

"Whit sort of shift is that ye wear?" he inquired interestedly, noticing my short, black silk spaghetti strap chamise.

"A nightdress," I replied simply.

"Is that whit it is named?"

"Yeah," I replied demurely as he was beginning to make me feel sheepish by the way he was gazing at me, given the inspired, mischievous smirk I recognized on his face.

"Come haur, *àille dhubh*." He reached an arm around me and pulled me over himself so I lay flat on top of his chest, facing him.

"Why?" I asked softly.

"I care tae hold ye," he said huskily. I felt his hands coming over my shoulders and stroking down my arms.

"Do you?" I responded faintly.

"Aye."

His fingers seeped into my ringlets at the back of my head as he compelled my lips down over his in a longing, soft kiss. I parted my lips and his tongue entered my mouth, dancing warmly and carefully over mine, quenching me.

"I shall never have enough of ye," he semi-whispered over my mouth when he released me from his kiss. I inhaled, breathing unsteadily.

"I still can't believe that you're here with me," I whispered. I leaned and placed my lips over his and kissed him in return. His large hands gently stroked up my bare thighs, sending tingling sensations throughout my body. He began easing my thighs apart to straddle his hips and positioned me at his groin. The sudden hard feeling of him distinctly pressing against my pubic bone, heated my blood and induced my belly to ache as the warmth spread.

His hand slid between us. Grasping his engorged shaft, he grazed it along my cleft, spreading me apart with the head. Mindfully brushing it to and fro, I sensed myself opening as he teased my clitoris and entrance. Searing warmth and dampness seeped between my thighs, and I naturally shifted myself more comfortably straddling his hips, ready to receive him. Aware of me, he ceased stroking himself against my entrance the moment I felt him opening me when gently inserting the head of his organ into me.

"Ye ken whit tae do," he uttered throatily and I smiled unevenly at him as I was adjusting to the bold sensation of him entering me. Slowly easing myself with care down on him, he began powerfully filling me to my core, holding me captive to him. A moan escaped my lips. He was deliciously deep and my body ached for him. "Och, ye receive me with such glory," he groaned as his hands roamed upward along my thighs and over my back until they removed my chemise. He groped my buttocks, and the heat from his kneading hands sent my blood searing throughout my body, torturing me with painful need.

"*Uhh...* Leif," I whispered shakily, helplessly succumbing to his luring touch.

"Aye. Take it," he uttered in a gravelly voice. He seized my waist and held me tight against him, deliberately rocking me. Forging himself into me, he worked his driving will over me, dissolving me as my depths welcomed him. Acclimating to the pressure of him far inside my depths, I felt him pushing against my cervix and rocking my uterus. Slowly, my body naturally began taking over from him and my hips swayed upon his groin. The sublime sensation made my breath flutter, and carried me off into a world only known to us.

"Leif," I breathed. He moved a hand over my flat belly and pushed against it, not harshly but firmly enough where I sensed the pressure of his hand pressing against his own organ inside me.

"I can feel ye," he groaned as I continued grinding myself on him.

"I know."

"Existing within ye soars my soul tae hights never knoon tae me before."

I closed my eyes, focused on the sensation of him deep inside me while deliberately rocking back and forth. His hands stroked up my abdomen and tenderly seize my breasts, cupping them as they caressed with care, gently pulling, and tugging my erect nipples. He caught them between his massaging fingers, teasing them as he lightly tugged and rolled them. My eyes remained closed, and it seemed as though time had suspended. I was enjoying the lucid feeling of him touching me, as no other thought but him existed in mind.

When I finally opened my eyes again, I gazed down at him, noticing his eyes turned toward the large vertical mirror attached to the barn door closing the closet. The room was illuminated in a soft warm glow from the lamplight on the nightstand by my bedside, and I could see him looking at my reflection, mesmerized. Catching a glimpse of myself in the mirror with my long ringlets hanging over my shoulders, our eyes met in the reflection.

"You're watching," I said breathlessly.

"I am," he rasped.

"Why?"

"I huvnae ever seen ye so magnificently when we couple."

I smiled at him in the mirror. He raised a hand over my shoulder, removing my long hair covering it, off to the other side. Now, he could completely see me naked over him as I continued making love to him.

I leaned toward his lips, kissing him, then trailed kisses toward his cheek and neck while he watched us. Pressing my elbows into the pillows beside his head for further support, I glanced down below while pumping myself over him and glimpsed at the rise and fall of my hips over his. His shaft emerged then vanished as it submerged into me again, and again. I watched him moving in and out of me with such pleasure. The vision of it hypnotized me— corresponding with the feeling of emptiness and fullness as the rhythm drove me toward climax.

"I love you," I breathed into his ear. He took my obscuring hair and cleared it from his face, suddenly shifting his gaze from the mirror toward me, locking our eyes together. Positioning my hair behind my shoulders, he then seized my face between his gentle palms with fingers immersed into my ringlets, and gazed into my heart as we silently stared at each other for a moment. Suddenly drawing my lips over his, he fervently shoved his tongue far into my mouth, consuming me with his kiss, stealing my breath.

"I loove ye more," he growled against my lips. I smiled and straightened from his insatiable mouth, further grinding my hips over his as my fingers mindlessly raked the light hairs on his chest. He returned his gaze toward the mirror and watched. I began tightening around him as my slick depths started gripping his thick, formidable shaft, closely reaching the end of my journey.

"*Ooh*... Leif. I'm coming," I panted.

"Come tae me, *àille dhubh*," he groaned.

Then, my insides abruptly began contracting into wild spasms, sending me over the precipice. My back arched as I seized. Motionless over him, I was held captive to the euphoric sensation enveloping me. My thighs radically quaked and I shook uncontrollably, soaring off into oblivion.

When I ceased trembling, I collapsed over him and before reality brought me completely down from rhapsody, Leif swung me around beneath him, inescapably caging me with his body as he vehemently began thrusting himself into my depths. I raised my hands to his shoulders, securing my legs around his hips, holding onto him as he wildly ebbed and flowed. Pushing himself farther inside me than I thought he could ever reach, he forged an undiscovered path.

He hardened further and I felt the full articulation of his shaft driving into me, sending electrical pulses throughout my veins, and igniting a raging flame incinerating my body. I raised my gaze and glanced down between us while he pumped over me. He turned his gaze downward also and we witnessed what he was doing to me. His robust organ driving in and out of me with fervor, and determination slick from the well found within my depths, enraptured us. It seemed magical while he appeared and vanished with each purposeful, yearning stroke, as he bore me open on every surge. Seeing myself taking all of him was deliriously spellbinding. I thought I would faint from the sight and feeling combined.

"*Uhh—you're amazing*," I panted as I tossed my head back into the pillows and wreathed beneath him, on the brink of climaxing again.

Each thrust made him firmer as he moved more rhythmically, and I knew himself to be on the verge of explosion. He vigorously pumped, and panted. It seemed he was hanging on by a single thread for a second longer, not wanting for it to end. Tiny beads of perspiration had formed on his brow and his heated skin was damp. I was aware of him beginning to buckle under the pressure to last another thrust. The stimulating sensation he was creating for himself within me was pushing him toward his annihilation as he struggled dominating the inevitable that was on the cusp of overcoming him.

I stared up into his eyes as his were locked onto mine, never once wavering, until he groaned a feral groan and they helplessly rolled back the second his head tilted backward.

"I cannae bare it. So, I come, Sylvie," he growled. Suddenly, he violently throbbed between my thighs, releasing himself and filling me with his essence flowing deep into my core, until I was seeping.

When he drained, he slumped over me and buried his head into the curve of my neck. He was heavily breathing as his hot breath caressed my heated skin. His heart was fiercely pounding against my breast. I wrapped my arms around him and lightly stroked his back with my raking nails, settling too.

Silence ensued between us as we listened to ourselves calming. But after a moment, he lifted his gaze and our eyes met again. An indolent grin came over my lips. His cheeks creased as his lips lazily curved upward also, and my smile widened. He dipped his head and softly pressed his warm lips over mine. When he broke from kissing me, he rested his forehead against mine, and I could still feel his heavy breathing flowing over my lips.

"Do ye have a latch upon the bedchamber door?" he asked.

"Yeah," I replied.

"Guid."

"Why?"

"I didnae discover it when I had closed it upon our entry."

"Oh—that's because it's small and unnoticeable, since it's attached behind the doorknob."

"'Tis fortunate the bairns didnae enter the chamber whilst we waur coupling," he recognized luckily.

"But, they're sound asleep," I replied, not too worried about it.

"Bairns sleep lightly."

"Sometimes. So, I guess we are *definitely* lucky." A nervous giggle escaped me. He raised his gaze to mine and I noticed the lax smirk on his face. It seemed an additional thought had crossed his mind.

"'Tis most fortunate that we are undisturbed. We cannae seem capable of remaining silent once we couple," he lightly chuckled, appearing somewhat relieved. "Yoo're an untamed and shameless, lass." He playfully slapped the side of my hip.

"Hey! It takes two to tango," I scolded lightly, feigning offense.

"Tango?"

"Yes."

"I huvnae a notion of whit ye mean," he chuckled a little again and mischievously slapped the side of my hip once more, creating a loud smacking sound, that didn't hurt.

"Leif!" I squealed.

"*Shhh!* Yoo'll awaken the bairns," he warned.

"But you just—"

"Silence." He suddenly held an ordering finger to my lips and cocked a warning brow, quieting me. I couldn't help the little giggle escaping me as I gazed at the playful smirk on his face also. "Now, be a guid lass and fall tae sleep."

He pecked his lips over mine and I subsequently sensed him disengaging from me. He rolled off to the side and drew me close against his broad chest, clasping me in his sound arms. I exhaled, feeling extremely relaxed and contented as I wrapped my arm around his chest, embracing him also.

It became quiet between us again as I listened to the hypnotic sound of his breathing and the beating of his heart. I reached over toward the lamp on my nightstand and finally switched it off. The room filled with moonlight entering through the windows instead, and within minutes we had drifted, succumbing to slumber at last.

Eighteen

Sometime in the middle of the night I had awakened and covered myself with my chemise that had been thoughtlessly tossed to the foot of the bed, and quietly removed myself from the covers, intending to check on the kids; it was my nightly ritual to do so—to make sure they were all right. When I arrived into their bedroom, I replaced the covers over them that they had kicked off of themselves while they slept, and kissed each of their heads before returning to bed.

Entering the master bedroom again, I carefully slipped back beneath the blankets and snuggled against Leif as he continued sleeping. He automatically rolled to his side and drew me close into his embrace, spooning with me in his sleep.

However, very early this morning as dawn was breaking, I awakened unexpectedly to the sight of Leila and Little Leif standing quietly at my bedside as I stupidly remembered that I hadn't locked the door when I had returned from their room last night.

"Hey," I muttered while rubbing my drowsy eyes, focusing on them. "What are you two doing up so early?"

"It's our birthday party today," Leila reminded me, bright-eyed and ready to begin the day.

"I know," I replied sleepily, gazing back at their excited faces. They stood expectantly at my bedside and leaned in close simply staring at me, waiting for me to remove myself from the covers to begin their exciting day. "It's still early, though. Why don't you rest a little while longer before we have to get up for school," I urged instead, lightly patting the empty space on the mattress beside me.

I naturally shifted a little more away from the edge of the bed toward Leif as he continued sleeping on the other side, making room for them to climb in next to me beneath the covers. They each crawled into bed and snuggled up beside me. It was usually what they did over the weekends with me as I tried sleeping in, or if they instead came down with a cold or stomach ache as they sought attention and comfort from me.

"Now, you two have to stay quiet and rest until it's time to get ready for school," I quietly cautioned them.

"Okay, we will," Little Leif promised.

"All right. In that case, you may stay here with me to rest a little more," I allowed.

I whipped the blanket over them and they began resting with me as I lightly returned to sleeping. Except, they wouldn't remain still and kept whispering to each other about their birthday party, that I found I couldn't fall back to sleep at all like I had wished. So, I simply lay there listening to their little conversation, making sure that they kept their voices low so not to awaken their father.

But soon I felt Leif closely stirring on my opposite side from the kids beneath the blanket to the sound of his children happily whispering to each other. I turned my gaze toward him, observing his eyes opening and he shifted his languid glance toward me. A lazily grin eased over his lips and a gentle smile came over mine.

"Guid morrow tae ye, *àille dhubh*," he said in a low voice and the children suddenly ceased speaking.

"Good morning," I replied softly to him. He slid an arm

beneath me and drew me close against him. "The children are here," I quickly informed him.

"Och! Are they?" He looked at me with abrupt surprise and embarrassment as his eyes widened with his cheeks flushing. His body went rigid beneath the covers as he stared at me, alarmed.

"I'm sorry. I completely forgot about locking the door. They sometimes get in bed with me just to say hello when they've awakened before me. This time, they're excited for their birthday party today—and they didn't realize that you're here," I explained nervously.

"I am unprepared fur them," he said, appearing clearly uncomfortable.

"Don't worry. I'm leaving now with them. We'll make breakfast while we wait for you to come downstairs into the kitchen," I responded apologetically.

"Very weel," he agreed, looking uneasily at me. So, I promptly gathered the children from out our bed and urged them to leave the room with me, closing the door behind us.

When we reached the kitchen, the kids desired pancakes for breakfast, so we began collecting ingredients to make them.

"Mom?" Little Leif began as we were arranging ingredients on top of the island.

"Yeah, sweetie?" I replied.

"How come you had a slumber party with Dad without us?" he asked innocently.

"Well, I—" I stammered, somewhat bewildered and unready for his inquisitive observation.

"Yeah, why didn't we all have a slumber party together?" Leila inquired also.

"Since your dad is with us from now on, his room will be my room too—and we need some privacy now. So, slumber parties aren't going to happen like they used to," I tried explaining.

"How come? Because he could use the room Grandad and

Nanna use when they're here, instead," he continued inquisitively, looking a bit put-out.

"But then, where will they sleep if he uses their room when they come to stay with us?" I asked.

"He could use the other one that nobody uses," he suggested apparently.

"Except, haven't you noticed that Grandad and Nanna share the same room together also?" I asked.

"Yeah," he recognized simply.

"That's because they're married and they love each other," Leila said obviously.

"Well, your dad and I love each other too. Don't you remember your dad saying that we were both married, also?" I asked.

"Oh. Yeah, I remember that," Little Leif suddenly recalled. He paused for a moment and I could see him wondering.

"Wouldn't it be okay with you for your dad and me to share the same room?" I inquired considerately.

Little Leif thoughtfully shrugged. "I guess so. I just don't want our slumber parties to go away, though."

"You don't have to worry about that, necessarily."

"Why not?"

"Well, we'll still be able to snuggle with each other for as long as you want whenever the time is appropriate. We just need to remember that because your dad's here now, that we've got to be considerate of him."

"How do we do that?"

"Well, he likes his privacy. So, whenever the door is closed, just know that he's in the room and probably doesn't want to be disturbed. But, you're always welcome to knock on the door first to see if it's okay for you to enter. Is that understandable?"

"I suppose so."

"Good." I gave him a gentle little tap on the end of his petite nose and he giggled. "What I wonder, though, is what am I going to do when you've grown into a big boy and don't want to give me a kiss anymore?"

"Don't worry, Mom. I'll always give you a kiss whenever you want me to," he said confidently, giving me an unheard of look.

"Then, I guess we'll always make each other happy. Won't we?"

"Uh-huh," he said, nodding his head for certain. I smiled at him and kissed the top of his head. Not to ignore Leila, I leaned and kissed her cheek too. She smiled, and the kids seemed contented now.

After we had mixed the ingredients and as I was in the middle of cooking the pancakes while the children waited eagerly in the breakfast nook to eat, Leif finally arrived into the kitchen freshly dressed for the day and joined us. He was striking. Attired in a pair of dark denim blue jeans he had decided to wear and beige pin-striped oxford button-down shirt, his hair unbounded and hung like gilded silk past his shoulders. I knew he would have liked to have worn a tie with his shirt, but I still had yet to teach him how to tie one when I had a moment to spare sometime later. So, for now, the slightly open collar at his neck made him appear relaxed, and attracted me to him as I gave him a little smile. He returned a subtle wink and a benign grin as he strode deeper into the kitchen, advancing toward me.

"'Tis delicious in haur. Whit is it that ye are preparing?" he inquired curiously when he arrived closely standing beside me at the stove.

"Chocolate chip pancakes!" Leila happily informed him.

"Och," he replied interestedly, turning his smiling gaze toward her.

"Are they ready, Mom?" Little Leif asked me, eagerly waiting to be served.

"Yes, they are," I said easily.

"Yay! I'm hungry!" Little Leif expressed anxiously.

"Me too!" Leila verbalized the same way.

"Okay, here you go," I said, swiftly plating their food and placing their plates before them on the table. I promptly fixed Leif's plate also as he now strode toward the table and took his seat with the kids, joining them. I observed him intriguingly admiring the kids while he steadied his gaze upon them when I placed his readied plate nicely in front of him. "I hope you don't mind a treat for breakfast," I said to him.

"I shall enjoy it as they," Leif said willingly, shifting his attention toward me. He then turned his attention to his food and gathered his fork between his fingers. But, he returned observing the kids again who were already enjoying their food. Once I served the kids their milk, and Leif a glass of mixed apple and carrot juice, I took my place at the table with my own plate and glass of juice. "Shall we not say a blessing?" he inquired oddly, appearing faintly disapproving.

"Yes, of course," I said certainly.

"I'll say it!" Little Leif abruptly offered and the both of them ceased eating their breakfast. Our son proceeded with the Sign of the Cross and we all followed his lead, then he began saying a sweet blessing that he'd learned from school. When he had completed it, I glanced at Leif and noticed the slight grin gently warming the expression in his eyes as he gazed at his son.

"Weel done, laddie," Leif complimented him, satisfied. Little Leif simply glanced at his father, a little unexpected.

"Say thank you, Leif," I prompted our son.

"Thank you," he replied innocently.

"Yoo're welcome, my son," his father kindly said to him.

"I want to say the blessing next time," Leila desired.

"Of course, you may," I nicely said to her, meeting her bright emerald gaze. She smiled widely at me, then proceeded eating her breakfast like her brother as he had already begun.

Silence ensued as we sat together enjoyably eating. But after a moment, the kids continued talking excitedly about their much-anticipated birthday party today.

"Mom?" Little Leif called my attention from observing his father enjoying his meal while I drank my juice.

"Yes, sweetie?" I replied, replacing my glass onto the table.

"Please don't forget to bring Yoda today when you pick us up. I want to show him to my friends," he reminded seriously.

"I won't forget," I promised.

"Okay," he replied, satisfied, as he took his cup of milk off the table and drank it.

"Are you walking with us to school today?" Leila asked their father.

"Aye. I shall escort ye," Leif said affably.

"Good. I want to show you my friends," she said gladly.

"I shall be pleased tae be newly acquainted with yer friends," he responded genuinely. I smiled and he caught me gazing pleasantly at him. A warm grin eased over his lips also, creasing his cheeks and brightening his glinting eyes.

"Do you know that we're having a birthday party today?" Leila asked her father. Leif shifted his smiling gaze back toward his small daughter.

"Aye. I reckon that I micht have heard a word of it," he said pleasantly.

"Oh," she replied simply.

"Do you know that you both share the same birthday with your father?" I told them. Their eyes widened suddenly with surprise.

"We do?" Little Leif responded with clear astonishment.

"Yes, you do," I said surely with a nod.

"*Ooh,*" Leila expressed, looking significantly amazed.

"Isn't that nice?" I asked.

"That's the best!" Little Leif happily declared, very impressed.

"You're our twin," Leila stated to their father. Leif chuckled, obviously humored. "You can share our birthday party with us because of it!"

"Why, that is most gracious of ye. I am most obliged, my wee birdie," Leif said to her. She smiled at him and her happiness was plainly perceivable on her face.

"All right, let's focus on finishing our breakfast so we're not late for school," I suggested nicely, redirecting their attention to the final bits of food on their plates.

"Okay," Little Leif complied easily, and stuffed his mouth with remaining pancake as Leila gulped the last of her milk.

Nineteen

After breakfast had been completed, I rushed the kids upstairs to their bedroom and assisted them in dressing. When they were attired in their school uniforms and nicely groomed, they returned downstairs to keep their father company while I swiftly went to dress myself for the day. Once I had freshened myself in the bathroom, I quickly threw on a pair of dark, denim blue jeans and a peach, fitted cap-sleeve, scalloped neck blouse, then promptly arranged my long ringlets, tying them into a loose ponytail. Finally, I rushed downstairs ready to take them to school.

With light sweaters over their shoulders and petite backpacks placed on their backs, the four of us emerged from the house into the cool morning air. It was an overcast morning with low lying clouds created by the marine layer from the ocean not too far from here. But it was forecasted today that the sun will have burned off the clouds, revealing bright, sunny, blue sky for the remainder of the day.

As we walked to school, the kids talked about their usual curious topics with me. Leif simply listened to our discussion, seeming charmed or intrigued, or maybe both, while he paced along with us. I knew he didn't understand some of our conversation, but he paid close attention to what his children were saying, regardless.

"Mom?" Little Leif started curiously.

"Yeah, sweetie?" I responded.

"Why did the meteor kill all the dinosaurs?" he inquired—for what seemed to me to have been the millionth time he had asked that question—as it was one of his favorite topics of discussion.

"Well, there are a bunch of asteroids that fly around in outer space and they're always bumping into each other and crashing into things, and sometimes they hit planets. And, the one that hit Earth was a huge enough one to change the Earth's environment. So, because of that, the dinosaurs couldn't find the food they needed to eat, and they all died," I explained simply.

"Will a meteor ever hit us?" he asked.

"I don't think so," I said unlikely.

"Yeah, 'cause God won't let it," Leila said confidently.

"Do you think a Tyrannosaurus Rex or a Brontosaurus was nicer?" he asked.

"A Brontosaurus because they ate plants!" Leila answered freely.

"Yeah, I suppose you might be right, sweetie," I said to her as I held both of their hands in mine while we walked along. The conversation continued as such for the duration of our stroll, and I wondered what Leif was thinking as he heard us discussing. I caught his gaze when he glanced at me and he warmly grinned, causing me to smile in return.

Soon arriving at school, we walked through the pedestrian gate beside the parking lot fence. We continued toward the back of the school until entering into the junior high school courtyard where all of the schoolchildren congregated according to their grade levels. Parents had already gathered around the perimeter beneath the awnings to see their children off to school this morning as usual. Leif and I came to stand beneath the awning near our children's class, patiently observing them as they happily spoke with their friends while in line.

Heather, and Maria, a widowed mother who reminded me of Jaclyn Smith from the original *Charlie's Angels* TV show, and who had not yet met Leif, caught my attention as they waved at me while approaching us. They were joined by Autumn and her husband, Glen, as they greeted each other while advancing in our direction. Autumn and Glen were both noticeably tall and good-looking. A laidback couple who had met in collage, they had gotten married right after they had graduated. Glen, at one time was a professional baseball player, but since then had settled into the real-estate profession. His wife, Autumn, made a living as a marketing agent for a cosmetics company. Leif hadn't yet made their acquaintances either, and when they arrived with Heather and Maria close enough for a conversation with us, they cordially introduced themselves to him.

The awkward feeling never left me from yesterday when I had introduced Leif to Heather. So, I stood there before my friends knowing they had already begun gossiping about the sudden reappearance of him into my life, and of our feigned elopement to each other, as they gazed at us with friendly, but inquisitive expression on their faces.

Proceeding to wish each other good morning, Heather commenced a light conversation about the weather, kids, and sporting events. Glen, Autumn, Maria, and Heather were buoyant and lighthearted as they engaged me in the topics. Leif, however, remained quietly listening and observant of my friends while they surrounded us. Aware that he didn't relate to anyone, I was also subconsciously uncomfortable for him. Regardless, he was polite when Glen attempted discussing with him the latest Laker game until the morning bell rang, bringing our conversations to a close.

After school announcements, prayer, and saying the Pledge of Allegiance, Leif and I escorted our children to their classroom building, then commenced our way off school grounds as we began strolling through the neighborhood on our return home. Naturally slipping my hand into his, he clasped it as we strolled silently together while enjoying our walk.

"One haur is raither familiar with the other, is one not?" Leif remarked thinkingly as we comfortably paced.

"What do you mean?" I asked curiously.

"My meaning is that thaur isnae any inhibition betwixt people, it appears," he noted.

"You mean they're informal," I understood, pondering him.

"Aye."

"Well, I suppose so, generally. I guess people are just more casual with each other nowadays—respectively."

"'Tis quite apparent."

"Does it bother you?"

"'Tis merely a matter of respect tae regard one formally," he commented.

"Well, people still respect each other here—it's just more informal. That's all. There's no intentional harm by it. Society is just generally less reserved now. I'm guessing it's because people don't regard class structure like in the past, and prefer being made easily available to each other—as in their accessibility. And since there's no legal pedigree hierarchy here anymore, it puts everyone on the same level in a way. Plus, it not only makes people more at ease with one another, it makes things even when people simply approach each other on a whole," I replied thoughtfully.

"'Tis an observation," he remarked.

"I understand the difference, though—your meaning, I mean. So, if you feel that you wish for me to introduce you more formally to people, I'll do that."

"I reckon 'tis of nae consequence, *ceisdein,* as I am untitled within this society, nonetheless. When in Rome, do as the Romans do," he said, turning his gaze toward me.

"I just want you to feel comfortable, that's all," I replied, meeting his eyes.

"I am making an attempt."

"I know," I acknowledge. "But I don't want you feeling pressured to be accepted. I know what it feels like. I simply don't wish for your feeling uncomfortable around my friends, or family. So, please let me know how you're feeling, because I'd like to ease your discomfort in any way that I can." He didn't respond except quietly returned to gazing ahead as we continued strolling along. He appeared to be pondering. Noticing him, I asked, "Do you feel worried about your acceptance here with me?"

He returned his gaze to me. "It micht seem that yer friends are raither accommodating. Therefore, I dinnae feel unwelcome. Although, I do gather their inquisitiveness regarding me."

"Yes, they are curious about you, certainly. It has everything to do with your sudden appearance into my life, mostly. Not where you're from instead. It's also surprising to them, according to their suppositions, that we've eloped. Even still, I'm glad that you feel welcomed by them. But are you offended by their lax mannerism toward you?"

"I cannae say that I am affronted by them at all. Indeed, they are most amiable. I merely made an observation. 'Tis all."

"That's reassuring, because they really do like you."

"Do they?"

"Definitely."

"'Tis comforting fur ye tae inform me. Yet, we have only met, therefore how micht they make a sudden judgment of me? Do they not perceive my being a misfit amongst them, nonetheless?"

"You're exotic to them."

"Exotic? Am I?"

"Of course."

"I can scarcely be deemed so," he disagreed, giving me a quizzical look.

"But, you're a rarity to everyone here. So don't be surprised," I assured with a little smile. "Your uniqueness attracts them. Originality goes a long way with anyone here. Besides, they've never met anyone so genuinely proper and polite—and that charms anyone too. So, you shouldn't worry."

"Certainly?"

"Yes."

"Ye solace me."

"Good. Please don't be concerned in the slightest," I supported. He grinned at me in response, encouraged, and I smiled back at him, also appeased.

But when I shifted my gaze ahead, my parents entered my mind again, immediately throwing my pleasant mood back into apprehensiveness. Among the many things demanding my attention today before the kids' birthday party started, was the necessary call I had to make to my parents—finally. The mounting pressure to inform them about Leif, letting them know that he was here with me now, as they deserved to know, was quietly unsettling me. I had so many concerns: a large one being them realizing that I had lied to them, and another was that I primarily hoped they'd accept Leif and love him too.

Still, since they knew absolutely nothing about him due to my refusal to ever reveal anything about him to them—never even once divulging his name—I knew I was headed for turmoil with my parents like I had incurred with my brother—which would be conceivably worse. And, despite the fact my parents knowing something of my invisible relationship with a man they'd never met, they recognized it had to have been substantial proven by my kids' existence, although they never pressed me with questions. But I was ultimately scared of their reaction to the truth about me and Leif after years of assuming, and for the fallout that was going to occur.

Since my return home from disappearing, I was aware of their constant wondering about the details along with the man I'd become involved with. While they never pressed the issue with me, for which I was extremely relieved, I nevertheless couldn't help recognizing their silent, and severe, concern for my situation.

Instead, however, my circumstance was never discussed—likely from their fear, as well as my own, of upsetting the placidity between us by exposing the shame they might be feeling due to my unmarried circumstance. Or, perhaps they feared the potential revelation that something actually horrible might have in fact happened to me during my absence. Maybe it was all of it, I considered.

While they didn't insist upon my telling them any information about it in the wake of my disappearance, it seemed they were being extremely patient with me, though. It seemed they were preferring to wait until I was ready to discuss my episode with them. But with each passing day, it had become easier for us to avoid the discussion altogether as we submerged ourselves in the distractions of our daily lives, leaving the issue on the periphery to be visited one day. In the meantime, my parents clearly expressed and demonstrated their love for me and the kids, reinforcing my security and which shunned some of my uncertainty along with critical feelings about myself as I hid the truth.

However, given my secrets and lies I had told them explaining away my pregnancy with the twins, everything was now coming to a head—finally. My parents were sure to ask me many pertinent questions regarding Leif, since he was now here. So, I wasn't positive how I was going to answer them. Except, what I did know was once they discovered I had lied to them in some regard about my relationship with him, they weren't only going to be disappointed, but I also assumed they were going to be considerably angry.

Recognizing this, I found myself unexpectedly forced to having to speak with my parents about my relationship with Leif, exposing a minimum of the truth as it pertained to him specifically, while ignoring the overall plight of how we met in the beginning. And, finally speaking with them about it was going to have to be as soon as today, since they were taking the kids to Disneyland tomorrow for their birthday—and I was panicked; I didn't want my parents inadvertently learning of Leif's presence through their grandchildren before I had the opportunity to tell them myself. I only wondered about the most opportune time to tell them when I arrived home. And, I hoped for privacy when I spoke with them to spare Leif as much as possible from the likely oncoming disruption between my parents and me.

Twenty

When Leif and I returned home, I offered him a cup of tea with another *National Geographic* magazine when we entered the den, encouraging him to make himself comfortable without me. I also turned the TV on for him to watch, and explained how to operate it whenever he decided to switch from reading. Leaving the TV sound on low with the Travel Channel airing, it gave him the opportunity to watch something light and interesting.

Once satisfied that he had settled comfortably into the den, I subsequently excused myself from his presence without his concern. Retrieving my phone from my back jeans pocket as I withdrew from the room, I now proceeded stepping outside into the backyard. I unthinkingly paced around the lawn for a moment, hesitant to finally making the call I was forced to do. Until, I found myself by the swimming pool at the back of the yard where I ceased moving, after entering through the gate.

I dropped into one of the pool chairs before the water, feeling almost already defeated. But as if experiencing an out-of-body instance, I watched my finger automatically dialing my mom's phone number, compelling me to face my burden. Putting the phone to my ear, I nervously held my breath while listening to it ring, fabricating in my mind what I was going to say to her as my heart jackhammered in my chest.

"Hello?" Mom answered promptly. I suddenly exhaled, feeling extremely insecure.

"Hey, Mom. It's me," I started, aware of my nerves as my fingers were trembling while holding the phone. Abruptly, all of my contrived thoughts flew from my head, and I didn't know how to begin.

"Oh, hi sweetheart," she said pleasantly. "How was your trip to Boston?"

"It was good," I replied.

"Oh, that's nice," she responded. "How are the kids?"

"They're great."

"I'm certain they're excited for their party today, aren't they?"

"Yeah, they are—very much."

"Be sure to take a lot of pictures for us, won't you?"

"I will."

"Your dad and I will be over at your place at eight o'clock tomorrow morning to pick them up for Disneyland," she reminded.

"Okay."

"We should be back by five on Sunday—if not earlier. We'll call you to keep you updated on our time."

"That sounds good," I said, abstracted. "Mom?"

"Yes, sweetheart?"

"Um, there's something I've got to tell you," I started unnaturally.

"What is it? Is everything all right?" I discerned her voice quickly responding to my irregular tone. She was surely concerned now.

"Yeah, everything's fine—I suppose," I said shakily, trying to control my emotions as my eyes began welling.

"You suppose? What's going on?"

"I'm sorry," I said meekly, struggling to maintain my composure.

"I don't understand. For what? Why are you sorry?"

"For what I've done," I blurted.

"I'm confused, sweetie. What did you do?"

"I lied."

"About?"

"I lied to you and Dad—about what you guys know, or don't know, about the kids' father," I said shakily.

"Oh. I see…" she responded, pausing momentarily. I felt the gravity of her presence through her silence over the phone, and I shook more. "What is it that you told us about him that is a lie?"

"First, before I say anything about him, you must believe that I was never raped during the months I was gone—because that's absolutely the truth," I prefaced.

"If you say that it never happened to you, Sylvie, then we believe you."

"It never happened."

"I believe you," she guaranteed. "So, explain to me what this is about, sweetie."

"I told you that I had been involved with a man without you and Dad knowing about it when I had returned pregnant with the kids. Remember that?"

"Yes, I remember."

"That's true too."

"Then, what is it that you've lied to me and your father about?"

"I let you believe the reason why I had disappeared was because I thought you'd be ashamed of me for having an intimate relationship with someone without being married to him."

"I see."

"The thing is, is that I know you and Dad have expectations of me, and that you both hold certain beliefs. Because of that, I didn't want to embarrass you or shame you—and that's sort of why I've held back telling you anything about what happened to me with the kids' father."

"I see. I'm so sorry to hear this. I regret that you feel that you've felt burdened because of how we feel about certain things regarding morals and social mores. But you should always know, sweetheart, that you're our daughter and we'll always love you no matter what mistakes you might've made. Or, believe that you may have made," she said endearingly, causing me to breakdown and snivel.

"I also let you believe that Matt was the reason I couldn't maintain a relationship with anyone else, and that's why I left the kids' father. Except, that's not the reason," I replied unevenly. Tears perched in my eyes. I blinked and they slipped down my cheeks.

"You said that you needed time to sort things out—to clear your head," Mom remembered.

"Yes, I told you that... But it was an excuse."

"Then, what was the real reason?"

"It—" I broke off, hesitating, knowing that I could not tell her the absolute truth while letting a lull come between us instead.

"What broke you two apart, sweetheart?" she urged, resuming the conversation.

"It was because of—um..."

"Was he abusive?" she inquired carefully, speculating the worst.

"No! He was extraordinarily giving and kind," I responded suddenly, extinguishing any negative ideas coming to her mind.

"Then, I remain confused. Why did you break up with him, if that's not the case?"

"The distance... The distance between us proved to be too great to overcome—at the time."

"I see. Well, how far away did he live from you?"

"Too far."

"I understand that long distance relationships can be a

hindrance, and sometimes it can influence couples' decisions on whether to stay together. But, if Matt wasn't who was troubling you while you were in this particular relationship with their father, and if you say that your relationship with this man was wonderful, then couldn't there have been a way for the both of you to work it out?" she asked.

"Well, um… he's, uh—he's been looking for me since we've been separated… and he's here now," I sniveled, careful not to answer her question directly.

"What do you mean that he's here now? You mean he's here in L.A.?"

"Yes," I exhaled unevenly as my vision blurred with salty tears. Mom suddenly became quiet for a moment, and I wondered what thoughts were running through her mind, precisely.

"To see you?" she resumed.

"Yes."

"I see… What's his name?"

"Seamus Stewart," I answered.

"That's an unusual name," she recognized.

"He's from Scotland."

"Oh. That *is* a distance," she validated. "How long has he been in L.A.?"

"Since yesterday."

"He just arrived?" she responded with more surprise.

"Yes."

"So, he obviously knows about the children now," she fathomed especially.

"Yeah."

"How did he take the news?"

"He loves them, tremendously," I told her.

"He wasn't shocked? Or upset in anyway?"

"No. He sort of presumed that I'd become pregnant. And, he's really receptive to knowing that he's a father."

"I must admit that I'm very stunned."

"I know."

"This is so surprising," she said seriously. "I would have expected him to have some sort of adverse reaction to unexpectedly knowing about his new status. Wasn't he upset with you for hiding from him the fact that you were ever pregnant?"

"He's not holding it against me."

"Isn't he?"

"No. He's just happy that he found me," I replied honestly.

"Hmm... So, has he already met the kids?" she inquired curiously.

"He has."

"Well, I don't see how he couldn't love them. Especially, now that he knows that they're his," she said thinkingly. "The fact that he's been seeking you out for so long and hasn't any concern about suddenly being a parent, you do understand that he's going to want to be a father to them by being in their lives from now on. Don't you?" Her tone turned graver, which only made me more insecure and nervous about her reaction.

"I know," I said shakily.

"And, he has a right to do that," she acknowledged soberly.

"I know."

"How do you feel about his involvement now?"

"I'm okay with it."

"Are you? Because it could be difficult between you two since you've been separated for so long now—and now with the kids factored in, it will add a certain level of intensity to your relationship from the start as you and he try reconnecting with each other," she warned clearly.

"But I think we can work it out," I sniveled.

"Well, I'm glad that your convinced of it. Your optimism makes me hopeful that you mean to show some kind of commitment, especially since you said that your relationship with him was a healthy one. And bearing that in mind, it can only stand to benefit the children. So, obviously you've seen each other since he's arrived into town. Were you aware that he was coming to see you here?"

"No. He just suddenly appeared."

"I see… I'm sure his sudden arrival comes as a great shock to you—more than anything. I have to say that I can't help being as astounded as you are, though. But I can only imagine what you must be feeling… Curiously, though, which part of town is he staying? Is it by the airport so that he can easily meet up with you?"

"In fact, um, he's staying with us," I disclosed nervously, trying to keep my sniveling quiet.

"He is?" She sounded exceptionally surprised, in addition.

"Yeah."

"Won't that put any pressure on the kids, though?"

"Well—I—I didn't think they'd be troubled, since they've missed having him around at all."

"Only, that's what you're thinking. Honestly, put it into their perspective and think about it. How did they actually react when they first saw him?"

"I'll admit that they were uncertain at first—when they met him. But, since their meeting, they seem really glad now that he's here at the house with them."

"So, you don't have any concern about the kids' reaction to him?"

"I don't. They're getting along so nicely. It seems they're bonding well with him already, and they're so happy to have him with us—finally."

"That's very reassuring. But I'm sure they must have had some questions, however—at least," Mom said.

"Yeah, they did ask me some things. But when I explained a bit about their father, they seemed comforted by what I'd told them."

"Well, that's certainly encouraging. What did you tell them?"

"Essentially, that he's been wanting to meet them for such a long time and it was only now that he had the opportunity to do it," I explained briefly.

"Hmm... And, that's eased their minds?"

"Yes, it has. They seem to really enjoy getting to know him as he gets to know them as well," I said.

"Well—again—that's encouraging," she considered. "I know it's early since you've just reunited with him, but would you know what his plans are at all?"

"He's planning on being together with us—for good," I said.

"Really...?"

"Yeah."

"He means to live here?" Mom asked.

"Yes."

"And, he doesn't plan on taking the kids anywhere with him?"

"No. He would never do anything like that."

"Well, I'm sorry for having had to ask the question. But it's important to know. So many estranged couples wind up kidnapping their own kids from each other. You know that."

"Yes, I'm aware."

"So, your positive answers about him dispels my greatest fear..." She paused again for a moment, and I knew she continued thinking as she considered what I was telling her. "So, I'm wondering if you mean to cohabit? If so, you'll need to get married for the children's sake. Otherwise, it isn't a healthy situation for them." Her tone was noticeably disapproving over the thought.

"I know," I said.

"Then, what do you mean to do?"

"Well, um... I need to also tell you, Mom, that—uh—we're already married," I disclosed unevenly.

"What? Since when?" she questioned, flabbergasted.

"Since the beginning of our relationship," I divulged.

"Oh, honey," she gasped. "Why didn't you ever tell your father and me any of this?"

"It was spontaneous—and I didn't think that you would understand," I wept.

"Oh, sweetie." Mom deeply sighed. "You didn't have to run

away because of your relationship, and hide any of this information from us. We would have understood and tried to help you. I'm so terribly sorry that you felt so pressured to keep such an important secret like this from us... Oh dear... I'll admit that I'm a little disappointed. But, I'm really sorry for not letting you know enough just how much we love you, and that we're always available and open to you—that you could come to us at any time to talk about *anything* bothering you, and that we'd support you... You've got to know how much we love you, sweetheart."

"I know you love me," I wept.

"Do you? Sylvie, for goodness' sake—you're our daughter. We absolutely love you. We are your parents, and we always will be—despite the fact that you're grown and are proudly independent. You should never believe that we don't love you. Please don't think otherwise.

"And, yes—we as your parents naturally hold certain values that aren't in fashion these days. While that's true, it doesn't mean that we'd ever disown you for having an unmarried relationship with this man that resulted in you having our grandchildren... We'd do anything to make sure that you and our grandchildren are safe and happy, and that your mind is at ease with us. You've got to trust us, sweetheart. You've got to trust that we love you. Put all nonsense aside. Do you understand?" she said.

I wanted nothing more right now but to tell her the entire truth of the real ordeal of my disappearance, and how Leif and I truly met; I was on the cusp of telling it all to her. But something held me back.

"Do you understand me, Sylvie?" she asked again, aware of my pause.

"Yes, I understand, Mom," I replied, sniffling.

"Good. It's so important for you to know this," she said seriously. "All right. Now calm down. I can hear you crying over the phone. Everything's going to be okay. I promise. All right?"

"Okay," I sniveled, trying to do as she said. I took deep breaths and wiped the streaming tears from my eyes with my fingertips.

"Good girl. Try to calm down now. As I said, everything's going to be all right. It's very easy to misconstrue things in your mind and blow things out of proportion when you've kept your thoughts and feelings pent up for such a long time. Give me and your father a chance to respond to this. We'll work this situation out together, okay?"

"Okay," I gasped while continuing to clear my vision.

"Now, please, continue telling me everything there is to know about him. You said his name is Seamus Stewart, right?"

"Yes."

"And, he's from Scotland also?"

"Yeah."

"Did he immigrate here?"

"He's not a citizen," I sniffled, informing her.

"But you said his intention is to remain here. So, he must have a green-card?

"He actually doesn't."

"Oh, dear—I hope he's not here illegally, then."

"His important identification records have recently been lost," I explained as closely to the truth as possible.

"Oh, how unfortunate. Well, do you have the marriage certificate at least?"

"No—he kept it with his records."

"It's missing too?"

"Yeah."

"But you can get a copy of it. Right?"

"That'll be very difficult for us to get."

"Why is that?"

"Because, we didn't get married in the States," I told her.

"You didn't?"

"No."

"Sylvie, I want to understand. Did you leave the States when you left us?"

"I didn't think that I was ever going to leave anybody," I said shakily, trying to curb the tears still streaming down my face. Mom drew in a long breath and released it.

"Sylvie, my dear, dear sweetheart. I'm so extremely sorry," she responded empathetically. "I didn't know how much pain you were in after Matt died... Why on earth didn't you ever tell any one of us about it? You didn't have to suffer alone in silence to the point where you felt that you had to suddenly abandon us. We were so terrified when you unexpectedly left without a word or trace. None of us had any idea where you'd gone. Your father was utterly beside himself with grief, thinking you'd been kidnapped and left for dead," Mom said unevenly as her voice cracked now with tears.

"Please forgive me, Mom. I can't tell you how truly sorry I am. I'm so very, *very* sorry—more than I can ever say to you—that I ever scared you and Dad—everyone. Kyle's so angry at me right now because of what's happened, after he found out. He can barely look at me. I never thought any of this would happen, and I'm sorry that I've caused everyone any pain because of me...

"Yes, it was very hard for me losing Matt. But I've come to accept him no longer being here, and I've let him go. So, I refuse now to let the past negatively affect my present, and I want to have a fulfilling future. I know that I can have that now, because I've found that with Seamus. I'm really, *really* happy when I'm with him—and he loves me just like I love him. I'm sorry... Mom? Forgive me. Just forgive me. I never meant to hurt any of you," I sobbed.

"Shhh, now... Okay—let's both settle down before both of us make an entire mess of ourselves crying," she said shakily. "It's going to be okay, sweetheart. Everything's going to be okay. We'll work it all out, just as I've said. Everyone's going to be all right— including Kyle. So don't worry about him. I'll also have a word with him to help settle things with him. He loves you like we do, so he'll come around. Now, let's just focus on you and the kids, first, before anything else by getting Seamus squared. Okay?"

"Okay," I breathed.

"Good. Now. Let's see if we can get him some kind of a state ID card. I know they offer those to undocumented immigrants in this particular state. So, let's start there. Then, once he obtains a legitimate ID card, then you both can apply for a marriage license at the clerk's office. We need to make your marriage official in the U.S., so there will be no issues with the government. And, once that's cleared, then you can focus on having him apply for a green-card—that will also allow him to earn a living here. We can tackle citizenship sometime later. Does that sound reasonable to you?"

"It does," I replied, feeling quieted now—and hopeful—and thankful that Mom could think on her toes with legal advice.

"Good," she said with satisfaction. "So, continue telling me more about him. What is his profession?"

"He's a retired military serviceman," I disclosed.

"Is he, really?" She replied, sounding pleased by this revelation. "Well, he'll have something in common with your father. Your father will appreciate that information about him. What else can you tell me about him?"

"I don't know—I think that might be it... except, he's extremely reserved and polite—a little old fashioned, believe it or not... and he's a little older than I am," I informed her.

"Interesting. Well, politeness goes a long way. Certainly, a good quality to have. How much older is he than you?"

"Eight years."

"Oh, that's not by much," she said encouragingly, overlooking the age difference. "What else can you tell me about him?"

"I can't think of anything else."

"All right. Well, I suppose, we'll find out more about him when we meet. I'm thinking your father and I should have you both over for dinner next Friday. Can we plan for that?" she invited.

"Yeah," I agreed.

"Wonderful. Bring the kids, of course. No need to hire a babysitter. I don't trust them anyway."

"Okay."

"Good."

"Thank you so much, Mom."

"For what, sweetheart?"

"For everything."

"No need to thank me. I'm your mother. It's what I do. Now, wipe your tears. Everything is all right," she reassured.

"Okay."

"Good. That's much better. Now that we've had this conversation, there's no need for anymore worry. I'm going to talk to your father, and we're all going to get together for a nice dinner. Does that sound promising to you?"

"Yes—it does."

"Great. Now, let's put this aside and focus on things you need to do in order to prepare for the kids' birthday party in a few hours."

"All right."

"First of all, do you need any help with preparations from me?"

"Oh, no, it's okay, thank you. Everything's already prepared. I just need to run errands to pick up my orders for it, that's all."

"Okay, then, I'm going to let you go so that you can take care of it."

"All right," I agreed.

"Are you going to be okay, now?" she asked compassionately.

"Yeah, I believe so."

"I'm glad, sweetheart."

"I love you," I told her.

"I love you too, sweetie. Never forget it," she said unequivocally.

"I won't."

"Good. Now, you go on ahead and enjoy the rest of your day with the kids—and with Seamus, of course. I'm assuming he's joining in on the fun."

"He will be."

"Okay. Then, enjoy your whole family being together, all right?"

"Thank you, Mom."

"Don't mention it, sweetheart. Enjoy your day."

"All right. You have a nice day too."

"Thank you, honey. I will. Bye-bye, now."

"Bye, Mom." I hung up the phone, feeling indescribably alleviated. It was remarkable—actually. This conversation with Mom went unexpectedly better than I had been originally anticipating, and I found myself breathing again. An inexpressible weight had suddenly dissolved from my consciousness, and with it behind me now, I could actually concentrate on what the kids needed from me for today.

I took a moment to clear my appearance as I straightened from my seat on the pool chair. When I felt that I'd sufficiently compose myself, I tucked my phone back into my pocket and proceeded away from the pool, walking again over the lawn toward the house.

As I immediately returned indoors, I went to the downstairs bathroom to further clear my appearance by refreshing my face with cool water. When I had finished, I noticed the redness over my cheeks had disappeared, but it lingered obviously in my eyes. Incapable of altering that detail, I nevertheless decided to withdraw from the bathroom to locate Leif, knowing he preferred accompanying me on the errands.

Entering the den where I had left him, he was staring at the TV with captivation while currently watching the Travel Chanel.

Immediately noticing me, however, his eyes shifted from the screen toward me and he straightened from the sofa to his feet, acknowledging me.

"How are you enjoying watching the exploration of New Zealand, is it?" I asked as I reached for the TV remote on the ottoman.

"'Tis most intriguing. I have unimaginable insight into a bonnie land which I hudnae knoon existed," he said amazingly.

"Yeah, it's great learning about a different place from afar when you can't actually go there to see it for yourself," I agreed, holding his gaze with an uneven, little smile. He stared at me for a second, searching my eyes, and the expression on his face turned into concern. I almost glanced away from him, but he forced my gaze to his with transfixed eyes.

"Yoo're troobled. Whit micht it be, *ceisdein*?" he inquired keenly, studying my face.

"I, um—just finished speaking with my mom over the phone," I replied nervously as I gazed back at his scrutinizing eyes.

"Aye?" he prodded, desiring to know more.

"We had a conversation about us—you and me—being together now that you're here," I disclosed.

"Och," he realized. "Whit was yer mother's reception tae this news?"

"I thought she would be angry with me for keeping you a secret."

"Thus, was she vexed?" he asked, intently observing the expression on my face.

"No," I replied, shaking my head a little.

"Quite fortunate."

"Yes."

"I ken that ye have been troobled of late by the anticipation of yer parents' responses regarding our matter."

"I have—very much."

He nodded in acknowledgment, although I could see him pondering. "Micht ye care tae elaborate upon whit else was spoken betwixt ye?"

"Well, I also told her that you are here with me to stay... and, that we're married even though we don't have any records to show for it."

"'Tis true that our accounts remain at *Taigh Gràs*. I huvnae any proof tae display of our wedding tae honor yer parents," he replied pensively. I sensed his earnest concern over it as his eyebrows drew together.

"But my mom suggested for us to marry again in spite of the fact that we already are—for official reasons that exist here. We could have a current certification of it so no one would have to worry about our legitimacy."

"Aye, of coorse. I do agree tae this validation. Yer parents' wishes are weighted and must be honored," he replied unquestionably. I nodded a little in accordance.

"It's a bit ironic," I expressed ungracefully at a sudden thought.

"How do ye mean?" His brow furrowed, appearing puzzled.

"The number of times we will have gotten married now."

"Och," he realized. "Be it as it will."

"Yeah," I replied, nodding. "You're right."

"In whit regard?"

"You told me that my family loves me."

"Was I mistaken?" A faint grin curled his lips and his eyes warmed with encouragement. I perceived the heartened expression on his face, and I smiled a little too.

"No—you weren't mistaken," I replied, shaking my head a bit.

"Then, ye mayn't worry henceforth. Whit will come of it otherwise?"

"Still."

"Aye?"

"Well, there is a dinner planned for next Friday when you'll meet them in depth."

"'Twill be my honor. I shall very much anticipate this affair, at last."

"Your confidence encourages me."

"Grant yer parents a bit of fair leeway. Ye may find yer concern is all fur naught."

"But I just can't help feeling nervous about it, though."

"Our meeting will fare accordingly."

"How are you so sure?"

"My inkling is that should yer mother be as fair as yerself, and if yer father micht be as agreeable as yer brother, then we shall all engage pleasantly."

I smiled gently at him, inspired by his optimism. "You once told me that I give you strength."

"I recall weel my saying so, fur ye do indeed provide me such grace."

"Well—you give me strength also," I said.

"A pleasure tae note." He gently grinned at me. "Ye also once said tae me that ye and I are a balanced union."

"I clearly remember that," I replied softly, suddenly feeling my cheeks grow warm as I was struck shy.

"Indisputably, we are," he reinforced in a tender voice. My lips automatically turned upward a little as I gazed correspondingly at him with a hint of bashfulness surfacing. He carefully raised a hand to my cheek and I sensed him warmly caressing it. He gazed steadily at me for a moment without either one of us saying a further word, and I perceived the support he was offering me in his vibrant eyes. I also saw devotion and warmth, and I smiled unevenly at him, aware of my attraction to him rising all over again.

"Well..." I began, lightly clearing my throat as I broke the small lull.

"Aye?" His hand slipped from my cheek and slid over my

shoulder, falling away from me as he maintained his unwavering gaze to mine.

"There are several errands I have to make—for the birthday party," I mentioned, noticing the flush in his cheeks.

"I shall escort ye," he offered politely.

"Thank you," I appreciated nicely.

"Certainly."

Turning from him now, I leaned to return the TV controller on the ottoman after turning it off, aware of him watching me. I sensed his silent eyes rolling down back, over my backside and linger while facing away from him, aware of the attraction between us, knowing he wanted to touch me. When I straightened from the ottoman and glanced at him again, our eyes met. A slow grin swept his lips and his eyes were soft.

"Must ye attire yerself in such breeks?" he asked candidly in a mild tone.

"A gown these days would be worse for me to wear," I replied sheepishly.

"In whit manner?"

"It would be as good as only wearing a shift."

"Tae our detriment?"

"Very much so. Don't you remember the way you kept ogling me in my dress the first time we'd met?"

"'Twould be precisely tae my detriment instead, apparently," he said, smiling at me.

"As revealing as they are to you, my pants keep us both safe from your wily distractions."

"My wily distractions?" He briskly chuckled, suddenly amused.

"Always," I giggled, enlivened by his reaction. "You're forbidden to try playing any of your games with me right now."

"Then, I am defeated," he replied, appearing playfully disappointed.

"Pull yourself together, soldier," I giggled again. His eyes abruptly widened and his upturned lips remained grinning. "Now, let's go." I gently snagged his fingers with mine, urging him to follow me out the room. The grin lingering on his lips spread distinctly across his face, and I reciprocated his smile as we left to complete my tasks, forgetting my troubles had existed at all.

Twenty-One

I drove us through parts of Los Angeles while making my errands to various stores to collect supplies for the kids' party. After obtaining snacks, fruit platters, drinks, balloons, party favors and stopping off at a local bakery to acquire the cake, we finally returned home where I started arranging things. The kids had early dismissal on Fridays, so I had to be certain that most of the arrangements were completed before we picked them up from school.

Balloons had been festively scattered throughout the ceilings on the first floor of the house, and Leif was fascinated by them floating everywhere. Occasionally, he tugged on a string to one balloon while sitting in a chair at the island facing me, and observed it bob up as it returned to the ceiling.

"Whit makes it buoyant?" he asked me, wondering in fascination.

"Well, it's filled with an element that's lighter than air called helium," I explained to him.

"Helium," he echoed curiously.

"Yes."

"Och," he responded blankly, not quite understanding the

concept as his brow lightly drew together. He released the string to the balloon he was toying with and let it bob up to the ceiling again, captivatingly observing it. After a minute of thoughtfully staring at it in silence, he returned looking at me and watched while I was in the process of making sangria for the adult guests. "Whit is it yoo're preparing?" he asked interestedly.

"Sangria. Here, please try some." I poured a bit of it into a glass that I'd swiftly retrieved from the fresh dishwasher for him to sample, and gave it to him as he remained sitting at the island in front of me. I also poured myself a small glass to taste test, and we watched each other sipping the beverage for a moment. "Well?" I asked, anticipatory, when he drew the glass from his lips.

"'Tis raither flavorful, indeed," he complimented, appearing pleased with a wink and smile.

"I'm glad that you like it," I replied, smiling back at him. His grin lingered as he continued drinking from his glass with eyes remaining on me. My gaze fell from his when I set my glass on the counter and proceeded slicing lemons, limes, and oranges to place inside the drink container with the sangria. As I worked, I was acutely reminded of the intensity of his penetrating eyes whenever he gazed at me. The look always compelled my shyness and deep attraction toward him, and the excitement I felt for him never failed to cause butterflies in my stomach as my cheeks warmed. I knew he could perceive me right now. I was feeling like a silly schoolgirl, to my embarrassment.

"'Tis quite an affair," he remarked as he was finishing his drink and observing all the prepared food spread over the countertops when he finally took his gaze off me.

"Yes, it is," I agreed.

"Micht this be a common presentation fur them?"

"Yes, it's an annual occasion that I do for them."

"A grand gesture toward our bairns."

"I can't help but to do it for them—they enjoy it so much," I replied, looking up from the fruit I was slicing, meeting his gaze. I smiled at him and his piercing eyes smiled back at me. The ruddiness in his masculine cheeks appeared, and I felt myself warming further by the discerning of his gaze adhering to mine. Awkwardness filled me with unexplained bashfulness and I nervously broke his gaze again as I glanced at the clock on the stove. But my attention compulsively returned to him, and the sultry grin remaining on his face continued making me aware of him observing me. "You're looking at me," I commented gently with an uneven little smile.

"I am," he admitted confidently.

"Why?"

"Ye ken why." The sensual grin crept over his face again, curving his soft-pink lips. I was aware of myself smiling in response as I dropped my shy gaze from his and returned to slicing the citrus fruit before me. Silence ensued between us while we proceeded quietly observing each other in familiar companionship, both aware of the powerful pull of our attraction for the other.

Once I had completed slicing all of the fruit, I turned from him at the island countertop to put the heap into the drink and placed the entire filled glass beverage dispenser into the refrigerator for it to chill. While it was set to chill, I requested his assistance outdoors on the back patio and we began arranging wooden child-sized rectangular tables and chairs that I had rented for the occasion. When they were nicely organized, we covered the tables with festive birthday printed tablecloths and finished their appearances with whimsical plastic jars of colorful rock candy centerpieces. As we concluded decorating the columns supporting the overhanging trellis beams with colorful pastel streamers, I grabbed my phone from my pocket, sensing the time, and looked at the clock.

"We should probably leave now in order to arrive at the kids' school in time for when they're dismissed," I suggested, noticing the time.

"As ye wish," Leif agreed readily.

So, we returned indoors and I gathered Yoda into my arms

from off the floor and snatched up my keys from the console table in the foyer, prepared to leave the house. Stepping outdoors from the front door, I locked the door behind us and we started on our walk together for school.

ARRIVING A LITTLE EARLY BEFORE THE DISMISSAL BELL rang, we were going to wait with other parents who had also come at this time to pick up their kids from school. As we approached the picnic tables, Heather, Autumn, and Dave were already engaged in light conversation when they noticed us and waved for us to join them. When Leif and I arrived at my friends, Dave turned toward Leif and struck up an easy conversation about the weather and sports. Given Leif was unfamiliar with American pop-culture and sports, instead of discussing, he politely listened instead as Dave mostly carried the conversation—which seemed not to faze Dave since he was naturally verbose.

Tuning in a little onto their discussion as Heather and Autumn continued with their own conversation, I discreetly observed Leif seeming interested in what Dave was saying to him when he intermittently asked Dave curious questions regarding his chosen topic of conversation—that being the sport of baseball. Leif cordially nodded in response as he tried understanding Dave's interest in the sport, and Dave appeared encouraged to explain more about it to him. When I returned my attention to Heather and Autumn, I realized they'd been watching me also when they both smiled simultaneously as I looked at them. I smiled back at them, and their curiosity over the kids' puppy I was holding resumed.

The dismissal bell finally rang, and the children began emerging from their classroom building. As the group of children approached us to sit on the picnic benches according to Ms. Lambert's instructions, they had become easily distracted due to the new puppy I was holding in my arms. Instead, the entire class of children began swarming around me like guppies in order to catch a glimpse of Yoda and to pet him. Little Leif and Leila instantly noticed me also and rushed in my direction with their friends, eager to share Yoda with them.

"I'm sorry for the distraction," I apologized to Ms. Lambert.

"A puppy, huh?" she replied, giving me a wan smile.

"Yeah, my parents gave him to the kids for their birthday," I said.

"How sweet. Well, you beat me. I can't top a puppy," she joked. I giggled, and she smiled as she turned to instruct the children to be careful, and to also calm themselves, while they excitedly surrounded the little animal.

After each child had the happy opportunity to pet Yoda, I finally gathered Little Leif and Leila from the benches where they'd gathered with their friends, before Leif and I started away from the school grounds with our kids. As we started away from the benches, the kids and Ms. Lambert waved goodbye to each other. Then, we proceeded making our way off campus through the parking lot and onto the sidewalk. Heading for home now, the kids romped with each other along the way while pacing slightly ahead of us. They were happy. And, so was I.

"Thanks for bringing Yoda, Mom," Little Leif said cheerfully to me.

"You're welcome, sweetie," I replied.

"Can I hold him?" he asked eagerly.

"Sure, you may. Just be careful not to drop him."

"Okay. I'll be very careful." He reached up to take him from my grasp, and I leaned to place the puppy securely into his arms. During the whole walk home, the kids cheerfully expressed to us the events of their day while in school, along with their excited anticipation for their quickly approaching party this afternoon.

Twenty-Two

Guests began arriving promptly on the hour for the party, and our house quickly took on the noisy air of festive excitement while kids cheerfully ran throughout the house amid conversations between congregated parents. As I was in the kitchen refilling large bowls with tortilla and potato chips, and replenishing salsa and hummus in smaller serving dishes, I noticed Leif had disappeared among the many guests crowded around me in the kitchen. A little concerned about it, when I had finished replenishing snack trays and speaking with several parents about soccer games and karate classes, I went to search for him.

Suddenly thinking he had become overwhelmed with so many strangers around, I regretted having left him to mingle on his own. He had little yet in common with my friends and acquaintances that I didn't wish for him to feel any more pressured to be charismatic, since I was certain he was feeling well out of his element to fit in.

Having a strong hunch of where he might be found, I went upstairs and headed toward our bedroom. Arriving at the closed door and opening it, I stepped passed the threshold into the room and discovering him comfortably seated on the spacious window bench, petting the puppy in his lap.

"Hey," I acknowledged carefully, closing the door behind me.

"Hullo, *ceisdein*," he said, immediately lifting his gaze from Yoda to me. He seemed a little surprised that I had found him in here by his slightly raised brow.

"Are you all right?" I asked concernedly, pacing toward him.

"Aye, I am," he said certainly.

"Then, why are you here all by yourself?" I asked strangely.

"I brought the puppy into our bedchamber, so he wulnae be trampled by the guests," he said.

"Oh. That's a very considerate idea," I realized.

"Aye. He's wee and the bairns waur startling him by their fondness fur him. They wouldnae let him be. Therefore, a respite fur him is in order."

"Thank you so much for rescuing him."

"Aye, of coorse."

"So, how's the puppy doing now?" I inquired, seating myself beside him on the bench.

"He appears tranquil presently."

"Oh, good. I'm relieved."

Leif dropped his gaze toward Yoda as I moved a caressing palm over the animal's soft head and proceeded petting him while Leif also gently rubbed his paw. "Whaur ye in search of me?" he asked, returning a steady gaze toward me.

"Yeah, I was," I admitted, looking at him again.

"Is thaur anything the matter?"

"No—well, I mean, I thought there might be something wrong—with you."

"A matter with me?"

"Yeah," I replied, nodding.

"Why micht thaur be any matter with me?"

"Well—I thought that you were escaping."

"Fleeing?"

"Yeah."

"From whit or waur?" His brow furrowed slightly.

"From here."

"Whyever micht I?" I shrugged a little, observing the confused look on his face mixed with surprise. "I didnae ken that I was a captive," he joked, now grinning at me. "Pray, forgive me. I am indeed yer servant."

I smiled back at him and benignly said, "That's not what I meant."

"Then, whit micht ye mean?" he asked curiously.

"I was thinking that you might be eluding the guests," I clarified.

"The guests?" His brow slightly drew together again.

"Yeah." I nodded a little.

"Och. Pray, forgive my slight. It is not intended in the merest," he apologized.

"It's okay. I don't feel that you're being at all rude. I understand if you need a break from being around so many people you're not acquainted with all at once," I replied sympathetically.

"I beg yer pardon, *ceisdein*."

"No, it's okay. I really understand."

"I fear not."

"What do you mean?"

"I reckon that I have been mistaken. I am not seeking refuge from yer guests, *mo ghaol*. 'Tis as I said, that I merely entered our bedchamber tae safeguard this besieged puppy. That is all," he explained.

"Oh."

"Aye."

"I was thinking that you might be feeling overwhelmed with everything new around you."

"I see."

"Yes. So, I was just making sure you're all right."

"Yer world is all quite novel tae me, tae be certain. Yet, I am faring weel. Thaur isnae any need fur yer over concern of me. I assure ye that I am alrecht. Although, I am heartened by yer consideration, and I thank ye all the same fur it."

"You're sure you're okay, then?" I continued regardless, to be completely certain.

"Indeed. All is weel," he assured. I smiled at him again, glad that he felt this way.

"You're incredibly brave. I was terrified when I was out of my element in your time," I said, remembering.

"I recall how fearful ye waur, indeed. I deeply regret that ye waur ever imperiled," he replied. "It ails me that ye remain burdened by this recollection."

"It doesn't bother me so much anymore since it was a while ago. But, I'm especially able to think less about it, because you're here with me now."

"I am rewarded by the affection ye still hold fur me."

"Well, of course I'll always love you. You know that," I said gently.

"Ye swore it tae me."

"I did—because it's true."

"Aye." He grinned affectionately at me and I reciprocated with a gentle smile too. "I have never looved any other lass but ye."

"I haven't loved any man the way I love you."

"Then, we remain."

"Nothing's changed."

"I perceive it. Forever bound are we."

"Forever." I smiled again at him, deeply feeling the distinct connection between us. "So..."

"Aye?"

"I just don't want you feeling overwhelmed and alone here, that's all."

"I am nae longer alone, *mo ghaol*. My heart rejoices, presently."

"Mine too."

"I perceive it in yer bonnie eyes," he said. "Yet, 'tis as I have said

—that thaur isnae any reason fur concern in my regard. Whilst indeed I am apart from whit is common tae me, my experience with ye haur is one of a different nature than from yers whence the time we had met. Instead, I am welcomed haur without suspicion or qualm. Thus, I dinnae fear that I am in any jeopardy. I beg tae differ from yer claim that I am brave, since I have landed in yer realm when all that I have done is rescuing this poor puppy." He grinned at me again, and I couldn't help the tender smile spreading my lips.

"But you are brave—for many reasons," I said, returning to being more serious. "The fact you're a warrior—that you've rescued me from harm numerous times. But most recently, you've risked yourself by traveling through time not knowing what to expect, or where you might land in order to be with me again. You're incredibly brave, Leif. More than anyone."

"I merely do whit is demanded of me, *mo ghaol*. That we remain together is paramount tae my existence, aside from my praising God," he said sincerely. I nodded a little, giving him a smile once more. I observed him carefully remove Yoda from his lap and place the baby animal gently on the floor. The puppy trotted toward the tufted area rug and comfortably lay himself over it. "Now that the wee pup appears weel contented, I shall withdraw from the bedchamber tae better acquaint myself with the lads." He straightened from the window bench and reached for my hand, collecting it into his. He lightly pulled me up to my feet and now I stood close before him. "All is weel," he repeated encouragingly and bestowed a small kiss over my knuckles. I smiled, reassured, and he winked at me, causing me to giggle a little.

"Let's go," I said, softly grinning at him.

"Your Grace," he replied politely, gesturing with his hand for me to lead the way for us out of the bedroom. I curtsied before him, then turned for the door. Reaching for the knob, he opened it for me and I stepped out the room into the hallway. Closing the door after us, he followed me through the corridor, leaving Yoda safely concealed from the company. Striding through the hall, we came downstairs together where he separated from me to mingle with the guests.

So, I returned making my rounds throughout the house to restore empty food trays with fruit, dips, and chips. While I was replenishing fruit platters over the dining room table, unbeknownst to several discussing mothers congregated by the sliding glass doors overlooking the patio in the backyard, I overheard some of their gossip.

"Yeah, she's married," Maria confirmed easily while gazing out the windows, locating her daughter playing on the swing.

"She is?" another mother named Jasmine responded, obviously surprised.

"Yeah, even Heather didn't know that she was married until yesterday when she first met her husband," Maria said, turning her gaze toward Heather standing in their circle.

"Yeah, I didn't know," Heather confirmed, shrugging her shoulders, as their shocked and inquisitive eyes turned toward her.

"You and Sylvie talk a lot, don't you, though?" Maria asked, apparently curious.

"Yeah, we do," Heather said.

"See? I told you. They're best friends out of all of us. So, if anybody would've known anything about them getting back together, it would be Heather. Weren't you so surprised when she told you about him?" Maria asked interestedly.

"Of course, I was. As shocked as all of you guys are now," Heather admitted.

"So, what did you say to her when she told you about him before you met him?" Jasmine inquired.

"I didn't know what to say, actually—except just to be encouraging for her, really," Heather replied.

"What was it like when she introduced him to you, though?" Jasmine continued inquisitively.

"Obviously, I was stunned to suddenly meet him when she

brought him to school with her the other day. And, when she told me that they'd eloped—well—I couldn't have been more surprised," Heather answered.

"I was shocked too," Autumn said also.

"Yeah, she never once told me a thing about her relationship with him since I've known her. So, I had just as well assumed they had a bad relationship that ended on bad terms, and that's why she never mentioned him. Too painful—you know?" Heather responded.

"I get that," Maria said objectively.

"So, were they separated because it was bad and they suddenly decided to reconcile after so long?" Jasmine inquired strangely.

"She said it was the long distance that kept them apart, actually," Heather informed her.

"Oh. But if it was only the distance that was the problem, couldn't they've worked it out, regardless? I mean that sounds like an excuse to me not to commit," Jasmine said suspiciously.

"He's from Scotland," Heather informed her.

"So? Obviously, they managed to date each other despite where he's from. I mean they could've just stayed together if they wanted to. Right? They could've just chosen which part of the globe they were going to commit to live together. It would've seemed," Jasmine said realistically.

"Maybe she didn't want to leave her family to be with him. She's very close to her family, you know," Heather speculated.

"Or, maybe he's also close to his family and didn't want to move across the Atlantic. That would be a huge move," Maria acknowledged accordingly.

"Yeah," Heather agreed, nodding her head.

"Sure, it's a huge move. But if he really loved her, I think he would've followed her here, and would've committed to her earlier," Jasmine said skeptically.

"Well, he did eventually follow her here—and he married her.

So, I don't think he's a bad guy. Some guys just need time to reflect, actually," Heather said.

"Reflect for four years? C'mon, who are you kidding? I'm not saying he's a bad guy, but any guy who takes that long to commit likely prefers to play around," Jasmine determined.

"Well, I don't think she would've eloped with him if she felt that she couldn't trust him—especially because of how protective she is over her kids. She's never once dated *anyone* since I've known her. Let alone ever casually admit that she found any strange guy was good-looking in passing," Heather countered.

"Speaking of good-looking, he's definitely got a sexy accent to match his looks. Perfect eye candy if you ask me," Maria giggled.

"Wait. You've met him too?" Jasmine responded surprisedly, shifting her eyes toward Maria.

"Yeah, yesterday," Maria said.

"I guess I'm late to the game, then. I have no idea what he even looks like," Jasmine replied.

"You can catch a glimpse of him right over there," Autumn informed Jasmine, pointing toward the large window before them in the direction across the backyard lawn at the stone laid fire pit where her husband, Glen, stood talking with Leif. Jasmine peered through the window at the outdoor crowd and spotted them.

While Maria was a widow, who didn't date much, Jasmine was a divorcé who sprung free from a noncommittal marriage she blamed on her ex-husband, and was definitely on the prowl for excitement with any guy she found interesting and attractive.

"Wow! He *is* hot," Jasmine confirmed. Giggles fluttered between them.

"He kinda looks like a young Paul Newman, I think. But he's got a more impressive physique. I bet he's rebellious with that long hair of his too," Autumn agreed.

"He sure does. He's totally gorgeous," Jasmine confirmed as her gaze locked onto Leif.

"You know what's kinda funny, though?" Heather asked.

"What?" Jasmine asked, maintaining her attention on Leif.

"Sylvie, looks really similar to Elizabeth Taylor, only tanned," Heather remarked.

"Oh yeah! She does. Did you ever see *Cat on a Hot Tin Roof*?" Maria asked agreeably.

"Yeah, I've seen it. A very long time ago, though," Heather replied with Maria's enthusiasm.

"Maybe they shared the same disfunction in their relationship also," Jasmine said pessimistically.

"Don't be such a downer, Jasmine," Maria chided.

"Well? He could be like the character, Brick, in the story, you know?" Jasmine justified.

"He hardly has that kind of disposition from what I can tell when I'd spoken with him," Heather said.

"Then what's he like?" Jasmine asked curiously with her gaze still frozen on Leif.

"He just seems really reserved," Heather noted.

"Like how?" Jasmine asked.

"He seems extremely old fashioned. Very polite, really," Heather said.

"I'd say more old worldly," Maria said, giving her opinion.

"That's sexy. Don't find many men like that these days. Unless, he's a prude," Jasmine laughed suddenly, and Maria giggled.

"He doesn't look *anything* like a prude," Autumn contradicted, and more laughter sputtered around.

"So, what's his name?" Jasmine asked curiously.

"Seamus," Heather informed her.

"Nice. So, he's her kids' father..." Jasmine commented thinkingly, realizing the fact.

"Yeah, obviously Leif looks just like Seamus," Maria remarked.

"Yeah, he does," Heather agreed. "Leila looks more like Sylvie, though."

"Yeah, she's totally adorable," Autumn said.

"I think so too," Heather agreed. "Well, if anything, I really do hope it works out between the both of them."

"We'll see. As they say—time will tell. I just know that if her situation had been mine, I would've never let a guy like him leave my sight. All is fair in love and war," Jasmine declared.

"Go take a cold shower, Jasmine," Maria teased, inciting laughter to escape from the surrounding women. Jasmine suddenly shifted her gaze from Leif to Maria.

"You're one to talk, Maria," Jasmine scoffed.

"I'm not the cougar, remember?" Maria joked.

"Cougar?" Jasmine replied exceptionally.

"Yup," Maria said.

"He was twenty-one," Jasmine justified.

"You'll be thirty-nine next month," Maria reminded, smirking at her. Jasmine scowled and giggles flittered around the group, at which point I decided to finish replacing the fruit platter over the dining room table and discreetly left the room. Somewhat surprised by their conversation, I nevertheless expected that I'd be the center of their gossip at one point, and although I supposed that I should have been uneasy about it, I found that I really didn't care. Leif and I were together again, and I was immensely happy about it. Nothing, or anyone could ever dampen this reality—or drive a wedge between us—I believed.

When retreating from the dining room, I unexpectedly bumped into Dave as he was coming through the threshold.

"Hey, great party," he said enthusiastically.

"Thanks," I replied cheerfully.

"Yeah, Jake is having a good time," he said about his son.

"I'm so glad."

"Where's Seamus? Couldn't find him anywhere a second ago. I'd like to talk some more baseball with him. He seemed interested in it when we were talking about it earlier at school. Thought he might consider Little League for Leif some time, if you'd both be interested."

"Oh, sure. He's outside right now talking with Glen."

"Great. I'll catch up with them."

"Sure."

"See ya," Dave said genially and passed by me when I heard the doorbell ring. I rushed in the opposite direction to answer the front door. It was the pizza-man delivering our large pies, and he helpfully brought them into the kitchen for me. After tipping him and as he was leaving, Leila promptly appeared beside me with her friends, excited and very ready to eat as I was proceeding to bring forth the disposable plates.

"Why don't you and your friends let everyone know that pizza's here," I said to her.

"Yippee! Okay!" she expressed cheerfully and ran out of the kitchen with her friends. It wasn't long before all the children had gathered around the stretched tables out on the patio and seated themselves in their small chairs as Maria, Heather, Jasmine, and Autumn began helping me serve them pizza slices.

When I had finished pouring the children petite cups of lemonade, I happened to glance up from the last cup I was pouring and noticed Leif gazing at me with an ale in hand as he was leaning against the door frame to the sliding glass doors belonging to the living room. He furtively grinned at me, and I reciprocated before turning away for the kitchen to organize the rest of the pizzas to serve the adult guests.

Once the adults had been served their slices with sangria, ale or beer and settled down either eating with their children, or with other parents, Leif appeared into the kitchen as I was stacking empty pizza boxes over the counter.

"Hi," I said, glad to see him.

"Hullo, *ceisdein*," he replied mildly as he moved toward the island where I was standing with the pizza boxes.

"How are you enjoying the kids' birthday party?" I asked, observing him bringing the rim of his ale bottle to his lips and sipping.

"'Tis a merry affair," he said after drawing the bottle away from his mouth and swallowing.

"I'm glad you think so," I replied. "Have you eaten yet?"

"Nae." He shook his head a tad.

"Oh. Well, would you like a slice of pizza?"

"Is it whit all are eating?"

"Yes."

"Then, I shall take it."

"Sure." I moved to collect a paper plate from the corner of the island and placed a large slice of cheese pizza from one of the boxes that still had a pie in it. I handed the plate to him and he simply stared at it for a second, seeming a little baffled. "You eat it with your hands," I encouragingly informed him, discerning the questioning look on his face.

"Och," he realized immediately as I decided to snatch a slice for myself, feeling quite hungry also, and took a healthy bite out of it. Leif's eyes abruptly widened when he saw me carelessly chomp down on my piece, then grinned at me, amused. "Yoo're famished," he joked lightly.

"Yes, I am," I giggled a little, nodding in accordance while chewing.

"As am I," he admitted and took a large, ripping bite out of his slice of pizza also. I watched him chewing and swallowing his food, and smiled at him as I continued eating mine. An eyebrow arched over his eye as he considered what he was eating, and he grinned again when he took another big bite. We quietly observed each other eating for a moment as guests' voices resonated from outside into the kitchen where we were standing. Within a minute, Leif had devoured his full pizza slice, to my surprise, before I had completed mine.

"You like pizza as much as the kids do," I remarked jokingly.

"Aye, 'tis unusually palatable," he agreed, and helped himself to another slice. He took a swig of ale again, then bit into his pizza enjoying a second slice. Sipping more of my sangria, I continued finishing my own piece when our son entered the kitchen with his friends.

"Mom, when can we do the piñata?" he asked excitedly. I glanced at the clock on the stove, realizing it was growing late in the day.

"Let's have cake first. Then, we can do the piñata," I recommended.

"Yay!" he cheered.

"Are you ready for cake now?"

"Yup!" he said eagerly.

"All right, I'll be there in a jiffy. Let everyone know that we're having cake soon."

"Okay!" He and his excited friends promptly turned out of the kitchen as they hastily dashed returning outdoors, where everyone was still gathered at the tables.

"Whit is a piñata?" Leif strangely asked me.

"It's a paper mache creation filled with candy, and it's used for a game where the kids hit it with a stick while blindfolded, until all of the candy spills out of it. Then, all the children grab as much candy as they can get to eat," I explained.

"Curious," he responded with a quizzically interested look on his face. I smiled at him as I moved to unbox the marble-fudge buttercream cake with Star Wars and Hello Kitty toppers, and placed candles on it, to his intrigue. When I was finished arranging the candles, Leif helpfully collected the large cake from the counter for me upon my request, and we went outside together with him following me until I suggested the area for him to place it on one of the tables. He mindfully set it over the table where our kids had been sitting, and they happily cheered when they recognized their pretty cake. After promptly lighting the candles, all the guests sang the birthday song to our children.

Once Little Leif and Leila simultaneously blew out their candles to everyone's applause, the cake was promptly sliced and served for everyone's enjoyable consumption before finally hitting the piñata, to all of the kids' delight.

The party lasted well into the evening with some guests remaining as they continued relaxing in the yard in chairs beneath the trellis, or by the fire pit. At this time, light conversation persisted and nice mingling between parents took place with drinks. Little Leif and Leila continued playing with their friends outside in the dark on the swing-set, or inside their playroom while Leif and I sat with our guests surrounding the flaming fire pit. The conversation turned toward sports, light banter and politics between the men, and the women discussed their careers and their kids. While discussions were taking place around us, however, I noticed Leif mostly listening with interest as he reservedly sat beside me. Although he was observant, he seemed relaxed and interested by the people around him, and I believed he was enjoying himself as he learned more about them.

It wasn't until close to eleven o'clock, though, when our remaining guests finally left our house for their own. Once the house had emptied and settled from company, I decided to promptly bathe the kids to ready them for bed. But prior to tucking them in for the night, they begged to open their presents before going to sleep. Having the heart, I allowed them to do so on this occasion and within minutes, their gifts had been delightedly unwrapped.

When we finished admiring their presents, with their father's curiosity included, I tucked them into bed and was glad to bring myself also to rest for the evening, at last.

Twenty-Three

I awakened sometime in the middle of the night to check on the kids as they slept in their bedroom. After covering them again with blankets they'd accidentally kicked off while sleeping, I left their room for my own. When I returned into my room and began entering into bed again, I noticed Leif was now gone from the covers. Glancing toward the bathroom, noticing it unlit and vacant, I realized he'd left the room.

Curious to know where he'd gone, I removed myself from bed and as I was pacing for the door, I caught a glimpse out the window and saw him standing outside in the backyard. He was bathed in moonlight, dressed in a robe, and appeared as a sculpture while standing still, save for the breeze animating the hem of his robe. He was simply gazing up toward the sky at the moon. I moved from the window and continued toward the door, leaving the bedroom for the staircase.

When I arrived downstairs, I proceeded through the hallway and entered the living room. The sliding glass doors to the backyard were already open, letting in the temperate night air and light breeze which stirred the linen drapes. As I came through the opening between the doors, I entered outside beneath the trellis onto the patio and stole beside him standing close by the edge of the lawn. He didn't seem aware of me until I lightly slipped my hand onto his firm bicep, distracting his attention from the moonlit sky, finally.

"Och, hullo, *àille dhubh*. I believed ye waur asleep," he said, appearing a little startled to see me as he stiffened and swung his gaze down toward me from the sky.

"I just awakened to check on the kids," I informing him.

"Och," he realized, immediately relaxing to my touch now.

"Why are you up?" I wondered curiously.

"I cannae sleep," he answered.

"Why?" I looked at him with some concern. He shrugged a little. "Are you all right?"

"I merely cannae rest."

"Oh. Is there something on your mind?"

"Ye mean am I troobled?"

"Yeah."

"I cannae say that I quite am. Merely, mayhap a bit of rum micht soothe me tae rest at last."

I glanced around at the illuminating street lights surrounding us, and assumed maybe they might be the matter causing him to remain awake. Then, a jetliner loudly flew overhead, making me also consider that the air traffic from the airport quite possibly stimulated him from sleeping.

"Sure, I'll bring a glass for you," I responded, agreeing to his request. I remembered purchasing a bottle of rum for him when we made errands earlier during the day for the kids' birthday party. So, I left him to go inside for the kitchen. Promptly locating the rum tucked in the corner on one of the counters when arriving into the kitchen, I retrieved a glass tumbler from the cupboard and poured him some of the liquor. When I returned outside, I found him in the same place where he had been left still gazing up at the night sky.

"Why can I not see the stars?" he asked oddly as he received his filled glass from me.

"The city lights are so abundant and bright that they reflect in the night sky and drown out the stars' brilliance," I said.

"Och…" He took a large swig of rum from his glass.

"Come on," I hinted suddenly, stepping away from where he stood, urging him to follow me deeper into the backyard.

"Whaur micht we go?" he inquired as he began striding after me.

"Let's relax by the pool," I suggested simply. He strode with me past the lawn and fire pit until we entered the gated pool area. Strolling over the cemented deck, I chose a spot to sit near the edge of the pool and slipped my bare feet over the ridge into the lukewarm water. He moved to sit himself close beside me, adjusting the length of his silk robe and dipped his bare feet into the water also.

The pool lights were on and glowed beneath the water, making it appear like neon turquoise. We silently gazed up at the sky together, picking out what few stars we could still see while admiring the brightly shining moon. The atmosphere around us was quiet and tranquil, except for the occasional jetliner flying in its flight path over us as it was landing, disrupting the placidness in the air.

Leif glanced away from the moon for a moment when he took another swig from his glass, seeming to enjoy his rum.

"How does it taste?" I inquired simply, observing him drink.

"It has an irregular flavor. Not as pungent. Nonetheless, raither pleasant," he answered easily.

"Oh," I replied, smiling at him.

"Micht ye care fur a bit?" he offered politely.

"Sure," I accepted, curious to understand what he meant, though it remained not my preferred drink. He passed his glass to me and I took a little sip. Still not an avid alcohol connoisseur anyway, I nevertheless recognized this rum was smooth and not as potent as the kind I had remembered drinking when I was with him in the eighteenth century.

"Weel? How do ye fancy it?" he asked interestedly, once I'd swallowed it.

"You're right. It's different." I nodded in agreement, wincing a little, not liking the hard taste of liquor. "It's one of the best Jamaican rums I found," I mentioned with a scratchy voice.

"Is thaur more than one sort?" he inquired curiously.

"Yes, a number of different styles and brands," I informed him.

"This land is full of plenty," he remarked, impressed.

"Self-enterprise is the reason," I replied. He nodded a tad in response, and took another swig, enjoying the taste.

It became quiet for a moment between us as we sat companionably with each other in the dark, now observing our feet slowly swirling in the glowing pool water. He took his time savoring his rum while I silently watched my gently moving feet beneath the water, entranced by the way they moved beneath the surface as I enjoyed the resistance the water created against them. I sensed Leif watching my feet too as I slowly moved them around.

"Were you thinking of home when you were first standing on the patio looking up at the moon?" I asked him, breaking the silence between us.

"Aye," he said.

"You miss it, then," I acknowledged, turning my eyes toward him. He placed his glass down beside himself on the deck and fastened his eyes to mine.

"I mean tae take ye and the bairns with me tae *Taigh Gràs*," he disclosed carefully, though sounding definitive. Despite discerning some of consternation on his face, I also perceived his compassion for me. Still, I was immediately worried.

"You do?" I knew he would eventually say this, and I was scared that he had, hoping all along the idea didn't exist. Afraid of how strongly he felt about this prospect despite experiencing the advantages my world had to offer us, seriously disturbed me. Also, since I'd told my parents that he was here to stay with us, giving them the impression that we'd never leave them, pierced me with sudden alarm.

"I wholly wish it. Ye and the bairns belong thaur with me," he said honestly, gazing earnestly at me.

"I see..." My heart sank with worry and I felt my brow knitting.

"Yet—" he started but interrupted himself, as I perceived him carefully forming his thoughts.

"But what?" I pressed pensively.

"I ken that I cannae merely retrieve ye from haur as soon as I wish," he said. "Yer family ought tae be considered as I am weel awaur. We must inform them delicately. I am certain they will miss ye—"

"Yes—very much," I interrupted, maintaining his gaze cemented to mine.

"I am also awaur that our bairns together are very weel within yer family's care. Although, 'tis in a manner uncommon tae me," he said, also realizing this truth. I nodded in acknowledgement, and he paused thinkingly. "Ye do understand that my utmost concern is the welfare of my family?"

"Yes. I know. So is mine." I nodded again.

"Aye. Of coorse." He nodded accordingly also. "However, I intend tae have my family return with me tae *Taigh Gràs.*"

"Why? I'm curious and would like to know."

"'Twould be fur the best."

"I understand your wish. But is returning to *Taigh Gràs* the most prudent thing to do?" I asked worriedly.

"It is," he replied, convinced.

"But you literally just arrived here and we're finally together after so long. I fear that you haven't given this era a chance to live in, yet. We could be happy here. There are so many advantages to living here that can't be provided for in the past," I tried explaining.

"Aye, so it appears. Despite it, I am of strong mind that returning us would be tae our truest benefit," he said.

"Would it?"

"Without a question."

"I'll say you're right on a very important account which should weigh differently on your wish."

"Whit micht it be?"

"Our kids will miss my family, tremendously, since they've known them their entire lives and have never been apart from them —ever. And considering this fact, the adjustment for them to leave my family in order to live centuries ago could be harmful to them. I mean, also consider the medical disadvantages they would experience if we lived at *Taigh Gràs*, at least."

"Aye," he said thoughtfully, looking intently at me which carried his sensitivity toward me clearly expressed on his face. "Nonetheless, I have gravely pondered it, *mo ghaol*. Yet, I remain persuaded that the benefit outmeasures the drawback." He became silent as he continued thinkingly gazing at me.

"How? Our wellbeing could be jeopardized if we go. How could you protect us if that's the case?" I said.

"I grant yer assertion. However, thaur seems tae be perils with all occurrences. Regardless, I remain a capable man who can protect his family. As far as warding off illness, I reckon ye have the wit tae safeguard us in that respect," he replied respectively.

"With what materials?"

"With materials which already exist in the past."

"But, they're archaic and not precise ones that have been invented yet."

"Have ye not considered the nature of endangerments which may befall us upon any practical occasion? Let us not live our lives determined by fear, but be brave tae live at all."

"But, why increase the risk to our lives by returning to the past when it's safer here?"

"Is this place such a refuge?"

"Compared to the past, I believe so, yes."

"Let the Lord Almighty forbid, I may be trampled by horses whilst crossing a street within the year of our Lord seventeen sixty-eight, and ye may be overrun by a horseless carriage of a sort within this current year. Therefore, the risk tae our lives is similar," he reasoned. "Furthermore, micht ye be concerned over the war with France, ye neednae worry as it is done. The war is over. It has been fur five years yet. Tell me, has all war ceased tae exist in this era?"

"No," I confessed, shaking my head a little.

What about the impending Revolutionary War, though? And, the Yellow Fever outbreak? What about the other diseases? Smallpox? Plus, no kid should have to live through war. It's one thing to be removed from it because of media, but quite a different situation when it's experienced in your own back yard.

So many precarious thoughts swirled in my head, and I was on the cusp of telling him.

"Precisely. The world still battles—so I have read within plenty of yer broadsheets," he continued justifying, stopping me instead. "Whit about famine and disease, has it all been eradicated from Earth? I fear not. Fur I have seen suffering exists still in this new world as we rode through this great metropolis. Nae matter how great or minute, risks do indeed currently prevail. Any little peril can cause great tragedy. Thus, I am much inclined tae risk ourselves in my era whaur I can see tae our safety and happiness."

"So, you see yourself not being happy here?" I asked sadly.

"I am certain, fur as long as I remain haur in this future century, that I shan't have the ability tae acquire my proper position within this society. I am yer provider and protector, Sylvie. I am ignorant in the ways of this society. I huvnea any means or clout. How shall I endeavor?"

"But, I'm a professional. I have a medical career that can support us," I countered realistically, sounding hopeful.

"Nae," he said, shaking his head, disagreeing.

"Why? When it's true that I can sustain us?"

"Micht it be practical, however?"

"I think so."

"Truly think on it. Is it?" he pressed honestly. My brows furrowed as I really thought about it. "Thaur is a true burden that cannae be disregarded."

"But I'm not complaining—and I won't complain if I'm the sole breadwinner between us."

"Yet, ye will," he contradicted.

"I think that I will be able to manage it, though."

"Nae. I dinnae concur. The notion of it has not been realized by ye. Therefore, ye speak imaginatively and without truly knowing."

"Well, I think that I might have some idea about it since I've been managing alone with the kids for a number of years now," I differed.

"I reckon resentment may settle within yer spirit if my mouth waur added tae be fed," he said candidly.

"I would be willing to—"

"Hear me forth," he interrupted. "Consider that I am my own man, firstly. I am not reliant—particularly upon my wife. I am abled bodied and more than willing tae tend tae my family. Need I tell ye that my dukedom remains intact? Fur indeed it does. I am landed and I am immensely wealthy. Thaur isnae a reason within the wide world why I cannae, and ought not, provide fur ye when I can. The burden tae bear fur our family isnae yers but mine. So long as I draw breath."

"Then, you could never be happy here," I realized, feeling gravely downhearted.

"I shall flounder before I fail," he said bluntly. I suddenly became quiet, distressed about the unfortunate situation we were now in. "I must also return tae Amity, lest we forget."

"I know," I muttered, reminded. I swallowed hard. "How soon must you see her again?"

"Mayhap, not till we wed—fur yer family's sake," he said contemplatively.

"After that happens, is that around the time you were thinking we'd leave for *Taigh Gràs*?" I asked somberly.

"We huvnea yet arranged fur the wedding, have we?"

"We haven't," I replied. Knowing he preferred to have a priest officiate instead of a judge at the courthouse, I wasn't sure how soon we could have a wedding. "I'll need to speak with Father Hanley who knows me well, from the church I used to attend before my current one and that my parents still belong to, about scheduling a time for it. I know weddings and baptisms are booked far in advance. So, I'm not certain about how soon we can have a ceremony."

"In which case, once we have spoken tae the priest, we shall proceed accordingly with our return," he said pensively. "I am weel awaur that ye will miss yer family, Sylvie. Yet, all isnae lost."

"What do you mean?"

"I perceive that ye are in need of my reminding ye that because of yer wondrous instrument, time fur our sake may be managed. Therefore, we may return tae visit yer family at any moment we so choose. Consider this fact, and merely think upon the notion of our family living at *Taigh Gràs* with the opportunity fur our return haur again. Will ye not also contemplate this?"

I just stared at him in silence, knowing that he could perceive me thinking along with the worry and dejection on my face.

"Will ye not ponder it?" he asked again, waiting for my response.

"I'll think about it," I agreed quietly.

"Fine," he said, nodding his head a little.

Silence drifted into existence and ensued between us as our eyes lingered on each other's for a thoughtful moment. The other's willingness to understand and for the happiness we both desired to maintain between us was perceivable.

I broke away from his gaze and quietly watched my feet

swirling around beneath the water for a minute longer when I felt his gaze finally turning down toward my feet also. We both silently observed my swimming toes when I thought about submerging myself entirely into the pool to simply drown away my conflicted heart. The urge to distract myself from thinking anymore about our conversation overcame me. So, without a care, I withdrew my chemise off my body and slipped into the lukewarm water, submerging myself, completely.

"Whit are ye about, Sylvie?" Leif asked strangely, wondering what I was doing.

"I want to swim for a bit," I replied, swimming away from him at the edge. He didn't respond as I kept breaststroking farther from him toward the opposite end of the pool. The water felt cool against my naked flesh, and the feeling was nice as I moved across the area. I was glad to escape from the depth of our discussion, needing the diversion to settle my worry and pacify my mood.

As I reached the deep end at the opposite side, I grappled the ledge and turned my gaze toward where I'd left him. Discovering he had disrobed also and had slipped into the water after me, he was already swimming in my direction. When he arrived close to me, he snagged my waist, wrapping a muscular arm around it. Tugging me close against his naked body, I naturally encircled my legs around his lean hips. I could feel him formidable, and erect as he pressed himself between my thighs.

"You caught me," I said unevenly, smiling a little at him.

"Indeed, I have, *àille dhubh*," he replied in a low voice, smiling a bit too. He proceeded moving us toward shallower water. Wrapping my arms around his neck, my breasts pressed against his broad, sculpted chest as the water gently eddied around us. Guiding us toward the side edge of the pool where he ceased us, he gently pushed my back against the wall and supported me in his enfolding arms. I lessened my grip around his neck and eased slightly backward to look directly into his eyes. "Whit sort of game are ye inciting, siren?"

"I'm not playing any games," I said softly.

"Are ye not?"

"No. I'm not." I shook my head a little.

"Then, explain yerself."

"I just wanted a swim to relax me. That's all."

"Dinnae fret, *ceisdein*. I wulnae stand fur yer heart tae be in woe."

"Except, it is."

"Permit me tae assuage it."

"Okay."

"Whit will ye have me do tae ease yer spirit?"

"I suppose anything you can think of will make me feel better."

"Micht a kiss assist?" he asked sincerely. I gave him a little smile, suddenly feeling persuaded by the attemptable look on his face.

"Maybe," I considered.

"Then, let us see." He leaned his soft lips over mine and bestowed a gentle, benign kiss. "Thaur now. Any better?"

"A little."

"In which case, micht ye care fur anither in order tae make it entirely weel?"

"Possibly." I smiled a little more at him, seeing his genuine eyes.

"So be it." Softly pressing his lips over mine, he tenderly kissed me again. But this time his lips moved more intently over mine as they lingered with growing warmth. After several smaller kisses, his mouth parted from mine.

"Thaur. How micht we be feeling presently?" He inquired, gazing at me with an affectionate, coaxing grin.

"Better," I confessed, aware of the heat flooding my veins now as I smiled sheepishly at him.

"All better?" he continued.

"Nearly," I said, and the grin on his face grew.

"Do ye recall the previous occasion ye charmed me in this manner?" he asked gently with our eyes so closely gazing at each other, slightly changing the topic.

"Yes, I remember," I said faintly, feeling weightless in his arms with my legs wrapped around his hips, floating before him.

"Whit occurred?" he asked, leaning forward slightly and nearly brushing his lips against mine.

"We got shot at," I whispered. He chuckled lightly.

"Aye. We had. Whit else do ye recall?" His breath was warm and sweet from the scent of rum as he spoke, and I felt the heat from it coming over my lips.

"I fell off the rocks and you dove into the water to save me," I remembered also.

"Indeed, I had. I wisnae going tae lose ye. Whit else micht ye recall?"

"We had fun swimming around by the waterfall."

"Aye, 'twas joyous. Was it not?"

"Yes, it was."

"I recall it too weel."

"So do I."

"Splendid. Whit else comes tae mind?"

"You started making love to me," I whispered, feeling shy in front of him as my mind vividly drifted back to that moment between us.

"That I did, indeed," he semi-whispered.

"We were interrupted, though," I mentioned, winded.

"A pity. Was it not?"

"Yes, it was."

"Nae interruptions this occurrence, however," he promised, brushing his lips against mine now, making me forget my worries. He gently started kissing me again. But now his kisses were hotblooded and I secured my arms around his neck, pressing my body against his. I automatically parted my lips for him and his tongue slid inside my mouth. He began kissing me with unfaltering, deliberate wanton desire, reminding me of how we were together—and *who* we were to each other.

My blood ran warm, heating me throughout my body, and I anxiously raked my fingers through the silky hair on his dampened crown, desperately needing the warmth of his touch. His lips broke from mine and ravenously trailed toward the side of my face, ruling my patience as he determinedly kissed my cheek and neck.

"Leif," I breathed between his lips as they returned over mine.

"Nae," he rasped. "Ye will refrain till I permit ye."

Minutes seemed to suspend as he continued teasing me with impassioned, desirous kisses. His heated lips moved over my cheek and neck again, burning my skin as they trailed over my flesh. His tongue escaped his mouth as his lips fervently tugged and sucked the delicate skin on my neck, hurting me a little.

"*Uhh*," I gasped, accepting the pain. I yearned to receive him to quell the molten ache between my thighs. Moving his lips upward toward my mouth again, he deliberately caught my bottom lip between his teeth and drew it into his mouth, suckling it with fervor, stealing my breath. When he released my bottom lip, his tongue returned into my mouth, exploring it. His dancing tongue discovered mine and sucked, catching my breath from me once more.

When his arms released my waist, his hands found my breasts. They began groping my stiffened nipples between his fingers while I steadied my arms around his neck. For a moment, I held on to him before withdrawing my embrace and abruptly gripped the edge of the pool with my palms, securing myself against the wall instead. Arching my back, begging him to enter me, I anticipated him between my legs as they remained encircling his hips.

His head dipped below my chin, catching my nipple into his mouth and began fervently suckling, causing me to gasp. A delirious moan eluded me. His kissing mouth moved over my breast and teased my nipple between his teeth. His mouth scorched me, and I thought I was going to die. Feeling it roll within his ravenous mouth, he arduously paid it attention and it grew tender by the fire burning within him. When he was satisfied with what he'd done, he moved to the next nipple, attentively bestowing the same unabashed affection to it, as it was not to be ignored. He continued painfully teasing it, making it ripe and sore, and causing me to moan while my blood raged for him.

The water around me no longer felt lukewarm, but hot like a sauna, and it seemed I might melt away.

He finally eased up a little, removing his insatiable mouth from my second breast. His massaging hands moved downward, one firmly seizing my waist and the other moving further below between us. I felt him seizing his shaft, then rubbing the tip between my cleft several times, separating me, and teasing my clitoris when the entrance to my yearning canal was exposed to him.

The moment his massive organ began opening me when finally pushing into my depths, suddenly forced me into a rapturous dream. A satisfying sigh escaped my lips, and he groaned with pleasure. Sensing my flesh enveloping him as he surged into me with one deliberate thrust, euphoria began consuming me. I became lifeless—like putty in his hands when he began driving himself into me.

"*Mo ghaol*," he rasped, bringing his lips over mine once more and securing a second fierce hand on my other hip. When he withdrew his mouth from my lips, he proceeded slowly thrusting himself into me, determining the optimum rhythm between us.

"Leif," I sighed, adoring him filling me as he drew the heat from my depths and burning a path for himself far inside me.

"Say it again, so that I ken 'tis nae dream," he moaned.

"You know it's no longer a dream," I uttered breathlessly.

"Prove it tae me," he panted.

I buried my fingers into his hair and pulled my lips to his, kissing him with all my zeal, opening my mouth for him to consume. His tongue immediately entered my mouth and claimed it all over again, kissing me with abandonment. Moaning, I returned his vigor, kissing him, doing as he desired, showing him the proof. He groaned from his gut as we kissed.

When we released our lips, panting, he dug fingers further into my hips, fastening me to him, hurting them a little as he proceeded forging his way deep into me. He penetrated my depths with intense force, reminding me of all that we'd ever shared and confirming the reality of our reunification.

"Do ye recall whence I took ye in the wood?" he panted.

"Yes," I moaned.

"Whit did ye say tae me then?"

"I told you that I loved you. That I was yours. Forever."

"Aye. Hence, whit did I say tae ye in return?"

"You said that you loved me, too. That you have me. That I belonged to you and we were bound forever. You told me that you were giving me everything you had to give to me, and for me to take it," I replied unevenly.

"Thus, are ye taking it?" he groaned.

"Just as you're giving it to me," I panted. I noticed a euphoric smirk slowly curving his lips. He appeared intoxicated and my own lips curled too.

"It being so, take every bit of it."

"I will."

"Yoo're my lass." He continued vehemently thrusting himself into me like a steel piston, his organ opening me to receive him whole on each surge as it kissed my cervix. He had claimed my soul as he had claimed my body, so I was reminded of him as I knew him when he thrust with ease into me. "I revere ye so as ye receive me. Yoo're taking it entirely weel. My cock relishes within ye."

"You're making me blush," I uttered sincerely, feeling him easily gliding in and out of me. A light chuckle eluded him.

"I told ye once not tae hide yerself from me. Do ye recall?"

"I remember."

"Thus, why are ye bashful of me?"

"I don't know."

"Micht it be since I ken ye like nae other man?"

"Maybe."

"Yet, ye hide from me still," he said, grinning.

"What's the difference when I know you'll always find me?"

"Aye. Ye have a notion." The sluggish grin on his lips widened across his face as his eyes were glazed with ecstasy. "Ye must ken how I venerate ye."

"*Uhh*," I gasped when he pumped inconceivably deeper into me as he suddenly seized my legs and crimped me against his chest, pressing me hard against the wall. A sharp pain shot through me and electrified my uterus as I oddly craved his entrance into it. It seemed he would breach it as he forging his way through me, further conditioning my body to receive all of him like the time we'd spent in the woods. "Would it be a secret to you if I told you now how much I love the way you feel inside of me?" I uttered with bated breath.

"'Tis glorious that ye tell me so," he replied huskily. I felt my lips slowly turning upward into a smile again. He caught the expression on my face and listlessly grinned.

In and out, over and again he continued thrusting. I thought I was going to perish as he pushed me closer toward the apex. I heard his own breathing unevenly escaping him while he concentrated on his self-dominion over me.

When he finally released my legs from being crimped, I naturally swung them snugly around his lean hips, trapping the electrical sensation of his rapid thrusts inside me. His hands continued tightly gripping my hips as he possessively fixed me to him. My uterus was stirring with little charged pulses, causing my fortitude to buckle, and I knew that he could clearly see what he was doing to me.

He forced my gaze and I stared back into his eyes as the pool's light reflected and cast shadows on his exalted face. It seemed he was a ghost locked in paradise.

He began moving more vigorously, quickening the tempo. The water sloshed and lapped over my suspended breasts, and I knew he was going to let us go at last. I was beginning to contract around him, compelling my disintegration. He perceived me, and I saw him too. He hardened like stone, and was also close. Moving more rhythmically now, in and out of me, again and again, pulling me along with him, in a moment I knew he was soon going to arrive at his end.

Suddenly, my insides thunderously charged, uncontrollably pulsating, unrestrained as vivid spasms overtook me and launched me into pristine rhapsody. The world dissolved around me and I only existed in bliss with my throbbing cervix and canal. Leif's mouth abruptly slackened, releasing an audible groan that originated from the pit of his gut. A moan eluded my lips as I froze. Confining, wild sensations electrified my nerves deep within and throughout my body as he seized, violently exploding into me. I shuddered and he poured himself into my chasm, filling my depths with his essence the moment I drowned in ecstasy.

Afterward, we slumped against each other as my grip slipped from the poolside, and I returned my arms around his neck. I felt him heavily breathing on my cheek and I sluggishly held onto him, embracing him. We tightly held each other, the both of us gasping, as we remained joined for moments longer. When Leif finally straightened only a little, I felt him slipping out of me, leaving me empty.

"Sylvie," he mumbled heatedly against my cheek, still heaving from his release.

"Yes?" I replied under my breath, listlessly smiling at him.

"Yoo're a perilous siren," he said, and I giggled.

"You don't have the right to blame me."

"Whyever not?"

"Because you're wicked," I said.

"Aye, I am raither libertine, am I not?" he chuckled, admitting it.

"And so, you've corrupted me."

"I huvnae quite debauched ye," he differed a little.

"Haven't you?"

"Hmm. Mayhap, I have a wee bit."

"I told you so," I giggled.

"Yet, thaur is more tae come from me," he teased, chuckling some more. I nervously giggled, wondering what else he would do to me.

"Is there?"

"Aye. Thaur is aplenty which awaits ye as I please tae serve ye."

"Shame on you, Your Grace," I giggled again.

"I huvnae any guilt. Therefore, I am not ashamed, Your Grace," he replied, grinning widely at me.

"Then, I'm worried."

"I beg yer forgiveness. I didnae disclose that my weakness fur ye will indeed lead tae yer debauchery as I am a most passionate man."

"I should have already recognized this flaw of yours when we were courting, since you did in fact seduce me then."

"Might ye truly perceive it a flaw?"

"Well, maybe not really. But the fault is mine."

"How micht it be?"

"I let myself be charmed by you," I teased and he laughed.

"Ye waur smitten with me?"

"Of course, I was."

"Yet, I was besotted by yer very existence as I drank the air ye breathed. Ye bewitched me in a manner that I had never experienced by any other lass."

"Really?"

"Aye. I was helpless fur ye, and had tae tooch ye before any other man would claim ye. Ye waur mine," he said. "Whit was I tae do?"

"Give yourself a favor?"

"By favoring ye."

"I guess I'm so lucky, then," I teased a little.

"I wouldnae have ever slighted ye by not granting ye my affection," he taunted in return.

"You're outrageous!" I laughed.

"Am I ghastly?" He was smiling ear to ear.

"Without a doubt."

"A fine compliment fur which I thank ye. I shan't ever wish tae be the cause of yer boredom."

"Likewise," I giggled.

"Yoo're most welcome."

"You're such a rascal!"

"Ye compliment me," he joked ironically. "Now, come haur ye ill-begotten nymph." He fully straightened from embracing me as he suddenly shifted me into both of his carrying arms, making me giggled again.

Leif carried me across the rest of the length of the pool until we arrived at the steps in the shallow end where he placed me down onto my own feet, at last. Climbing the steps together out of the water, we emerged dripping wet. Despite being soaked and without towels to dry ourselves, I promptly covered my nudity with my chemise without a care, and he replaced his robe over his gleaming naked body, concealing himself.

We subsequently started away from the glowing pool and stepped through the surrounding gate. Passing the fire pit, we crossed over the lawn for the house. As we silently returned indoors for our bedroom, peaceful contentment pervaded between us. Both of us satisfied from our intimacy knowing we completely loved each other to the depths of our existence, fused us without a flaw.

Twenty-Four

Early next morning, while Leif was sleeping, I had awakened in time to properly receive my parents when they arrived to pick up the kids to take them to Disneyland. The kids were thrilled to see their grandparents when they entered through the front door, and my parents where bright and cheerful to see them also. I had given my parents a petite suitcase packed with the kids' belongings for the weekend. As they were all eager to leave, swift kisses and hugs passed between us while I wished them all a safe farewell.

When they promptly left me and entered my parents' car parked in the driveway, I watched them through the foyer window carefully pulling away from the house. I was happy for them to have this enjoyable time together. Observing their excitement for themselves as they were ready to leave for the amusement park this morning, my parents were certain to arrive there early enough to check into the resort in order for them to see the sights before most of the arriving crowd.

Now that they had gone, I returned upstairs into the bedroom and noticed Leif still sleeping. As I mindfully crawled back into bed beside him, he stirred and awakened. An indolent grin eased over his lips as he viewed me through the slits of his groggy eyes. I leaned and pressed my lips over his, delivering an innocent kiss.

"How did you sleep?" I quietly asked.

"Raither weel, many thanks tae ye," he replied sluggishly. I placed a hand over his masculine cheek and tenderly stroked it. He clasped my fingers and drew the back of my hand to his lips, then wrapped an arm around my waist, pulling me close against him. "Whit may we anticipate fur this morn?" he implied while giving me a suggestive look. I smiled and shook my head, amused.

"Is that all you think about?" I teased.

"I fault ye fur it," he joked.

"Of course, you do," I replied ironically, giggling. He lightly smacked my buttocks, facetiously, causing me to suddenly yelp, and he chuckled. "Was that necessary?"

"'Twas fur yer cheek," he justified. I glowered at the playful look on his face. "'Twould please me immensely tae have anither swim," he requested rakishly as I sensed his hand slipping past my buttocks and discovering my cleft between my thighs, and beginning to spread me open.

"But, Your Grace, shouldn't we have breakfast first?" I asked instead, sounding innocent.

"Yoo're famished?" he asked, smirking.

"I'll be a waif soon if I'm not fed."

"Very weel," he sighed, dissatisfied, though the devilish smirk remained on his lips.

"Well, you don't want me to eat a horse instead, do you? Because, I'm close to doing it."

"Indeed not."

"Thank you. I'm in your debt," I quipped.

"Of coorse ye are, and I shall collect yer debt quite soon," he remarked in a joking tone. I sensed a palm seep into the back of my loose ringlets as he drew my lips down over his. He gave me a simple peck and released me. I smiled at him as our eyes met again.

"So, what I was thinking that we could do today, that I think you might enjoy, is to take Heather's idea and more appropriately tour the city to see the attractions. Then, have a picnic on the beach," I said, submitting the idea to him. His brow lifted in surprise and he slightly pursed his lips in consideration.

"I reckon that I micht fancy such a notion. Shall we have the bairns in our company?" he responded interestedly.

"My parents have them for the weekend. They took them to Disneyland to celebrate their birthday," I informed him.

"I see... Whit is Disneyland?"

"It's an amusement park."

"Och," he replied cluelessly. "Whit micht be an amusement park?"

"It's a park full of entertainment where people go to be amused."

"A sort of favored forum as a theatre?" His brow furrowed making him appear confused and disapproving.

"Not quite."

"How micht it differ?"

"It's nothing like you're imagining. It's amusement strictly catered toward children and families."

"Och." He nodded, better understanding as his face relaxed with approval now. "Raither innocent, then."

"Yes."

"Very weel."

"So, it'll be just us together until sometime later tomorrow."

"It seems fair."

"Good. Now, let's have some breakfast before I wither away."

"I shan't ever permit it tae occur."

"You almost did just now by keeping me in bed."

"I submit tae ye my dearest apology, Your Grace," he said, grinning boldly. I giggled in response, noticing the roué look lingering in his eyes.

"You're full of mischief," I accused.

"I never claimed being an angel," he chuckled, as we started from bed.

"You make me nervous," I replied, smiling at him.

"Do I?"

"Yeah."

"How micht it be, since yoo're free spirited?"

"I'm not as wild as you think I am," I responded matter-of-factly as he followed me toward the doorway to the bathroom, intending to shower.

"On the contrary," he disagreed actually. "I have witnessed yer behavior that is antithetical tae any lass that I have ever knoon."

"Really?" I gave him a skeptical look.

"Aye."

"I'm not so sure about that."

"Are ye not?"

"Well, you've known some questionable women in your past long ago. Not that I'm comparing myself to them, but I'm sure they wouldn't be categorized as *demure*."

"Och, weel, be that as it will. They waur indeed properly behaved lasses."

"They were?"

"Aye."

"Even in the bedroom?"

"Mundane."

"You're incredible!" I laughed, shaking my head incredulously.

"Yoo're correct by saying thaur isnae any comparison betwixt them and ye."

"Why?"

"Yoo're from Olympus."

"So, I'm a goddess?"

"Which cannae be restrained."

"Then, you excuse my free spiritedness after all?"

"As I brave tae tame ye with my enthusiasm fur ye, ye micht master me weel, consequentially."

"Fair enough."

"I reckon so."

I gave him a sidelong glance and caught the fiendish smirk on his face. I giggled again and hopelessly shook my head as we entered the bathroom, ready for us to wash.

ONCE SHOWERED AND DRESSED, WE ENTERED THE kitchen and Leif sat in the bay window in the breakfast nook reading the *Wall Street Journal* while I prepared us scrambled eggs, bacon, and toast with glasses of fresh orange juice. When I had finished the preparations, we sat eating our breakfast and enjoying our companionship in light conversation over articles he had just read in the Journal.

After our meal was completed, I gathered the dishes, placed them in the dishwasher, then collected the picnic basket and packed it with a nice lunch. When the basket had been entirely arranged, I collected the large picnic blanket, a couple of beach towels, and the beach umbrella as Leif assisted me loading everything into the minivan.

Now ready to leave, I locked the front door and we entered the vehicle. I then backed us out of the driveway, excited to share today with him.

I drove us through the neighborhood heading east on surface streets toward downtown Los Angeles. When we arrived in downtown, we visited the area inside the vehicle as I meant for us to tour the greater part of the city as planned. Leif was mesmerized while gazing out of his passenger side window when we passed many pedestrians walking along sidewalks between the skyscrapers. Continuing to meander on busy downtown streets through Little Tokyo, I found our way onto Sunset Boulevard until it turned into

Hollywood Boulevard, and made our way west toward Hollywood.

We passed through Thai Town along the way and crossed Vine, entering the strip where all the tourist sightseeing sights were located in Hollywood. Proceeding along the strip on Hollywood Boulevard, I finally made a right turn onto Laurel Canyon Boulevard and followed the serpentine road north as it wound through the Santa Monica Mountains.

When we came over the mountain pass, we arrived in Studio City and I took us onto the 101 freeway due west, heading toward the ocean. We passed through North Hollywood, Encino, Woodland Hills, finally making our way out of those towns into Ventura County.

Driving through horse country in Calabasas, we continued winding our way through the Santa Monica Mountains, passed Agoura Hills and Camarillo until we finally saw the ocean ahead. I veered onto Pacific Coast Highway and followed the road going south along the expansive aquamarine Pacific Ocean.

After having spent several hours in the car, I decided for us to stop at last at Point Mugu along the ocean and have our picnic on the beach. When I found a parking spot, we unloaded our belongings from the car and climbed a slightly rocky slope down toward the sand until we arrived close to the shoreline. Pitching the beach umbrella open and laying the blanket beneath it over the sand, we finally sat ourselves comfortably on it beneath the shade.

The location was beautiful and fairly remote with few beach goers, and some surfers in between. But Leif was significantly unaccustomed to the way people dressed here in general. However, as he observed the scant attire on beach goers in public, his eyes uncharacteristically bugged out when they glued to bikinied women and bare-chested men sunbathing on the sand, or enjoying themselves in the waves faintly attired.

"When in Rome," I reminded him, smiling a little. He still

gave me a flabbergasted look, and I couldn't help the giggle eluding me.

"'Tis as if one has shipwrecked upon a desolate island without a soul about tae leer. Yet, fur one who strictly witnesses these naked Romans, one cannae help but see scandal," he expressed shockingly. I laughed and he observed my amusement as the expression on his face turned quizzically humored.

"Oh, c'mon! It's not that bad," I laughed, perceiving his reaction.

"'Tis most indeed atrocious."

"For all of your Greek and Roman exposure to their ideals, literature and art, how do you suppose they actually dressed?"

"Aye, weel, they waur attired in either tunics or togas."

"But athletes were naked during the Olympics or when they fought in the colosseums. Besides, the sheerness of the material they used to dress themselves made them appear as good as nude, anyway. And since you're actually well-traveled, what about when you were in Guinea? I'm guessing the natives there were scantily clad, too. Weren't they?"

I looked at him sincerely and he pinched his lips into a line as he narrowed an eye on me, feigning vexation and appearing stumped for words. I smiled, amused, since he was cornered by my logic.

"Weel, if *ever* I waur tae catch ye within secht disrobed in public as these new Romans haur—Heaven help me," he responded offhandedly, certainly flustered.

"Heaven help you?" I replied, giggling.

"Aye."

"Why?"

"I shall have a fit and perish!" he expressed obviously. I burst out laughing, completely entertained.

"If I wore a swimsuit in this setting, it'd be entirely innocent," I said, laughing.

"Innocent?" His brow shot up and his eyes widened in question.

"Yeah."

"Not according tae any man."

"But you just admitted to me last night, plus hinting at it again this morning, that you are libertine. So, I'd just as well assumed that you'd be relaxed about this society's loose dress standards."

"Libertine am I as it pertains tae the privacy within my own bedchamber. Yet, as it regards the public, it is a different occurrence altogether. The public ought have standards of propriety in place of the exhibition of debauchery fur all tae witness. Whilst I am nae pietist, I do say thaur is a time and place fur it all, respectfully," he explained. I couldn't help smiling at him as a thought suddenly occurred to me.

"Are you afraid to show your knees to everyone?" I teased. His bottom lip suddenly gaped a little and his eyes widened again as a brisk snort eluded him.

"I shall not offend anyone by doing so," he replied priggishly.

"But you have nice, strong knees to show off," I goaded, though I was also sincere.

"I shall not," he refused bluntly.

"But I love them."

"Precisely my point."

"What is your point?"

"Whilst ye admire my knees, yer figure is mine alone tae behold," he said.

"Well, I distinctly remember you having no qualm about us swimming naked in the forest," I recalled, still smiling at him.

"'Twas a different affair," he countered with confidence in his voice.

"Yeah? How so?"

"'Twas private."

"Not any more private than your brother and cousins sneaking up and discovering us," I said. He smirked at me and faintly shook his head, appearing unimpressed and amused also.

"Even so. We waur withdrawn from the public forum," he said. Now, I smirked at him this time and shook my head.

"It was still in the open, though—for anyone to see," I replied, nevertheless.

"Hmph. I fathom that should ye have it in mind, ye would heedlessly frolic unrobed into this very sea as a nymph precisely like ye had done last nicht into the swimming bath. Ye would tempt me as weel as every other satyr about."

"Oh, my goodness! Do you really think I'm that wild?" I laughed, looking shocked at him.

"Untamed and wanton," he said, holding back an evident chuckle.

"In that case, I have my doubts you can tame this goddess," I teased again. He chuckled abruptly and his cheeks flushed, his vibrant blue eyes sparkling. "Am I proving to be too much for you to bear after all?"

"I beg yer pardon?" he questioned while chuckling.

"You heard what I said."

"Thaur is more time yet fur me tae meet that challenge with complete pleasure."

"You would have to be from Olympus also in order to do that."

"Ahh, of coorse! Have ye not already questioned whether I am?" He bantered back. I gave him a little quizzical look. "Recall the time we had spent together in the wood?"

"I do clearly remember that," I replied, no longer laughing now, flashing back to the memory of us together as my feelings for him at that time had been conjured. I felt my lips settle into a soft smile as I held his unbreakable gaze.

"Only one from Mount Olympus could harness ye," he said. I gazed at him, staring at his striking face, and thought he could actually be from that mythical place. I smiled bashfully at him. "We have only yet begun, *àille dhubh*."

The confident grin curving his lips was magnetic as he potently returned staring at me. He had me, and he enjoyed me. His love for me was stirring. It ran toward depths not yet known as the future held us in its palm, and he was certain to show me exactly how far his love for me extended. I knew it was limitless. So, I was rendered feeling shy, sitting before him, as I wondered in what other ways he would demonstrate his passion for me and bring me to this complete understanding.

"What will you do to me, Leif?"

"Adore ye till my last breath, Sylvie." The look in his eyes was warm with endearing affection as he gently gazed at me with a grin now that had grown soft and subtle. A pause ensued between us and the conversation drifted. Our gazes lingered together for a moment and the grin on his face slowly grew again, spreading calmly and confidently. I diffidently glanced away from him down to the cheese and grapes on my plate over the picnic tray before my folded legs.

"So..." I began again, changing the subject as I returned my gaze to his. It seemed his eyes had never left me as I found him still staring at me when our eyes met again.

"Aye?" he replied easily, as I watched him taking a sip of wine.

"You're retired from the army now," I mentioned, beginning to nibble on some cheese and grapes.

"Aye," he said, nodding.

"That's good."

"Aye." He mindfully placed his wineglass down over the tray before himself, and lightly snatched up a cracker between his fingers, taking a bite out of it.

"I know that it was something you had been looking forward to," I remarked thoughtfully.

"Indeed."

"Do you still have your business venture?"

"I do."

"How is it progressing?"

"It prospers verily weel, indeed," he said positively, finishing his cracker.

"That's good," I replied, nodding accordingly. "Now that the war is over and since you've been retired from serving in the army, I'm assuming that you've finally received your inheritance?"

"'Tis most unfortunate that I huvnae yet received any of it," he said, appearing earnest now.

"But why?"

"My correspondences regarding it huvnea yet been answered by the Crown," he informed me.

"Why not?"

"The king takes time on his decision. Raither simply," Leif said. My brow knitted in bemusement.

"I don't understand. Wouldn't it be an easy decision for him to make? Especially, because you've honorably served your end of the agreement with him?"

"'Twas never an agreement, but an order. The king never agrees tae his subjects. He commands them. And on his whim, he micht fancy a promise tae them if he pleases."

"Oh," I realized. "But, didn't he make a kind of promise to you, then? That if you served in the army until the war ended, then you'd be discharged and he'd relinquish all of your wealth to you?"

"He reminds me that I still possess my titles and lands in Scotland, and therefore I must be grateful. However, he will retain all of my coin. Therefore, whit coin I once had has been absorbed by the king's coffers as he claims it fur the debt I owe tae him fur my betrayal, due tae Laird Loudoun's public accusal of me," Leif explained.

"I remember... You said that he called you a Jacobite," I recalled.

"I am a Jacobite. A fact that remains."

"Yes, but you didn't fight for the Cause."

"It disnae matter. The gist being that the king has consumed every bit of my coin and threatens that if I waur tae profit from my dukedom, he will seize it entirely and leave me with naught," he informed me.

"Really?" I looked at Leif in shock.

"Aye."

"Then, he's essentially left you penniless."

"Aye."

"So, it doesn't matter if you have land or not, since you can't basically use it," I said unbelievably.

"Correct."

"What does that mean for all of the property you own in Massachusetts, then?"

"'Tis irrelevant."

"I don't understand."

"He wulnae seize it, because I refuse to benefit from any of my land of which he will be awaur. Though many spies remain about me, I shall not grant one the merest opportunity tae accuse me of betrayal and have it forfeited from me."

"Then how on earth are you not destitute if the king continues to claim all of your money? I haven't the slightest idea how you can be immensely wealthy as you've said, if you can't use your land."

"Precisely why I discreetly collect rent from my land in Northampton, and my possession of vessels fur trading, and that I am a venturer as weel as a merchant. As a result of my success in these schemes, I have gained extensive means."

"Still, what if the king discovers that you're producing dividends? He could seize all of your fresh profits, too, couldn't he?"

"He very weel could."

"Leif, this sounds horrible. I don't see how we could be financially secure if we were to live at *Taigh Gràs*," I said concernedly.

"Despite his attention upon my dukedom, the king hasnae the merest notion of how I micht conduct my private affairs away from England, in spite of spies as near in Boston. Nor, does he truly have a care, because the Empire is mired in debt due tae the war, whilst Parliament quarrels about it all. All of this commands his greatest deliberation."

"But, what if spies report to him about how you're making money, though?"

"It makes not a difference."

"Why not?"

"He is in fact already awaur of my mercantilism as I have disclosed this information tae him tae circumvent his spies, in order that his opinion of me be better regarded with favor. Furthermore, so long as I pay the tariffs, he remains satisfied."

"For now."

"Aye."

"Well—that part of the problem might be potentially solved regarding money—I guess. But, what's the political climate like? Hasn't it gotten worse since after the war?"

"The Crown has levied several heavy acts recently tae replenish the budget due tae the war which has forced men's ire. Thus, aye, men are not pleased," Leif answered.

"How angry have people gotten?" I asked curiously.

"Quite irate that they express their displeasure in meetings, broadsheets and circulars," he informed me. "Tariffs have risen upon goods—paper, sugar, glass, tea—merely tae mention but a few. Though England has won the war, her coffers are depleted, hence the king pressing subjects tae compensate fur the loss of her wealth."

I nodded in acknowledgment, thinking. "What else is happing in Boston?" I asked contemplatively.

"Subjects must quarter His Majesty's army," he disclosed.

"Still?"

"Aye."

"I thought that they would've returned to England after the war."

"Not merely. They have remained fur a number of reasons. However, more soldiers continue arriving into the city."

"Why?"

"'Tis insurance that order remains amongst subjects."

"Is there that much unrest?"

"Thaur was an eruption due tae the levy of the Townsend Acts. Yet, the city has come tae rest since troops are present," he said. I nodded thinkingly again.

"Do you believe it'll truly be safe for us to return there?" I asked with uncertainty.

"'Tis safe. Disturbances, if any, are constrained tae the North End. They are remote from *Taigh Gràs* and from waur neighbors lie."

"That's good to hear, I suppose." I nodded a little once more, slightly encouraged.

"Fear not, fur the city is indeed safeguarded from disruption despite the many dregs attired in uniform," he assured.

"Dregs," I noted skeptically, remembering what had almost happened to me in Northampton.

"Aye. Thaur are many of them," he acknowledged unfortunately. "However, the punishment fur their offenses is great should they disobey officers. Many of them dinnae seek tae risk their fate pertaining tae discipline."

"War is coming," I muttered, letting the concern slip from my lips. His eyes held onto mine, and he steadily looked at me as a flicker of alarm crossed his expression. "I remember from my history classes." He didn't respond any further but kept his gaze glued to mine without the sign of fear instead. "It's not just the war, but there're medical issues that are concerning to consider about us living there."

"Shall we be in fear of it all?" he questioned.

"What do you mean? Specifically?"

"Tae live at all is a risk. Will our security be entirely sound living haur? Can ye verify it and swear tae it?"

"You know that I can't promise that."

"'Tis impossible."

I nodded faintly in response, remembering the inhumanity of their punishment. I also thought it couldn't have been any less safe being there than it was living here when reconsidering present day local crime statistics occurring in this city.

I glanced away from him toward the ocean rushing over the shore with waves, and the conversation between us drifted into silence. After a moment, I returned looking at him and realized he had been gazing out at the ocean also when he turned his eyes back toward mine again.

"Are you enjoying yourself here today?" I asked, changing the topic.

"Verily," he replied. A tender grin eased over his face, making him appear contented and relaxed as our previous conversation was forgotten.

"I'm glad," I responded gently.

"Micht ye be enjoying yerself equally?"

"Very much."

"I'm greatly pleased." He reached a hand toward my face and I sensed his gentle fingers caressing my cheek, then carefully moved a stray ringlet tendril off my face, tucking it behind my ear. "My angel," he half-whispered, staring intensely into my eyes, before letting his palm slip away from my face. I smiled diffidently at him, feeling the warmth of my deep affection for him, and we continued picnicking naturally at ease with one another, despite the hidden worry I felt about our returning to his era.

WHEN WE HAD FINISHED OUR LUNCH, WE CONTINUED enjoying ourselves by taking a relaxing stroll on the sand by the shoreline, and everything felt indisputably perfect at that moment as thoughts of our earlier conversation regarding his era had dispelled.

During our stroll, we took our time returning to our picnic area. When we finally arrived to it again, we proceeded packing our belongings and went to the car, placing them inside. Once we also had ourselves inside the car, I continued driving us south on Pacific Coast Highway along the edge of the ocean, through Malibu headed toward Santa Monica.

When approaching Santa Monica, the pier could be seen in the distance with the roller coasters and rotating Ferris wheel on top. Leif curiously asked me about the pier as we came closer to it, since he had never seen one like it until now. I explained to him that it was a place of entertainment and that our kids really enjoyed it whenever we came to this part of town. I also told him that this was the city in which I worked and had my medical practice. He seemed impressed and interested as he intently listened to me speak about it all.

I continued telling him that before I had disappeared that this was where I had lived. But once I had returned with our children, I moved to Westchester, since I needed a larger house that was less expensive to purchase than my former modest two-bedroom adobe bungalow located here in Santa Monica, which I had rented, could provide for us. While he listened to me speak about my life before and after my disappearance, he was engrossed by the realization of my previous life.

As I took us through Santa Monica, I found my way onto Lincoln Boulevard and headed south until we returned to my neighborhood in Westchester. It didn't take long thereafter when we reached the area and were now pulling into the driveway, finally returning home.

The sun was now setting as Leif and I began unloading the car from our belongings and taking them back inside. When we had soon completed this task, we entered the kitchen where I began warming left over lasagna for us to have for dinner. Once dinner was shortly prepared, I arranged our dining places in the dining room and we closely sat eating together.

"Whit is it we are eating?" he inquired interestedly.

"It's lasagna," I informed him, observing him place a mouthful between his lips. "It's an Italian recipe."

"Is it?" he replied after swallowing.

"Um-hm." I took a sip of my sparkling water and replaced the glass over the table in front of me.

"'Tis delicious," he commented.

"I'm glad that you approve."

"I do always agree with your cuisine."

"Thank you," I appreciated. He grinned and winked at me, causing me to smile.

Twenty-Five

Late Sunday afternoon my parents returned with the kids from Disneyland. I rushed from the den where Leif and I were relaxing with cups of tea in front of the TV to answer the front door. Letting them inside the house, full excitement erupted as they entered. I noticed many souvenirs my parents had purchased for the kids and was taken by amused surprise. Mickey and Minnie Mouse balloons bobbed against the ceiling. A purple Padawan light saber and pirate sword swung around in Little Leif's hands, and a glittering Cinderella tiara embellished Leila's onyx ringlets while she spun around in her new Snow White princess dress and shoes, while Mom placed a gift bag full of smaller trinkets on the foyer bench by the window.

Leif appeared from the den, no doubt extremely curious about all of the noise emitting throughout the house. He paced through the hallway, arriving to stand next to me, observing the surrounding happy commotion in the foyer. My parents instantly noticed him, and I promptly introduced them to each other, feeling extremely nervous about it. While my heart was hammering in my chest, I simply smiled at my parents as their eyes bounced between the both of us before settling onto me.

"How are ya, Sweet Pea?" Dad asked me.

"Good, good—I'm great," I replied, suddenly stammering.

"Glad to hear it," he said easily.

"You?"

"Oh, we're great, too," he assured good-naturedly. I nervously glanced at Mom and she smiled nicely at me, then turned a friendly eye toward Leif.

"It's nice to finally meet you, Seamus," Mom greeted pleasantly.

"The pleasure is certainly mine, Master and Mistress Esperanza," Leif replied genteelly. Mom subtly glanced at Dad with a nice little grin. I knew she instantly noticed Leif's uncommon reticence and polite demeanor, and I hoped she wouldn't find him eccentric. Her affable glance returned looking at Leif as Dad cordially extended his hand to him. Leif appeared slightly clueless for a second but quickly recovered as he promptly took my dad's hand. I observed them shaking hands as Mom's gaze remained unwavering on Leif. By the look in her eyes, I perceived her forming her immediate impression of him as she amicably stared at him, and hoped for her approval along with Dad's.

When Dad and Leif finished shaking hands, silence between us all suddenly descended and we simply stood there in the foyer awkwardly gazing at each other, wondering how to begin a conversation.

"How was Disneyland?" I clumsily started.

"Can't you tell?" Dad chuckled in his good-humored nature as the kids cheerfully jumped around him, attaining his attention. I was glad Dad's attention was so easily diverted from Leif by the kids, as I wondered what his first impression of him was also. I sorely hoped he would find him agreeable, knowing he would compare him to Matt.

"Looks like your trip was a blast," I remarked, feeling a modicum of relief by the kids' distraction around us.

"Oh, yeah," Dad agreed without reservation.

"Mama!" Leila called, attracting my attention from my parents.

"Yes, sweetie?" I answered, looking interestedly at her.

"I saw the real Snow White and she said that we looked like each other, and that I was her twin!"

"Is that right?" I replied, charmed.

"Yeah! And, Granddad and Nanna took a picture of us together," she expressed happily.

"Oh, I'll have to see that," I said, smiling at her.

"I saw the real Darth Vader! And, we did the Jedi Training and I fought Darth Mal and won!" Little Leif eagerly expressed with the same happy excitement.

"Wow! That sounds exciting!" I responded, captivated by him.

"All right, Sweet Pea," Dad interrupted, calling my attention back to him. He drew me by the shoulders and delivered a peck over my temple. "We'd love to stay for a while, but your mother and I are going to take off now. We're beat. Hope you understand."

"Sure," I said. "Thanks so much for taking them."

"It was loads of fun. Wish we could bottle up the kids' energy and sell it," he chuckled lightly. Mom and I giggled, and I caught a grin spread over Leif's face as he was closely observing us engaging each other.

"Imagine that? Marketing that kind of product would be too easy," Mom said smilingly as she reached for me also, giving me a hug and kiss on my forehead. "Hate to run, sweetheart, but your dad's right. We've had our fill. Don't think us rude or anything for our short visit with you. But we'll be very happy to see you all on Friday as we're really looking forward to it."

"All right. We'll see you Friday," I said, feeling easier about the prospect as I sensed her early approval of Leif.

"Everyone enjoy the rest of your day," she said, acknowledging Leif again with eye contact and a smile. Leif respectfully dipped his head slightly toward her in response and Mom glanced at Dad again, catching his supportive eye.

"Thank you so much again, for entertaining the kids. Enjoy the rest of your day also. You guys get some rest," I replied nicely to my parents.

"Thank you, sweetie. We will," Mom assured.

She smiled at me again and gave the kids a kiss each on the cheek before turning with Dad for the front door. Leif and I were left with a pair of excited children bouncing around the foyer as they played with their new toys. I noticed the pirate hat on Little Leif's head and the large plush Minnie Mouse toy enfolded in Leila's arms while they twirled and jumped around us.

"We saw Captain Jack Sparrow too!" Little Leif told his father as he suddenly stood still before him.

"Who micht he be?" Leif curiously asked his son, looking cluelessly at him.

"He's a pirate," Little Leif told his father.

"A pirate!" Leif responded, appearing significantly astounded as his ultramarine gaze abruptly widened and darted toward me. The look on his face was combined with disapproval and alarm.

"He's a fictional character," I clarified, reassuring him with a little giggle.

"Och," Leif quickly understood in relief, nodding his head accordingly.

"Captain Jack Sparrow is funny! He drinks a lot of rum," Little Leif said cheerfully.

"Does he now?" A golden eyebrow arched over Leif's eye and his lips subtly curved in amusement.

"Yeah," Little Leif responded.

"I see. Being a pirate, he is then a villain," Leif replied, appearing plainly entertained.

"What's a villain?" Little Leif asked curiously.

"An evil man in a tale," Leif told his son.

"Oh. No, he's a good guy," Little Leif simply informed his father.

"In whit manner is he guid?" his father asked quizzically as he stared admiringly at his son with a grin.

"He has lots of friends and people like him, because he fights bad guys," Little Leif explained.

"Truly?" his father inquired incredulously.

"Uh-hu. Have you seen *Pirates of the Caribbean* before?" Little Leif inquired curiously.

"Weel, I huvnae been tae the Caribbean Sea as of yet. Therefore, I huvnae seen any pirates from that particular region of the sea," Leif explained. Little Leif furrowed his brow at his father, appearing clearly puzzled.

"He means have you seen the movie depicting the story," I clarified, smiling at them.

"Och," Leif realized.

"No, sweetie, your father hasn't seen the movie," I said to our son.

"Oh," Little Leif responded thinkingly.

"Can we see it then, Mom?" Leila asked suddenly as she continued twirling around beside us in her princess costume.

"It's *may* I, sweetie, not *can* I. And, yes, of course you may see it," I responded pleasantly to her.

"Yay!" she exclaimed excitedly. She suddenly ceased spinning like a top and slipped her small hand into her father's, tugging him. "C'mon! Follow me!"

Leif looked surprisedly at me as a grin simultaneously curled his lips. I shrugged a little, intimating for him to do as she wished while she continued tugging his hand.

"Alrecht, I shall," he agreed, returning his affable attention toward her, and allowed her to lead the way for him through the hallway toward the den. Noticing them walking away, Little Leif ran after them, joining as they paced. Following them also, when we entered the den, everyone took their places on the large sectional sofa and made ourselves comfortable, eager to share the movie with their father.

WHEN MONDAY CAME THE FOLLOWING MORNING, LEIF and I walked the kids to school before I went to work. I wondered how he might manage being left alone at home for the first time, although he had the puppy for company. Concerned for his comfort, I made certain to have prepared food for him to eat throughout the day, so that he wouldn't be overwhelmed with the responsibility of feeding himself by using the kitchen appliances he had no familiarity of using. I also was sure to supply him with a stack of current newspapers, a wide selection of magazines, and books I had pointed him to, kept in bookcases in the den for his reading pleasure. Lastly, in case he preferred to watch a bit of TV, I had written instructions for him describing how to use and navigate it.

Believing he was now poised to occupy himself well without my company, I felt better about leaving him alone while I returned to my pediatric practice and while our kids were in school for the day.

This was the arrangement for him for the time being until he acquired his state ID card. Having his ID card would also allow him to pick up the kids from school for me instead while I sometimes remained later at work.

While the thought of obtaining an ID card for him as soon as possible laid at the forefront of my mind, I soon made arrangements to take a day off work in order to bring Leif to the Department of Motor Vehicles and apply for his card. Understanding the lead period for the card's arrival into my mailbox would be within a month's time, I also decided to take the opportunity to visit the rectory with him for an impromptu meeting with Fr. Hanley to explain our intentions to marry. As pleased as Fr. Hanley was to learn of this news, he promptly encouraged us to visit his secretary in order to schedule a date.

So, we did as Fr. Hanley advised. His secretary, Mrs. Cartright, was just as happy to learn of my unexpected engagement and readily assisted us in narrowing a time frame for the wedding to occur in the future, since the church had already been booked for this spring and summer. She noted that couples were generally encouraged to have moderate engagement periods anyway for them to grow accustomed to the understanding of marrying each other. With that in mind, she immediately presented to us the first date available in the fall for the ceremony. We promptly accepted November eighteenth, the week before Thanksgiving.

As this date was chosen, Leif seemed pleased; I knew it brought back the memory for him of the time we had originally gotten married, and it pleased me too.

Twenty-Six

When Friday evening came, I was nothing but a bunch of rattling nerves as Leif and I arrived with the kids for dinner at my parents' house. Regardless that my parents had appeared to enjoy their first encounter with Leif when they'd returned from the amusement park—brief though it was—the nervous anticipation for this dinner tonight with them was nearly too much for me to conceal.

After my phone conversation with Mom last week about Leif now being here with me seemed to have ended positively, I still remained unsure about how much they'd actually gravitate toward him and like him. He was in fact noticeably different in speech and mannerism from everyone else with whom I associated. I hoped my parents wouldn't perceive that being a hindrance and label him too eccentric for the good of our compatibility as they regarded his sincerity.

I kept thinking: *you're just overthinking things, Sylvie. Get a grip... Mom and Dad aren't even close to being pre-judgmental. So, why the presumption about them? Still, they're conservative—so... but so is Leif. So, there's that. They should have something in common with him regarding their outlooks. Except, they want to know every-*

thing about him. I know they're wondering why he suddenly reap-
peared now into my life instead of earlier despite the lie I had told
them about us... In spite of their cordiality, they're going to pick him
apart. I know it... Ugh, this could go so wrong.

My rattled thoughts slightly centered as we entered my parents' house. Mom and Dad were happy to receive us, with particular whimsical attention to the kids as they gave each one giant bear hugs. The kids were also excited to see their grandparents and were thrilled to have their puppy along with them for the evening. Once greetings were exchanged, the kids took their puppy and naturally made themselves comfortable inside the family room before dinner was soon to be served.

When we finally sat at the dining room table to eat, between distractions from the kids' lighthearted banter with Dad, I remained internally jittery from anticipation. This gathering was crucial. I kept wondering what the conversation between Leif and my parents was going to be like as we were about to address the elephant in the room.

"So, my wife has filled me in on some facts about you, Seamus. One being that you're from Scotland?" Dad started, now turning his attention from the kids toward Leif. Dad looked interestedly at Leif while he drank a sip of beer after shifting his playful attention away from the kids.

"Aye, I am indeed from Scotland, Master Esperanza," Leif replied respectfully.

"What part of Scotland are you from?" Mom inquired inquisitively while serving the kids' their plates of roast beef, mixed vegetables and mashed potatoes.

"I originate from the Highlands. A place knoon as Skye, Mistress Esperanza," Leif replied politely.

"Oh, how nice. That's quite a distance, isn't it?" she recognized nicely.

"Aye, it is," Leif replied courteously, taking a sip of Cabernet

Sauvignon from his glass which Mom had automatically served him without asking his preference.

"I understand that you're planning on staying here in the States," Dad commented directly. Leif briefly hesitated as he glanced at me sitting beside him.

"My intention is tae remain devoted tae yer daughter, Master Esperanza," Leif said with confidence, not answering the question directly as he shifted his gaze back to Dad.

Dad kept his eyes locked onto Leif, and I was aware that he had observed Leif's slight falter when Leif looked at me before answering his question. Dad was a hard man to persuade, especially when it involved the protection of his family, and I sensed his critical analysis of Leif begin just then.

"I'm curious to know what made you decide to seek out my daughter after so many years have lapsed?" Dad frankly asked Leif.

"I have never forgotten the value of whit yer daughter has brought tae my existence, sir. It has taken me this length of time tae discover waur I micht locate her, efter all," Leif began sincerely. "It was a tireless task in my search, yet I was determined fur us tae be reunited. Should it be of any solace tae ye, Master Esperanza, I have never abandoned yer daughter. I never shall. Not in the present. Nor, in future." Leif appeared plainly earnest, matching Dad's candor. Dad's gaze instantly shifted toward me, unsettling me as I knew he perceived my guilt.

"Sylvie has hinted to her mother and me what might have happened between the both of you. Losing Matt wasn't easy for Sylvie," Dad said somberly, turning his eyes back toward Leif.

"I truly understand 'twas difficult fur her tae experience, certainly," Leif said with an honest expression.

"I assume that she thought it was probably easier for her to protect you from her grief," Dad responded, sounding sympathetic in his voice. But the expression on his face was impassive, and I knew he disapproved of the way I had managed myself with Leif.

"That's what I believe also," Mom inserted compassionately. "I don't think it was her intention to cause any misunderstanding or to hurt you in any way, Seamus, when she parted from you. Truly, I don't. It's not like her at all to consciously be disregarding. People grieve differently and sometimes it takes longer for them to recover than it does others. Sometimes people who are grieving feel as though they must guard themselves in order not to feel the pain, or trust others enough in order not to feel pain again, when they simply need time to heal."

"Still, she should have explained to you the situation she found herself in. You had a right to know about it, and she should have given you the opportunity to honor your relationship with her—specifically when she realized she was expecting. I apologize for that." Dad said to Leif, seeming a bit nettled now as he speculated what I must have put Leif through, and for the scandal that had been mitigated by todays' society's generally loose moral standards.

"I understand yer position as a father tae yer daughter, sir, however apologies are unwarranted as I am not affronted in truth. I do indeed understand the circumstance. My opinion of the only matter which needs forgiveness is time, fur it has stolen Sylvie and me apart from anither fur too many years. Nonetheless, I rejoice presently that we are reunited at last," Leif said genuinely.

Dad became silent for a moment and Mom remained quiet also as they caught each other's glances from opposite ends of the dining table. I could only focus on the hammering in my chest and heat in my cheeks from the tremendous guilt I felt as I squarely received the blame for my supposed situation with Leif.

"Then, I'm assuming, in that case, you'll have no opposition to finally legitimizing your relationship with her," Dad resumed, responding to Leif's optimism.

"The question of our wedding is moot, fur we are already wed as I do hope that ye are already weel awaur, sir," Leif said.

"Forgive me. I didn't mean the insult. I'm merely driving home the point to both of you that her mother and I were left in the dark regarding the gravity of your relationship," Dad replied.

"Indeed. Quite understood. Nor I either meant any slight tae ye, Master Esperanza. It grieves me most sincerely that I didnae have the proper opportunity tae seek yer daughter's hand in marriage," Leif replied honestly.

"But we just recently spoke with Father Hanley about officiating a wedding between us at Saint Monica's, and we scheduled a date," I interposed carefully into the conversation. My parents' eyes shot toward me and I swallowed hard.

"Really?" Mom responded, sounding pleased.

"Yes," I said, fixing my attention onto her, gravitating toward her approval.

"That's wonderful," Mom said, smiling at me. Her gaze then shifted toward Dad and she gave him a hopeful look.

"Yet, prior tae Sylvie and I proceeding with this new wedding, I must nonetheless pursue yer blessing fur her hand upon this moment," Leif requested as he steadily gazed at Dad. Dad paused momentarily and suddenly I found myself no longer breathing while anticipating his reply. He was thinking while he held Leif's gaze, and I feared the unexpected possibility of him denying Leif's request—despite everything that had already occurred between us. As I stared at Dad, waiting for his answer, I understood the fullness of the depth of injury I'd caused him and Mom by never having had them informed of the fact that Leif and I had been married.

"What's your position, Sylvie?" Dad asked decidedly, shifting his serious eyes toward me.

"My position?" I stumbled.

"That's right. What is it?" Dad pressed.

"Well—I—I'm committed to my relationship with Seamus," I stammered, surprised that Dad's attention suddenly turned toward me.

"Are you?" he questioned.

"Yes, I am, of course," I replied certainly, nodding accordingly.

"I ask you because your mother and I need to be assured—for the kids' sake—if you understand my meaning. The time to be completely honest with us, by being most importantly so to yourself, is now," Dad said to me.

"I'm truly committed, Dad. I want nothing more than to be with him," I said truthfully.

"I hope it's more than you're feeling responsible, or obligated," he replied.

"No, it's more than that," I said undoubtedly.

"Then, why?" he asked directly.

"Because, he makes me happy and I love him," I responded really. Dad nodded in response, still thinking, and paused momentarily.

"I understand your desire to ask me for my blessing, and it is my wish to grant it as long as the relationship you have with my daughter is equally desired by her. I know time's passed and that things between the both of you now must be great, but let's be honest and set the rose colored glasses aside for a moment.

"You both have matured since the last time you've seen each other, so I'm assuming things will be considered more seriously this time. Whatever differences you both may have had in the past must be appreciated from a united front on your end as a whole. Otherwise, what's the point? It makes no sense to commit when there's no real unity in confronting challenges as a couple—now, or in the future. There's no such thing as a white picket fence regarding families, households, or relationships between people, as reality would show. But anyone can strive for making the best out of any situation, or relationship—so long as it isn't harmful.

"So, the more you're willing to accept that life has its challenges, the more likely you'll be able to overcome those challenges as a pair. Copping out of promises after the choice was first considered and then had been made to commit is dishonest. And you know how I feel about dishonesty. It's a character flaw I don't tolerate. Neither should anyone else. So, it's important to rise to the occasion and take life by the bullhorns in order to achieve fulfillment out of it. Do you catch my drift?" Dad turned his eyes toward me and I knew exactly to whom he was directing his words.

"I know, Dad."

"Are those issues resolved?"

"Yes, completely."

"In that case, I trust you," he said, meaning it. I nodded in response, then Dad turned his attention toward Leif. "But while my wife and I are still admittedly rather disappointed in being ignorant to the fact that you had eloped, I now see no reason why we can't forge a solid relationship with each other from here on into the future. If you agree to commit to this family by dedicating yourself to my daughter, and because she's expressed her willingness to promise herself to your relationship with her, then I will fully give you my blessing."

"I thank ye most sincerely, Master Esperanza. Ye chasten and honor me, fur I am yer daughter's most humble and devoted servant," Leif replied with polite earnestness filled with gratitude. Dad nodded in response, accepting Leif's vow.

"Lastly, since we've come to this understanding between us, I'd prefer it if you were to simply call me Leo and my wife would also agree if you'd call her Bernadette," Dad required candidly in an amicable tone now.

"Yes, there's no need for formality. Especially, since we're family," Mom agreed definitively with a smile.

"As ye wish," Leif responded adequately, nodding once in accordance.

"Good," Dad said, satisfied. "So, when's the wedding date?"

"November eighteenth," I interposed again, catching Dad's attention. "It was the earliest date that could be scheduled for us for it."

"All right. That gives time to prepare, which is fine," Dad replied, satisfied again. "Now that the issue is settled, let's continue enjoying our dinner." He scooped up some mashed potatoes with a small slice of roast beef onto his fork and began eating.

"So now that we're getting to know you, Seamus, why not give us a little history? Tell us how you first met Sylvie?" Mom asked inquisitively.

"I first encountered Sylvie upon a desolate road. She explained that her car had broken. She was alone upon the road and therefore I safeguarded her from those who would bring her peril," Leif explained.

"That was very considerate of you," Mom said thankfully.

"'Twas my duty tae transport her tae safety," Leif replied.

"Well, we can't thank you enough for assisting her. Anything could have happened to her in that case, and we're just fortunate that it had been you to help her. Never know what people's motivations are these days," Mom responded.

"Can't argue that," Dad said certainly. "Bernadette also tells me that you're a retired military man?"

"Aye, I am a retired major in the British army," Leif confirmed as he began eating the food on his plate now, following Dad's lead.

"I'm a retired colonel myself from the U.S. marines," Dad informed him, more at ease.

"Sylvie has told me of yer honorable military service," Leif responded interestedly.

"Did she?" Dad looked surprised, briefly bouncing his eyes toward me.

"Indeed," Leif assured simply.

"I see. Well, I served as a surgeon for many years and was honored to do it. Hell of a job trying to put those boys back together," Dad said as he remembered his time in service.

"Aye," Leif agreed, politely nodding.

"So, where did you serve?" Dad attentively asked Leif.

"He was in Afghanistan," I blurted, lying for Leif instead.

"No surprise there. That was my last tour also. Lost several good friends in that fight. How about you?" Dad responded, keeping his eyes on Leif.

"My brother perished in battle," Leif answered, reminiscing.

"Oh, you had a brother who served also?" Dad asked.

"Aye," Leif replied.

"What was his name?" Dad inquired.

"His name was Finley. My elder brother," Leif informed him.

"Where you guys in the same unit?" Dad asked curiously.

"We belonged tae the same regiment, aye," Leif responded simply.

"My condolences to you for the loss of your brother," Dad said sympathetically.

"Thank ye most kindly, sir," Leif appreciated. Dad nodded thoughtfully, appearing compassionate.

"War's an ugly demon," Dad condemned, relating to Leif.

"Aye," Leif agreed also.

"How's it been for you since you've been back from fighting?" Dad asked.

"I care not tae dwell upon it, as it brings nae benefit of solace tae me," Leif admitted.

"I know what you mean," Dad sympathized. "It's much easier to try to forget about it. But, if you're ever in the mood to share stories, I'd be interested to exchange some."

"I shall bear the offer in mind. Thank ye," Leif appreciated again.

"No need for thanks. It's what we veterans do for each other," Dad replied with fraternity. Leif nodded in accordance. "So, what do you do with yourself now that you're out of the army?" Dad continued interestedly.

"I have delved deeply into mercantilism," Leif disclosed.

"Interesting. You're a capitalist. You'll have something in common with Sylvie's brother, Kyle. I'm supposing your interests are American?" Dad asked.

"They are," Leif replied.

"What do you invest in?" Dad inquired with intrigue.

"I have investments in various commodities particular tae textiles, copper, paper and sugar," Leif revealed.

"Interesting. No stock in tech or medicine?" Dad asked curiously.

"I cannae say that I have," Leif responded plainly.

"Well, I guess construction and retail are solid for now until the market begins slowing down as predicted. But tech is always a sure bet because of the military. So are pharmaceuticals, since the demand is solid—you know, because people's health is always in question. You might want to consider talking to Kyle about expanding your portfolio. He's sure to help you with that," Dad advised kindly.

"Thank ye fur the consideration," Leif replied politely.

"Of course," Dad responded, glad to assist.

"So," Mom began, inserting herself into the conversation now when she looked at me and Leif, "where do you think you'll go on your honeymoon?"

"Well—I—I don't think I've really thought about it… I don't know—maybe Hawaii, I suppose," I regarded awkwardly.

"Oh! Hawaii would be so nice!" Mom responded enthusiastically. "Such a lovely place. We were there several years ago. It's a perfect destination for a honeymoon."

"I shall like very much tae see Hawaii," Leif said, encouraged, as we gazed at Mom's delighted face.

"Then, I guess that's where we'll go," I agreed spontaneously, as we both forgot about returning to *Taigh Gràs* for a moment.

"Wonderful! I'm sure you'll both have a great time there together," Mom replied, looking supportively at us. "I know it's very early on to consider, but your wedding date will quickly approach, so have you considered how intimate you'd like the wedding to be?"

I shook my head a little in response.

"Well, start considering it, sweetheart, so we can plan," Mom suggested.

"Okay—well, since we're thinking about it now, I feel that I'd like for a small ceremony this time," I replied thoughtfully.

"I agree. A small wedding this time with just family and close friends will be nice to have," Mom said.

"Nanna?" Little Leif innocently interrupted, finally.

"Yes, sweetheart?" Mom said, turning her attention toward her grandson.

"I finished eating all my veggies," he said, showing her his empty plate.

"Yes, I see," she replied nicely, noticing his plate.

"Do you have dessert I can have now?" he asked her.

"Yes, I do, in fact," she said pleasantly.

"What is for dessert?" Leila inquired interestedly as she was finishing the last of her mashed potatoes.

"It's Neapolitan ice-cream," Mom revealed.

"What's that?" Leila asked strangely.

"It's chocolate, vanilla and strawberry ice-cream all together," Mom informed both of them.

"Yummy!" Little Leif expressed enthusiastically.

"Yeah, yummy!" Leila agreed.

"Well, if your mother helps me bring your plates into the kitchen, then you'll both receive your desert in a jiffy," Mom said to them as she bounced a hinting eye toward me. I had just completed the last portion of food on my plate also and excused myself from the table, gathering my plate from it as I understood her cue. Readily following her indication, I assisted collecting the kids' plates and proceeded with Mom out of the dining room, leaving Dad and Leif alone in conversation among themselves.

When we entered the kitchen, I began rinsing the plates in the sink, intending to load them into the dishwasher as Mom collected fresh desert bowls from one of the cupboards. I heard her go to the freezer and pull the door open to retrieve the ice-cream. When she had it, she arrived closely standing next to me at the counter and set the couple of bowls with the tub of ice-cream over it. I turned a curious eye toward her, and she caught my glance with a knowing little smile.

"Well?" I quietly prompted her.

"He's extremely lovely, sweetheart," she replied truly.

"You really like him?" I responded with utter relief, feeling myself smiling with her.

"I love him," she said.

"What about Dad? You know how scrutinizing he is. Do you think he likes him too?"

"I believe he's extraordinarily impressed with him. Liking him is not even close to being an issue for him, because he already admires him," Mom disclosed. I sighed and fully smiled, gladdened by her. "It seems the kids are very comfortable with him also," she observed.

"Yeah, they're already attached to him. They love him as much as he loves them," I said.

"I'm so happy to hear it. And, I'm so very happy that you and he found each other again," she replied in a heartfelt tone.

"Me too, Mom," I replied as she turned directly facing me and slipped her hands over my shoulders so that we looked at each squarely in the eyes.

"Your father and I have dreamed for so long for your happiness, sweetheart. I'm incredibly elated you've found it, finally. You haven't any idea the happiness I feel for you. You deserve to know what joy is, of all people, sweetie," she said truly. She drew me into her arms and soundly embraced me.

Embracing her in return, my eyes welled with tears and I began to cry, understanding and feeling her deep heartfelt feelings for me. I heard her sniveling too and the both us wept from complete happiness. "We better stop all this sniffling before we make a mess of ourselves. Your dad and Seamus won't understand, and are going to think we're just a couple of silly drama queens if they discover us," she joked. I giggled and she gently drew me away from her, clearing my watery gaze with the pads of her thumbs as she now held my face between her soft hands.

She lightly kissed my forehead when my tears had cleared, then quickly cleared her own appearance also. Checking each other as we collected ourselves, we smiled at each other when we were satisfied, then resumed with what we were originally doing. As I quickly finished loading the rinsed dishes into the dishwasher and washed my hands, I helped her complete scooping out ice-cream into the desert bowls for the kids.

After she returned the ice-cream tub into the freezer, I followed Mom back out of the kitchen and into the dining room, each of us holding a bowl full of freshly scooped ice-cream for the kids. A tidal wave of indescribable relief came over me as I felt wholly at peace by my parents' reception of Leif when returning into the dining room.

As I realized this, a profound feeling of the love my parents had for me filled my heart while we served the children their dessert. It was a realization that I hadn't really acknowledged until now. The feeling it brought me was the knowing of unconditional love as I returned to sitting at the table, and quietly observed my parents and Leif continue genuinely engaging each other in amiable conversation. As I watched them, my security returned and contentment calmed my nerves, finally bringing my wild pent-up fears to rest.

Twenty-Seven

It's been a month now since Leif arrived from 1768 and living with us. Every day since has been filled with contentment and happiness as if we'd never known the fear and loneliness of separation. He and the kids have been inseparable with every weekend filled with fairytales told, games played, trips to the parks and children's museums—activities galore to fill the calendar for the rest of the year. Every weekday he and I took the opportunity to enjoy a morning stroll as we walked the kids to school before I left for work during the day. While I wasn't thinking about him as I tended to my pediatric patients, I spent time giggling on the phone with him during lunch as I ate alone in my office.

A smile came to my face as I thought about our recent days together while now sitting on the edge of the tub in my bathroom at home, waiting for the results of the pregnancy test I'd just taken. I was a day late receiving my menstrual cycle when it always appeared like clockwork, and anticipated the test result with nervousness.

Suddenly, the door moved ajar and Leif appeared, stepping into the bathroom and our eyes met, catching me off guard.

"Hi," I said unevenly, startled to see him.

"Och, forgive me. I wisnae awaur of yer presence as I came tae use the pot," he apologized, surprised to see me also.

"No—it's ok—come use it," I stammered, waving him inward.

"Very weel," he accepted, closing the door behind himself. He proceeded unzipping his fly and began reliving himself in the toilet while I remained sitting on the tub's edge. His eyes turned toward me and I smiled nervously at him. "Whit are ye about?" he curiously asked, noticing my demeanor.

"Well—I—I think there's a chance we might be parents again," I replied. His brows drew together, appearing questioningly.

"I am puzzled, fur how micht we be parents again when that is who we are already?" he asked strangely.

"I mean that there's a chance that I could be pregnant," I clarified. His eyes abruptly widened and his mouth gaped. He quickly finished relieving himself, flushed the toilet and zipped his pants before fully turning toward me with undivided attention as he raked a hand through his long silky hair.

"Bairned," he said, realizing the possibility.

"Yeah," I replied, nodding a little.

"Is it true?" he asked, shortly excited as he grinned with a heartened look.

"Well, I don't know yet," I answered cautiously.

"Why do ye not ken?" He suddenly looked curious as the grin curving his lips slightly diminished.

"It's very early to know for certain. That's why I'm taking a test for pregnancy in order to find out," I explained, observing him briskly washing his hands now in the sink.

"A test? Ye mean an examination?"

"In a manner, yes."

"Shall I remove myself whilst ye execute this examination?" He toweled his hands dry and looked directly at me.

"No, it's all right. You don't have to go anywhere. The test is right here resting beside me on the edge of the tub," I disclosed. He stepped forward and I gathered it between my fingers to show him.

He peered at it, grimacing a little, not understanding. "It's an indicator," I said, pointing to the window on the wand for him to see. "When this portion of the stick is exposed to urine, it causes a reaction and measures a female hormone called Human Chorionic Gonadotropin. If the hormone is present, then a plus sign will appear in this window, meaning the result is positive and I'd be pregnant. If not, then a negative sign will show instead, indicating that I'm not."

"Och..." he replied, slightly clueless to my explanation. "Hence, an integer symbol appears determining whether ye are bairned or not as a result of the content within yer urine."

"Yes."

"Clever," he said, impressed as he understood now. "Has a symbol yet appeared?" He leaned slightly closer to see the wand's window as I was holding it in view before us.

"Not yet, it seems. I only urinated on it less than a minute ago. It takes about a minute for the sign to appear," I informed him.

"Och," I understood.

"Would you be happy if I were pregnant again?" I asked curiously.

"Whit sort of inane question are ye asking?" He responded, returning his eyes to mine, giving me an incredulous look.

I shrugged a little, almost apprehensive to raise the subject.

"I was just wondering," I replied meekly.

"Why must ye wonder when ye ken that I would rejoice?" he asked obviously. "Would ye not be jubilant as weel as I?"

"Of course, I would be," I replied certainly.

"Then, yer question tae me is puzzling," he said oddly.

"I was just wondering that if you had the chance to defer having a child, would you consider it?" I asked honestly. I didn't think he could have given me an even more incredulous look, but he did as he stared at me. Then, the look in his eyes suddenly became stern.

"I recall that we had a similar discussion long ago whilst we waur journeying tae Fort William Henry," he remembered.

"I remember that," I replied, clearly remembering.

"I expect that ye do recall it as weel as I," he said undoubtedly. "The concern at the time was the risk of yer being bairned whilst under the duress of perilous conditions as we waur at war."

"Yes, it was a concern."

"Indeed, a most grave one. Yet, whit other concern could be matched presently, when thaur is none?"

"You're right. There isn't any concern that could compare to that," I admitted.

"Then, why ponder this question at all?" he asked plainly.

"I'm thinking about it because if there's a chance that I'm not pregnant then we can postpone having another child so that we could fly to Hawaii for our honeymoon. Otherwise, if it turns out that I am pregnant now, then we won't be able to go since I'll be too far along in my pregnancy to safely fly there," I explained.

"'Twould be a mere inconvenience that is all, would it not? Tae delay our honeymoon would bring us nae harm."

"Except, I was really hoping that we could go—to celebrate and enjoy each other alone before... well—you know—before we have to leave for *Taigh Gràs*," I tried explaining. He suddenly cocked an eyebrow and gazed inquisitively at me.

"Ye have contemplated *Taigh Gràs*?" he asked curiously.

"I have."

"Micht yer final sentiment be in agreement?"

"I just want us to be together, Leif—that's it, primarily—and I want you to be happy no matter where we choose to live," I said sincerely.

"I care fur yer happiness as weel."

"I know you do."

"Micht ye believe in truth that you could be content at *Taigh Gràs*?"

"I believe so. I was actually very happy when I was there with you. I don't see how that could ever change. It's beautiful there."

"I wished fur ye tae be gleeful as ye once waur when we first resided thaur."

"I was very happy being there. I'm sure I'll be just as happy there again."

"'Tis my wish fur ye tae be so. Ye forgot yer former life whilst we waur thaur fur a period, I reckon," he said, reminiscing.

"That's because I had you."

"As I had ye."

"Yeah. So, I'll be happy there again."

"So, shall I. Ye restore my heart." His eyebrow came down to rest normally above his eye, but the inquisitive expression turned solid with conviction. "However, as we continue tae address this new question before us, I say 'tis an honor and a privilege tae be blessed with bairns."

"I agree with you," I responded, perceiving his earnestness along with the added pensiveness in his unwavering eyes. "I'm just asking would it hurt us to wait?"

"I am unsettled with the prospect of toying with procreation," he said bluntly.

"Why?" I asked, wanting to know exactly.

"I reckon 'tis dishonoring tae manipulate the will of God. 'Twould be sinful," he answered with certainty. "'Tis not whit I desire."

"What do you desire instead?"

"Tae have whit God bestows upon us."

"But we do have that—and we'll continue to have whatever He gives us."

"It unsettles me."

"Why?"

"He may grant us naught henceforth should I permit ye tae toy, and I fear punishment fur it," he replied gravely that corresponded with the gaze he was giving me.

"You believe that God will punish us," I echoed, understanding him.

"Certainly."

"But He didn't punish us for using my cycle beads. In fact, He blessed us with healthy twins."

"I presume 'tis because I have devoted my prayers tae His forgiveness," Leif responded unequivocally. I suddenly realized the true guilt he felt, and I felt horrible he was burdened by it.

"Please don't think of us having sinned when we were just using the knowledge God gave us found in medicine to benefit my safety," I replied truly.

"Yet, waur is the peril presently which warrants such action?" he asked realistically.

"There isn't any," I confessed.

"Precisely."

"Well—then..." I drifted for a moment, thinking, disappointed, as I broke away from his gaze, glancing at the blank test.

"Aye?" he prompted, sounding thoughtful, and I returned my eyes to his.

"Then, if it turns out that I'm not pregnant now, I will likely be so between now and the time for our honeymoon, which means there's a considerable chance that we may never go to Hawaii before the baby's born. And as I continue thinking about it, we'd also likely have to postpone returning to *Taigh Gràs*, because quantum leaping while pregnant is a heavy risk—given my experience with the twins the day they were born when I returned here," I said.

"I hudnae considered this new peril... Aye, transporting through time is most uncomfortable at best upon the body," he recognized. I nodded in agreement.

"So, knowing that, would you feel more comfortable now if we waited to have another child?" I asked carefully. He paused and pensively gazed at me for a moment.

"Whilst I am eager fur anither bairn, in truth, 'twould not be worth a tragedy if ye waur in such a state," he said genuinely.

"I don't think so either," I agreed.

"Aye..." He paused meditatively again. I bit my lip, wondering what thoughts were running through his mind.

"So? What are you thinking?" I prodded patiently.

"I reckon it wise tae act prudently once more in this case as we must transport ourselves through time," he said thinkingly. "Yer welfare is my utmost concern, and I shall never risk the fate of my bairns. Born or unborn."

"I know," I replied carefully.

"However..." he started, then paused as he caught himself.

"However?"

"Yer cycle-beads waur lost tae the brook," he remembered.

"It's okay," I dismissed considerately. He nodded slightly in acceptance, pondering while maintaining an unfaltering gaze to mine.

"Micht ye string anither?"

"Are you agreeing to the delay, then?" I wondered.

"Aye," he said simply. I nodded correspondingly.

"Except you should know that I'll be using medicine this time for it, instead," I informed him.

"A remedy?" His brow furrowed, seeming suddenly concerned.

"Yes."

"Remedies fur such matters are poison. I shall not permit yer use of any sort of a solution," he forbade adamantly.

"It's not what you think, though."

"'Tis exactly whit I ken of such nostrums. The lasses who ingest them are quick tae perish. I prohibit it," he said strictly.

"But you're forgetting how far medicine has advanced. I promise you that I won't die if I were to take that kind of medication," I swore.

"If not, ye will most certainly be left barren," he challenged, unpersuaded.

"That's not true," I replied, shaking my head a little.

"'Tis indeed true."

"Yes, solutions of that kind from the past were very harmful to women. I'm not disagreeing with you at all regarding that. But you must understand that medicine has greatly advanced for women since then, and they've benefited from it. I can promise you that if I were to take this kind of medication for preventing pregnancy, I will not be left sterile. Numerous women today use birth control that isn't harmful to them to prevent pregnancy. And when they desire to have children, they simply stop taking the medication and it results in having healthy pregnancies and babies," I explained.

"Indeed?" His eyebrows lifted and he looked shocked.

"Yes," I assured.

"Yoo're raither persuasive in yer seamless argument," he replied, as I could see now that he was considering me.

"That's only because what I'm telling you is true," I said.

"It wulnae hinder yer ability tae have more bairns? Nor will it curse them upon birth?" he pressed.

"I'm confident that it won't," I guaranteed. He nodded slightly again, still seemingly thinking.

"Do ye still regard my expectations of yer duty tae me?" he asked, noticeably serious.

"Just like you've sworn yourself to me," I replied honestly.

"Then, thaur will be nae further inquiries deeming whit has been vowed betwixt us. Ye have therefore sworn tae me that yer life will remain intact. So long as yer welfare and the welfare of our offspring are safeguarded from any harm by consuming this remedy of which ye speak, then I shall grant yer wish tae take such precaution fur this occurrence alone," he said, finally agreeing.

"Thank you," I replied genuinely. He nodded slightly, still appearing pensive, though.

"Yet, if any harm is brought upon ye as a result of this decision, this agreement may never be forgiven in the eyes of our Lord and I shall bear the brunt of this blame," he continued.

"Don't worry. The precaution we're agreeing to take will not kill or harm me, or our future baby, in anyway and I certainly believe will not toss us into Hell since we won't be causing any injury or suffering," I mollified.

The conversations edged into silence briefly as we gazed at each other. I perceived him pondering still as he wouldn't release me from his intense gaze. "Do you have any other concerns about it?"

"I have named them already," he said.

"Okay," I said, nodding a little.

"I merely ponder presently that in the case yoo're already bairned whit micht we do but await the bairn tae be born before dreaming of our return tae *Taigh Gràs*," he said, appearing a bit concerned.

"You're worried about Amity," I fathomed.

"She has been my ward since Finley's demise. I vowed tae Beth that I would manage Amity's welfare as Beth understood that she couldnae obtain the appropriate opportunity that the lass deserves," Leif said. "Though she cares fur her presently in my stead, she mustn't believe that I have abandoned her. I fear it could be so, if I remain fur too long."

"So—then—if it turns out that I'm pregnant, does that mean you'd return without me?" I asked worriedly.

"It micht be so," he disclosed, acknowledging the possibility. I couldn't believe what I was hearing as I looked at him suddenly deeply perturbed.

"I understand your obligation to return—but for us to be separated again... despite the fact that you said time could be manipulated. What if something wrong happens?"

"Fear not."

"Anything could happen, Leif. A simple accident could occur to either one of us while you're on the other side, and we'd never know about it until it was too late—if we're lucky," I replied as my imagination took flight. "We could potentially be separated forever."

He crouched and knelt before me, taking my hand into his and maintained a steadfast gaze to mine.

"I vow tae very much take care, fur I ken that ye will also. In the event that we must separate, ken weel that we shall always be reunited much sooner than before our deaths. I swear it," he guaranteed.

"I don't like talking about our possible separation at all. It frightens me," I responded quietly.

"I swear it," he reiterated, vowing it to his core, I perceived. I nodded a little, breaking from his stalwart gaze and glanced coincidentally at the test I was still holding in my hand.

"Oh, my goodness," I said under my breath, surprised.

"Whit is it?" he asked strangely, noticing my sudden reaction.

"It's negative," I answered, showing him the result.

"Yoo're not yet bairned," he realized.

"No," I replied, shaking my head a tad.

"Och."

"I guess we're in the clear for now."

"Then, we shall see Hawaii efter all."

"Yes." I smiled a little as we gazed at each other, and he seemed unworried. I drew my arms around his neck and I sensed his embrace enveloping me, feeling relieved that the potential for our separation had disintegrated.

When we released each other, he straightened from me and I stood from my seat on the edge of the tub, dropping the wand into the wastebasket by the toilet. As I moved toward the sink to wash my hands, he pressed a gentle kiss on the top of my crown, settling the subject.

That night I received my period, and injected myself with Depo-Provera contraceptive.

Twenty-Eight

Time moved swiftly, it seemed, as we became consumed with the daily particulars of living as a whole family. July silently arrived and the fourth was today. Leif wondered about the day's special occasion as we made preparations to celebrate it. When I mentioned some of the history behind the holiday, he remembered what I had told him long ago while I was with him in the past when I revealed my origins to him. He realized now that we were celebrating Independence Day, and the thought struck him particularly. I perceived by the ruminative look on his face that he was contemplating our future. Despite it, I smiled at him to stymie the heavy thoughts entering his mind and lighten the mood as I was assembling our belongings for outdoor enjoyment into tote bags. He grinned a little at me and resumed helping me with the packing.

We decided to spend the day at my parents' house in Santa Monica and had walked to the beach for a day's relaxation. Though, it seemed half of the city had the same idea in mind and appeared at the beach too. Leif wasn't used to the abundance of individuals around him and found the sport of people watching curiously intriguing.

Attired in a nice white, long sleeve, linen shirt and board shorts that I'd made a great effort in convincing him to wear, he and I waded in the waves with the kids dressed in swimsuits while my parents sat nearby relaxing in their beach chairs beneath a large sun umbrella, watching their grandchildren play.

Occasionally I caught Leif's glance skimming over my body as I was dressed in a modest black swim-dress. I subtly grinned at him, feeling sheepish by his attraction, knowing that he believed the manner in which I was dressed was highly risqué—as was everyone else, and more so, as countless individual women were clad in thong bikinis. But he didn't appear offended as our gazes met. Instead, his face flushed and I noticed his lips warmly curl into an engaging grin which creased his cheeks.

The sun was bright and hot, heating my skin, and illuminating the hazy cobalt sky as it washed over Leif's golden hair in a gilded halo. Except for the lack of curls on his crown, he appeared like Apollo who warmed the Earth with the sun as he pulled it with his chariot across the dawning sky, while Leif was gazing at me, warming my blood.

He approached close beside me and I anticipated his hand slipping affectionally onto the back of my neck. But he only remained standing close and motionless beside me, refraining from a mere touch. I was aware of his inhibition to display intimacy with me in public.

"You're staring at me," I said self-consciously to him as I kept my eyes on our romping kids in the wet sand, feeling his warm gaze transfixed on me.

"I am," he said surely in an even voice.

"Why?"

"How can I not?"

"You're making me bashful."

"Am I?"

"Yes. You are."

"Yet, ye bewitch me, and so I must."

"But you've seen me before."

"Not in this manner," he said certainly. I turned my gaze up to him and our eyes met. His ultramarine eyes were soft and glinted by the sun. His lips were unexpressive as the appearance on his face was genuine. "My blood stirs as I gaze upon ye." His voice suddenly became nearly too low that I almost didn't hear him over the crashing waves and our kids happily screaming in the water not so far away from us. I smiled and the corner of his mouth tilted upward into a little half-grin.

"Did you ever lose hope?" I asked, wanting to know.

"Never," he said.

Leila was heard abruptly screaming and we turned our gazes toward her as she was seen trotting toward us.

"Dad!" she expressed excitedly while approaching.

"Aye, lassie?" Leif responded attentively, observing her as she arrived standing before us.

"Will you help us make a sand castle?" she asked expectantly, looking up at him.

"I shall," he replied, grinning warmheartedly at her.

"Yay!" She jumped up and down with further excitement. Grabbing his hand, she tugged him to follow her out of the shallow waves where we stood. I glanced in the direction where she was pulling him and noticed Little Leif at the shoreline already with his sand pail in hand catching waves inside of it. "You too, Mama! C'mon!" she yelled over her shoulder, glimpsing back at me from behind. I started from the water, following, and met them in the wet sand just beyond the approaching waves crashing at our toes as they cheerfully began building their castle. I sat beside them on the soaked sand and joined them, enjoying the companionship of me and Leif being playful with our kids.

As we enjoyed the beach, the hours imperceptibly passed and eventually I moved away from them while they continued romping along the shoreline, constructing in the sand, to join my parents as they continued relaxing in chairs underneath the shading umbrella. We contentedly watched the kids playing with Leif as he attentively engaged them while the sun dipped lower toward the horizon over the ocean.

Sometime later, Mom suggested the time had come for us to leave the beach for their house in order to have dinner prepared. But the kids were disinclined to part from the water and wished to enjoy themselves for a while longer. However, once our belongs had been packed, I corralled the kids from the shore and we began our trek over the warm sand, heading for my parents' house.

When we arrived there, I promptly bathed the beach away from the kids and dressed them into their pajamas for the evening. Ready for dinner, they rushed away from me, darting out of the bathroom and into the hallway on their way to meet Leif and Dad outdoors in the backyard, where burgers and hotdogs were being grilled. Following them out into the backyard onto the patio, they began playing with their puppy already outside, and I was happy to see Leif and Dad conversing as Dad tended the grill.

They each had a beer in hand and the mood between them was casual and friendly. Tidbits of their conversation was overheard as I briefly glanced around the area looking for Mom. It seemed they were discussing British military history. A topic comfortably geared toward Leif and obviously interesting for Dad. Noticing everyone happily engaged, I withdrew indoors when I found Mom in the kitchen chopping vegetables for a salad and willingly offered my assistance to her.

Soon everything for dinner had been prepared, and we eagerly settled ourselves at the picnic table by the grill on the grass away from the patio near the gated pool, to eat. While Dad shared some of his war stories with Leif, the kids laughed and joked with each other, and Mom was sure to discuss wedding plans with me.

"Mom?" Little Leif called my attention away from my mother as he was eating his hotdog.

"Yes, sweetie?" I replied, turning my gaze toward his.

"Are we going to see fireworks tonight?" he wondered, gazing at me with big blue eyes.

"Of course. You'll see plenty of them tonight," I answered.

"I can't wait to see them!" he anticipated cheerfully.

"Well, it'll be dark soon and then they'll start," I said.

"Yay!" he expressed excitedly, dancing a bit in his chair, causing me to smile at him.

"I can't wait! I can't wait! I can't wait!" Leila sang expectantly after drinking some of her milk. "How fast will the sun go down?"

"In a bajillion hours!" Little Leif exclaimed, mimicking exasperation.

"That's too long to wait! I'm gonna pop like a balloon!" Leila replied with large emerald eyes.

"Speaking of things that pop, how would the both of you like to playing with bubbles after you've finished eating to help pass the time before fireworks?" Mom asked, smiling pleasantly at them.

"You have bubbles?" Leila asked, suddenly excited for this new idea.

"Sure, I do. I bought bubbles yesterday for you two to play with, and a bubble machine that looks like an elephant for you to enjoy," Mom informed them.

"Does the elephant blow bubbles out of his nose?" Little Leif asked interestedly while laughing at the idea.

"You guessed it!" Mom replied.

"Goody! I'm almost done eating my hotdog now. So, I wanna see it!" Leila responded, showing us her small piece left to eat.

"Take your time, so that you won't choke," I warned her.

"Okay," she agreed, nodding also.

"Well, I just have one more tiny bite left," Little Leif said, showing us the small remainder of his hotdog also.

"It looks like two bites to me," I said.

"Nope!" he disagreed, shaking his head, and stuffed all that was left of his hotdog into his little mouth. "See?" he asked with stuffed cheeks.

"I do see! Chew carefully," Mom said, warning him also. "I'll follow that lead and set up the bubbles for you now."

"Goody, goody gumdrops!" Leila exclaimed happily.

Laughing, Mom excused herself from the table and began arranging the bubble machine for them over the lawn. The kids hastily completed their meal and dashed from their seats at the table, running toward their grandmother where she was pouring bubble solution into the machine. In a second, the machine had been filled and she turned it on for them to enjoy. Bubbles quickly appeared into the air, delighting the kids as they chased them around the yard. Bubbles began floating over the table also as Dad and Leif conversed, catching both of their attentions. Leif turned his gaze toward the origin of the bubbles, witnessing the kids cavorting to catch the buoyant orbs flying around them, and chuckled at the novelty of it like Dad, as he too was entertained by his playful grandchildren.

Within an hour the sun began setting, changing the dimming blue sky into darkness. No cloud coverage from the ocean existed tonight and the crescent moon illuminated brightly over the city as it hung low in the horizon.

Suddenly, the first firework blasted colorfully into the air above us. Quickly gathering ourselves, we sat in Adirondack chairs over the lawn to watch the display. Little Leif removed himself from his chair and slipped himself comfortably into my lap, cuddling against me as we watched the celebration, and I noticed Leila also crawling sleepily into Leif's lap for comfort. She cozied up against his chest as we sat next to each other and I glanced at him, smiling at the sight of him affectionately holding his daughter in his arms. He caught me looking at him and a warm grin curved his lips, inciting a greater smile of my own. I shifted my gaze, looking back up at the exploding fireworks overhead, filled with contentment that my family was happy and complete as we enjoyed this time together tonight.

Celebrating Independence Day this time struck me

profoundly while gazing up at the fireworks now; the realization of all the sacrifices made in order for this day to be observed was an absolute blessing in many, many ways—as the thought of our future also flickered in my mind.

WHEN THE FOURTH OF JULY'S CELEBRATION WITH fireworks concluded, the night had comfortably settled into the calming later hours. The kids were exhausted and undoubtedly ready for bed. So, I took the opportunity to assist Mom in tidying up after ourselves in the kitchen before Leif and I bade my parents goodnight for the evening. After placing the kids inside the mini-van, Dad and Leif shook hands and I exchanged affection with my parents before Leif and I left with the kids for returning home.

By the time we arrived at the house and I pulled the car into the driveway, the kids were fast asleep. Leaving the car, I carefully gathered Leila into my arms and Leif collected Little Leif into his as we quietly entered indoors. Climbing up the staircase, headed for the kids' bedroom, he and I mindfully placed them into their beds, beneath their covers. After turning on the nightlight and leaving their door ajar, we left their room for our own.

Cleansing the salty beach day from ourselves, I went to shower and Leif bathed relaxingly in the tub. It was a long joyful day, but I was glad this time had come where I could wash and finally relax.

After showering and dressing for bed, I realized Leif had finished bathing before me and found him already resting beneath the covers as I re-entered the bedroom. With an arm crooked behind his head against the pillows, his eyes were closed, I noticed, while I strode toward my bedside. He looked as peace-fully sleeping as much as I desired to rest at last. Turning down the covers on my side of the bed, I then leaned over my nightstand and reached a hand toward the illuminating lamp to turn it off.

"Leave the lecht, *ceisdein*," Leif requested unexpectedly. I shifted my eyes over my shoulder toward him and realized that he hadn't yet fallen entirely asleep after all.

"I thought you were sleeping already," I responded a little surprised, suddenly removing my fingers from the lamp switch.

"I am awaiting yer arrival," he said, looking at me through the corners of his languid eyes.

"Oh. I'm sorry for keeping you awake. I'm in bed now, so I won't disturb you from sleeping any longer," I apologized.

"Nae matter fur remorse."

"Thanks."

"I am raither already disturbed from sleep."

"You are?" I asked, suddenly worried, knitting my brows as I oddly looked at him.

"Aye."

"What's wrong?"

"I must have a word with ye before we shall rest."

"What is it?" I asked curiously.

He mindfully slipped a sturdy arm beneath me and rolled me over him so now I rested flat on his chest, closely gazing back into his eyes. I noticed his idle eyes begin smiling as the corner of his mouth curled into an intentional little smirk, making him appear mischievous.

"What are you up to?" I asked suspiciously, smiling oddly at him also as I began realizing his flirtation.

"I mean fur a reprimand," he said.

"A reprimand?" I questioned dubiously.

"Aye."

"Who will you reprimand?"

"Why, ye of coorse."

"Me?"

"Aye."

"You're not allowed to reprimand me. Besides, I didn't do anything wrong."

"Ye did plenty inapt, and I am indeed quite permitted tae reprimand ye fur it." The smirk on his face altered into a substantially wide grin, exposing the pearly gleam of his teeth, and creasing his cheeks. I giggled nervously. "Thus, ye will obey me. Is it understood?"

"But Your Grace, what have I done to warrant this response from you when I don't even know what offense I've caused?" I asked innocently, sounding extremely proper in tone while gazing closely into his vibrantly dark blue eyes.

"I have warned ye about the fit ye will cause upon me should ye be nude fur all tae witness," he said, sounding disapproving despite the contradicting smirk on his lips.

"Nude?"

"Aye."

"What in Heaven's name are even talking about?" I looked incredulously at him.

"Today. Upon the seashore. Ye waur nude before all in public," he disclosed.

"Oh," I giggled guiltily.

"I had granted ye fair warning whit would occur if ever I witnessed ye in such a state."

"But I can't be blamed for that. When in Rome, remember?"

"Och, a tragic excuse," he scoffed, feigning displeasure.

"I was in my swimsuit—a modest one at that, mind you—essentially clothed and appropriately dressed for the occasion," I contradicted. The smile on his face remained, and I couldn't help the smile on my own lips as we stared into each other's eyes.

"Nonetheless. It so seems the male condition cannae withstand the lure of yer beauty despite when yoo're attired fully. Therefore, the fact that ye waur bare skinned whilst at the sea before plenty strange beasts of the male persuasion who leered at ye, merely served their temptation tae ravish ye," he said.

"Their temptation to ravish me?" I questioned, giving him a ridiculous look.

"Indeed," he replied unequivocally. I smiled suspiciously at him again when a sudden thought entered my mind.

"Are you jealous?" I inquired curiously.

"Granted that I am voluptuary within the bedchamber, yet I shall never share ye with anither man," he swore.

"Our hearts are locked to each other's. Don't you remember that?" I asked. His hand slipped into the back of my loose ringlets and he drew my lips down over his, gently kissing me with yearning.

"I ken," he half-whispered against my lips, kissing me.

"Then, don't worry. I'd never be with anyone else even if my life depended on it," I muttered over his supple mouth.

I parted my lips to catch my breath while kissing him in kind when his tongue slipped into my mouth, dominating it with ownership, stealing the very air from my lungs.

Twenty-Nine

One August afternoon, after gathering the kids from our swimming pool and latching the surrounding gate to the area, the kids decided to remain in the back-yard to play on their swing set on the lawn. So, Leif preceded me indoors to use the bathroom as I continued lightheartedly engaging our children while gathering our damp towels before bringing them indoors into the laundry room. When I had finished collecting them all and bantering with the kids, I left the kids to themselves and proceeded inside the house for the laundry room. But as I left the room and began toward the kitchen to prepare snacks for us, I unexpectedly heard voices emanating in the foyer by the front door. Recognizing their voices, I instead wandered in that direction curiously wondering about the reason for Jasmine's unanticipated visit while she was conversing with Leif.

"So, yeah, I hope you'll come," she was overheard saying in a flirtatious tone as I was making my way out of the kitchen through the hallway, and approached them by the front door.

"Hey, nice to see you, Jasmine. This is a surprise. What brings you by?" I asked politely as I greeted her.

"Oh, hey, Sylvie," she replied, appearing pleasant, which didn't exactly match the insincere smile and look in her eyes. She suddenly reached and gave me a shallow embrace, then just as quickly released me. "Sorry for my sudden surprise visit, but I was just telling Seamus that I was having a pool party to celebrate the last days of summer vacation before our kids start school again soon."

"Oh, sounds like fun," I responded, casually studying her face for any glimpse of depth.

"Yeah. So, I invited Seamus—and, you too, of course—to come to the party," she said unnaturally. "Bring the kids too—obviously."

"Thank you. That's nice of you. When is it?" I asked.

"Next Saturday. I know it's short notice. But I decided to have it impromptu. You know? I'm a little whimsical as you already know." She smiled unevenly. "So, do you think you'll come? Say that you will. It'll make me happy."

I wasn't certain that I actually wanted to attend her party. I sensed her attraction to Leif and I wondered about how genuine she was being with me as I silently questioned her motivation. She was never shy of her feelings when it involved her own interests regarding men in general, and my tapping intuition now suddenly made me feel uncomfortable with her—though I hoped I was mistaken and wished to give her the benefit of the doubt because we were friends.

I smiled at her, shirking my intuition, and not wanting to appear weird when I realized my pause to her question. She and Leif were obviously anticipating my reply and sensed my hesitation by the looks on their faces as I met Leif's wondering gaze, aware of her watching me also.

"Please say you'll come. It won't be the same without you there," she resumed encouragingly, insisting. I returned to looking at her, and smiled a little as my disinclination nagged at me while suddenly trying to conjure a gentle and realistic excuse that was polite for not attending, to simply spare her feelings. But I drew a blank. "So, you'll come?" she persisted eagerly again.

"Y-yeah. What time?" I stammered, feeling pressured.

"Noontime."

"All right. We'll see you."

"Great! I'm so looking forward to it. It'll be a blast," she responded enthusiastically. "All right. Well, don't let me keep you. I'll be off now."

"Okay."

"Bye." She abruptly turned from the front door and started away down the steps away from the porch. I watched her walk along the path and leave through the picket gate as it latched behind her when she entered onto the sidewalk, then I closed the door. A small sigh escaped me. I turned my eyes toward Leif as he remained standing beside me in the foyer and he looked at me somewhat curiously.

"Micht thaur be a matter?" he asked, noticing my demeanor.

"No—well—I'd rather we simply spend our time alone together than go to her party," I admitted.

"Why micht that be?" he inquired unusually. I shrugged a little, not wanting to divulge the full reason.

"Well, I know that you're not too fond of crowds," I started. "And, her parties are always full of people and overbearing music. I just don't wish for you to feel overwhelmed or anything like that."

"I see."

"Yeah, so. On second thought, you know what?"

"Aye."

"Maybe, I'll just cancel our going and make up some excuse for us not being able to attend, instead."

"Nae, ye have already given yer word that we shall be present. I shall fare. Dinnae be concerned," he contradicted. I paused for a second, studying the assuredness on his face.

"Are you sure?" I considered.

"Quite. I shall be alrecht. I'm growing accustomed tae yer era," he said, unfazed by the challenge.

"Okay. Only if you think you'll not mind the crowd. It could be overstimulating," I warned, nevertheless.

"'Twill not be a concern. I may assure ye. Have I not been subsisting weel thus far?"

"Yes, you've been managing very well."

"So?"

"All right." I nodded. "We'll go to her pool party."

"Very weel," he agreed. "Now, explain. Whit micht a pool party be?"

"A festive occasion at a swimming pool where everyone can swim and enjoys grilled food, or sandwiches, and drinks. Things like that."

"A garden party of sorts," he likened.

"Of sorts," I agreed.

"Sounds quite jubilant," he remarked.

"Yes."

"Was it not kind of Mistress Jasmine fur the invitation?" he regarded.

"She likes having parties," I answered instead.

"Does she?"

"Yes. The more, the merrier, is her philosophy," I said in a faint, ironic tone.

"I see," Leif replied, catching my inflection. He gave me a considering look as his brow scarcely drew together.

"I should probably start making snacks for everybody. I'm sure you're all hungry by now," I suggested, preempting his impulse to question my unusual reaction regarding her.

"Och, aye," he replied, suddenly reminded of food. "Mayhap, I shall proceed tae the pot before returning outdoors with the bairns whilst awaiting tae graze a wee bit."

I nodded and he winked at me, then turned, starting his way through the hallway, heading for the bathroom. So, I proceeded out of the foyer and went to the kitchen. While preparing snacks, the thought of going to Jasmine's party didn't exactly settle with me well for reasons that felt rather nebulous. I couldn't quite articulate what I was feeling at the moment, but what I knew was that I wasn't comfortable. Still, I disregarded myself, believing everything was in fact all right.

WE ARRIVED THE FOLLOWING SATURDAY AT JASMINE'S house, which merely lay several blocks away from home within the same community. As we meandered our way through the front gate to her house and followed the audible sound of chattering and laughter toward the back of it, I noticed a select number of guests attending from school and the neighborhood as we rounded the side of the house and entered into the backyard.

Jasmine had many friends and acquaintances through work and socializing as a result of her involvement in exclusive charities throughout town, along with the elite beach club to which she belonged. So, I expected her house to be full of different guests with their kids from these associations. Instead, those attending belonged to the small parent circle to which I belonged from school that I'd recognized along with several loosely acquainted neighbors. And while she had explained that the party was to celebrate the last days of summer before school began, I also expected more familiar families from school to be here as well, but weren't —to my surprise.

"Oh, hey! I'm so glad you guys made it," Jasmine expressed excitedly as she immediately noticed us entering the yard, and left the people she was conversing with to greet us instead. "I was wondering when you guys were going to show up."

"Are we late?" I replied, a little confused.

"Nope. Just thought you'd show up kinda early like the other girls." She gave me a superficial hug and light kiss on the cheek, then turned toward Leif and threw her arms around him with a tighter hug and kiss also over his cheek.

Startled, Leif suddenly stepped a little backward from her and instantly flushed, clearing his throat as Leila and Little Leif happily darted from us to join the friends they'd recognized already playing in the pool. Simultaneously, Heather and Rick along with Autumn and Glen, including Maria, appeared and surrounded us as they also gladly greeted the both of us. As the men were exchanging handshakes, friendly hugs passed between the women and me.

Cordial banter began and I became slightly distracted from my other friends, noticing Jasmine focusing her intrigued attention on Leif. He and the men were lightly conversing when her attention turned toward him and seemed coquettish. She smiled at him without any regard as she started speaking to him. But my observation was interrupted the moment Heather and my other friends resumed talking to me.

As we were lightly catching up with each other, I casually glanced away from them toward the pool in order to catch a glimpse of some of the kids in the water. I saw mine splashing around as they playfully swam with medium-sized inflatable doughnut rafts over the water with their friends. Leila caught my attention and waved at me as she joyfully screamed and laughed while attempting to climb on top of one of the brightly colored inflated rafts.

"Hey, let's move to sit by the pool so we can talk and watch our kids at the same time," Maria suggested to us, noticing my line of sight.

"Great idea," I agreed. When I turned toward Leif to inform him that I was now locating myself by the pool with my friends, with the assumption he'd soon be joining me when he finished talking with their husbands, Jasmine suddenly placed her palm over his bicep and massaged a caress before I had uttered a word to him.

"Wow, just like I thought," she giggled.

"I beg yer pardon, Mistress Jasmine?" Leif questioned, immediately turning his unexpected attention toward her from the men who had his attention, obviously caught off guard.

"You're strong enough," she smiled blatantly at him as he gave her a weird look and flushed again. His brow shot up along with the hue in his face. I knew he'd been stricken with instant discomfiture as he looked at her. "Here," she said confidently, reaching for the beach towels and full tote bag he was holding and retrieved it from him. "I need a man strong enough to help me carry the heavy food trays and punch containers from the kitchen, and place them on the serving tables out here," she continued saying while passing the packed items from Leif to me to hold now.

"I guess we're chopped liver," Glen joked, alluding to the other guys as he watched her favoring Leif.

"You know better than to say that, Glen. I thought I'd spare enslaving the rest of you this time and give you a well-deserved break," she teased.

"She always puts us guys to work for her during every function she throws," Rick said ironically, informing Leif.

"Thanks for your benevolence for not enslaving us. Never knew it was possible," Glen taunted Jasmine, giving her a light, sarcastic smirk.

"Well, I figured you've already been hazed," she replied, smiling at Glen.

"So, it's Seamus' turn now?" Rick jokingly inserted.

"If you're jealous, I'll enlist you too without hesitating," she said to Rick.

"Not fair," Rick said.

"How?" she asked.

"You're conveniently making the rest of us look bad," Rick accused.

"I don't see how," she responded.

"Apparently, if I decline to help you, then I'm a rude guest and won't appear chivalrous like Seamus here," Rick remarked.

"Go help her, Rick," Heather nudged in an exasperated tone. "But the second you start your antics with him, Jasmine, you'll have me to deal with," she warned half playfully, appearing nonchalant at the same time.

"Uh-oh. Cat fight?" Glen joked, feigning hopefulness as he raised his brow and continued smirking.

"In your dreams, buddy," Autumn injected, scowling at her husband as she also rolled her eyes.

"It was worth a try, anyway," Glen chuckled, shrugging his shoulders, dismissing the idea. Autumn delivered a playful jab, elbowing her husband in the chest.

"Ouch! She's brutal," Glen claimed lightheartedly as he rubbed his chest, pretending to be injured.

"Gotta keep you in line," Autumn warned him.

"Sure, Boss," Glen teased. "But while Seamus and Rick are helping Jasmine, I'll be designated the *loaf.*"

"The loaf?" Jasmine responded with a large smile.

"Of liverwurst," Glen clarified.

"Paté is a delicacy," Jasmine insisted as she countered him.

"I hate liver. In case you hadn't already known," Glen said.

"You do?" Jasmine's eyes widened, seeming surprised.

"Yeah. So, it's anything but luxury cuisine in my book. In fact, it's beneath Rocky Mountain oysters—and, I don't even entertain the idea of ever consuming those," Glen said.

"Wow, such passion. Fine, I'll include your labor with the others. I wouldn't want you to feel equated to the food you hate," Jasmine replied to him with a wink and smug smile. Glen grinned at her and Autumn sighed as she lightly shook her head.

"You guys better behave. That's all I have to say," Autumn said, referencing her husband and Jasmine. Jasmine laughed and shook her head at Autumn, giving her a frivolous look.

"Don't worry, he's in good hands," Jasmine replied flirtatiously as she looked directly at me.

"With all the spies around here, I'm sure everyone will be on their best behavior," Maria chimed in, pointing her comment toward Jasmine with a smile that appeared innocent but wasn't.

Maria turned her glance toward me and the smile on her face heartened with distinction and genuine sincerity. Her expression buoyed my reassurance as I inferred her silent support of our friendship. She then returned to looking at Jasmine and so did I. The look on Jasmine's face slightly altered as the coy smile half vanished when her eyes bounced from Maria to me.

"Now that you've got help to expedite the appearance of food, don't let us starve, Jasmine. You know how kids are especially worse when they're hungry. And since they're swimming, they'll be like brainless piranha," Maria continued saying to her.

Jasmine faintly narrowed her eyes on Maria, understanding Maria's awareness of her hidden intentions.

"Since when have I ever been so negligent, Maria?" Jasmine said, steadying her eyes on Maria.

"There's always a first time for everything. Knowing that, consider me your best friend for preventing that potential," Maria responded with a drop of snark.

"I couldn't be luckier." Jasmine smiled superficially and the irony in her eyes couldn't have been more obvious. "Would any of you girls like a drink?"

"Someone said you were serving Strawberry Daiquiris," Heather inserted as she was closely listening to our exchange. No doubt she'd clued in on the surfacing tension between Jasmine and Maria.

"Of course," Jasmine replied, turning her attention toward Heather now, giving her a more genuine smile.

"I'll have one of those," Heather said.

"Make it two," Autumn requested.

"What about you, Sylvie?" Jasmine asked, returning to looking at me.

"Sounds good to me," I agreed simply.

"Fine," Jasmine replied, then shifted her gaze toward Maria. "How about a Midori Sour, Maria? I know it's your favorite."

"A far cry from straight Midori, right?" Maria jabbed with a giggle.

"Not my favorite," Jasmine said, rolling her eyes.

"Oh, I forgot. It's a Martini on the rocks," Maria replied, giving Jasmine a little knowing wink. "Shaken, of course."

"You know me so well, Maria."

"Friends would know, Jasmine."

"I'll have your Midori Sour served up right away."

"Your hospitality is amazing. But don't let me skip ahead of the line. You know how I frown on preferential treatment," Maria replied flippantly. "Don't go through any trouble on my account. Everyone's going to be starving soon if food doesn't make an appearance first."

"You're so thoughtful, Maria," Jasmine said insincerely, dismissing her when she turned her attention toward our husbands again. "I'm giving you handsome boys a workout. Food and drinks are in the kitchen and are ready to be placed on any of the serving tables around the yard. Thanks in advance. Let's go."

Motioning for them to follow her indoors, they proceeded after her except Leif, who hesitated with a skeptical look in my direction. Meeting his glance, I gave a small uncertain shrug with the same smile as the other guys began leaving us behind.

"I guess the more who help her, the quicker we can sit by the pool," I said to him in a considerate tone, aware of my friends observing us both.

"Aye," Leif agreed.

"I'll be by the pool watching the kids," I informed him.

"Certainly." He then turned from me and proceeded following the other guys with Jasmine in the lead for indoors.

When I returned looking at my friends, realizing their staring at me, a beat of silenced came between us. We simply stood facing each other without a word for a second, aware of Jasmine's questionable demeanor. The awkwardness was apparent and small smiles of sympathy passed over my friends' faces.

"We saved you guys a couple of chairs over here," Heather said to me, breaking the lapsing discomfiture in the air as she pointed to the area by the pool that was shaded by a large umbrella. "It's near where all of our kids are, so you can watch yours perfectly fine from where we'll sit."

"Great. Thanks," I appreciated.

"Yeah, sure. Come on," she replied casually.

I began pacing with her and my two other friends toward the pool where they located the seats they'd originally left to greet me and Leif when we had arrived. Heather showed me the couple of empty seats she'd saved for us among the group, and I placed my tote bag on one of the chairs, and sat in the other as my friends proceeded returning themselves into their chairs also.

Light conversation began between us as my attention frequently turned toward my cheerful kids splashing in the water, to ensure their safety while they played with their friends.

"Did you hear about Jasmine and her pool boy?" Heather asked us, capturing my attention from the kids.

"I can't say that I have," I suddenly responded with shock as I looked at the knowing little grin on her face.

"Yup. The woman has no boundaries—apparently," Autumn replied ironically, appearing also in-the-know.

"She's the very definition of a *cougar*," Maria scoffed.

"I'm aware of the other guy," I responded, a little puzzled.

"The one who was barely twenty-one, right?" Autumn asked me.

"Yeah," I said, nodding.

"That's yesterday's news," Autumn said.

"You mean there's someone other than him?" I asked curiously, giving her an odd look.

"Her pool boy is the current flavor of the month and he's nineteen," Autumn informed me.

"Nineteen?" I gasped as my eyes helplessly bulged.

"That was my reaction," Maria said, agreeing with me.

"It still doesn't keep her from flirting with our husbands, though," Autumn resented.

"I don't know. You might not have to worry about that anymore now that she no longer seems to find them novel," Heather said with a little skepticism.

"What do you mean?" Autumn questioned with apparent doubt.

"No offense, Sylvie, but your husband has stolen the show," Heather explained.

"Has he?" I replied with some caution.

"Everyone adores Seamus. Haven't you noticed? Even the guys have man crushes on him," Heather revealed.

"Yeah, he has that *je ne sais quoi* quality about him. Mysterious. You know?" Autumn determined.

"It's the old fashioned manly chivalrous air he has I think that everyone's attracted to," Heather speculated.

"Yeah, that's it. He's just unusually polite and respectful," Autumn agreed.

"Thank you for saying that," I acknowledged sincerely.

"Are all the men like that in Scotland?" Maria asked curiously.

"Where he's from, they are," I admitted.

"Well, sign me up. I'll go wherever he's from to find my own," Maria joked, and giggles flittered between them.

"Good thing our husbands are with yours in Jasmine's presence, though," Heather warned.

"Strength in numbers," Autumn agreed.

"Well, I'm not worried about Seamus. And, I doubt that

Jasmine would stoop so low," I responded confidently, feeling secure. Certain looks passed between them, expressing doubt.

"It's just good to be aware, Sylvie," Autumn notified.

"It's always good to be aware whenever it involves Jasmine," Heather supported. "She bates any guy to see if they'll bite. And even if they don't, if she's got her eye on them, she'll throw herself out there to undermined them. Ever since she's been divorced, she's been on the hunt."

"She doesn't care how young or old he is, married or not," Maria recognized also. "It's like she's sexually unhinged, or something."

"Definitely that," Autumn agreed. "I caught her shoving her boobs in front of my husband's face when he was sitting here a minute ago by the pool without me."

"What did she do?" I replied, really surprised.

"Well, before you guys showed up, I had stepped away to use the bathroom and when I was making my way back to join Glen again, I spotted her having a conversation with him. While Glen was showing her his phone, she leaned her boobs against his head as she took a look at the pictures he'd just taken of our kids in the pool. And she wasn't wearing the sarong that she's wearing now. Instead, she was just wearing her *very* skimpy thong bikini which barely covers her nipples and her ass. She might as well just be wearing pasties and a ribbon up her ass under that sarong," Autumn derided defensively.

"I was actually impressed that she appears relatively modest in her sarong for this pool party—considering the Brazilian bikini she was wearing at the beach party you threw for everyone last summer, Autumn. Remember that?" Heather gossiped.

"How can anyone ever forget it," Autumn replied intolerably.

"Rick jokes about it. He teases that Jasmine escaped Hefner's mansion," Heather giggled, making Autumn laugh.

"Are you sure Flynt isn't missing her, instead?" Maria joked also, causing more laughter and inciting a cautious grin from me.

"Speaking of which, take a look over there at the table farthest from us," Heather mentioned, noticing Jasmine approaching Leif just as he'd set the large sandwich tray over the table as Glen and Rick were positioning heavy coolers filled with chilled juices and sodas beside it. Jasmine leaned to place the fruit salad bowl next to the sandwich platter with her eyes fixed on Leif, and made an inaudible remark which drew Rick's lighthearted response, inciting Glen to chuckle. But Leif remained unmoved, though he seemed to have said something polite to her. She replied and pointed behind herself toward the house from where they'd just come. Leif then turned from her and proceeded his return toward the house where he briefly vanished.

Within a second, he reappeared, holding another massive platter full of sandwiches and placed them on a separate table where plates, napkins and pitchers of lemonade had already been stationed. As Jasmine had been watching him while still talking with the other guys at the first table, she excused herself from them and began approaching Leif when she glanced our way and happened to catch my staring at her. A careless smile crossed her face, and she shifted her gaze toward Leif again as she continued in his direction.

When she arrived at him by the second table, her eyes turned toward me again and the smile remained over her expression. Returning to looking at Leif, she said something inaudible to him and he gently tilted his head toward her out of cordiality, then withdrew from her, heading in our direction now.

As he arrived standing before us, he noticed my friends and I staring at him with some curiosity.

"Mistress Jasmine requests that I inform ye that the food is prepared fur serving," Leif said, informing us.

"Oh," I responded simply.

"Great," Heather said also and my friends started from their pool chairs to gather their kids out of the water as they thanked him.

"I'll let our kids know that there's food now, in case they're ready to eat," I said to Leif. He nodded a little and I stood from my chair also, stepping from beneath the umbrella out into the sun where he was standing. He kept his attention adhered to me as I moved toward the pool and caught the kids' attention while they played in the water. Moving toward me, Leif stood with me at the edge of the pool as my friends were gathering their kids' attention too.

"Watch me swim under water, Dad! I can hold my breath like a whale," Little Leif yelled excitedly from across the pool and immediately dipped himself beneath the water, swimming toward us until he reached the pool's edge where his head bobbed upward and appeared. Before I could encourage him out of the water, he dipped himself beneath the surface and swam along the edge of the pool away from us.

"I can do that too! Watch me," Leila squealed giddily, ready to impress her father also as she also caught our attention.

"Wait, but aren't you hungry now?" I asked, apprehending her impulse to follow her brother.

"Yup!" she replied enthusiastically with anticipation.

"Then, have a morsel, birdie," Leif encouraged her.

"Okie dokie." She stretched a hand up toward me when she swam to the pool's edge where we were standing. I reached for her little hand, assisting her as I pulled her forth from the water with Leif's help. Easily taking her from me, Leif gathered her into his arms and I moved along the pool's ridge in the opposite direction, following Little Leif as he swam until his head popped up from the water at the other end. He smiled at me and laughed as he waved from afar.

"Did Dad see me?" he asked excitedly, very proud of himself as I arrived to him.

"Yes, he's watching you right now, of course," I replied as Leif now arrived standing beside me with his attention glued to our son, while still holding Leila in his arms.

"You saw me?" our son eagerly asked him.

"Yoo're indeed as impressive as a whale, laddie," Leif answered with a mesmerized grin.

"I can do it again. Watch me this time go longer!" he screeched happily, ready to impress his dad further.

"Aren't you hungry now, though," I asked instead and he looked at me with sudden consideration.

"Yeah. Can I have pizza?" he abruptly desired now.

"How about a sandwich? There're so many different kinds. I'm sure you'll find one that you'll like," I encouraged.

"Okay," he accepted easily.

"All right. Climb the ladder beside you and come out of the water," I instructed. He shifted toward the nearby ladder and began climbing it out of the pool. As he neared the top rung, I leaned for his arm and assisted him completely out of the water. Leif set Leila down upon her little feet and the kids began trotting away together from us toward the gate's opening. "Make sure the both of you walk. Don't run," I promptly ordered them while they quickly moved over the wet deck, hoping they wouldn't slip on it. They suddenly slowed their paces, but still continued hurrying themselves away from the pool area as Leif and I proceeded following them.

As we arrived at one of the food tables with plastic plates and sandwiches, Heather and Rick appeared beside us as everyone's kids were helping themselves to eat. Light conversation began between us all as Leif and I also served ourselves. When we returned to our chairs by the pool to eat, the conversation between everyone remained pleasant and light. And although Jasmine had been the original topic of discussion between my friends and me, the indifference my friends had for her returned as she joined our company by the pool with our husbands. But, my sudden suspicion of her nicked the back of my mind as I observing her buoyant friendliness toward Leif in particular while generally engaging everyone else in conversation.

Furtively observing her certain glances at him, Leif seemed absolutely unfazed by her. In fact, he was utterly impassive. Save for the frequent occasions when she addressed him during our group conversation, he responded to her in his typically polite manner as if nothing was astray.

Aware of his reaction to her supported my confidence, and repelled any creeping suspicious thoughts about her so that I enjoyed the present occurring around me in the company of my family and friends.

Thirty

The months have blurred with wedding plans underway, and today is Halloween. The children were permitted to wear their costumes to school for today's celebration. Little Leif disguised himself as Darth Vader and Leila dressed as Princess Leia. Much of the day was festive for them in the classroom with presented snacks, treats and projects provided and shared by parent volunteers. I took off from work early in order to participate in their class function, since I was designated to bring snacks for the children in the classroom.

Leif accompanied me, witnessing the occasion, to our kids' delight. He seemed to find the classroom activities merry and enjoyed observing our kids and their classmates, while I participated in distributing the children their snacks onto desks before them. As I was passing food out to the children, I happened to glimpse in Leif's direction and noticed him pleasantly conversing with Glen and Dave by the windows. He had grown accustomed to their company and appeared comfortable in this setting like other parents. I surreptitiously smiled at him, and he caught my glance. His lips furtively curled upward while he was speaking to his new acquaintances, making my heart warm.

When evening came, after dinner, as I was preparing our kids to go trick-or-treating, Little Leif sought his father in the den while he was reading a magazine. He was eager and ready to have his father join us for the last celebration of the day.

"Are you coming trick-or-treating with us, Dad?" he excitedly asked his father. Leif unexpectedly looked up from the article he was reading at his son.

"Trick-or-treating?" Leif responded inquisitively, looking surprised at the sight of his son remaining disguised in his costume, now holding his candy bucket, ready to go. "Yoo're prepared tae go about souling?"

"Souling?" Little Leif asked, strangely looking at him.

"Aye. 'Tis whit it is named in my period," Leif informed him.

"Oh," he replied simply.

"What's souling?" Leila asked curiously, as she suddenly made her appearance also as Princess Lea.

"Yeah, what is that?" Little Leif echoed.

"'Tis when one goes about their neighbors' abodes reciting holy verses fur their dead in order tae receive a soul-cake from one's neighbor," Leif explained.

"Like a prayer?" his son curiously asked him.

"Quite like it," Leif said.

"But no one's ever asked us to say a prayer. We just say trick-or-treat to them and they give us a bunch of candy," Leila said.

"Certainly?" Leif responded curiously, raising his brow, now gazing at her.

"Yup!" She nodded her head.

"What's a soul-cake besides?" Little Leif continued inquiring, knitting his little brow also.

"Have ye never heard of whit a soul-cake is?" Leif asked the kids, appearing rather surprised.

"Nope!" Little Leif replied, shaking his head, absolutely.

"Me neither!" Leila replied in the same manner, looking curiously at their father.

"Weel, permit me tae enlighten ye. A soul-cake is a wee spice cake with raisins within it, and every one eaten frees a soul from Purgatory," he explained. "Presently, bairns listen tea me weel as I serenade tae ye this ballad...

"Soul, Soul, a soul cake!
I pray thee, good missus, a soul cake!
One for Peter, two for Paul
Three for Him who made us all!
Soul cake, soul cake, please good missus, a soul cake.
An apple, a pear, a plum, or a cherry, any good thing to make us all
merry.
One for Peter, two for Paul and three for Him who made us all."

The kids looked mesmerized at their father with grins ear to ear as he'd charmed them with his song.

"Can we make some soul-cakes?" Leila asked, fascinated, and smiling happily up at her father when he had concluded singing to them both.

"I'm sure I can find a recipe somewhere online for how to make them," I interposed pleasantly, listening to their conversation.

"I can't wait to have some!" she expressed excitedly, swinging her treat bag from side to side around her little hips.

"But I can't wait to go trick-or-treating first! Let's go before all the candy's gone!" Little Leif urged impatiently.

"All right, let's get our sweaters and then we'll go," I consented.

"You're coming with us, right Dad?" our son asked him again.

"Indeed. I shall escort ye," Leif replied amiably.

"Yay! Let's go!" Leila said, jumping up and down in front of Leif.

"Yeah!" Little Leif agreed and swiftly turned from us, dashing out the den for the foyer. Leila quickly followed her brother, disappearing past the doorway, leaving me and Leif alone to patiently follow after them.

"Why is our lass not attired frightfully as our lad?" Leif curiously asked me as we were stepping out into the hallway.

"Scary things frighten her that's why she's dressed like a princess," I explained.

"Och," he replied, nodding a tad. "Would it not, however, benefit her tae appear frightful tae ward off that which will frighten her?"

"Don't worry. Nothing bad will happen to her. She'll be holding my hand the whole time we're out."

"I speak of the possession of spirits," he clarified.

"She has my mother's rosary tucked into her pocket, since she always carries it with her when we go out on Halloween. Mom gave it to her so that she wouldn't become scared by people in scary costumes when trick-or-treating," I said, assuaging his concern, knowing not only how religious he was but superstitious too, despite his reasonable mind. Leif nodded in response, acknowledging my answer. I didn't want him becoming distracted by thinking about the vulnerability of Leila's soul because of the way she was dressed for Halloween. So, I slipped a comforting palm around his bicep and gently tugged on his arm in order for us to catch up to the kids waiting for us by the front door. "Let's go and have fun."

I knew he was skeptical. But I also knew his skepticism would wane as I meant for him to delight in the safe, innocent fun this hour had to offer us. He gave me an impassive look and nodded a little as the kids opened the front door, ready for us to enjoy Halloween night.

By the time we had finished our festive trick-or-treating and returned home with the kids' treat bags full of candy, they swiftly dove into their candy and were quickly hyped on sugar. Curtailing their sweets intake, I was able to have the kids finally settled from their jubilance in roughly an hour later. As expected, they had grown tired and were now ready for bed.

After escorting them into their room, once they'd been prepared for bed, and tucking them beneath their blankets, I returned downstairs and finished dispensing the rest of our designated Halloween candy to the last of the trick-or-treaters that came to our door. When I put the empty candy bowl in the kitchen on the island counter, I came into the den and discovered Leif relaxing with a book in his lap while enjoying a glass tumbler of rum.

"What are you reading?" I asked curiously as I approached him, finally ready for bed.

"'Tis named *The Great Gatsby*," he informed me.

"Oh, F. Scott Fitzgerald," I recognized instantly.

"Aye."

"How are you liking the story?"

"'Tis a decadent tale, it seems," he said.

"It's a tragedy."

"My sense also that it micht very weel be. 'Tis intriguing."

"Yes, it is," I agreed. "Did you enjoy yourself with the kids tonight?"

"I raither fancied it, aye."

"I'm glad," I replied, smiling at him.

"Will ye not join me as I read with a tale of yer own tae read?"

"I'm afraid I won't last a minute longer. I can barely keep my eyes open," I said, yawning.

"A pity."

"Why not join me in bed as you read? I can keep you company as I fall asleep."

"A guid notion," he considered, as the corner of his mouth curved into a suggestive smirk.

"Rascal," I remarked, shaking my head with a little smile too.

"Ye spurn me," he chuckled as the book snapped closed in his lap and he stood from his seat in the chair.

"I would never do such a thing, Your Grace," I replied faultlessly.

"Then, I am deeply enticed," he said straightforwardly when I unexpectedly felt a little pinch on my buttock cheek. I suddenly yelped and gawked at him in surprise.

"Wicked man," I declared, giggling as I looked at him with wide eyes.

"I have informed ye many a times that I am nae angel," he replied, grinning rakishly.

"You're incorrigible, and a complete mischief," I chastised, feigning a serious look as I narrowed my eyes on him.

"I find that ye do enjoy me, however," he said smugly.

"I have no idea what to do with you," I laughed.

"Come tae bed." He pinched my buttock again, causing me to screech. He chuckled as his eyes lit suggestively, and his face flushed from amusement.

"Leif!"

"Aye?"

"Quit!"

"Why shall I?"

"You're distracting me!"

"Guid," he chuckled again. I unbelievably shook my head at him. "Come tae bed, I say, lest I toss a hand upon yer crease."

"You won't dare!"

"Would I not?"

"Unbelievable."

"On the contrary. I shall proceed gladly making a believer of ye, fur I assure ye that I can make the experience most pleasurable fur both."

"Never mind! Okay, okay—I'm moving. Geez," I giggled and

scurried away from his ability to goose me again as I rushed out the den ahead of him. Hearing his chuckling from behind while he followed me through the house toward our bedroom, reminded me of his youthful disposition and roused my spirit, as I couldn't help my own laughter in anticipating him.

Thirty-One

November was suddenly here, and Leif and I successfully acquired our marriage license. Although, a small wedding had been planned, much of what was left of my free time had been consumed by properly arranging for it. Fortunately, the ceremony had been scheduled to take place at the church months ago and the venue for the reception was set conveniently to take place as a garden party in our own backyard at home. The band had been arranged and the menu had been ordered along with the party rentals and fresh flowers. The final item that needed my attention was my last dress fitting.

It was a very lovely pink champagne, silk taffeta, nineteen fifties style dress. The bodice was a sleeveless, shallow V-neck and fitted around my torso with a matching, slender belt encircling my waist. The knee length, A-line skirt attached to the bodice flared, nicely complimenting my physique and made me feel quite dainty in addition to the matching pumps I was wearing on my feet.

When our wedding day arrived at last, I wore my hair up in a loose braid and tucked into an elaborate bun at the nape of my neck with red and pink roses among jasmine blossoms. As I walked down the aisle with my father as he presented me to Leif waiting for me before the altar, I arrived standing at his right side, feeling happy and comforted after all that we'd been through. And, that my parents were supportive and joyful for us, brought me entire fulfillment and closure over it all.

Once Dad had kissed my cheek and smiled at me, he retreated from us and found his place next to Mom sitting in the front pew with their grandchildren. I turned a glance up at Leif and demurely smiled as he met my gaze, admiring his strikingly handsome appearance. His soft-pink lips warmly curled upward into a pleasant grin, creasing his handsome cheeks and he flushed as he stood by the altar dressed in his Royal Stewart plaid tuxedo kilt, reminding me of the day we were married by Reverend Stansfield in 1756.

Father Hanley proceeded with the ceremony, beginning with a blessing and prayers. Once our previous rings and vows had been exchanged, the Offertory took place and after the Eucharist the ceremony drew to a close. Leif and I signed the marriage certificate with Father Hanley, and my parents signed as witnesses. Subsequently, the wedding party and guests arrived at our reception venue for a fun evening of special food, drinks, and dancing.

Leif and I sat at the wedding table nicely conversing with my parents. Dakota and Kyle had also come to share in the event, displaying their approval and support for me and Leif after the tension we'd experienced with each other earlier. Although we hadn't been provided the proper opportunity to reconcile before now, I was extremely happy and grateful that they had chosen to attend this special occasion. Invited by us and with extended encouragement from my parents, it was the first time that I'd seen or spoken to either Kyle or Dakota since last spring when Leif arrived unexpectedly at the Rockport's house looking for me. Though hurtful and uncomfortable truths had been addressed by Kyle to me the last time I'd seen him, I was consoled to me see him here with us today.

The children had inquired earlier about the excitement

surrounding our wedding event as they questioned the reason for their father and me to marry again, after he'd told them that we were already married the day he first met and introduced himself to them. To calm their curiosity, I had simply explained to them that this occasion was in celebration of our wedding anniversary. The explanation easily laid their inquisitiveness to rest, and they were happy to celebrate.

While our children sat comfortably and contentedly in each of their grandparents' laps as we ate and drank, the band started playing music and I slipped my hand into Leif's. Attracting his attention, he shifted his gaze toward me after taking a sip of champaign and grinned benignly.

"You do remember how to rumba, don't you?" I asked furtively. His brow raised as he set his flute back down over the table before himself.

"Are we tae dance it presently?" he asked reservedly, appearing a little unexpected.

"Yes," I replied, smiling.

"Will it not be scandalous?" he asked as I sensed his hesitation.

"Not at all," I replied encouragingly.

"I shall be forward in my presentation fur all tae witness," he said, looking skeptical.

"That's the point," I responded.

"Och. Weel, I see. As ye wish, of coorse," his acquiesced in a warm tone that only I understood. A little grin broadened over his face, making him appear slightly shy and boyish. But when he subtly winked at me and enfolded my hand into his, he suddenly seemed confident, bolstering his dashing appearance as he took charge. Proceeding from his chair, he assisted me to stand from my own seat at the table, and lead us out onto the dance floor in the center of the lawn.

Arriving in the middle of the dance floor, to everyone's onlooking anticipation, he naturally bowed toward me and I automatically reciprocated with a curtsy before he took me into his arms and proceeded leading me into the rhythmic box step to the rumba as the singer of the band crooned *The Way You Look Tonight*.

When we had concluded our dance, Leif returned us to our table as the music became lively with a contemporary beat. I knew he wasn't persuaded at all to freely bouncing around to modern music, so we sat happily with each other in conversation as guests began merrily filling the dance floor and danced to the carefree music. The kids eagerly removed themselves from their seated grandparents at this moment and cheerfully joined their Uncle Kyle and Aunt Dakota, who happily received their niece and nephew into their dance out on the floor.

As my parents also joined in dancing, enjoying themselves, Leif and I pleasantly made our rounds together greeting and conversing with our guests who remained seated at various tables on the sidelines of the dancers, delighting while they dined.

It was a special, celebratory day as guests savored each other's company during the gala. I was happy that the event was intimate; it gave everyone the opportunity to meet and socialize with various individuals, fostering new friendships. After the buttercream frosted wedding caking had been cut and served, the evening grew late with continued celebration. But it wasn't until the hours waned into the late evening when guests began leaving and the reception ended, Leif and I had tucked our exhausted children into bed at last.

As we were leaving the kids bedroom and were passing the top landing of the staircase, Kyle and Dakota unexpectedly appeared at the bottom of the steps on the first floor and noticed us. Dakota waved at me, catching my attention and I ceased pacing with Leif. He also stopped his stride and noticed Dakota climbing up the stairs toward us with Kyle following behind her.

"Hey," Dakota greeted affably as Leif and I moved aside for them on their arrival on the top landing with us.

"Hi," I replied, smiling, extremely glad to see her. She suddenly reached for me and drew me into her arms with a snug embrace. As she held me for a moment, I noticed Kyle stretching a hand toward Leif. Leif reciprocated and they both shook hands.

"I'm so very happy for you," Dakota softly said into my ear while hugging me.

"Thank you," I replied in the same tone while embracing her also. "I'm so happy that you came."

"We wouldn't have miss it for all the world. Thanks so much for inviting us," she said while releasing me from her hug and looking dearly into my eyes with a smile.

"Well, of course. I was hoping you'd come. It wouldn't have been the same without you," I said.

"We want to offer our sincerest congratulations," Kyle submitted humbly as his gaze bounced from Leif toward me, then back toward Leif again after they shook hands.

"We are most grateful, Master Kyle," Leif said obligingly.

"Yes, thank you, Kyle," I responded also, perceiving the earnest expression on his face. He nodded a little in acknowledgment as he shoved his hands into his pants suit pockets, then returned looking at Leif.

"Would you mind if I spoke with Sylvie for a minute, Seamus? I promise I won't keep her long," Kyle asked respectfully.

"But of coorse," Leif agreed absolutely.

"Thank you," Kyle appreciated, then turned his gaze toward me. "Is there somewhere we could go for a second?"

"Sure," I responded easily as Dakota began a casual conversation with Leif, attaining his attention from me, when I moved from them to lead Kyle through the hallway into one of the nearby guest bedrooms. As we entered the vacant room, I switched the light on and carefully closed the door behind us, lending privacy. We stood quietly facing each other for a second, and a modest smile came over his sincere face.

"You look beautiful," he started solemnly as the gentle smile faded.

"Thank you," I replied in a soft voice.

"I just want to finally apologize to you for being such a dick to you back in May," he said.

"It's okay," I replied.

"It's not okay," he said definitively.

"I only meant that you were right about me. I've kept things from you—from all of you—because I was—"

"It's okay. You don't have to explain anything," he interrupted. "I've been meaning to talk with you for some time since I lashed out at you, but I wanted to see you in person instead of just talking over the phone." I nodded in response, quietly listing to him. "I know losing Matt was hard on you. It was hard on us too—he was a great guy—but seeing you go through all of that... was very difficult. I shouldn't have blamed you for how you reacted—I was just worried that we'd never have you back. I just wanted you back, Sylvie. That's all."

"I know. I'm sorry for being closed off... and for pushing you away," I replied.

"I know it wasn't your intention."

"No."

"I think about sometimes being in your shoes—if I ever lost Dakota. I'd be devastated. I don't think I'd be the best guy to be around if it happened to me. So, I get it," he said. "Time's a funny thing."

"What do you mean?" I asked strangely.

"Just how it's the only thing that provides us the opportunity to really heal from things—like grief—and how it changes us," he said.

"Oh," I replied, nodding. He paused for a minute, nodding his head a bit also, seeming thoughtful.

"You're happy."

"Yeah."

"I can definitely see it—on both of you."

"You can?"

"Without a doubt."

"That obvious?"

"As it should be. It's been a long time."

"Yes, it has."

"I hope the happiness you've found with Seamus lasts you a lifetime, Sylvie," he said in a croaky voice. I moved toward him and wrapped my arms around his neck, feeling suddenly overcome with emotion as a knot developed in my throat and my vision blurred with tears. "If anyone deserves to be happy, it's you, Sylvie," he semi-whispered as I sniffled against his cheek, feeling his arms coming around me with affection.

"Thank you, Kyle," I sniveled.

"You don't have to thank me for anything," he replied unevenly.

"Yes, I do.

"For what?"

"For being my big brother."

"You're my little sis. Of course, it goes without saying that I love you."

"I love you too."

We embraced each other for a solid moment until our arms mutually slipped from each other, and we simply stood in silence before ourselves clearing the tears from our faces.

"I'm always going to protect you, Sylvie. No matter what. You know that, right?" he continued.

"I know," I replied meekly.

"Even if it's from yourself," he said. "But now I know that I don't have to worry too much about you anymore. I say too much, because you're my sister and I'm always going to worry a little— even if you glow like the sun like you are now—that's just what brothers do for their sisters who they love." He paused for a moment, seeming to collect his thoughts as well as his composure. Then he resumed saying, "I know you and Seamus are more than compatible. It's obvious that you two have a unique bond—that you care for each other in a way that most couples could only dream about having with their spouses, let alone with the people they just date.

"So, I can't express how glad I am that you and Seamus have found each other, and that you've decided to be together again. I know what you have with him is solid—and good. I also know that I'm a little winded right now when I'm not normally, but that's what I wanted to tell you—that I'm very happy for you—and that I love you." He gave me a little encouraging smile, and I perceived the heartened sincerity that was earnest in his expression.

"Thank you, Kyle—for saying this to me. It means so much—and, I love you too," I responded with a shaky voice, on the verge of tears again.

"You're gonna turn me into a sap again. Don't do it. Image is everything to a guy," he lightly joked and I giggled.

"I'll spare your ego," I teased a little, smiling a tad also.

"That's all I ask." A warmhearted grin eased over his face.

"I understand."

"You're a good sister for protecting my pride. If Dakota had any hint of me crying, she'd coddle me like a kid who scraped his knee. Can't have that."

"She'd mean well, though."

"Nope. A guy's a guy. I'm the one who does the protecting."

"But I'm protecting your ego. So, there's that."

"Touché." The smile curving his lips settled comfortably on his face. "I guess we're good, then."

"Yes, we are," I affirmed. He gave me an affectionate pat over the shoulder, and I wrapped my arms around his neck, hugging him once more.

"So much for my ego," he croaked as he reciprocated my embrace that was heartfelt and wept again.

"Sorry," I replied.

"No, you're not."

"I know," I replied and he snorted, faintly chuckling.

When Kyle and I finally released each other from embracing again, we cleared our appearances once more before withdrawing from the guest bedroom. When we entered the hallway, returning to Leif and Dakota, they were found standing in conversation right where they'd been left at the top of the staircase. As we approached them, they turned their attention toward us and I noticed the calm look in Leif's eyes and the inquisitiveness in Dakota's.

"Everything all right?" she asked Kyle, undoubtedly noticing the leftover red in his eyes. She glanced at me and smiled uncertainly, noticing the same look in my own eyes.

"You bet," Kyle assured her.

"Okay," she replied acceptably, nodding also, as her gaze bounced over to me with the same question.

"Yes, everything's great," I promised.

"Good," she said, satisfied. She slipped a palm around Kyle's bicep and gave him a sympathetic smile before looking at me and Leif. "Well, I know it's late in the evening and I'm certain the both of you must be exhausted, so Kyle and I will head to your parents' house now. We wouldn't want to keep them waiting any longer, since we're staying with them."

"Of course," I agreed nicely.

"We'll see you there for Thanksgiving dinner before we fly back home to New York the day after," she said.

"All right," I replied, nodding in acknowledgment.

"So, have a great night, and we'll see you soon." She swung her arms around me and we embraced again as the four of us bade each other a good night before separating for the rest of the evening.

WHEN LEIF AND I ENTERED OUR BEDROOM TONIGHT, closing the door behind us, I glanced at him as he proceeded removing the bowtie from around his neck while beginning to undress himself from his tuxedo kilt. He caught my glance and steadily held it, ceasing to undress further. He gave me an encouraging look, prompting me and I gently smiled.

"How is it that you're so often right about things?" I asked demurely, amazed.

"I dinnae ken that I am," he replied honestly.

"But you are. So, how is it that you know so much?" I inquired curiously. He shrugged a tad, genuinely considering my question.

"I reckon that I merely attempt tae measure the circumstances posing themselves tae me," he answered sincerely.

"Hmm..."

"Why do ye inquire?"

"Because I think you're extremely insightful."

"Och," he replied simply. "I do my best tae perceive whit is beyond the apparent."

"It seems so, and I greatly appreciate you for that."

"Yoo're most welcome. Yet, I wonder. Have I recently aided ye in any manner?"

"Yes. You have. You've done so much for me."

"How have I aided ye?"

"You reminded me how much my family loves me. You told me that I shouldn't give up on them—that I should trust them and give them a chance to show their love for me. And, to believe that they did love me in spite of my secrets that I've withheld from them, and the betrayal they felt because of that. All of that made me realize the strength we have as a family," I told him. Leif approached closer toward me and placed his palms gently over my shoulders, assuring that I remained looking at him as he stared transfixed into my eyes.

"I am greatly pleased that I have served ye weel in this manner, and that the matter betwixt yer family has been solved. Ye are beloved by them, immensely, and 'tis certain that the fondness which is shared betwixt ye will never diminish. Do ye recall the Stewart Clan motto?"

"Courage grows strong at a wound," I remembered.

"Befitting a Stewart of which ye are indeed," he said unequivocally. I smiled diffidently at him and he carefully placed a palm on the side of my neck. I sensed the pad of his thumb gently stroking my cheek. "His Grace is most honored to have Her Grace for his wife."

"Thank you, Your Grace," I replied softly, feeling suddenly shy before him. He grinned, and I smiled also. Leaning a little, he pressed his supple lips gently over mine, kissing me with a tender heart.

Thirty-Two

Thanksgiving Day came the following week and quickly passed with time celebrated and relished at my parents' house. It was the first time ever in years that not a single family member had been absent while gathering for this day. We'd come together as a whole, and immense placidity, gratitude and joy was all I knew. Everything was perfect.

As this holiday marked the beginning of the Christmas season with its observance closely approaching, Leif and I agreed to make honeymoon plans for after New Year's Day. Instead, we wished to spend his first Christmas with our kids together. So, it was arranged with my parents to leave the children with them in January while Leif and I honeymooned the month in Hawaii. And, arrangements at work had been made for my absence for my colleagues to cover my patients by their understanding and happiness for me, to which I was extremely grateful to them.

But while Leif seemed to anticipate our vacation to Hawaii with favor, I also perceived his desire to return to *Taigh Gràs*. Relieving Beth from Amity no doubt was on his mind, along with every other responsibility to which he was committed also needed his tending.

And as I also thought about eventually returning to *Taigh Gràs*, the pressing realization of having to inform my family of my move weighed on me, unsettling my mind and heart with each passing day as the time was quickly approaching. Having originally told my parents that Leif was here to stay in L.A. with me and the kids, I knew they were cemented to this expectation and were going to be deeply saddened when learning this promise was going to be broken. The idea of moving my own family far away from them was hard enough. But moving us to a different century where there would be absolutely no contact at all with them was an unbearable thought.

I struggled pushing the reality of it from my mind, but it continued edging into my thoughts again. Contemplating it, I found myself stuck in a horrible predicament. I had no idea how to solve the problem. Any which way I looked at it, there was no solution without causing them significant disappointment as there was no choice but to adhere to the agreement I'd made with Leif to root our family in a place where he could ground us with his stability.

Many families move far away from each other for job opportunities, don't they? Some to different continents altogether. So, what's the difference if the location happens to be in a different century? Right? Especially, if we can find our way back to each other? Hopefully...

Hopefully. The operative word. I only hoped conditions would permit us to be so fortunate to return here to visit them. At least the possibility existed, however. I was grateful about that.

Still, aside from my close relationship with my parents, they had an even closer bond with their grandchildren. The only grandchildren they had and knew were going to be ripped from them. The mere thought of it anguished me, nearly making me want to cry. Except, the only thing which prevented tears, was my realization of the possibility of our returning to see them again as I likened the distance and journey to living and traveling from one continent to the other. It was an idea with which I could cope, while fixating on the inevitable prospect of moving inconceivably far away from life with my family. Thinking of it this way tended to settle my spirit, considerably.

WHEN SCHOOL CLOSED FOR THE CHRISTMAS HOLIDAYS, one night close to Christmas Day, Leif and I took the kids Christmas tree shopping. We spent the evening hunting for the perfect tree at one of the local Christmas tree lots. Once we found it, we ended our search with cups of hot cocoa with whipped cream from a local coffee shop before returning home.

As Leif unloaded the Christmas tree from the minivan and bustled indoors with it, he brought it into the living room just as the kids and I had desired. The next morning, he assisted me by bringing the Christmas decorations from the garage into the house, to the kids' excitement. When the boxes containing the decorations had been arranged before the tree, the four of us began happily spending a good portion of the morning trimming it and concluded by embellishing the rest of the house afterward.

After our attention fell onto decorating the house, we finally returned into the living room to admire our tree with the angel on its pinnacle. At that moment, I turned the Christmas tree lights on and the boughs illuminated, heightening the cheer on the kids' faces. They instantly hurrayed at the sight of the brilliant tree, and I caught the gleeful smile in Leif's eyes since he was impressed by the novelty of the embellishing lights as they blinked.

"Do ye recall our prior two Christmases?" he asked me as we stood close together near the back of the living room observing our kids' joyful reactions while they bounced by the tree.

"Yes, I remember," I replied fondly.

"'Twas the merriest period of my existence," he remembered warmly.

"Mine too," I said.

"Yet presently, I ken even greater happiness when I thought it couldnae be had," he responded as he gazed at his happy children jumping around with excitement, while Christmas music gently played in the background from the radio. I shifted my gaze from our kids up toward him, and he turned his sparkling eyes down toward mine. I smiled. He affectionately grinned in return, and I slipped my hand around his bicep. Sliding an arm around my shoulder, he drew me snug against his sinewy body.

"'My bounty is as boundless as the sea, my loove as deep; the more I give tae thee, the more I have, fur both are infinite,'" he said, quoting Shakespeare. My smile widened, and I felt my blood grow warm as I suddenly felt self-conscious. I knew he could see the flushing hue emerging in my cheeks. I would have glanced away to curb my unexplainable abashment, but he had locked his eyes to mine, preventing me. His lips curved into an endearingly, confident grin, spreading evenly across his face, and he appeared satisfied.

"Is Santa Claus coming to our house tonight, Mama?" Leila asked innocently, abruptly interrupting while hopping toward us.

"He's coming tomorrow night," I answered pleasantly, adhering my attention to her.

"Oh! I can't wait!" she cheered eagerly.

"Me too!" Little Leif expressed in the same anticipatory manner.

"May I have a candy cane? Pretty please?" Leila pleaded.

"Just one. And then, we have to brush our teeth before bed," I stipulated. Since the candy canes were small, I saw no harm in it to treat them.

"Yay!" She rushed back toward the Christmas tree, plucking a candy cane from one of the boughs.

"May I have one too?" Little Leif asked hopefully.

"Of course, you may," I said easily and he swiftly joined his sister at the tree, snatching one for himself too. As they began tearing away the wrappers from their candy, they plopped themselves on the floor by the tree and contentedly sat eating their treat as they played with their puppy, Yoda.

"Have ye a wish fur yer birthday, *mo ghaol*?" Leif asked me in a low voice, calling my attention away from the kids back toward him.

"No. I can't say that I have," I said simply, meeting his gaze.

"Indeed?" His brow lifted, seeming considerably surprised.

"Well, I have everything that I want right here, right now, with you and the kids together," I said sincerely.

"'Tis certainly a blessing," he agreed. He wrapped a hand around mine and brought it to his lips, bestowing a tender kiss on my knuckles. Then, returning his gaze toward the kids while they continued enjoying their candy and playing with Yoda, he peacefully observed them for moments longer, and I knew he was happy too.

❦

EARLY CHRISTMAS MORNING, AT THE BREAK OF DAWN, I was stirred from sleep when I sensed the weight of two light, little bodies pouncing over me and Leif while wrapped in each other's arms.

"Och," Leif moaned in his sleep.

"Wake up! Wake up! Santa came!" Leila expressed excitedly as she crawled over me.

"Yeah! Santa came, Mom! Wake up, Dad!" Little Leif said also in the same happy manner.

"Okay, let Mom and Dad have a moment," I said drowsily, still tired from wrapping many presents and assembling a pair of bicycles with Leif's assistance from last night when the kids slept. "Tell you what, why don't you check in the living room to see if Santa ate all of his cookies? While you're doing that, Mom and Dad will get ready to come downstairs shortly for you to show us everything."

"Okay," Little Leif agreed gladly.

"Okay," Leila complied eagerly also, and they both hastily scampered off of the bed, running out of our bedroom, disappearing as the pitter-pattering of their little feet dashed away through the hallway. I shifted in Leif's arms, glimpsing at him, and an indolent smirk eased over his lips as he viewed me through the languid corners of his eyes.

"I have been stampeded awake by our son," he muttered groggily, appearing humored.

"Leila trampled me pretty well too," I giggled and he chuckled lightly.

"This is Christmas morn in the Stewart household, is it?" His voice sounded more deep and tired than usual this morning, likely because he was as exhausted from last night as I was.

"Yes. This is what it's like every year. Except now, they're even more thrilled because they get to share it with you," I replied, yawning as I covered my mouth with my palm.

"I am most heartened tae experience this glorious day with my family at last," he replied sentimentally as a yawn overcame him also.

"Well, let's start enjoying our day. I'm sure the kids can't wait much longer for us to join them," I encouraged and leaned toward him, sweetly pecking him on the lips. A crooked grin tilted his mouth again and he winked at me this time. I smiled knowingly at him and lightly shook my head, discouraging him. He chuckled a little in response.

"Aye. Let us rise tae witness this merry stir," he agreed, resigning himself. I began removing myself from his arms and emerged from the covers as he flung them off himself when he withdrew from bed also. As I slipped my house robe over my chemise, Leif covered his nakedness with a soft flannel robe and we started our way toward the bedroom door left ajar by the kids.

Once we came down the staircase onto the first floor, we entered the living room and discovered the kids already tearing into their presents with wrapping paper remnants strewn across the floor. Not to miss a single captured moment, I promptly retrieved my phone from the mantelpiece above the fireplace and started taking pictures of them while they continued opening their gifts. As I was taking pictures, Leif contentedly sat on the large sofa quietly watching our happy children excitedly discovering their presents.

"Look! Santa Claus brought us bikes! Mine is blue. My favorite color," Little Leif expressed merrily as he came to sit astride on the seat, showing it off to his father.

"So, it appears. Father Christmas has spread his good cheer tae ye, indeed," Leif responded, grinning at him.

"You must have been a really good boy all year for him to have brought you such a nice gift," I said brightly also.

"I tried my hardest!" Little Leif said wholeheartedly.

"That's all he would ask for," I supported.

"I got a bike too!" Leila chimed, pointing to her new shiny purple bike with pearl streamers on the handlebars.

"Whit do ye presume of it, birdie?" Leif asked her with a charmed smile. She shrugged her little shoulders, not quite understanding his question.

"Tell us what you think of it?" I asked, clarifying the question for her.

"I love that it's a princess bike! It's got a crown on the basket at the front of it," she sang cheerfully.

"Splendid!" Leif chuckled, and she smiled brightly at him.

"May we go outside and ride it? I wanna do that now," she wished eagerly.

"Sure. Let's change into some play clothes first, and then you both may go outside to ride your bikes," I permitted.

"Yay!" she screeched excitedly. Without any delay, she and her brother darted from us out the living room. Running up the staircase, heading directly for their bedroom, they were ready to dress themselves.

I smiled and glanced at Leif still seated comfortably on the sofa and caught his grinning face. "Would you like some tea or coffee?" I offered him.

"Aye, tea will pleasantly suffice, *ceisdein*," he said, straightening from the sofa. He strode toward me and naturally pressed a kiss on my crown before we paced together for the kitchen.

Once our tea was soon prepared, I sat with him in the bay window nook at the breakfast table and we enjoyed drinking tea together. But before we had completed it, the kids came rushing past the threshold into the kitchen full of giddy anticipation, dressed and prepared for riding their new bicycles outdoors.

Without a moment to spare, they impatiently urged me and Leif from our seats to join them outdoors. Happy to obliged, Leif and I removed ourselves from our places at the table to quickly attire ourselves appropriately for the occasion. Once he and I hastened to our bedroom and changed into sweats for me, and jeans and a shirt for him, Leif collected their bicycles and the four of us went outside for them to enjoy riding a little while early this crisp morning.

When we came out onto the sidewalk, I assisted them onto their bikes before they promptly began pedaling them away with training wheels attached. The kids were quickly independent as they rode along the sidewalk, while Leif and I stood by the picket fence pleasantly observing them. I made sure to have my camera ready at my disposal, and proceeded taking plenty of pictures and videos of them happily peddling themselves along.

Conscious of the time, however, after an hour of outdoor fun for them, I encouraged the kids to return inside to play with their other Christmas toys while I started making breakfast for everyone. When breakfast had been served and eaten, we promptly prepared ourselves for our attendance at church.

As we arrived inside church, we were promptly greeted by an already packed vicinity with holiday parishioners. The atmosphere was welcoming and joyous with plentiful brightly decorated Christmas trees and poinsettias adorning the alter. Because of the unusual amount of people crowding the pews, it was difficult to find an open pew where we could sit together as a family while scoping the nave with our eyes. Noticing us, one of the ushers kindly escorted us upstairs into the balcony with other parishioners where there were some empty pews for us to sit, and also where the pipe organ was located, emitting lovely music by the organist. A treat for us all, since this location was typically closed to anyone who wasn't the organist.

In about an hour, church had concluded and the children were eager to return home to continue playing with their Christmas toys. Later that afternoon, the kids were allowed to gather a couple of their new toys, along with Yoda, to bring with them to visit my parents' house for Christmas dinner. When we arriving at my parents' house, they elatedly greeted us as the delicious aroma of specially prepared food filled their house with further Christmas warmth and cheer.

LATER TONIGHT AS LEIF AND I HAD JUST COMPLETED preparing ourselves for bed, I reached for my vanilla hand cream placed on my nightstand and proceeded distributing it over my hands to moisturize them while sitting up in bed, grateful for the beauty of this Christmas Day. As I thought about how happy I was over how today was spent surrounded by everyone whom I loved, my thoughts suddenly spoiled with dread. The idea of separating from my family with our children in order to live at *Taigh Gràs*, spiraled me into a pit of discouragement, which dampened my spirit.

The need to broach this subject with my parents was daunting. But there never seemed to be an opportune time to bring this matter to their attention, though the time for this conversation was encroaching. The pressure to speak with them had mounted to the point of causing me a severe heartache, actually rendering me somewhat ill to my stomach.

"Leif?" I started carefully, turning my glance toward him as he relaxed with his arm crooked behind his head against the pillows while reading a news magazine.

"Aye, *ceisdein*?" he responded peacefully, shifting his gaze from what he was reading toward me, meeting my eyes.

"Well—I've been thinking about our returning to *Taigh Gràs*," I said thoughtfully.

"Och?" He lifted his brow in interest and placed the magazine down flat over his bare chest, maintaining a steady gaze to mine.

"Yeah," I replied quietly, nodding a little.

"Whit of it?" he inquired as I perceived his gaze searching me.

"My family—particularly my parents—are still under the impression that we'll be living here and nowhere else," I disclosed.

"Are they?" Now he seemed uneasy as he propped himself up against the headboard, matching my eye level, alerted.

"Yes. They are," I replied, nodding a little again.

"How micht it be that they are not informed already?" he asked, looking surprised.

"Well, at first—before you and I had ever even discussed living away from them—I had told my parents that you'd come here to permanently live with me and the kids," I prefaced.

"I see," he acknowledged.

"Yes. So... they were really glad to understand that was going to be the case. But when you and I had talked about us leaving here for *Taigh Gràs*, I didn't know how to tell them that's what you and I had discussed, because I knew they'd be significantly upset by the prospect of losing us—especially the kids, since they're so close to them.

"And because the idea of moving had come up so soon from when you had first arrived, I just felt I couldn't tell them at that point. And with every day passing, it only seemed to become harder to tell them... Plus, the time to have a conversation with them about it never seemed opportune—because the focus was on planning the wedding," I explained. "Also, now that the holidays are here... it's just—I can't seem to bring myself to broach the subject without making them extremely sad."

"I see," he responded, intently listening to me. He nodded a little in conjunction, seeming earnestly contemplative.

"I also know that you've grown anxious to return to the past, because of your obligations," I said.

"I must," he replied seriously. I nodded in acknowledgment. "'Tis a quandary with which we are presented, apparently at present, indeed. It pains me tae see yer torment."

"I just don't know how to rectify it—except maybe I just need more time in order to tell them of our plans."

"Yet, our honeymoon quickly approaches. How much more time micht ye require?" He inquired sincerely. I released a heavy sigh, wishing that I had several more months after our honeymoon to address the issue with my parents in order to cushion the blow and prepare them for the reality of it. But I knew Leif wouldn't agree to staying the extended time as I was well aware of the pressure he felt to return.

"I can't honestly say how much more time I'll need that feels reasonable to everyone," I replied, shrugging a little.

"Hmm," he muttered pensively as I perceived him deeply thinking with staid eyes.

"Otherwise, I don't know how to spare everyone's disappointment, and possibly another conflict," I said, feeling distressed.

"I am in accordance with preventing discord within yer family. Yet whilst ye have agreed with me 'tis ideal fur our family tae reside at *Taigh Gràs*—fur we shall—I believe that I have arrived upon an unexpected resolution that may meet everyone's benefit," he said sensibly.

"What do you have in mind?" I asked, considering him.

"Why do ye not instead accompany me on leave tae visit Beth as it pertains tae Amity's welfare during the time taken fur our honeymoon? In this case, we shall alleviate a portion of yer concern regarding our separation, and I may utilize this opportunity tae minister my duties which press me, which would otherwise be neglected," he posed, giving me a realistic look.

"But won't we miss Hawaii, then?" I responded disappointedly, considering the option.

"We shall return tae see it as weel," he replied with optimism.

"How? From my experience of quantum leaping, we can't return in the same month from when we originally leaped," I said oddly.

"Yet, we may do so a month from the time we had," he said for certain.

"Really?"

"I have done so."

"You have?"

"Aye."

"How have you been so precise when I was thrust five months ahead from the original time I'd leaped?"

"Recall letting yer instrument slip from yer grip tae the ground once the process began those many years ago?"

"Yes, I remember that," I replied, nodding.

"Doing so permitted time tae transport ye slightly off course as in a vessel blown from course upon the sea," he compared.

"Oh," I replied, realizing the novelty of his comparison as I gazed into his reassuring eyes.

"Therefore, ensuring the instrument remains upon one's person whilst traveling will determine an accurate delivery much like a compass would do," he further explained.

"Really?"

"Aye."

"Oh," I replied, simply amazed. I abruptly started feeling hopeful as I understood the probability from this idea.

"Hence, we shall enjoy Hawaii efter all upon our return—permitting that yer parents will extend their generosity tae mind the bairns fur anither month," he said.

"So, we would be needing a two-month vacation, instead?" I fathomed.

"Aye."

"Hmm... Well, I won't want to burden them for that long, though. Also, I have to consider my work colleagues' burden as they substitute for me. But as I'm really happy to consider it—I'll ask my parents, still. Maybe when we return here for Hawaii, we could simply stay there for two weeks instead of using the whole extra month. That way, I'm positive my parents will likely agree to the two-week extension watching the kids. I'll still need to speak to my colleagues about the schedule change, though, as I hope for their flexibility and understanding. Luckily, they're such nice people—and, I've often covered for them too through the years. So, maybe they'll help me now," I responded hopefully.

"Then, we shall pose the question tae yer parents as promptly as the morrow, and pray that they will consent tae our wish. As fur yer physic responsibility, discuss the matter soon with yer associates as weel," he said, equally positive.

"Okay," I agreed, satisfied. "Then, once we return from

Hawaii, I'll have a much better chance informing them of our relocation. I'll also have the time to think about how I'm going to gently break the news to them as much as possible. I know they're going to be upset regardless, but hopefully that'll be enough for them to understand."

"Aye. I shall assist upon attaining a resolution fur this matter as weel, although the notion fur explaining this tae them has not yet sprung tae mind. I shall ponder it, however. Bare in mind I fathom thaur must be a resolution to our predicament, in spite of it. Rest easy, alrecht, *mo ghaol*?"

"All right. Thank you so much for helping me with this."

"Nae matter. Whaur thaur is a will, thaur is a way. Therefore, fret not any longer regarding it." Leif gently grinned encouragingly at me. However, I was continually bothered by another thought. "Still ye contemplate," he said, noticing the look on my face.

"Yes," I replied, nodding.

"Tell me."

"Will we ever see my family again—once we leave?"

"We shall upon yer whim whenever it is permissible," he promised.

"Permissible?"

"Aye, season permitting."

"Right," I understood, suddenly feeling better about the possibility.

"Micht our spirits be uplifted presently, knowing this will be the case?" He gave me a little inspiring smile.

"Yes, I do feel better, now—surprisingly. Thank you for promising me everything," I replied, now contented.

"Anything I micht do tae ever be of assistance tae ye is my duty and pleasure."

"Thank you."

"Nae need," he said unequivocally, and my spirit had settled. "Merry Christmas, *mo ghaol*. Rest weel, now."

"Merry Christmas, Leif."

He reached for my chin and tenderly caught it between his thumb and forefinger when drawing my lips toward his. After bestowing a reassuring, little kiss on my lips, I smiled at him as he withdrew. He proceeded to press a final kiss on my temple, cementing my confidence and his vow over the situation.

THE NEXT DAY I MADE A PHONE CALL TO MY PARENTS, asking them for the favor I needed regarding the two-week extension to care for the kids while Leif and I honeymooned. Fortunately, Mom and Dad agreed to this impromptu arrangement. The reason being they not only constantly enjoyed the company of their grandchildren, but that they strongly wished for me and Leif to completely celebrate our wedding with this honeymoon without any qualms.

I was also able to reach out to my colleagues to inquire about the favor I needed to extend my vacation. And as I'd hoped, fortunately they understood as they considered my long traumatic history with Matt, and the constant devotion I'd committed to the medical practice with them in the aftermath of my recovery, they were more than willing to grant me this favor as a result of their understanding and happiness for me found in my new marriage to Leif.

Considerably relieved by my colleagues' favorable responses, I was particularly relieved by my parents' willingness to watch the kids for this extended period to give me and Leif the opportunity needed to fix our responsibilities. I was extraordinarily grateful to my parents. This chance granted me and Leif the space needed to formulate our explanation to present to them our intention to relocate, as well as give them the opportunity to have some time to absorb the knowledge and reality of it.

Until then, though, I was simply glad that time had been stalled for all of us to remain here, together as a whole.

Thirty-Three

A week later.

Leif and I had been invited to Heather's and her husband, Rick's, New Year's Eve party. I spent the last hour preparing to leave our house as I lightly placed make up on my face and dressed in my nineteen fifty's, silk sateen, plum, halter neck, knee length dress with matching pumps. I arranged my hair in a high ponytail which hung loose down my back with wispy, ringlet tendrils escaping the sides of my face. After reinserting the teardrop pearl earrings Leif had given me centuries ago for my birthday, that I'd rarely removed, I scrutinized my final appearance in the barn door mirror, and was pleased.

Shifting my gaze away from the mirror, though, I glanced at Leif as I grabbed my black, patten leather clutch and noticed a warm grin easing over his curving lips while he was staring at me. His own appearance was captivating, I noted. Attired in his Royal Stewart plaid kilt suit, I couldn't help the smile spreading over my own lips.

"Yoo're bonnie," he complimented, striding toward me. Arriving close, he lightly grasped my elbow, ready to escort me.

"Thank you," I responded, sensing his lips coming over my temple. "You look very handsome."

"Thank ye, *ceisdein*," he replied kindly. "Shall we take our leave, presently?"

"Yes, I'm ready."

"Very weel."

He guided me out of our bedroom, through the hallway and down the staircase until we met my parents, who were babysitting for us this evening, in the den watching a movie with the kids. Receiving raving compliments on our appearances from our closest admirers, I smiled as we affectionately bade our children and my parents goodnight for the evening before leaving them for the party.

Heather and Rick's house wasn't too far from ours and when we arrived, we were gladly greeted by unacquainted guests who answered the front door and let us inside. As Leif and I entered the house, it hummed with loud music and audible conversations among crowds of animated attendees. Meandering our way through the festive gathering, we discovered Heather in the kitchen pouring wineglasses full for several guests who were keeping her company at the island.

"Oh, hey guys!" she greeted us enthusiastically, noticing our approaching, and placed the wine bottle on the island in front of herself.

"Hi," I replied, also glad to see her when she and I hugged each other. Leif politely presented a French wine and cheese basket I'd purchased for her and Rick for the occasion, once we'd released ourselves from hugging.

"Oh, wow! Thank you so much! You guys didn't have to bring us anything," she appreciated, admiring the basket from us as she glanced at it.

"Of course, we did, and I hope you enjoy it," I said pleasantly.

"It looks amazing! Thank you," she accepted gladly, and Leif moved to place the large heavy basket on the side counter for her that was cleared of food trays and wine bottles. "So, how was your Christmas?" she asked me as Leif was returning to us from the counter.

"It was great! We spent it with my family. How was yours?" I replied.

"Awesome! Ours was good too. We went to Rick's sister's for dinner. His parents were there too, visiting from San Diego," she said.

"Very nice," I responded, nodding accordingly.

"It was. So, can I offer you two some wine to start with? The veal for the French onion sliders is almost ready for assembly, and Rick is outside right now monitoring the duck and lamb roasting on the Gaucho grill. Tell me what you'll have? I've got Bordeaux, Champagne, and Chardonnay," she offered, smiling at me.

"I'll have Champagne, thanks," I replied.

"You got it," she said easily, and snagged a couple of fresh wine-glasses from the large cupboard behind her. Grabbing the Champagne bottle from the other counter, she poured a glass and politely passed it to me.

"Thank you," I said, receiving my glass.

"Of course," she replied. Then, she turned her attention to Leif. "What about you, Seamus? What will you have?"

"Anything French and I shall be pleased," he said graciously, lightly bantering. Heather smiled at him.

"You're in luck because that's all we have," she joked in return.

"I shan't be disappointed in this case," he remarked.

"Nope." She shook her head.

"Permit me tae sample a portion of yer Bordeaux," he requested politely. I knew that he didn't favor the effervescent taste of Champagne once he first had the opportunity to drink it at our recent wedding reception, despite the fact it is a French wine.

"For sure," she said agreeably and promptly poured a glass of the red wine for him to have. She smiled at him again as she passed him the glass. Receiving it, he gently swirled the contents a little, then brought the filled wineglass to his lips and sipped a bit from it. Observing him as he drank and swallowed it, I wondered what his reaction to this vintage would be, knowing he was familiar with this kind of wine when he lived in France while in his youth. Once he withdrew the glass from his lips, he raised it slightly before her, politely saluting.

"'Tis agreeable," he said certainly.

"Great! I'm glad you like it," she replied. "There's plenty more, so don't be shy. Make yourselves at home. We've got a live band playing in the backyard, and if you're craving to snack while waiting for the main course, there's a caterer serving light dishes in the living room. So, help yourselves."

"Thank you so much," I responded.

"Don't mention it. Have fun!" she said. "Gotta make my rounds now, or people will accuse me of neglect and call me a bad host." She giggled and shrugged carelessly, then swept out of the kitchen, leaving me and Leif with the other guests already engaged in different conversations.

Except, Leif and I decided to make our way out of the kitchen, meeting new people as we passed through various crowded rooms while slowly meandering toward the backyard to hear the band. Heather and Rick had a nice large property on a hill impressively overlooking the city. Every location indoors, aside from her son's room, was full of animated guests as lively music emitted from the band playing outside in the spacious backyard.

There were many guests I had recognized as parents from school, and although Leif remained formal in group settings, he and I socialized well together as we mingled among friends. When he encountered Rick tending the large flaming grill outdoors along with Glen and Dave, he seemed more at ease while also enjoying his wine as the four of them conversed with each other. But the unique manner in which Leif was dressed attracted interest and inspired conversations with him about his appearance—particularly among the women standing around him eavesdropping on the conversation between him and the other men.

As Leif and I drifted from each other while socializing with different acquaintances, I went to the caterer in the dining room and gathered a plate to snack from, meeting Maria as she was doing the same for herself. She and I kindly struck up a conversation about our kids' Christmas experiences this season and while we were speaking, I happened to notice Jasmine.

Watching her through the window overlooking the backyard approaching Leif and his surrounding male company, she joined their conversation and my suspicion was raised. Maria noticed my divided attention as we were speaking with each other and followed my line of sight, observing Jasmine too as she was mostly conversing interestedly with Leif. After a moment, I glanced away from them and so did Maria, returning our attention to each other. Maria smiled awkwardly at me and an automatic insecure little grin crossed my lips, impeding the confiture of our original conversation.

"Everyone loves your husband," Maria remarked with a nervous little giggle as Autumn and Heather arrived standing beside us, joining our conversation.

"That's for sure," Autumn agreed, overhearing Maria.

"Maybe you could get him to convince my husband to wear a kilt," Heather joked.

"Yeah, mine too," Autumn joked also, and the girls giggled.

"There's a Scottish shop that sells kilts in Coronado," I informed them, smiling a little sheepishly.

"Really?" Heather replied interestedly.

"Yeah," I said, nodding.

"That's in Rick's parents' neck of the woods," she realized.

"Too bad Halloween's over," Maria said ironically.

"Who needs Halloween for anything?" Heather giggled.

"Apparently not you," Autumn teased.

"And that's a good thing," Heather mocked lightheartedly.

"Didn't say it wasn't. Nothing's wrong with a little added spice in the bedroom," Autumn replied, and the girls continued giggling, slipping me knowing little glances. I felt my cheeks growing slightly warm and dropped my gaze to the delicious food on the plate in my hand. I scooped up a bit of seasoned tortellini in olive oil onto my fork and placed it into my mouth.

"So—how were your Christmases?" I asked once I had chewed and swallowed my bit of food, changing the subject. They smiled at me and the subject was easily changed as they began exchanging their recent Christmas experiences.

When my friends and I nearly had our fill from the caterer, main courses began circling among the guests by servers as it was being served à la carte straight out of the oven and hot off the grill, enticing us to begin partaking in the meal.

Once we had completed eating, we wandered through the socializing crowd in the house and found our way out into the capacious backyard, watching the band play as we continued drinking wine, bantering, and giggling. As a busboy came around collecting people's empty plates and glasses while guests stood around socializing, he approached us and we gave him our empty wineglasses also. Next, we found ourselves hurrying toward the playing band as we began dancing and having fun with the music.

While enjoying ourselves dancing, the crowd grew thick with more people participating around us and loud cheers erupted from everywhere, it seemed, when the band enthusiastically began playing *Deadbeat Club* by the B-52's followed by *Love Shack*.

But when the band began playing *Don't Stop Believin'* by Journey, the crowd grew even more lively as we were joined by the animated husbands of my friends into our dancing group. The jovial atmosphere distinctly reminded me of the fun parties I'd participate in during college. I was having a blast and didn't want it to end.

As I was enjoying myself dancing, I coincidentally caught Leif by a glance as he was standing by the outdoor fireplace at a distance. He was gazing at me with a new glass tumbler of rum in hand still talking with Jasmine. The whole time I was dancing, his eyes were fixed on me as he stood there conversing with her. But my dancing friends distracted my attention, and I returned to them. Smiles, laughter and singing passed between us as we danced, completely diverting my attention with enthusiasm.

When the song faded and a slow one took place, I finally wandered breathlessly off the dance floor and spotted Leif still standing with Jasmine in conversation where I'd last seen them. I decided to walk toward him, wondering if he wanted to dance with me now. While approaching, she noticed me and curtailed her discussion with him. Leif grinned receptively at me when I stood before them, and I smiled at him. He promptly set his tumbler containing the last portion of rum in it down over on one of the stone ledges to the large flaming fireplace.

"I beg yer pardon, Mistress Jasmine," he said courteously, suddenly turning toward her, "however, I shall seek my wife's company presently."

"Oh, sure," she said unexpectedly as Leif took my elbow and guided me away from her.

"The band's playing a slow song now. Would you like to dance with me?" I asked as he was gently steering us through the crowd now. I glanced over my shoulder at Jasmine looking at us as we were leaving her. She bit her lip and narrowed her eyes, appearing clearly annoyed. Jealousy was amplified on her face while she continued staring after us, until we merged into the surrounding crowd. I realized there for a second, that she and I were not true friends, and it stung.

"If it pleases ye, I of coorse fancy a dance with ye," Leif said agreeably, returning my attention to him.

"Let's go," I urged, smiling at him instead. I slipped a hand into his and led him with me out onto the dance area before the band. Mingling us between the already dancing couples, I placed hands over his shoulders, and he naturally placed his palms around my waist. Following my lead, he began gently swaying with me to the band soulfully singing *If You Don't Know Me By Now*.

While slow dancing, I gazed up into his unwavering deep blue eyes and noticed them glinting from the abundant surrounding suspended Chinese lanterns and Christmas lights hanging above us. A slow grin turned his lips upward with one corner higher than the other, making him appear roguish. I sensed him unexpectedly pulling me close against his body, surprising me a little, contradicting his reserved disposition in public. He leaned his lips to my ear and said in a low distinct voice, "Ye have earned yerself punishment this evening." He noticed my eyes suddenly widen when he returned looking at me, and the devilish grin on his face deepened.

Maintaining his close gaze, I couldn't help feeling slightly embarrassed as I subtly asked, "What have I done to earn any kind of reprimand?"

"Ye are weel awaur of yer offense," he said confidently, and suddenly I clued into his meaning.

"Am I too bold?"

"Yoo're quick tae realize how lurid. As yer guilt determines."

"What will you do to me?" I giggled nervously.

"Ye will learn precisely in bed," he replied confidentially. My eyes abruptly widened again, and the fiendish grin on his face spread completely, exposing the pearly gleam of his teeth.

He drew me tighter against his body and I could feel him hardening against my pubis as we slowly swayed to the music. I smiled nervously at him and the implicit look on his face remained unaltered. But as we danced, it seemed as if the world around us had disintegrated, leaving just us alone together. I was aware of my blood running warm as he kept his gaze locked to mine. Keeping me firmly gripped against his body, I wondered what he had in mind for disciplining me, exactly. My nerves began tingling and a little lightheadedness came over me as the warmth coursing throughout me stirred the heat between my thighs, causing a little ache embedded within my sex.

Nothing else was said between us as we continued dancing, but the look in his eyes conveyed his yearning, and the feelings in mine expressed willingness to receive it.

When the song ended, so did the dreamlike ambiance, and another livelier one took its place. We ceased dancing and the world emerged around us again with noise and chatter from surrounding enthusiastically dancing guests. I slipped my hand into his and we paced together toward a more secluded area in the yard on a slope. Locating an area to rest, we sat ourselves on a low stone wall in front of the gazebo, which was only several further strides away higher up on the gradient.

"What do you think of this party?" I asked him while watching people mingling and dancing with each other below from us on the lawn ahead.

"This ball is closely prurient of the highest nature," he answered, observing the attendees also. I turned my gaze toward him, smiling a tad, a little humored.

"Why closely and not completely?" I replied curiously.

"Fornication is lacking," he said candidly, meeting my gaze. He smirked at me and I giggled.

"You sound experienced," I said.

"Quite sincerely," he replied.

"When you were in France?"

"London also, once I had arrived from France."

"Now I'm the one who's shocked."

"Stunned ye mean?"

"Quite," I giggled a bit. He chuckled a little too, amused by my reaction.

"Yet, I have told ye that I am not an angel of a man," he reminded.

"I do remember you saying that—a while ago."

"Aplenty a time I have informed ye that I am thus. Yet, forgive me fur not saying that I am indeed so debauched in more ways than one."

"I'm learning that may very well be the case."

"A willing pupil is admirable."

"Pupil? Me?"

"Aye."

"I never thought of being your student."

"However, I am yer master."

"Hmm. Then, what do you plan on teaching me that I haven't already learned from you?" I inquired innocently.

"The nature of pleasure," he said with a rakish grin.

"But you've already given me that lesson. Haven't you?" I smiled back at him.

"Not entirely."

"There's more?"

"Perpetually."

"Oh," I giggled nervously.

"Ye will learn and be satisfied as I serve ye till I draw my last surviving breath upon Earth."

"That doesn't sound like a punishment."

"Say thus as I torture ye whilst in my arms."

"What do you have in mind—specifically?"

"Ponder my bed."

"What about your bed?"

"Yer cunt will be at my command as ye beg fur my mercy tae alleviate the strain of pleasure which is certainly tae overcome ye," he said bluntly as the fiend look in his eyes flared.

"Leif!" I gasped, scolding him as the sudden heat of embarrassment flushed my face. He briskly chuckled.

"Ye huvnea the reit tae claim propriety," he said, laughing.

"Yes, I do," I differed quickly, sensing my curling lips betraying me.

"Yoo're mistaken."

"I'm not. Why do you say that?"

"Yer conduct this evening is utterly without shame, and will be fittingly rebuked."

"I see. Except, I haven't done anything out of the norm from anyone else here at this party."

"Have ye not?"

"Nope."

"Yet, ye arenae common. Yoo're upheld tae a higher standard as ye are my wife, mind ye."

"Excuses. You're making excuses to seduce me."

"Am I indeed?"

"Indeed, you are. And, you know it." I narrowed my eyes on him and he grinned widely.

"'Tis most true that ye are of a higher standard. 'Tis my duty that I must remind ye of yer proper place when ye falter."

"Falter?" I gave him an exceptional look.

"Aye."

"Oh, my goodness. You are too cunning for your own good," I teased, wagging a reprimanding finger in front of his face. He chuckled again.

"Moreover, as it pertains tae my excuse tae bed ye, need I remind ye of who I am tae ye? Permit me tae answer, instead. 'Tis yer master who speaks. A fine noble who proceeds without mentioning. Yet, take note that I am a most generous one, nae less. My generosity within the bedchamber is my gift tae ye as I inform ye of all the corrections warranted upon ye."

"Really?" I giggled, entertained by his flirtation with me.

"Aye. I shall bestow knowledge of pristine delight as I gracefully liberate ye."

"Liberate me?"

"Aye."

"You mean debauch."

"As I adore ye. How else am I tae convey my rooted veneration of ye?"

"You are a master of words, it seems. And, of me," I admitted, smiling bashfully at him.

"Lest ye be remiss, yoo're my mistress and I am yer vassal," he replied genuinely, grinning only a little now.

"I forget how even we are."

"Indeed, we are so."

"May I tell you a little secret?"

"Pray do."

"It's slightly off topic."

"Very weel."

"Well, I will have you know that my friends want their husbands dressing in kilts now because of you," I said. His brow drew together a little in confusion. "It's true. They all have crushes on you—totally fancying you."

"Och!" he chuckled, realizing the humor. "I shall make ye awaur also, in the case that ye micht not already ken, that every lad who encounters ye is bewitched by ye." I gave him an ironic look and shook my head a tad, disagreeing. "Ye spellbind all who have been graced by yer presence. Particularly tonecht, as ye freely engaged yerself fur all tae admire and crave, whilst ye unabashedly whirled about in an untamed manner believed tae be dancing."

"It *is* dancing, and I was doing it normally like everyone else," I giggled sheepishly.

"Ye will be disciplined fur it," he said with a smirk. I giggled and lightly shook my head again. "Do ye mock me?"

"No. You're just incorrigible. That's all."

"I admire yer quick study of me, in which case." He grinned at me and I giggled again. But the grin faded when he continued saying, "Whilst we discuss the topic of yer friends, I shall say that they are tolerable."

"Tolerable?"

"Aye."

"Are you saying you're unimpressed or that you don't like them?"

"Yoo're above them."

"That's a little arrogant. Don't you think?"

"Nae."

"But it sounds like it."

"'Tis my sincere opinion. I recognize their sort, and find them common in circles I have already encountered, whilst yoo're a rarity in all facets within their company."

"How?"

"Yer honesty and yer compassion are yer foundation. Those qualities are from the heart."

"Oh," I replied simply, nodding a little in acknowledgement of his compliment.

"Yet, thaur is one of yer friends fur whom I dinnae have any care fur at all."

"Really? Who?" I was suddenly surprised by his candor about my friends.

"Jasmine is horrid," he said flatly, not at all appearing appalled, though.

"Oh," I replied, trying to remain unfazed. Except, I continued regardlessly to ask, "Why do you say that?"

"I say it fur not merely is she full of tripe, she is brazenly scandalous. An utter abomination of a trollop," he answered forthrightly.

"Do you really think so?" I gaped at him and he didn't seem to care at all.

"Of coorse."

"It's a little harsh to say, isn't it?"

"Ye neednae screen her as she wulnae grant the reciprocal grace tae respect yer virtue," he said.

"How do you know?"

"She and I are far from familiar, yet the lass addresses me as if we were."

"Oh."

"I ken every particular bit of her affairs—and they are sordid. She is forward and unabashed as she seeks dalliances with any lad who micht oblige her wishes—wed or not. Whilst I am nae pietist, the lass claims tae be yer friend when clearly she is not, and that warrants my criticism of her, and yer caution."

"So, she made an advance toward you?" I asked on suspicion, suddenly feeling betrayed by her.

"Her overture disgusts," he said in a revolting tone while sincerely gazing at me.

"I see..." I replied faintly, nodding a little as I shifted my gaze from him. I returned to looking at the animated crowd ahead of us. I knew that Jasmine occasionally pursued frivolous affairs, but I didn't think that she would dare set her sights on my husband—despite my inkling. I was sad and angered by it. I wanted to have a word with her just now, but couldn't given the lack of opportunity and the occasion.

Leif secured an arm around my waist and drew me close against himself, gathering my attention away from the crowd. Carefully clasping my chin with his fingers, he turned my gaze toward him. Our eyes met in the moonlight, and he leaned his lips over mine in a kiss that was reassuring and devoutly devoted. He continued kissing me with tenderness, and suddenly Jasmine was erased from my mind. Comforted, I smiled at the sincerity of his affection for me and his tongue eased carefully between my lips. Naturally opening my mouth further, it slid inward completely, causing my breath to flutter a little. He pulled me tighter in his embrace, forgetting our surroundings, as he was softly kissing me with care in the dark, secluded from everyone.

But footsteps were unexpectedly heard advancing in our direction along the stone pathway toward us. We broke from kissing and noticed a rather tipsy, laughing couple who were strangers coming closer.

"Oh, hey guys," the man in the couple easily greeted as he accidentally discovered us sitting comfortably on the wall.

"Hullo," Leif replied reservedly as we were observing them.

"The countdown is about to start," the woman between them informed us as she hung onto her male companion.

"It is?" I asked, surprised by the time.

"Yeah," she said drunkenly. "You guys have the right idea in mind being here all alone, away from everyone else. It's private up here. Anything can happen," she giggled. "Besides, you can also see all the city lights from the gazebo to enjoy too from there." She giggled again, sloppily kissing her male companion on the cheek. He gave her a sexual look and laughed also.

I glancing around us and admired the lighted city basin as Leif kept impassively watching them.

"Nice. Huh?" she said, observing the city lights too.

"Yeah," I agreed simply, glancing at the couple again.

"Well, we're headed up to the gazebo, so see ya," impatiently said the man as he tugged her higher up the slope inside the gazebo.

"See ya," I muttered ironically and Leif shifted his glance toward me. "What? Was that a little rude of me?"

"Anither reason fur yer punishment," he said discreetly. The tone in his voice was emotionless, but the look in his eyes was perceivable amusement. I smiled at him and a faint chuckle eluded his grinning lips.

He kissed my temple and it became quiet between us as we heard the couple laughing and giggling behind us inside the gazebo. No doubt kissing and making out had begun taking place between them. But after a moment, we could hear guests below the slope counting down the seconds to the new year with the lead singer of the band. Then, in a fleeting moment, everyone was heard shouting, "Happy New Year!" and party music instantly resonated in the midnight air from the band.

"Happy New Year, *mo ghaol*," I heard Leif saying to me as I was gazing at the guests celebrating below from us. I shifted my glance toward him and our eyes met once more.

"Happy New Year, Leif," I responded softly. I pressed my lips over his in a nice, warm kiss. His fingers wrap around the back of my head and he kissed me with further affection.

Thirty-Four

We didn't return home until very early the next morning before dawn. Knowing my parents wouldn't make the drive back to their house tonight after a long night of babysitting, they had agreed earlier to sleep the night at my house, and would return home the next morning on New Year's Day.

The house was dead silent when Leif and I arrived indoors. We quietly crept up the staircase and before I entered our bedroom, I went to the children's room to briefly check on them. After replacing blankets over them they'd kicked off in their sleep and gently kissing each over their heads, I retreated for my own bedroom.

When I entered the room, Leif had already begun disrobing his vest and shirt from his torso. As I proceeded undressing my sore toes from my heeled shoes, I sensed his fingers mindfully slipping over my back and unzip my dress from behind. Glancing at him, I smiled and slid out of my garment. The grin on his face was languid, coupling the sensual look in his eyes, and he seemed assured. As I smiled at him, I couldn't help feeling shy in front of him for whatever unexplained reason and I dropped my gaze from his. Distracting myself with my dress to hang inside the laundry bag inside the closet, I was fully aware of the focus of his attention which created nervous butterflies in my stomach, making me feel like a ridiculous adolescent girl.

Curious and a little worried about him adhering to his earlier playful threat to punish me, I was hesitant to return into the bedroom from the closet to meet him again. Clothed in my slip now, instead I went to the bathroom and refreshed myself for bed, prolonging the inevitable. But once I'd finished, and returned into the room, he had already tucked himself beneath the blankets.

However, wide awake as I had discovered him, his eyes locked onto me the second I emerged from the bathroom. Apparently, he was waiting for me to join him in bed. When I moved around the mattress for my bedside, I was conscious of his gaze following me until I was ready to enter beneath the covers. Except giving me a stern, provocative look he said, "Yoo're forbidden."

Suddenly freezing at the edge of the bed, I felt a curious little chill creeping over my skin by the command in his voice. The tantalized look in his eyes warmed my blood, strangely contradicting the hint of fear seeping into my consciousness. Ironically, I felt my lips automatically beginning to curl into a small, nervous grin. But his face remained unexpressive, except for the perceived clue of inspiration expressed in his eyes.

"If I'm forbidden, Your Grace, then where will I sleep?" I asked uncertainly, sounding naive to my own ears.

"Ye must earn yer place at my side this nicht, lest ye will sleep upon the floor," he determined unemotionally. Although said in a pleasant tone, I noted the unforgiving note in his voice.

"On the floor?" I questioned, a little shocked as I regarded his humorless expression.

"Ye arenae deaf, Your Grace. Correct?" he qualified formally.

"Yes, Your Grace, I am not."

"Then, heed me weel. Should ye do precisely as I say, ye will be permitted tae enter into bed whaur ye may sleep at my side. Fur, I shall warn that if ye choose not tae obey me, ye may lie upon the floor immediately tae sleep the nicht away. Thus, how micht ye choose?"

I stared incredulously at him, knowing he wasn't kidding. He was genuinely serious, despite the fact I understood he was playing a game of sorts. And since I didn't at all want to entertain the thought of sleeping on the cold hard floor—or anywhere else for that matter outside this room—despite the tufted rug beneath my feet, I took a step backward from the edge of my bedside and curtsied respectfully before him.

"What sort of game are you playing, Your Grace?" I inquired demurely.

"The sort ye will come tae understand. Now, how will ye proceed?" he replied in a mild voice.

"I choose to obey you, Your Grace," I said modestly.

"Very weel. Remove yer shift," he ordered directly. Tempted to ask him what exactly he had in mind for me to do in order to be allowed to sleep in bed, I bit my lip instead and did as he said, knowing better not to incite him further. Removing my nightdress, I carefully folded it and placed it over my nightstand.

Now standing entirely naked before him beside the bed, I observed him as his eyes slowly rolled over my body. A sluggish smirk tilted his lips and the pull of allurement ignited his gaze. I stood there for an undetermined moment watching him scrutinize me in silence, feeling vulnerable and exposed, wondering what sort of lurid thoughts were running through his mind.

"Place yerself before me at the center of the chamber. Ye neednae worry, fur the door is latched," he ordered finally.

I proceeded following his instructions and silently moved toward the foot of the bed, arriving to stand in the center of the room, curious about the game he was playing. Relieved that the door had been locked and that he had spoken at last, I wondered what he was going to say to me next. Unable to help the nervous smile on my face, he looked at me with a lascivious little smirk.

"Ye have conducted yerself in a most libidinous manner whilst tripping fantastically tae hedonistic music this nicht. Ye will suffer fur it," he said, appearing serious, despite the small smirk on his face. "Do ye recall the instant upon once ye first danced before me the rumba?"

"Yes, Your Grace, I remember," I answered demurely, agreeing to his mischief.

"Whit had I told ye once ye completed performing it?"

"You said that I wasn't allowed to dance like that ever again in front of anyone. Unless, it was with you."

"Aye. Yet, ye have now surpassed my order with utmost incredulity. Therefore, that ye quite understand the consequence of yer naughty behavior, ye will obey precisely every order I present tae ye tonecht. Is it clearly understood?"

"Yes, Your Grace," I replied meekly.

"Guid." He shifted himself upward in bed and positioned himself comfortably leaning among the pillows against the headboard with the blankets over his lap. "Hence, I shall proceed with this commencing admonishment. Ye will dance unabashedly fur me upon my immediate determination."

I stared at him for a second, hesitating, as I couldn't believe his request. Struck with obvious embarrassment and shock, I stood there wondering if he was truly sincere. Except, the actual look on his face gave me the distinct impression that he unequivocally meant it.

"Are you kidding me?" I blurted, regardless.

"Micht I appear jesting?" he returned.

"No, Your Grace. You don't."

"Precisely. Begin," he ordered again without any yield, observing my reluctance while waiting for me to comply. Compelled, self-consciously, and without another word, I lightly began swaying from side to side as his eyes adhered to mine. Filled with mortification, I couldn't move past the palpable silence in the room while he watched me simply swaying back and forth. His intense gaze distracted my concentration to vary my movement, and ignore the fact that I was attempting to dance seductively for him while entirely naked. I could clearly perceive his measured anticipation and lustful scrutiny as he was silently watching me. Aside from feeling extremely embarrassed, I began feeling quite stupid, too. "Yoo're failing, *mo ghaol*," he warned in a slightly gentler tone. "I ken that ye wulnae favor the floor."

"May I beg for a request, Your Grace?" I implored sweetly while continuing to sway.

"Whit micht it be?" he replied, unaffected.

"It might please His Grace to know that I will certainly perform much better to his liking if he would allow the sound of music to play also," I suggested politely.

"His Grace will be lenient as he permits whit Her Grace must do in order that he may be pleased," he said.

"Thank you, Your Grace." I ceased my swaying movement and returned to my nightstand where my phone was charging in the dock. I snatched up my phone from the port and promptly opened my music app, finding a list of favorite songs. After quickly deciding on one, I started the song and reinserted my phone into its dock as the music immediately began playing through the wireless speakers on the shelves. As the room resonated with Sade's sultry, smokey voice, I returned to my position in the middle of the room and proceeded slow dancing to the groove of *Lover's Rock*.

Gently swaying my hips while sedately stepping in place and slowly rotating with arms raised slightly above myself, I lightly snapped my fingers to the sensual rhythm and his gaze melded to mine. My self-consciousness remained, though, as I noticed the hypnotized expression on his face. He rested bare chested in bed observing me move, entranced with patent captivation and attraction as I rocked and swayed my hips, lightly snaking my body.

The sex appeal evident in his intense eyes filled me with sharp awkward sheepishness, and I felt insecure holding his gaze, since I'd never behaved like this with anyone before in my life. But a lazy grin began curling his lips and lingered with the stupefied expression on his face, enhancing my awareness of his attraction to me.

Abashed and no longer capable of maintaining his magnetized gaze, I broke from it when I closed my eyes and let the music drown me instead. Now that I was blind to his adhesive, burning stare, I submitted to the music alone and was carried away by the languid rhythm as Sade's lustrous voice absorbing me. Slowly gyrating, I rotated and swerved my hips, slightly raising my arms again while lightly snapping to the sleepy beat, peacefully lost in the music now. Time seemed to relax while listening to the song, and I automatically hummed and sang the lyrics, not wanting for it to end.

So, I kept dancing as the music played...

But when the music faded into silence, it seemed all too abrupt and my eyes opened. My gaze returned to his. The reality of him still staring at me in sheer allurement, filled my consciousness and suddenly I was really embarrassed again. Feeling my cheeks growing hot on my face, I wanted to disintegrate. The urge to run and hide in the bathroom was pronounced as I stared back at him. But his gaze locked me in place. Obviously flushed also, but for a different reason, he speechlessly gazed at me for a moment longer, gaping, and I wondered what thoughts he was thinking. I was tempted to ask, but I knew better than to break his rules. So, I simply gazed at him in silence also, waiting for his response.

"Come," he uttered, finally. He lightly patted the empty space over the mattress beside himself. Following his cue, I began toward the bed and he flung the covers off my bedside when I proceeded entering over the mattress. He also tossed the blankets off of his naked lap, revealing his large, swollen shaft, erect and ready. But he remained sitting motionless in bed with his back leaning against the headboard, while observing me settling over the mattress before immediately responding further. "Well done, *ceisdein*," he said finally. His voice was kind, and I assumed my punishment was over. "His Grace is pleased. However, yer lesson isnae yet completed."

"It isn't?" I inquired, looking at him surprised.

"I fear not," he said, gently seizing my chin between his thumb and forefinger.

"What else will His Grace have me do?" I asked as he drew my lips to his and began bestowing tender kisses.

"He will have ye lie upon yer back," he ordered, half-whispering between his kisses. "Do it fur me, presently." He withdrew his supple lips from mine, and I proceeded to lie on my back. He leaned over me and began carefully kissing me again on my lips as I sensed his fingers lightly brushing over my nipple. He started fondling it and it stiffen by his caresses. "I must make an inquiry of Her Grace as I am most curious of her answer."

"What would you like to know?" I asked strangely.

"Had she ever pleasured herself whilst separated from His Grace?" he asked while intimately gazing into my eyes and toying with my nipple. I hesitated answering him, because of my sheer embarrassment. "'Tis said tae be a sin tae do so," he said looking seriously at me, furthering my reluctance to answer him. "Yet, I understand man's weakness of will in succumbing tae desire." He tenderly pressed his lips over mine, kissing me again and my nipple ripened between his fondling fingers. I began growing warm throughout among his touch, and my depths were liquifying. "Answer me," he demanded softly between his gentle kisses.

"Yes, Your Grace, I did," I divulged quietly, feeling acutely abashed about it. I sensed his lips spreading into a grin against my mouth while he continued kissing me.

"Splendid," he moaned. "Show me how 'twas done."

His lips trailed from my mouth, passing my chin, wandering over my neck and lower until they latched onto the nipple he had been teasing with his fingers. My breath caught in my throat when his teeth lightly nipped it before drawing it completely back into his mouth and suckled. The sensation of his feeding tongue felt abrasive enough to sensitize the flesh, and would soon become over stimulated if he continued paying it much attention. But sucking it as fervently as he was, seemed fitting of his wanton desire this time as I sensed his lack of care for any restraint.

As he was relishing my nipple, a moan eluded my lips and I was quickly falling under his spell where all other thoughts vanished from my mind but him. Doing as he wished, I moved my thighs apart and placed my hand over my pubic area, ready to comply. But my nipple began aching as he was patiently satisfying himself with it, and the ailing tenderness he was rendering it felt oddly pleasurable, causing me to whine with bated breath.

At last, his lips withdrew from my nipple, relieving my anguish, and I glimpsed at its awfully swollen size. It was furiously red, nearly appearing nut brown and as large as any ripened berry. Given what he'd just done to me, I understood the warning of what was to come and knew there would be no mercy from him this time—closely reminding me of the time we had spent loving each other in the woods so many years ago.

He gazed at my nipple and smiled, gloating. He was in control and the look on his face was intentional, salacious, and engulfed in lust as he returned his dreamy eyes to mine. The fiend that I had not yet known in him was visible. I wasn't certain what to expect, and a little nervous smile came over me as I looked at him.

"As we proceed," he started in a low voice while glancing down at my hand resting over my pubis, then returned looking at me, "spread yer petals wide fur me and reveal tae me yer flesh with particular attentiveness tae yer clitoris, in order that I may witness it all as ye pleasure yerself."

I nodded a little and adjusted my hips, widening my thighs as far as I could despite my inherent feelings of modesty. I caught the smirk on his face while observing him shifting himself more comfortably below me to better see. Now with his vision watchfully fixed onto my pubis, I began exposing myself to him by spreading my flesh. Taking my index and middle fingers, forming a

V, I cradled my clitoris between them, and commenced slowly stroking it up and down, lightly adding pressure. Beginning to pleasure myself for him to witness, I glimpsed at his face and caught his gratified expression as I noticed a sensual grin indolently curving his lips.

Unable to keep my eyes open as I desired to perceive his reaction, the sensation of my massaging fingers on my clitoris drew my attention away from him as my nerves were becoming electrified. The rising pleasure overcoming me roused moans from my lips and my breathing grew irregular. Deliberately, up and down I stroked with small circular motions around my flesh with the pads of my fingers. Continued moans eluded my parted lips as the crescendo was nearing.

The thought of him watching me edged into my mind, and propelled me swiftly toward the summit. The crest was so close as I oddly realized myself enjoying performing for him. I could feel the ledge right before the fall, and when climaxing was soon within reach, Leif whispered into my ear, "Yoo're extraordinary. Bonnie as nae other lass," and began pressing soft kisses over my temple and cheek. But my breath caught in my throat when I unexpectedly sensed a long thick finger of his inserting into my entrance, interrupting my trance. Instead, his finger began pumping in measured strokes along with my own caresses over my clitoris. In and out his finger rubbed from within, drawing liquid from me and slicking my flesh, hypnotizing me more powerfully.

"I adore yer warm, wet flesh more than ye ken," he semi-whispered against my cheek as he kissed it. "Ye flow gloriously. Tell me?"

"Yes?" I breathed unevenly.

"Whit thoughts had ye whilst pleasuring yerself in my stead?" he rasped.

"I imagined it was you sticking your cock into me," I answered breathlessly, bluntly revealing myself.

"Ye longed fur me, then?"

"All the time."

"Ye craved?"

"I was starved."

"Desperately."

"Yes."

"Glorious." His voice was hoarse and gravely, and I was anguished for him. "Micht ye crave my cock inside yer cunt at present?"

"Very much."

"Yearn more fur it."

"How much more?"

"'Till ye have earned it."

"You're not being fair."

"Indeed I am. I shall give it tae ye when it pleases me upon yer earning it," he said and pressed his lips over mine again, kissing me with earnestness as his tongue thrust into my mouth, making me gasp.

"You're going to make me beg?" I asked while continuing to stroke myself as his finger kept pumping into me between his kissing lips over mine.

"Aye."

"Why?"

"I mean tae ken yer remorse. Once I perceive yer understanding the purpose of my discipline as ye express contrition, ye will reap the benefit of my cock," he said between his kisses.

I felt my clitoris hardening and the muscles within my depths tensing around his surging finger. On the verge of breaking pleasure, I was close once more to climaxing. Then when I sensed a second finger inserting into me along with the first, a jolt of electricity wired my nerves as he spread his fingers apart, widening my hole. The pulse shocked my depths, commencing the avalanche of uncontrollable shuddering euphoric throbs when he suddenly pulled his fingers out of me and removed my own fingers off my clitoris also. The sublime sensation of my beginning orgasm was abruptly interrupted, and my eyes flung open. I looked at him somewhat stunned and gasped at the sudden disruption. "Not as of yet," he commanded.

"But when?" I panted, disappointed.

"The pulse of my heart is hard of hearing, I see."

"I'm begging you now. Please."

"Pray whit?"

"Let me come."

"Upon my word as I fancy," he reminded. He reached for a couple of pillows and shoved them beneath my buttocks, raising my hips to him. "Be a guid lass. Ye will be rewarded should ye obey. Presently, spread yer legs wide and open yer petals accordingly fur me tae plainly see once more."

"Whatever you say."

"Address me accordingly."

"Whatever you say, Your Grace."

"Very weel. Presently, proceed."

Following his command, I spread my thighs as far as they could go and opened my cleft wide for him to see it all. His vision locked onto my exposed flesh and a gratified smiled curved his lips again. I then sensed the pad of his thumb pull the hood back on my clitoris. The sensation didn't feel exactly gentle, since it was quite sensitive to the stimulation I had already caused it. But he began stroking it with a bit of pressure from his finger, and I moaned from the mild soreness oddly pleasuring me.

I slightly raised my vision to see what he was doing to me and became entranced by his enthrall as he concentrated his attention between my thighs.

"Lie," he said without removing his eyes from my pubis. So, I dropped my head back again on the mattress without the support of a single pillow and gazed up at the ceiling, letting him use me, as I wondered what he was going to do. With my hips raised toward him, he proceeded titillating my clitoris with the large pad of his thumb when I sensed a thick finger of his circling my entrance before sliding into me. "The glory of a wet cunt. Yers has all the splendor," he commented as he proceeded pumping a finger into me once more.

I drew in a little breath, sensing his finger stirring the heat and dampness within my depths. While staring up at the ceiling, my mind began emptying again as the focus had been drawn between my legs. The sensation he was inducing began taking me from my surrounding reality as I succumbed to him and relaxed. My eyes closed and I moaned, feeling myself beginning to rise with sublimity all over again while he massaged and thrust his finger into me with measured control. Then, another finger was sensed working its way into me and the pair began working in tandem, pulling forth more wetness from within me as they surged rhythmically while his rubbing thumb stroked my clitoris.

Dire pleasure was expanding and mounting, and the room had grown silent that I could hear his fingers between my thighs. My sex ached and the pain was growing raw. I needed to be relieved by ecstasy, but I was tortured when his pair of fingers widen me from within, spreading me further apart for a third to join the stroking pair. I moaned from the pleasing sensation of myself being stretched when his pinky finally eased inward also. Feeling my muscles surrounding the girth of his palm as my body took it in, I whined at the sudden electrical pulse which seized my walls when the width of his palm moved in and out of me while his thumb persistently toyed with my clitoris.

Amazed at what he was doing to me, I was certain I wasn't going to last.

"Your Grace?" I panted euphorically.

"Aye," he rasped.

"I'm going to come," I said in desperation, catching my breath.

"Yoo're forbidden," he commanded while continuing to purposefully pump his hand into me.

I couldn't help reigning in the rhapsodic elevation occurring to me—as much as I tired. Forcing my thoughts away from what he was doing to me was futile when the attraction of my awareness was the exalted feeling happening within my depths. My muscles began tightening again, ready for the discharge imminently approaching.

He suddenly withdrew his hand entirely from me, deliberately leaving me empty, anguished, yearning, and suspended.

"Why?" I responded breathlessly, lifting my gaze to him, frustrated. He didn't answer except for the lazy smirk curling the corner of his mouth. He not only appeared wicked; he was exactly that. I dropped my head back to the flat mattress, utterly dissatisfied, and begging. A brisk chuckle eluded him, confirming the fiend in him and he didn't care.

I let my hands slip from my slick folds and my flesh closed as I whined from discontent.

"Should ye protest, I shall have ye suffer longer fur it," he warned, sounding deviant.

"I'm begging you now, Your Grace."

"Micht ye?"

"I am."

"Bear in mind every instance ye prance wantonly about in public, ye will suffer my discipline."

"With pleasure," I taunted.

"Ye have warranted yerself further punishment," he chuckled suddenly, and unexpectedly delivered a playful wallop on the side of my hip, creating an echo and causing me to screech.

"Leif!" I protested, giggling also. "You're possessed."

"By ye."

"By me?"

"Ye haunt me."

"How?"

"Ye own my soul. Yoo're the very reason my heart will pulse."

"Really?"

"Aye, ye ken it is true. Now, observe the manner in which ye possess me."

"What are you going to do?"

"I shall demonstrate. Now, silence," he ordered. "Or, yoo'll have anither slap."

So, I bit my lip, silencing myself, not truly realizing how much more passionately consumed he could be until now. But I felt his fingers take my pubis again as he spread my cleft wide apart for himself. Noticeably sensitive to the touch, I jumped a little, gasping as his thumb returned to my clitoris. Paying it close attention once more, it ached tremendously now. It grew hard and very swollen by his hand. Except, the pain continued strangely mixing with pleasure and I found myself being taken this way once more.

He messaged it again with the pad of his thumb. Slowly, over and around it, repeating the motion, adding a little pressure each time his thumb passed over it. I became wetter and my walls were slick for whenever he meant to enter me. The motion was driving me senselessly toward oblivion, crippling me with delight, as I surrendered to his touch again.

I moaned in pleasure as my breath fluttered. He was reigning over me and drawing me toward dissolution. The need for release was increasing once more. But I strove my damnedest to withhold myself, understanding it was what he was determining me to do.

"Micht ye care tae come?" he asked finally in a low voice, sensing my flesh again.

"I care very much to. Please," I gasped, finding the air to speak.

"Permitted," he granted, at last.

He kept stimulating my sore clitoris that was now raw, and wouldn't cease until I immediately broke on the waves of euphoria. It suddenly began pulsating, and the movement of his thumb stopped. Placing his thumb directly onto my pulsing clitoris, he applied gentle pressure to it. Faintly seeing him through my delirious eyes while breeching ecstasy was taking me, a devilishly grin crossed his face. Then, everything blurred as I was abruptly launched into rapture. My breath caught in my throat, as my thighs shut around his palm, entrapping the breathtaking sensation within my depths while I uncontrollably shook.

When I floated back down from rapture, he withdrew his hand from between my thighs and brought his glistening fingers into view. He gazed wondrously at them for a second, and I watched as his mouth opened wide for them to slide inside. He deliberately sucked on each one, cleaning the wetness off, completely.

Then, he grinned roguishly at me. Suddenly grabbing my hips, Leif carelessly threw the pillows beneath me to the floor. Still dreamy from climaxing, I scarcely wondered what else he was going to do to me when he yanked me toward the center of the bed and flipped me over onto my stomach. He took my waist and propped my hips up. A sudden, hard slap impacted my buttock cheek which resonated in the room. Catching me completely by surprise, my consciousness instantly returned to reality as I immediately screeched into the bedsheet. "Dinnae ever be rude tae others though they may slight from ignorance and find yer vexation," he chastised.

"What are you talking about?" I asked in shock.

"I am referring tae the couple tonight tae whom ye waur impolite whilst we waur in the garden by the gazebo," he reminded me, sounding serious.

"Oh," I realized meekly.

"'Twas beneath ye tae behave in a disagreeable manner without just cause."

"I'll remember that, Your Grace," I gasped, registering he had just punished me for another mistake I'd made. But this time, it felt uniquely pleasurable.

"Ye will learn from yer errors so long as ye are wed tae me," he said undoubtedly.

"Yes, Your Grace," I breathed into the bedsheet, accepting his direction.

Resting on my elbows with my hips raised and buttocks exposed to him, he pushed my legs apart, separating them wide. I felt my holes revealed to him, and anticipated him. When I felt a finger brushing over my sphincter and indolently circling it, then idle over it, I silently questioned with anxiety which hole he was actually going to take—as I wondered if he was fiendish enough to truly do it, and if I'd let him. As I felt his finger begin gently pressing against it, I automatically drew in my breath, fearful. Closing my eyes, I sensed his temptation—and my weakness for him. Stunning myself that I'd even consider it.

"Leif," I whispered, unable to help my concern.

"Ease yerself, loove," he replied calmly.

"But what are you going to do?" I asked worriedly, feeling his finger resting lightly on my sphincter.

"Naught which warrants yer apprehension," he answered.

Then, his finger drifted from that hole and arrived at my vaginal entrance. He poked it inside and pumped it several times before swirling it around, inciting a little moan from me. Slightly withdrawing it, he began working more fingers into me as I felt my entrance stretching around the girth of his palm once more. Except, I sensed that his thumb had not entered with the others and instead remained lightly pressing against my sphincter, scarcely spreading it open by the little pressure he was adding onto it.

"A wee virgin hole," he commented hoarsely, observing my sphincter again. My breath caught with trepidation, knowing he was truly tempted, and my muscles stiffened. "I shall never harm ye, *mo ghaol.*"

"Thank you, Your Grace," I breathed, beginning to relax again, knowing he was true to his word. "Did you ever take a woman like that?" I automatically asked as the words fell out of my mouth.

"I have," he answered honestly. I was surprised by his admission.

"Who?"

"Sevine."

"One of your courtesans?"

"Aye," he said. "She desired it and instructed me as I indulged."

"Oh..." I muttered. "Was it enjoyable?"

"She claimed it so."

"What about for you?"

"I had enjoyed the full extent of her body."

"I see... Do you want to use me like her?"

"Not presently."

"You don't?"

"Nae."

"Why not? What's the difference?"

"Micht ye be willing?" he inquired peculiarly, sounding surprised also.

"I'm curious. I'll admit."

"Are ye?"

"I feel like I am."

"I see."

"So, tell me. What's the difference between me and her if you've already done it before?"

"The difference being I may not care tae debauch ye in such a manner."

"Why?"

"I care tae use whit is common betwixt us, and I dinnae care fur ye tae become damaged."

"Damaged?" I questioned, interpreting the metaphor, and feeling a sting of insult.

"Aye."

"What do you mean?"

"I may injure ye, and I care not fur yer fear."

"Oh," I understood, suddenly disregarding my initial miscon-strued thought and considered his caring for me.

"Aside, ken that my possessing yer cunt satisfies me weel till the day I shall perish."

"Still, it won't ever become boring for you?"

"Whit a preposterous notion. Nae. Boredom of ye wulnae ever

come tae pass. Ye offer a new world tae me every moment that I live," he uttered with conviction.

"I do?"

"Yoo're a novelty at every turn," he replied.

"Really?"

"Ye will never fail my intrigue, or my heart. Whit ye and I share is unique unto us. No other shall ever steal whit is betwixt us. We are sworn and bound tae one anither. Recall?"

"Yes, I remember," I uttered softly into the sheet.

"Guid."

"Then, will you ever—if I wanted to—would you—"

"Should the moment ever be suitable."

"So, what if I told you I wanted to play one of your concubines now?"

"Temptress," he chuckled breathlessly. I giggled a little also at his amusement.

"I could be like one of those women, you know?"

"Mayhap, I shall not deny it. Yet, I am disciplined," he said instead affirmatively.

"Oh," I responded in a small voice, realizing his self-dominion wouldn't yield. I suddenly felt faintly disappointed and thought it was strange.

"Do ye fear me?" He asked unexpectedly.

"A little, Your Grace," I admitted.

"Trust me as ye have done, instead of fear."

"I will, Your Grace."

"Fine. Ye will delight as I serve ye, in which case. My reprimand of ye this evening caters tae yer need as weel as my own. Submit tae me, and reap yer reward."

"Yes, Your Grace," I agreed quietly, desiring him.

"Very well." He placed his free palm on my buttock cheek and rubbed it a bit roughly in a circular motion while kneading it, heating the skin. "Ye belong tae me. Do ye recall my saying so tae ye?"

"Yes, I do."

"I may do tae ye as I wish."

"By using me. I know."

"Aye," he said. "Every part of ye is mine. Mine alone."

"I know and I'm glad, Your Grace."

"I venerate yer body as I do yer soul. Do ye fathom?"

"You're going to seduce me, completely, after all. Aren't you?" I understood, yearning desperately for him.

"Yoo're indeed a temptress, and my temptation exists," he admitted.

"How will you do it?"

"By demonstrating my depth of loove fur ye as it exists."

"What will you do to me, eventually?" I asked curiously.

"Take ye as ye huvnae yet been taken, whilst I exalt yer existence."

"Do I weaken you so profoundly that you have to show me unusual things?" I asked, wondering about him as I was realizing the power I had over him too.

"My forbearance is dissolved by ye, aye," he confessed. "Yoo're the sole lass I have ever loov'd. Ye will remain thus till I am nae more. I am beholden tae ye."

"Why?" I asked curiously.

"Yer acceptance of me fur the imperfect soul that I am chastens me. I have sinned, Sylvie," he divulged seriously.

"How?" I replied, suddenly alarmed and stiffening among his touch.

"My lust for fornication debauched my youth," he disclosed sincerely. "I enjoyed courtesans I used, and discovered many pleasures with them without remorse. Yet, I never loov'd a single one."

"You didn't?" I was somewhat surprised to hear him say this.

"Nae."

"Why not?"

"I didnae ken loove till I had discovered ye."

"That deeply touches me," I replied mutedly, feeling my

muscles relax again as I was immediately heart-warmed. "I've known that you've had women before. It doesn't matter to me. I love you, as you know, Your Grace," I reminded.

"As I loove ye. However, ye dinnae ken the sensualities they had bestowed upon me in the act of copulation, and of which I have learnt tae convey as I reciprocate the deed. My yearning tae demonstrate my entire loove fur ye, *mo ghaol*, will transform ye as we proceed with wedded life as I am presently free tae express it in a certain manner."

"In what way?" I asked, aware of my vulnerability to him.

"Into a wanton siren of mine ye will inevitably become in my bed," he answered honestly without sounding ashamed.

"Oh."

"Are ye not aback?"

"I don't really think so—no," I responded truthfully also.

"Certainly?"

"No."

"Whyever not?"

"You're seriously persuasive because I love you," I confessed. "You also have very many admirable qualities that others don't have as far as the type of man you are. You're virtuous, honest, and true—naturally. You're also understanding with me, as well as kind and adoring. Your constant devotion to me chains me to you," I said truly. "Besides, I want to know everything about you. And, I want to enjoy what I learn about you. Still, you said you'd never hurt me, Your Grace."

"Trust that I shall not bring forth tae ye any harm," he swore.

"I believe you. Take me as you own me," I desired.

"Yer willingness inspires me."

"Does it?"

"Aye. I am most deeply honored."

"Why?"

"Yer granting the opportunity fur me tae entirely bare myself before ye without repulsion, qualm, or judgement."

"Yes, I suppose that's true."

"A high honor that I shall not ever betray," he said. "I vow endeavoring tae bring ye utmost joy. How micht this please ye?"

"It pleases me very much, Your Grace."

"Grand," he said truly when he affectionately pressed his lips onto my buttock cheek he'd warmed after rubbing it.

"May I ask Your Grace a final question?" I inquired politely.

"Permitted," he replied.

"Now that I will become your courtesan, what will that really mean for us, Your Grace?" I asked sincerely, feeling somewhat strange that I was regarding myself with the scandalous term.

"I shall never share ye with anither. If it is whit ye mean?"

"Yes, that's what I mean?"

"Yoo're mine alone, Sylvie," Leif repeated, clearly stipulating the fact. "Let it be understood that none other will ever have ye but I."

"That's reassuring." I exhaled in relief as the slight fear dissipated.

"Bedding ye like a concubine as I adore ye disnae mean that yoo'll be shared with anither. On the contrary. Yoo're a rare gift bestowed unto tae me, and yer gift is my bounty tae behold and treasure with veneration, and glory. I am certain the more I express my deepest affections fur ye, the more I shall become imprisoned by yer whims which finally seals my fate."

"What fate would that be?"

"Redemption and joy. Ye bestow the lecht which brightens my heart. Therefore, I have been fated tae a life of sincere companionship and sublimity. I experience utter joy at every hour whilst in yer presence. It redeems me from a cursed life full of melancholy, solitude, and repression. Thus, I am forever in yer debt," he said genuinely, sounding heartfelt.

"You don't have to thank me, Your Grace. You rescued me too," I replied admittedly.

"Dinnae mistake my lust fur virtue. I rescued ye, fur I wanted tae take ye from all other men. The reason was mine."

"Still, your selfishness generously saved me. So, there's that, Your Grace. You love me."

"Indubitably."

"I know."

"Ye do ken. Do ye not?"

"Yes. I do."

"A balanced union, are we?"

"Obviously."

"Apparently," he semi-whispered, reinforcing it.

"You're my master, and I love that you are," I agreed with bated breath, still conscious of his hand inside me. I widened my legs and elevated my hips a little more toward him, intrigued to give more of myself to him and aroused enough to invite him to have it all.

"Whit do ye desire?" he inquired.

"You."

"Whit do ye desire of me, precisely?"

"I want you to do what you want to me."

"I care tae use yer cunt fur the present. Shall I proceed?"

"Yes, Your Grace."

"Ye desire it?"

"Of course."

"Wretchedly?"

"Wretchedly."

"Splendid."

With his four fingers inside my canal, I was spread wide around them. He began pumping them, stroking me from inside, further arousing my depths. My walls grew slick as his fingers thrust, and the wetness between my thighs was heard. Gasping at the strange sensation, I understood with desire that I was his to be used in any way he pleased.

The movement was deeply titillating and I was stunned that I was enjoying it, and that my body could be worked and manipulated according to him. As the resistance of my flesh was being dissolved by him, I wondered how else he could manipulate my body to receive him in unconventional ways. The thought piqued my curiosity and increased my appetite for him to use me and be pleasured.

Commanded by the sensations he was executing within me, the gratification was unmistakable and started consuming my full consciousness. Delirious, moans eluded me and I was quickly escalating toward ecstasy.

Suddenly, he withdrew his fingers, mercilessly interrupting my hypnotic spell again. I moaned into the sheet, utterly frustrated. But his fingertips returned and stretched my vaginal hole wide open, and pleasure recurred. My walls involuntarily contracted, anticipating the same penetration when the unexpected heat from his breath came close to my opening. I sharply inhaled as his mouth covered my entryway and suckled a kiss before the sensation of his tongue thrust into me and flick around, licking me. Dancing and flitting, it joyfully darted and the resonance of his groaning between my thighs vibrated my depths, stimulating a deep-seated burning ache for the feel of him inside me.

As his tongue blindly moved, it struck nerves. The feeling was a little abrasive against my tender flesh. I began dripping from kisses and from my own lubrication. My chasm ailed, and I was breathing erratically, dying to have him buried within me.

"Please," I begged under my breath.

"Ye beseech me?" he rasped as his hot breath scorched my genitals.

"Yes," I inhaled deeply.

"Fur whit reason?"

"Your cock. I need it. Please, put it inside me now."

"Do ye reckon yer punishment just?"

"Completely."

Suddenly his hot tongue withdrew from my entrance along

with his fingers, and I sensed the head of his massive, stone-like shaft pushing into me instead. Grabbing my hips with strength, he abruptly surged deep into my depths with vehemence, striking my cervix and compelling the wind from me. Filling me to the hilt, a satisfying sigh eluded my lips.

"Micht this be better suiting?" he groaned coarsely from behind.

"Very much," I answered unevenly.

"Are ye grateful?"

"Extremely."

"Then express it appropriately."

"Thank you, Your Grace."

I suddenly gasped again at the sensation of him forcefully beginning to thrust. Moving, he boldly plunged himself without regard, reminding me again of my proper place in relationship to him—and telling me not to question this rule unless he allowed it.

He grabbed my hips, digging his hands into my skin and authoritatively surged inside me among his powerful might. I audibly moaned into the bedsheet, feeling pain while he rammed his unforgiving shaft into my uterus and worked his will over me. The moment distinctly reminding me of the time he took me in the woods, and I was living it again; the unavoidable pain emerging mixed with pristine pleasure, making this experience sublime.

Pleasure expanded further, eclipsing pain, propelling me on an escalating euphoric run. My blood felt molten in my veins as it hotly flowed throughout my body, scorching me. The heat in my belly radiated, liquifying me, and ached from the pleasure he was granting me.

"Yes," I breathed into the sheet when he was gratifying the yearning pang within my depths. "Yes" I repeated with every powerful thrust, submitting to the magnificent sensation he was creating inside my being.

"Aye," he groaned, pounding himself more vigorously into me.

He gave it and I took it. Over and again, he pummeled me. The room was silent except for the sound of our heavy breathing. His testicles slapping against me and the wetness between my thighs as he pounded resonated also. Moans escaped us, adding to the charged atmosphere, and the room permeating with the aroma of our union. Delirium enveloped us and everything seemed like a dream.

He gripped my hips tighter, and I thought his fingertips were going to burrow right through my skin. The pain grabbed me and I cried out, knowing that I was being bruised inside and out. His groan overtook mine as he moved with deepening veracity and visceral intent.

The bold sensation of his impaling organ in this position permitted the feeling of complete articulation as he withdrew and entered me again with distinction. Wanting more of him, I spread my thighs farther apart and raised my buttocks higher just to receive everything he was giving me, and he pulverized me without restraint. Conditioning me, he now was gliding in an out of me with such ease, his ramming vehemence kissed the limit of my cervix and churned my uterus without complaint.

The delirious sensation was nearly all too much to bear. I thought I would die when I would reached the summit and fall.

Breathing irregularly, I turned my head toward the mirror and discovered him watching himself pumping into me. His eyes suddenly shifted toward mine and our gazes locked onto each other's in the reflection. We watched ourselves as I rested motionless over the bed being taken—exhausted. I was mesmerized by his voracity while he drove himself into me, pummeling me to my disintegration and to his annihilation. I was his vessel and he was exerting me. His image in the mirror was resplendent while he was surging into me without shame.

He was powerful and exercised it without care, letting the rawness of the act itself take charge of him. He was animalistic as he rutted on me, and so was I as I submitted to him like his prey. I enjoyed him doing this to me while watching him in the mirror taking my lifeless body for his gratification.

I audibly yelped when he clutched the back of my ringlets and pulled them toward himself, forcing my head backward as he leaned and bit me with biting kisses over my neck. He nipped my skin and wildly sucked with trailing kisses over my shoulder also, breaking small capillaries and bruising my skin.

Helpless to him and groaning while he pounded me, my slick insides clamped down on him in uncontrollable spasms that electrified every nerve in my body, cramping my toes. Turning my gaze from the mirror as I began climaxing, I caught a glimpse of my bouncing breasts when I looked past my flat stomach and saw his enormous, velvety pink scrotum jarring against me. His testicles hung low and slapped against my wet genitals, appearing majestic as they dipped back and forth. I stared at them, hypnotized, and gave into the electrifying pulses charging my depths as it wildly contracted around his invading shaft, sending me through absolute rhapsody.

As I was soaring, I mindlessly turned my gaze back toward the mirror and a guttural groan escaped him. His lips slackened in the reflection, and his head tilted back as he seized. Releasing himself, he succumbed completely to the moment. Shooting his essence into my depths, he filled my chasm, spilling me over while I drifted downward from intoxicating bliss.

When he was drained, he abruptly slumped over my back, raggedly breathing into my loose ringlets, and I could feel his heated breath breezing against the side of my neck as his chest heavily expanded and constricted. Weakened, he pulled out of me and fell onto his back over the bed, heaving.

I collapsed onto my stomach, sensing the mixture of my lubrication and his seed pouring out of me with satisfaction. Aware of my sopping sex glazing my thighs as I rested, incapable of moving, he scooped an arm beneath me, pulling me close against himself. He tugged me over his gasping chest so now I lay stretched on top of him. I rested my head on his solid shoulder, listening to his heavy breathing and the pounding of his heart. His fingers seeped into my hair and began idly toying with it. They were gently combing through my ringlets as we lay quietly together, settling.

After a moment, his arm tightened around me. I raised my dreamy gaze to his and lightly clasped my fingers around his square chin, drawing my lips to his to place an innocent kiss on them. His mouth curved into a lazy grin when I withdrew my lips, and I noticed the amorous look lingering in his eyes as the devil in him had not yet fully disappeared.

"You're gloating," I teased, gently smiling at him.

"Have I not already warned ye about the fiend that I am?" he asked, teasing in return.

"I guess I'm just starting to realize how wicked you really are," I replied. He chuckled a little, making me giggle also.

"Did I not reward ye efter all, despite yer punishment?" he responded, looking victoriously at me now, arching an according eyebrow. I giggled again and started to roll off of him, but his arm immediately caught me and pushed me back over his chest. "Yoo're not permitted tae remove yerself from me as of yet," he lightly admonished.

"Whatever you wish, Your Grace," I giggled once more.

"Yoo're learning." He grinned once more and the expression on his face was relaxed, and adoring. He slightly shifted with me while over him, grabbing one of the disheveled blankets beside us and flung it over our naked bodies, cocooning us together. Then, I sensed his palm gently settling over my buttocks and thoughtlessly massage it. Resting motionlessly in comfort over his body, I listened to the normal beating of his heart, aware of his flaccid shaft idled against my thigh. "Ye have earned yer rest in bed."

"You're so generous," I quipped, smiling at him.

"I have told ye that I am."

"I won't forget it."

"A benefit."

"You're still unbelievable, though."

"I'm complimented. I shall endeavor remaining so, as I wouldnae care fur yer boredom of me."

"Then, I guess I'll be spoiled."

"Rotten tae the core." I glanced at him, catching him grinning boldly at me. I giggled and he chuckled. "Now that 'tis entirely settled, presently then, close yer eyes, *ceased mo chridhe*, and sleep weel," he urged gently.

"Pulse of my heart," I drowsily translated.

"Aye."

"I love you."

"I loove ye more," he said in a soft voice and gave a tender kiss on my crown.

"Thank you," I whispered, bringing an arm over his shoulder, and gently caressing his cheek with my palm. He took my palm into his and kissed the pad, then enfolded it to hold. Closing my eyes at last, I immediately began drifting into slumber, feeling satiated and glad that I had satisfied him perfectly well.

Thirty-Five

A couple of days later, I made a quick pitstop at the local grocery store after work. As I was leaving the store and about to enter the parking lot, Jasmine and I unexpectedly bumped into each other as she was advancing through the parking lot toward the store's entrance, where I was pushing my grocery cart upon leaving. Making eye contact, she waved at me with a generous smile. I reciprocated a cautious half-smile as she approached and stood before me. Suddenly caught off guard, I wasn't certain how to receive her.

"Hey, Sylvie! Fancy seeing you here," she joked as she leaned and gave me a light hug. When she released me, the cautious smile remained on my lips as I awkwardly tucked loose tendrils behind my ear without promptly responding. "Doing some grocery shopping after work?" she supposed.

"Yeah, a little," I replied.

"I need to pick up some wine, of course," she said, still smiling.

"Oh."

"Yeah, I'm having a little dinner party tonight. Nothing special. Just a few friends. Why don't you and Seamus swing by for it?" she invited.

"Thank you, but I don't think we can make it," I declined.

"Why not?"

"We've got other plans, unfortunately," I replied evenly.

"Really?"

"Yeah."

"Are you both going out to dinner or something?"

"No, actually, I'm making dinner for us. A special recipe for Seamus and the kids," I replied simply, glancing at some of the shoppers around us entering and existing the market's doors.

"Oh—well, why not just make whatever you're going to make tonight for tomorrow instead, and the two of you come over for some drinks and what my chef's making? Take a little break from the kids. You know? It'll be fun. Like always," she insisted.

"We can't. I promised the dinner for tonight," I answered, wanting to leave our conversation for my car, since I had no interest in encountering her at all. Her brow knitted a little.

"Seriously?"

"Yes. How are your kids, though? And, how is Ron enjoying Cannes?"

"Oh, who cares about Ron? As for my kids, well, that's what a nanny is for."

"I see. Well, I'm sorry we can't join you. I promised my family that I'd make them dinner."

"Oh." She dismissively shrugged. "Lucky for Seamus that he's got you for a wife." The tone in her voice, I noticed, was somewhat patronizing.

"He always tells me how fortunate he is," I said cooly, silently adhering to her backhanded compliment, feeling the added insult.

"How sweet."

"Yes, it is, thanks."

"You're so lucky that he spoils you. I hope you realize how lucky you are. I'd die to have someone like him. My ex, Ron, couldn't compare at all. But I suppose you do realize how fortunate you are, since you never let Seamus out of your sight." The generous smile she'd been giving me suddenly turned superficial.

"It's mutual—the commitment we share," I responded tersely, matching her shallow smile.

"That's darling."

"You know, Jasmine?" I started in a mild, civil tone, fully aware of strangers around us as they passed through the doors.

"Yeah?" She asked, looking curiously at me.

"I sincerely appreciate your honesty."

"My honesty?"

"Yes."

"About what?" Her lips slightly curled into an awkward little grin, adding to the curiosity on her face as she quizzically stared at me now.

"Well, it seems I've misconstrued your superficiality and flippancy, because it actually turns out that you're being sincere. I've misjudged you and I'm really sorry, since it's made me realize the fact that we're truly not friends," I replied, conscious of maintaining my friendly tone, aware of our public surroundings.

"What do you mean? Of course, we're friends, Sylvie." Suddenly she seemed surprised as her mouth slightly gaped.

"I'm afraid we're not," I responded simply, keeping the note in my voice polite.

"I don't understand."

"Of course, you do."

"Well, I can't say so. What did I do? Obviously, I've offended you somehow."

"There's no need for an explanation, because as I've said, you already know."

"Well—if it's Seamus—I didn't mean anything by it."

"Sure, you did."

"But nothing's happened, though. So, it isn't fair for you to accuse me of anything."

"It seems your guilty conscious is piquing for you, evidently."

"Sylvie," she started and paused for a second. Then, she resumed in an inconspicuous voice, mindful of our surroundings, "Don't you think you're being a little over reactionary? I mean, c'mon."

"Actually, I believe I'm being very fair."

"Really? Tell me what I did, then, to make you hate me."

"I don't hate you, Jasmine. I don't hate anybody."

"Then, what's the problem? Specifically?"

"You haven't honored our friendship. But, that's okay, you don't need me as a friend because you've got so many others. So, don't worry about our relationship. It's meaningless and isn't worth your being upset over it."

"Of course, I'm upset," she whispered loudly, seeming appalled as her face flushed.

"But you're really not. You simply don't care enough to be upset."

"How can you tell me that I don't care?"

"Because if you did care, you would've regarded our friendship with respect."

"You're saying that I've disrespected our friendship?"

"You did."

"How?"

"I'll let you reflect on that."

"What's there to reflect on? I haven't done anything to you."

"If that's what you wish to believe, then that's your prerogative. I've got nothing more to say to you."

"Really?"

"Yes. Except, I will offer you a bit of advice to consider not treating your other friends the way you've treated me, if you value them even a little."

"I just don't get it."

"I'm sorry."

"It's not like I jumped into bed with your husband, Sylvie," she chastised, gritting her teeth as she said it loudly under her breath to keep others around us from hearing.

"You didn't have to. But there's no need to dwell on it any further." I began pushing my grocery cart past her, but her hand sprung forth and grabbed the edge of my cart, preventing me from moving it ahead.

"You're ridiculous," she ridiculed, trying to remain composed as she forced me to remain with her. Wide eyed and with her blood visibly raising the hue of her face, she was noticeably seething. Shocked that she was blocking my path to proceed toward my car, I simply stared at her as I was further thrown off guard. "So beautiful, perfect, and sweet, aren't you? Well, that's cute, since you're also naive. Do you think I'm the only one who likes Seamus?"

"It doesn't matter."

"Doesn't it, though?" she questioned abruptly. I didn't answer her, because I didn't think it was worth trying. "Are you that naive to think I'm the only one?"

"Perhaps you aren't the only one, Jasmine. But you're the only one who's tested the waters to see your chances. And, that's more than enough for me to know," I replied calmly.

"Hooking up with Seamus was never my intention, since I was just being nice to him like everyone else. I was just trying to make him feel comfortable here as a foreigner, that's all. I'd think you'd appreciate that from me," she claimed anxiously.

"Of course," I superficially acknowledged with a hint of irony, knowing she was lying.

"Well, you should believe it too, Sylvie, instead of implying that I want to get into your husband's pants."

"Diffuse the issue all you want, Jasmine. It doesn't change your motive. Still, that's neither here nor there."

"My motive? How can you tell me what my motive is? You're not me."

"Thankfully. You're right, though. Only you know what's in your heart. Actions speak louder than words, as the adage goes."

"My actions have been good to you."

"I differ."

"But you can't just end our friendship. It isn't fair."

"What's fair is my freedom to discriminate against whomever I'm friends with. And, I choose to choose my friends carefully. So, as far as we're concerned, we won't be engaging with each other anymore. It's for the best, and I think you'll be happier too as a result." I smiled at her and she paused. She speechlessly looked at me for a minute, and I sensed her inability to comprehend what I was saying to her. "I'm sorry that your feelings are hurt. But maybe consider your other friends by respecting their boundaries so that you don't lose any more friends. In the meantime, take care and enjoy your dinner party tonight," I concluded, sounding sincere, and began edging past her with my shopping cart. Her grip on it slipped away, enabling me to completely move away from her into the parking lot.

As I pushed the cart of groceries toward my car parked in the closest stall near the storefront, I was aware of her eyes burning a hole through me. The sensation of her glare continued as I put my grocery bags into the trunk of my car and entered the driver's seat. While backing out of my parking space and putting the vehicle into gear, I caught a glimpse of her still staring at me when I drove out of the parking lot.

It wasn't until I entered onto the main street did I realize the magnitude of our encounter just now. Fury came over me as my heart began racing and adrenaline kicked in, trembling my nerves. I realized then that this sort of conversation with her was long overdue, and that I couldn't believe how long it had taken for it to occur as I imagined myself truly rebuking her with all the harsh words I wished I could say.

But since our encounter had randomly happened in the public vicinity, I was certain she understood my position now, nevertheless. Our friendship was done. And, while I felt better about this resolution, I also felt sorry that our relationship had devolved to this state. Believing Jasmine was my friend, I'd placed my trust in her for several years, and the betrayal now was all I felt.

As I considered her, my other friends currently entered my mind also. Only Maria stood out. I believed she was probably the only one out of the circle on whom I could probably rely if I ever truly needed a friend. That's likely because she had known what it felt like to have suffered a loss of a dear loved one as a result of her husband's fatal battle with cancer. It had grounded a common bond between us, and I knew she was genuinely substantial.

It's often said in life good friends can be counted on one hand —if you're fortunate. I knew that out of everyone, including Maria, Leif was my dearest and truest friend of all—and, that was enough for me.

Thirty-Six

Plans had been arranged for our departure to *Taigh Gràs* without our children attending, and corresponded with a portion of our honeymoon time in Hawaii. The remaining honeymoon period left upon our return was going to enable us to actually visit the island and arrive back in L.A. on time. To prevent any communication concerns from my parents as Leif and I left for our honeymoon, I had told them that communication from us was going to be unlikely, since our vacation location was remote and secluded, where cellphone reception wasn't available, and landline phones weren't connected to the hotel bungalows where we were staying. However, I promised them that I'd communicate with them on our arrival at our new airport location, and on our departure from the airport when the time came, including upon our return to Los Angeles from our plane landing.

So, everything pertaining to our absence had been seemingly coordinated.

Flying back to New England this time proved to be less nerve racking now that we were married and Leif had some proper forms of documentation to legally be in the country. When we finally arrived at Logan airport, I rented us a SUV and drove us out of

Boston westward toward the Berkshires. In approximately three hours, we returned to Williamstown and found the nearby location of our disappearances off the highway in the woods where the strange-looking, large basalt outcrop that was Crazy Eye was hidden. As I drove the SUV off the highway slightly into the woods, we were soon concealed from the road.

After parking the vehicle close to our exact destination, we emerged from it into the frigid January air when I popped the trunk open. Pacing toward the back of the vehicle together, we gathered our one luggage from the trunk, unzipped it and retrieved our clandestine clothing suited for our return to Leif's era.

Leif proceeded dressing himself in beige breeches, a white billowy linen shirt, a yellow ochre waistcoat, his tricorn hat, scarlet coat, and black great coat in which he had originally worn when he arrived. Retrieving the cheerful rose chintz bed-gown in which I had arrived here four years ago when I was pregnant with the twins that I had kept hidden from anyone to discover, I also began dressing for the era.

If our quantum mechanics theory was correct according to the use of my cellphone, which Leif continued to possess, then we were predicted to return to this current time period at this location roughly during this season.

As we were dressing ourselves for the era, my stomach quivered and suddenly I felt anxious as the realization coalesced that I was leaving my family again. But the added knowledge of leaving my children for this extended period made me nervous to leave them at all, despite knowing they were going to be well cared for by my parents. Separating from them not only by distance but by time, filled me with anguish and deep foreboding. I already longed returning to them before I had gone. As I was also not quite certain of what to expect when arriving on the other side, the reality of it only added to my grossly mounting apprehension.

"Are ye ready?" Leif asked me, interrupting my thoughts as he was gazing at me with himself dressed and prepared.

"Yes, I'm ready," I replied. He scanned my appropriate appearance and reached a hand toward my face, carefully placing a loose ringlet tendril behind my ear.

"This way," he said after he was satisfied by the way I looked.

Notwithstanding my jittery nerves, I was as ready as I ever was going to be for this journey. So, remotely closing the trunk and locking the vehicle, I hid the keys along with my old phone by tucking them away into the folds of my skirt. Observing us now prepared, gathering my elbow, Leif proceeded leading us away from the vehicle and we walked deeper into the woods.

HIKING AMONG THE TREES FOR APPROXIMATELY TEN minutes, we soon arrived before the basalt outcrop and faced the large eye in the rock. Crazy Eye loomed like a haunted structure damning anyone who would dare trespass near it. My skin chilled with cold perspiration and my heart jackhammered in my chest. Anxiety filled me as thoughts of my family along with anticipating the place in which I was soon going to arrive, swirled in my head. The devastating feeling of unexpectedly being yanked from my loved ones by time alarmed my constitution as the memories of it flooded back to mind once more. My head felt floaty and my awareness began to swim as Leif positioned us directly in front of the pupil.

"Have ye the older instrument?" he asked me as he held my new phone in his hand. I nodded and retrieved my old phone from my pocket. "Make it fail. We dinnae wish tae confuse the periods."

I nodded again and deactivated it. We watched the screen go dead, then I placed the phone back into my pocket.

"We shall shortly discover whether yer new instrument succeeds. Then, we shall ken the answer tae yer inquiry regarding the differences in either instrument—whether it matters or not which one will transport us," he said. "I am most eager tae discover this puzzle tae determine our destination."

"So am I," I agreed.

"Aye. If whit we postulate is true, then we may also rely upon the duplicate should the other nae longer operate, as I huvnae the ability to repair it. The aged instrument I have used currently, begins tae tire quickly and I continue tae fear that it may nae longer become useful."

"If it breaks while we're in your era, we could become trapped there," I realized, terrifying me.

"Correct. Hence, ye perceive my urgency tae find ye," he said.

"Do you remember how many times you used my old phone to leap?" I asked curiously.

"The times have been countless," he replied. "Why do ye inquire?"

"I was only wondering about how many uses of the phone it took before it started wearing out when you found me," I answered. "If we knew, then we could simply calculate how many times we could leap during the lifespan of the new phone—if it will work like a temporal compass, so to speak. Being aware of that, we could more conscientiously manage our traveling so that we wouldn't become accidentally stranded in any era."

"Aye," he said, understanding, nodding accordingly. He then reached an arm around my waist and proceeded securely winding a rope around us. Tying it, he continued saying, "We shall soon determine the consequences of this experiment, and begin figuring the use of yer new instrument, if it succeeds."

After securing the rope around us, I was held immovable against him. He wrapped his arms around me while holding my new phone and fastened me in his embrace as he peered over my shoulder, looking at the phone's screen. I felt him working the phone behind me, envisioning him setting the timer for seventeen hours, sixty-eight minutes and eight seconds. When he shortly finished, he further locked me into his embrace.

"Hold me, and never let go," he directed.

"I won't let go," I promised against his chest and tightened my arms around his torso.

As my heart hammered in my chest, certain he could feel it, I closed my eyes and took a deep breath, nervous like hell.

A light breeze began stirring, rustling the barren birch and maple boughs surrounding us above. The frosted atmosphere began to hum with a low frequency pitch. Within a second, a sudden sonic boom erupted the peaceful air and the earth began quaking, pulsing like a deep heartbeat. Silence emerged and overcame, muting all. A white luminescence began glowing everywhere, obscuring the enveloping snow-covered woodland scenery, heating us, until it quickly faded into blackness. The temperature suddenly dropped to a sub-degree and gravity took hold of us, rendering us immovable as it took us into a centrifuge. Gravity abruptly dispelled, and we free-fell mercilessly into nothingness...

Thank You For Reading

Curious to know more about Leif and Sylvie? There is more to come in a forthcoming novel which continues their saga.

Join the author's email list to receive newsletters for whenever E. C. Roderick publishes a new book, and more. Thank you and happy reading!

Scan QR code with phone to link to author's mailing list.

Enjoyed The Book?

You can make a difference!

If you enjoyed this book, it would be greatly appreciated if you would spend a few minutes to leave a review on the book's retailer page found on the website where you purchased this book. A simple written line or two for your review would be extremely helpful in spreading the word. For ebooks, click the link below to find your retailer. For print books, scan QR code to find your retailer. Thank you so very much!

Scan QR code with phone to link to your book retailer.

Acknowledgments

First and foremost, thank you to my husband, Alan, who believes in everything that I do. Without your support this story would have never been written. I'm immensely grateful to you for encouraging me in all of my creative endeavors and that you've inspired me to create them. I love you. Also, thank you to my family who have given me the same wonderful support. I love all of you.

Thank you immensely to my magnificent beta readers, who are my prized gems. Your input was highly regarded and strengthened this story, for which I'm entirely grateful.

A huge thank you to my great editor, Candy Leonard, for your attention to detail so that the manuscript read smoothly, and for all of your encouragement. You're incredibly appreciated.

Also, a wonderful thank you to Mary Ann Smith for using your impressive talent in creating the perfect cover for this story. I can't tell you enough how grateful I am for our collaboration.

Finally, but certainly not least, thank you incredibly to my readers. I treasure that you took a chance on a new emerging author like me and have followed this story from the beginning. Without you, I would not be able to bring more stories for you to enjoy and continue my love for writing while being with my family.

Thank you!

About the Author

E. C. Roderick is an award winning emerging author of romance fiction. TAKEN is her debut novel which begins the saga of Leif and Sylvie. As a classically trained fine artist who taught painting to adults and children for many years, she also spent time writing while raising her children.

When she isn't chasing after her children, or creating with a paintbrush, she is creating with her pen, developing strong characters in their environment for readers to enjoy.

Connect with E. C. Roderick by scanning QR code with phone.